Dear Reader,

Thank you for purchasing *Dead Run.* I hope it keeps you up turning the pages until the wee hours of the night.

I'd love to hear from you! And now—as opposed to 2002 when *Dead Run* was originally published—there are lots of ways for you to contact me. I'm active on Facebook and Twitter, and you may also email me at comments@ericaspindler.com or write to my snail mail address, P.O. Box 8556, Mandeville, LA 70470.

Thanks again for choosing *Dead Run.* To show my appreciation, I'm offering you a free Erica Spindler refrigerator magnet! Simply request one through Facebook, Twitter, www.ericaspindler.com or my P.O. Box, and I'll mail it to you.

Best wishes,

Erica Spindler

ERICA SPINDLER

DEAD RUN

MIRA®

Recycling programs
for this product may
not exist in your area.

ISBN-13: 978-0-7783-1283-3

DEAD RUN

Copyright © 2002 by Erica Spindler

For questions and comments about the quality of this book please contact us at
Customer_eCare@Harlequin.ca.

www.Harlequin.com

Printed in U.S.A.

This book is dedicated to the many victims of the September 11, 2001, terrorist attack upon the United States of America. And to all the heroes of that day and its aftermath: the firefighters, police, emergency medical and rescue personnel, Good Samaritan citizens and the passengers of United Airlines Flight 93. Thank you. God Bless.

Be sober, be watchful. Your adversary
the devil prowls around like a roaring lion,
seeking someone to devour.
—1 *Peter* 5:8

DEAD
RUN

PROLOGUE

Key West, Florida
Friday, July 13, 2001
11:00 p.m.

Pastor Rachel Howard peered out the bedroom's rear window, struggling to see past the sheets of rain. Thunder shook the one-hundred-and-twenty-year-old parsonage, followed immediately by a flash of lightning so bright it stung her eyes.

She shrank back from the ground-floor window, retreating to the absolute darkness of the room once more. She didn't want them, the ones who watched, to suspect what she was up to. They were coming for her. She didn't know who they were, only that there were many of them.

He was more powerful than she had imagined. Craftier. More vile.

She had underestimated his reach. An error. A fatal one, she feared.

Rachel squeezed her eyes shut, words from the Twenty-third Psalm running through her head, comforting her. Drowning out the litany of other voices, ones no one but she could hear.

Yea, though I walk through the valley of the shadow of death, I will fear no evil; for Thou art with me.

She planned to escape tonight and head to the mainland. Once safe, she would decide her best course of action. If she made it.

A sense of calm came over her; a momentary peace. In death his glory awaited. No matter the outcome of this night, the darkness would not have her.

Rachel opened her eyes and inched toward the window once more, clutching the envelope in her hands more tightly. Her friend would come despite the storm. He wouldn't let her down.

She prayed he wouldn't.

And she prayed she hadn't endangered his life by asking for his help.

She imagined their laughter, their tauntings. She amused them, she knew. Her Lord amused them.

Thunder boomed again, reverberating through her. In the flash of lightning she saw her friend dart across the garden, a shapeless figure in a rain-slicked poncho.

Moments later he appeared at the window. Gratitude and affection flooded her senses; tears stung her eyes. She lifted the window and handed him the envelope.

"Take it. Make sure my sister gets it." He nodded but didn't speak. "Now go, quickly."

He hesitated a moment, then turned and disappeared into the storm.

Rachel wasted no time. She grabbed her raincoat and

umbrella, purse and car keys, and slipped out into the night. Flower petals littered the path before her, torn from the canopy of branches above by the wind and rain, the bruised poinciana blossoms forming a kind of bloody carpet.

Her Toyota was parked around the back of the parsonage. She started for it, working to keep her pace leisurely enough not to call attention to herself. She didn't want them to guess what she was up to.

The rain beat down on her umbrella, sluicing over the sides, splattering at her feet. Her lips moved as she silently spoke the words of the Apostles' Creed:

> *I believe in God the Father Almighty, maker of heaven and earth.*
> *I believe in Jesus Christ, his only son, our Lord.*
> *I believe in—*

She heard a sound from behind her. She stopped and turned, heart thundering in her chest. "Stephen?" she whispered, voice trembling. "Is that you?"

The rain stopped. The wind died. She felt the breath of death stir against her face, its stench as foul as the grave.

With a cry, Rachel broke into a run. The parking area in sight, she stumbled on a loose paver. Her car keys slipped from her fingers, clattering against the walkway. She scrambled to retrieve them.

She closed her fingers around the keys. The bushes rustled; she heard a soft laugh. She twisted her head, looking back. Lightning flashed; she caught the glint of metal as it arced through the darkness.

"No!" She leaped to her feet and ran, tripping once but righting herself.

She reached her car, curled her fingers around the door handle and yanked. The door popped open. She heard them following her. Without looking back, she scrambled behind the wheel and slammed the door shut. She hit the lock and attempted to insert the key into the ignition, her hands shaking so badly it took her three tries.

Finally the engine sputtered, then turned over. Sobbing with relief, she threw the car into Reverse and floored the accelerator. The vehicle shot backward, fishtailing on the wet pavement.

Rachel shifted to Drive and gunned the engine. As the car leaped forward, she whispered a prayer of thanks. She had done it! She was going to make it.

Rachel dared a glance back, searching for her pursuers, unable to see past the wall of rain. She returned her gaze to the road. Her headlights fell across something blocking her way. A figure, she realized, standing in the middle of the road.

A scream ripping past her lips, Rachel simultaneously yanked the wheel to the right and jammed on the brakes. The car lurched sideways, sliding on the wet pavement, going into a three-sixty spin. Rachel fought to regain control of the vehicle, praying for a miracle. Knowing it was too late.

The vehicle jettisoned off the pavement. A tree rushed up to meet the car. Rachel threw up her arms to shield her face as the impact sent her flying forward.

CHAPTER 1

Liz Ames watched as coffee dripped from the filter basket into the glass carafe. She yawned, cursing snooze buttons, red-eye flights and coffeemakers that brewed at a snail's pace. She needed caffeine now, not five minutes from now.

She was going to be really late this morning, she acknowledged. What was with her? She used to be so punctual. So...perky. No matter how few hours of sleep she had gotten the night before.

Now she could barely drag herself out of bed.

Jared, her cheating weasel of an ex-husband, had happened to her, she thought, squinting against the light streaming in and around the edges of the closed blinds.

And in response, her personal and professional life had taken a quick, sanity-stealing trip south.

Even Rachel had gone south, Liz thought, thinking of her older sister who had accepted the call from a small nondenominational Christian church on Key West right in the middle of the crisis. She shifted her gaze to her answering machine and its frantically flashing message-waiting light.

She really should call her. They hadn't spoken in nearly a month, and their last conversation had been troubling for many reasons, including the fact they had argued.

Simultaneously, the coffeemaker gurgled, signaling it was in its final throes of brewing, and the phone rang. Liz grabbed her mug with one hand, the phone with the other. "H'lo?"

"Elizabeth Ames?"

The voice on the other end of the line was a man's. Liz recognized his official tone from the many calls she had made and received in her capacity as a licensed clinical social worker and family counselor.

"Yes," she responded. "Could you hold a moment?"

Without waiting for a reply, she set down the receiver, filled her coffee mug then added a splash of cream. She opened the cabinet above the sink and took out the vial of antidepressants her doctor had prescribed. *Modern medicine's answer to a cloudy day.* She shook one onto her palm, then downed it with the scalding coffee.

Wincing, she brought the phone back to her ear. "Now, how can I help you?"

"This is Lieutenant Detective Valentine Lopez, Key West Police Department. Are you Rachel Howard's sister?"

Liz froze. Finally, she pulled one of the kitchen chairs away from the table and sank heavily onto it.

"Ms. Ames?" the detective said again. "You are Pastor Rachel Howard's sister, aren't you? Pastor Howard from Paradise Christian Church on Key West? She listed you as her next of kin."

Next of kin. Dear Lord, no. "I am," Liz managed to say. "What's… Is Rachel all right?"

"I'm calling because we're concerned about your sister. Have you seen her recently?"

Her heart skipped a beat. "Not since she…since she left for Key West."

"And that was about six months ago?"

"Yes."

"When did you last speak with her?"

Liz closed her eyes, remembering. Rachel had been subdued and evasive. When Liz had confronted her, she had denied anything was wrong. She had claimed her pastoral duties had kept her from calling. "It's been a while. A month or so. We argued. I was angry."

"May I ask why?"

"It's personal, Detective."

"It's important, Ms. Ames."

"I'm going through…was going through a divorce. And one of my patients… I needed my sister and she wasn't available. I was angry." Her words sounded childish to her own ears and she felt herself flush. "What's happened? Is Rachel—"

"And that's the last time you talked with her?"

"Yes, but I don't understa—"

"So, you haven't heard from her in the past seventy-two hours? Not by phone, e-mail or post?"

"No, but—" She brought a hand to her pounding head and glanced at the machine's blinking message light once more. "I've been out of town since last Thursday. I planned to get caught up on messages this morning."

"I'll need you to contact me after you do."

The blood rushed to Liz's head. She tightened her grip on the receiver, suddenly terrified. "I don't think so, Lieutenant. Not until you tell me what's going on. Is something wrong with Rachel?"

"Your sister has disappeared, Ms. Ames. We'd hoped you might be able to offer us a clue as to her whereabouts."

CHAPTER 2

Liz stood in front of the Old Town storefront she had rented to serve as both her office and her living quarters. As she watched, the building's maintenance engineer hung her shingle above the door.

Elizabeth Ames. LCSW. Family Counseling.

She drew in a deep breath, working to quell her sudden attack of nerves. Duval Street, for heaven's sake. What had she been thinking when she had leased this property? The location was totally inappropriate for a counselor's office, the rent exorbitant.

The number-one tourist destination on Key West, Duval Street was often described as the longest street in America because it stretched from the Atlantic Ocean to the Gulf of Mexico. Liz glanced to her right, then left. People streamed around her, most wearing shorts and sandals, their exposed skin as pink as a well-boiled shrimp. Obviously, sunglasses, baseball caps and fanny packs were de rigueur here. As was transportation by bicycle or motor scooter.

She shifted her gaze to the street. Choked with a mix of bicycles, scooters, automobiles and the occasional Harley, traffic moved with the rhythm of a school of shiny kingfish. They had all come to enjoy paradise, to sample Duval Street's spicy gumbo of shops, bars, restaurants and art galleries.

Ironically, Duval Street was also home to the oldest church on Key West, Paradise Christian. Rachel's church. The last place Rachel had been seen alive.

Liz glanced to her right. She could see Paradise Christian's startlingly white bell towers over the tops of the banyan and cabbage palm trees. A bar called Rick's Island Hideaway separated her storefront from the church.

A lump formed in her throat. This was the closest she had been to Rachel in nearly a year. She missed her so much it hurt.

"Okay, yes?"

It took a moment to realize the maintenance man had spoken. When she looked at him, he grinned down at her, his teeth bright against the backdrop of his dark, leathery complexion. She guessed he was of Cuban descent, not a huge stretch of logic as Key West was actually closer to Havana than Miami.

"Yes," she replied, forcing a smile. "Perfect."

He climbed down the ladder. "Key West, she is like a mysterious woman, she gets in your blood and won't let you go." He flashed his startlingly white smile. "Or for you, a potent man. You will be happy here."

Liz let out a shaky breath and murmured her agreement, feeling like a complete fraud. She hated Key West already. It had taken her sister from her.

He closed the stepladder and hoisted it onto his broad shoulder. "Have a beautiful day!"

Liz watched him walk away, then wandered into the office and busied herself unpacking books and office supplies, filling drawers and shelves, trying to achieve organization out of chaos. Difficult to do when her emotions were more of a jumble than the contents of her moving boxes. One moment found her near tears, the next fueled by an awesome determination.

Her therapist had warned that she might feel this way. He had begged her not to come to Key West. She wasn't ready, he had insisted. She had suffered a nervous breakdown; she was emotionally fragile. Too fragile to be reliving Rachel's last days in an effort to discover what happened to her.

Guilt swamped Liz. If only she hadn't attended that convention. Rachel *had* called; she had left a panicked, crazy-sounding message. One about having uncovered illegal activities on the island, one that involved a teenager in her flock. She had been threatened. They were watching her, how many of them she didn't know. She was going for help and would contact Liz soon. She had ended the message by begging Liz to pray for her—and to stay away from Key West.

She fought the guilt. The urge to fall apart. She had completed the application process that validated her license to practice clinical social work in Florida. She had closed her St. Louis practice, rented out her house, stored all but the most essential of her belongings and moved with the rest down here. Ready or not, she had to do this.

Liz crossed the office, stopping at the front window. She stared blindly out at the street, thoughts filled with Rachel.

Where are you, sis? What happened to you?
And where was I when you needed me?

The last cut her to the quick, and Liz swallowed hard, struggling to focus on the facts as she knew them. Sunday, July 15, Rachel had failed to show up for church. Concerned, one of the congregation had gone to the parsonage to look for her. They had found the door unlocked, the house empty.

The police had been called. They had found no evidence suggesting foul play. No body. No blood, overturned chairs or other signs of a struggle. Her car had been missing, but her clothes, toiletries and other personal items had remained.

Because of the lack of evidence, they believed Rachel had either fallen victim to a bizarre accident or suffered a mental breakdown that caused her to run off.

The authorities leaned toward the latter explanation. For if Rachel had been involved in an accident, why hadn't it been reported? Where was her car? Her plate and license number had been faxed to every law enforcement agency in the state. Every hospital and morgue in south Florida had been sent her picture. Nothing had turned up.

She had been acting strangely, they said. The members of her congregation had reported that suddenly the tone of her sermons had changed from gentle and forgiving to fire and brimstone, all sin and no redemption. The messages had become so frightening that families with small children had stayed away, fearful their children would suffer nightmares.

Liz didn't buy it. Rachel was the most stable person

she had ever known. Even as a kid, her sister hadn't been affected by life's ups and downs, not the way Liz had been. Rachel had remained centered no matter the crisis she encountered: a new school, a broken relationship, a failing grade, their parents' constant bickering.

Not only had Rachel been able to put it all into perspective and move on, she had been there for Liz. Supporting and encouraging her. Shoring her up when fear or uncertainty had overwhelmed her.

Liz had asked once how she did it. She'd answered that her absolute faith in God protected her. She believed in his divine plan. And with believing, with faith, came peace.

So, what had happened to turn her sister from a gentle preacher, one who believed in sharing the story of God's great love and forgiveness, into the person the police described?

Liz suspected she knew the answer to that. The illegal activities Rachel had spoken of in her message. She had been frightened. She had warned Liz that "they" could be listening. That "they" meant her harm. That she was going for help.

Liz feared the "they" Rachel had spoken of had killed her.

She fisted her fingers. She had shared her sister's message and her suspicions with the police. Instead of convincing them to reopen their investigation, the information had validated their own belief that Rachel had suffered a mental breakdown.

A burst of laughter jarred her out of her thoughts. A group of teenagers had congregated outside her storefront. They appeared to range in age from early to late teens; one of them carried a baby in a papoose on her back. Unkempt, dressed in ragged jeans and tie-dyed

T-shirts, they looked like street kids. Throwbacks to the hippies of the 1960s.

The Rainbow Nation kids, Liz realized. Her sister had told her about them. Unlike sixties-era hippies, however, the Rainbow Nation was a highly organized, international network that even boasted a Web site. They traveled from one warm climate to another, panhandling for a living. Here, they had claimed Christmas Tree Island—an uninhabited spoil island created by dredging refuse and covered with pine trees—as their own. Rachel had wanted to minister to them, had promised herself that bringing them the Word would be one of her missions.

Had Rachel acted on that promise? Liz wondered, moving her gaze over the group, settling on the broad shoulders and back of the tallest of them. Or had her ministry on Key West ended before she'd had a chance?

As if the young man felt her scrutiny, he turned and looked directly at her, his dark gaze uncomfortably intense. A slow smile crept across his face, one that conveyed both amusement and malevolence.

Liz told herself to laugh or shoot him back a cocky smile. She found herself unable to do so. Instead, she stood frozen, heart thumping so hard against the wall of her chest that it hurt.

A moment later he broke the connection, turned and left with his friends.

Liz released a shaky breath and rubbed her arms, chilled. Why had he looked at her that way? What about her had earned his contempt?

She shifted her gaze slightly, taking in her own reflection in the glass. Thin, pale face. Medium-brown hair, green eyes, mouth slightly too wide for her face.

She used to be attractive, she thought. She had possessed one of those bold smiles, the kind that both inspired confidence and put others at ease. People had been drawn to her. They had liked her.

Where had that bold smile gone? she wondered. The self-assurance that had sometimes bordered on cockiness? When had she become so fearful?

No. Liz lifted her chin and gazed defiantly at her own reflection. She wasn't afraid. She had come to Key West for Rachel. She would discover what had happened to her, with or without the help of the police.

She would do it no matter the cost to herself.

CHAPTER 3

Thursday, November 1
11:35 p.m.

Larry Bernhardt gasped with pleasure as the girls made love to him. Two girls. Both young and agile, their skin creamy smooth and unmarked by time.

Both so young his being with them was a crime.

Larry arched and grunted, his orgasm building. The girls were bold, uninhibited. They writhed against and around him, their movements clever and quick. Mouths and hands stroked, sucked and fondled. Wet sounds filled his head as did the pungent smell of sex. The satin sheets rustled, slipping and sliding against their damp flesh.

Larry Bernhardt was a lucky man. King of the world.

As the senior VP of lending for Island National Bank, Larry lived like royalty—no earthly pleasure was beyond his reach. His palatial, oceanfront home sat on Sunset Key—a spoil island metamorphosed by developers into Key West's newest high-priced resort and living community. From his bedroom balcony he could watch the sun, a majestic ball of fire, sink into the ocean.

His sun. His ocean view. One only money could buy. An unholy amount of money. More than even a king such as himself could legitimately acquire.

His orgasm rushed up, overpowering him. Time stopped, the earth ceased to rotate on its axis; for that moment the sun, moon and stars belonged to him.

He exploded with a great cry, jerking and shuddering. His head filled with light, then darkness. And in the darkness, the creature waited, one of unimaginable evil. One that had come to devour him whole.

Larry screamed. He bolted upright in bed, the sound of his scream ricocheting off his bedroom walls. Frantic, choking on his fear, he looked around the room. He was alone. No girls. No party. He tore at the sheet, which was wrapped around his legs like a satin shackle.

Freed, he grabbed the half-drunk bottle of champagne from the nightstand, scrambled off the bed and raced to the master bath. He jerked open a drawer and frantically searched through the rows of medication vials for the one he sought. He found it and shook out a handful of the Quaaludes, then downed them with the wine.

Feeling a measure of instant relief, he wandered out of the bathroom and across to the balcony doors. Tucking the wine under an arm, he yanked the doors open. The ocean breeze engulfed him. He sucked in the moist, salty air. It cleared his head, chasing away the darkness and its waiting beast. Three stories below, the pool glittered in the moonlight. Beyond his walled compound, the ocean called. Larry shifted his gaze to the tile patio.

He was in too deep. He had allowed his addiction to grow into a monster. One with a demanding, insatiable appetite. One he was too weak to deny. He had forsaken everything decent to feed the monster, had partaken of every sin available to man.

He had allowed them to feed it. To grow it into the monster it was today. One he would never be free of.

One they would never allow him to escape.

Tears welled in his eyes, then spilled over. Tears of self-pity. Of a pathetic, lost soul. Of a man who had nowhere to turn, who knew that only hell awaited him.

Hell would be better than this prison he had created for himself. Better a puppet in hell than one here on earth.

His tears dried. A sense of strength, of purpose filled him. No more. He should have ended it long ago. He had wanted to, but he had allowed himself to be seduced.

Because he was weak. A small, weak and pathetic man.

No more, Larry thought again. He popped the vial's top, shook the remaining tablets into his mouth, then tossed the container over the balcony rail. Bringing the bottle to his lips, he took a long swig. Then another. And another.

Damn but he enjoyed good wine. He would miss it.

Setting the bottle at his feet, he crawled clumsily onto the balcony rail, palms sweating, heart thundering. Squatting, he held tightly to the metal, working to get his balance.

For once, he would not succumb. For once, he would be strong.

Let them continue without him. Let them face the mess; he hoped they all fried.

The darkness, its unholy creature, spoke to him. It soothed and cajoled, though Larry heard the edge of desperation in its plea. *Don't do it. Conquer your foes. You are king of the world. You can do anything.*

A giggle slipped past Larry's lips, high and girlish. He *could* do anything.

He could do this.

Larry released the rail and straightened. Lifting his arms, he fell forward. For a split second he imagined himself flying, his arms becoming wings, imagined the ocean breeze catching under those wings and carrying him away. Far away from this moment and himself. From his sickness and the creature who had fed it.

In the next second, Larry Bernhardt imagined nothing at all.

CHAPTER 4

Rick's Island Hideaway was the quintessential Key West bar: Jimmy Buffet on the sound system; killer frozen margaritas; a friendly clientele whose attire never veered far from shorts and Hawaiian-print shirts; walls hung with maritime paraphernalia, including a stuffed sailfish and a signed photo of Key West's most famous onetime resident, Ernest Hemingway. It was the same photo that could be found in about ninety percent of the Duval Street drinking establishments.

And last but certainly not least, a bartender who could charm the skin off a snake.

The ability to do just that came as naturally to Rick Wells as breathing. It was an ability, a gift, really, that Rick depended on but didn't pride himself in. There were many ways to hide from life, he knew. On a bar stool was one way. Behind a killer smile was another.

"What can I get you?" Rick asked the man who slid onto the stool in front of him. Judging by his starched and pressed shirt and obvious hangover, he was a tourist. And not one who had stopped in for a cup of coffee.

"Uncle Jack, black. Straight up."

Jack Daniel's, black label. At only 9:30 a.m., the coffee would have been a better choice, Rick thought. But he wasn't this guy's mother, wife or pastor. Rick poured the shot and slid it across the bar. "Big night last night?"

The man nodded, a ghost of a smile touching his mouth. "This place is all right." He brought the glass to his lips. "You don't happen to have a *New York Times* I could buy?"

"Tough to get the current *Times* here. They sell out fast for an exorbitant price. It's a matter of geography, my friend."

The tourist swore. "Great. My wife's going to be more pissed at me than she already is." He shook his head. "The older wives get, the less of a sense of humor they have."

"Couldn't say, my friend. That's not my area."

The man shot him an envious glance. "Not married, huh?"

"Not anymore," Rick responded, forcing a light tone, cursing the sudden tightness in his chest.

"Well, take it from me, it's true." The man downed the shot, then nudged the glass back to Rick for a refill. "No *Times*. Imagine that." He shook his head, his expression a cross between disbelief and bemusement. "You seem like a pretty with-it guy, how do you manage?"

"I don't mind giving up a few conveniences to live in paradise." Rick refilled the glass, a smile tugging at the corners of his mouth. "Besides, the news isn't going to change if I don't read it today. It'll be just as screwed up tomorrow. Or the day after."

"You've got a point, man. September eleventh fucked everything up."

"If you want news, I suggest the *Miami Herald*."

The tourist downed the second shot. "You wouldn't happen to have one, would you?"

"Sure do." Rick reached under the bar for his copy, which he had already read, cover to cover. He laid it on the counter. "Enjoy."

"Thanks, I—"

"Marty," a woman called from the bar's open doorway, her tone disgusted, "I *thought* you were finding me a paper?"

The man rolled his eyes at Rick and stood. "Got it, sweetheart." He tossed a ten-dollar bill on the bar, scooped up the papers, then hurried toward the door.

"Nice talking to you," Rick called after him, then smiled as Valentine Lopez strolled through the bar entry. Valentine—Val to everyone but his mother and the priest who had baptized him—was Rick's oldest friend.

"Well, if it isn't Key West's own version of Dick Tracy. I'm honored."

"You should be, buddy," Val responded, crossing to Rick. "Still wasting away in Margaritaville, I see."

"Everybody's got to have a talent." Rick grinned and motioned to the stool in front of him. "Take a load off."

The two men were "conchs," the tag given to Key West natives, though they came from very different backgrounds. Rick's family was a Key West import, his father a doctor, his mother a socialite from West Palm Beach. On a vacation to the island, his parents had caught what the locals called the "Key West disease." Before their week-long vacation ended, they had decided they never wanted to leave. His father had sold his Tampa practice and opened one on the island.

Val's family, on the other hand, descended from some of the original Cuban inhabitants of the island. His ancestors had been involved in both the cigar-making and sponging industries. Val's father—now deceased—had been a shrimper. A noble occupation though not a particularly lucrative one.

The two boys would probably never have met, let alone become as close as brothers, if they had grown up anywhere else. But despite their disparate means and backgrounds Rick and Val had fallen into an unshakable friendship. A friendship tested only once: when Rick married the girl of Val's dreams.

Val sat. "Got any coffee back there?"

"The best café con leche on the island."

"My mother would argue with that."

"Second best, then. No way I'm getting into a pissing match with that little woman. She's tough."

Rick went about preparing the Cuban espresso and hot milk. "How are things down at the department?" he asked, raising his voice to be heard over the roar of the espresso machine.

"Let me put it this way, when you decide to grow up, let me know. I could use you."

The Key West Police Department consisted of eighty-one sworn officers and twenty-two civilian personnel. Val was the ranking detective on the force and one of five officers who reported directly to the chief of police.

"Use me? Geez, things must really suck."

Val sobered. "I mean it, Rick. You're a cop. One of the best I've ever—"

"Was a cop," Rick corrected. He set the *con leche* in front of his friend. "A long time ago."

"*Are* a cop," Val repeated. "It's in your blood. It's what you—"

"Joke's over, Val," Rick muttered. "I suggest you not go there."

"It's been more than three years. You need to let them go."

Emotion rose up in Rick, nearly strangling him. "Don't tell me what I need. Don't you...dare tell me that I need to do that. I'll never let them go. Never."

Silence fell between the two men. Until three years ago, Rick had been a detective with the Key West Police Department and before that with the Miami-Dade force. He'd had the reputation for being smart and fearless, a seasoned hotshot with a killer instinct and an unwillingness to say die.

Tragedy forced Rick out of Miami. His wife had been diagnosed with ovarian cancer and only a handful of months later, he found himself a widower. And single father to a grief-stricken five-year-old son. Despondent, in need of friends, family and a better place to raise Sam, he'd returned to Key West.

Val had quickly gotten him a spot on his team at the KWPD. Although it had been a big adjustment to go from lead detective on complex and high-profile murder cases to investigating open-and-shut burglary and assault cases, Rick had been grateful for the opportunity. And for the small-town pace.

His peace had been shattered only a matter of months later: two armed men had broken into Rick's home in the middle of the night. Shots had broken out and Sam, awakened by the commotion, had gotten caught in the cross fire.

Ballistics had proved that Sam had been killed by one of Rick's bullets.

Val pushed his coffee away and stood. "I've worn out my welcome this morning."

"Don't be a jerk." Rick scowled at the other man. "Drink your coffee or I'll have to kick your ass."

Val sat, a smile tugging at his mouth. "Kick *my* ass? You wish. You're out of shape, my friend."

The truth was, the two men were as different physically as they were genetically. Val was small, with a wiry build and the coloring of his Cuban ancestors. Rick was big—six foot three—with blue eyes and fair hair.

"You think?" Rick looked down at his gut. "Can't pinch an inch."

"It's all about training, my friend. My body's a lethal instrument, while yours—"

Rick burst out laughing. "By any chance, is that the line you use with the ladies? Because, well…I think I should warn you, it's pretty cheesy."

Val, still single and a self-avowed playboy, grinned. "To you, maybe. But to the ladies, pure nectar."

"Excuse me while I puke."

"I know it's hard to take. But it's true, I'm a chick magnet. I could fix you up." The corner of his mouth lifted. "We could double-date, like we did when we were in high school."

"Pass on that, buddy. Thanks anyway."

"Jill's gone," Val murmured. "Almost four years now."

Rick averted his gaze, staring at the open doorway

and the brilliant rectangle of light beyond. "That guy who was leaving when you walked in, he was complaining about his wife. Envying my single state. And all I could think was how not a day goes by that I don't wish she'd lived long enough to make my life a living hell."

Val swore softly. "I'm sorry, man. I didn't mean—"

"Forget it. It's my problem."

Several moments of strained silence passed between them. Val drained his cup. "Gotta go, crime calls."

"Anything interesting?"

"Missing person."

"As in *poof,* gone?"

"Don't know for sure." Val stood. "The supervisor of Island National Bank's processing center didn't show up for work yesterday. A friend and coworker tried to reach her and couldn't. When she didn't show up for their morning run this morning, her friend called us."

Rick frowned. "That's Naomi Pearson, right?"

"Yeah. You know her?"

"I'm a bartender. I know almost everybody on the island." He searched his memory for how or when he had first met her. "I financed the Hideaway through Island National. I think I met her one time when I was up there. I hope she's okay."

"I'm sure she is. Probably met some guy and took off." Val saluted. "Give me a call sometime. I'm in the book."

CHAPTER 5

Saturday, November 3
4:30 p.m.

"Hey, boss man," twenty-year-old Mark Morgan called as he entered Rick's Island Hideaway. "What's shakin'?"

Rick sat with his back to the door, head angled toward the television mounted from the ceiling behind the bar. He was watching the five-o'clock local news.

He glanced over his shoulder at him and smiled. "Not much. There was an anthrax scare up in Homestead. A jealous husband sent his soon-to-be ex a letter containing a powdery substance."

"Which turned out to be?" Mark asked.

"Cornstarch. But the hoax closed the entire office building where the woman works. What's with these people?"

"No joke. Sick."

Rick glanced back at the tube. "It's official. Fantasy-Fest attendance was way down this year. No surprise there."

Fantasy Fest, a nine-day adult Halloween celebration that culminated in a huge costume party on Duval Street, was the wildest thing Mark had ever seen. "If attendance was down this year, I'd hate to be around when it's up."

Rick snapped off the TV. "Libby called. She's running late."

"No problem. I'll clock in."

Libby, one of the nighttime bartenders, was consistently late. The original party girl, she stayed up all night and slept most of the day. In anticipation, Rick had begun scheduling her an hour before he needed her.

Mark smiled to himself, crossed to the time clock and punched in. That's the kind of guy Rick was. Flexible but demanding; a laid-back perfectionist, if such a thing was possible. He wanted what he wanted but wasn't averse to finding a roundabout way to get it.

Mark liked that about his boss. He enjoyed working for him. He figured God had been looking out for him big-time when he sent Rick Wells his way.

Like a lot of folks on the island, Mark was relatively new to Key West. Two years before, he had graduated from high school in Humble, Texas, concluded much to his family's dismay that he'd had enough of school for a while and set off to see a bit of the world. After bumming around the Southeast, he landed in south Florida, then Key West.

He had found Rick's Island Hideaway by chance. A Help Wanted sign in the window had propelled him inside. Rick had hired him on the spot. Mark wasn't sure if Rick had given him the job because they'd hit it off right away—which they had—or because Mark didn't touch alcohol, a rare commodity on this island.

"How was your day?" Rick asked from the doorway.

Mark thought of Tara, his girlfriend of three months. He had beeped her half a dozen times throughout the day, but she hadn't responded.

Had she tired of him already?

He lifted a shoulder, feigning indifference. "It was pretty cool. How about yours?"

"Good. Business was steady, but not nuts. Val stopped by."

"Great." Mark slipped on an apron and headed out to the bar. Florida law required a person to be twenty-one to serve alcohol, but he did just about everything else around the Hideaway, from washing glasses and replenishing stock, to mopping behind the bar and sweeping the walk in front of the Hideaway. It wasn't a glamorous job, but then Mark wasn't qualified for glamorous.

"Anything in particular you want done first?" he asked Rick, who had followed him out front.

"Glasses, then straighten up for the rush. Wipe all the tables and chairs, sweep the floor."

"You got it, boss."

Mark worked in silence, his thoughts turning to Tara once more. They'd met shortly after he'd gotten the job at Rick's. He'd been working; she'd been out partying with her friends. They had looked at each other and something had happened—it had been instant and electrifying.

Love at first sight.

Problem was, she was only seventeen and still in high school. A senior, she would graduate in May. Worse than her age, however, were her friends. She was part of a closely knit group, more a club than simply a clique of friends. They partied, used drugs and were sexually active. They espoused ideas that went against Mark's upbringing, materialistic ones about the existence of only the here and now, about living for today not tomorrow, about enjoying the moment and all it had to offer.

Once he had learned what she was a part of, he'd told her it was over between them. But she had begged him to see her again. She loved him; she would break away from her friends, distance herself from their beliefs.

So far, she hadn't been too successful at doing that. But then, it didn't seem to him that she had tried all that hard.

Is that where she had been all day? he wondered, hoisting a tray of clean glasses onto his shoulder and heading out to the bar. Running around with her friends? Seeing other guys? Partying the way she used to?

Anger rose up in him, swift and white-hot. He fought to get a grip on it. Anger was a powerful, destructive force. One of the seven deadly sins. The one he had to battle often. The one that had gotten him into trouble before—big trouble.

Tara had changed, he told himself. He had to believe in her, he had to trust. He loved her.

Mark sighed. Tara didn't understand his religious convictions; he didn't understand her lack of them. Raised in a strict Southern Baptist family, the church had played a major part in his childhood. In fact, in first grade he had announced that when he grew up, he was going to be a preacher. His conviction to do so hadn't wavered until just months before his high-school graduation.

Suddenly, he had felt called in another direction.

His change of heart had both shocked and dismayed

his family. They'd begged him to reconsider, had asked their pastor to intervene. But Mark had held fast to his decision. He had argued that he needed to experience sin firsthand before he preached against it. After all, how could he counsel others on spiritual strength if his had never been tested?

Mark loaded the glasses onto the shelves behind the bar, aware of Rick at the other end, chatting with a pair of tourists about the area's best bone fishing and where to hire a guide. He swallowed hard and acknowledged the irony of it all: he was knee-deep in sin and spiritual warfare, and most days, not faring so well in the battle.

Glasses done, Mark moved on to the tables and chairs, aware of time passing, and that the trickle of customers entering the bar would soon be a surge. Libby had arrived and was flirting with a pair of guys drinking shots and beer. Locals, Mark recognized. They came in a couple times a week, always together and always wearing matching Miami Dolphins caps.

So, where had Tara been all day? Why hadn't she returned his pages?

She had been acting strangely of late, jumpy and distracted, crying a lot. She'd lost weight and looked tired all the time, with dark circles under her eyes.

Maybe she didn't really love him. Maybe she loved her friends and their wild lifestyle more.

Business grew brisk, and Mark managed to put all thoughts of Tara aside until a lull offered him the opportunity to call her.

Using Rick's office phone, he dialed. At the sound of her voice, twin emotions of relief and anger cascaded over him. "Where have you been?"

"Nowhere," she answered immediately, tone defensive.

"I paged you five times today. You didn't call me back."

"The battery's dead. Geez."

A twinge of guilt speared through him. He quashed it by mustering indignation. *After all, she could have called him.* "Did you do it today? Like you promised? Did you tell your friends you didn't want to see them anymore?"

"Why are you acting this way!" she cried. "I didn't do anything wrong! I didn't even see my friends today."

He let out a sharp breath, wishing not for the first time that he had broken it off with her when he discovered who her friends were. "You made a promise to me, Tara. You haven't kept it."

"It's not that easy! You don't understand."

"Is it me you don't want to be with anymore, Tara? Is that what you're trying to tell me?"

"No! I love you, you know that." Her voice broke. "But today…I—"

She bit the words back and emotion balled in his chest, part frustration and part despair. *Another of her excuses. Why of all the girls in the world, had he fallen in love with her?*

"I'm so tired of this conversation, Tara. So tired of you claiming you love me then turning around and—"

"I have to go."

"Don't do this to me, Tara. All day I worried and now—"

Rick popped his head into the office. "Need you out front, Mark. Wrap it up."

Mark nodded and held up one finger, indicating he needed just a moment more.

When the other man had exited the office, he returned to Tara. "Please, babe, talk to me."

"Meet me later." He heard her parents in the background calling to her. "Our regular place."

He fought frustration. "Are you sure you can get away? Last time you didn't show."

"I'll be there. I—" her voice cracked "—I love you, Mark."

Before he could respond, she had hung up. Mark held the silent receiver to his ear a moment, conflicting emotions roiling inside him. Finally, he hung up and hurried back out to the bar area. Rick looked at him, brow furrowed with concern. "Everything okay?" he asked.

Mark hesitated. Rick was his friend. He was a smart guy. He would be able to help. Offer advice, support.

Mark opened his mouth to respond, the whole story—of how he and Tara had met, her wild friends, his doubts about her—springing to his tongue. From the corners of his eyes he saw Libby glance their way, obviously curious.

Mark thought forward, to the possible consequences of unburdening himself to Rick. Tara was underage. He didn't think Rick would go to her parents, but if he did...anything could happen. He could be arrested for contributing to the delinquency of a minor.

Her parents would tear the two of them apart.

Mark hadn't even met them yet. Tara had been almost rabid on the subject, growing hysterical the couple of times he had tried to push the issue. They were strict, she said. They wouldn't want her to date an outsider, an older boy. Fearful word would get back to them, Tara had insisted they keep the seriousness of their relationship a secret from everybody, even her friends.

Mark swallowed the words and forced a smile. "Everything's just great, boss man. Thanks for asking."

* * *

The lush, walled garden at Paradise Christian Church had become Mark and Tara's personal Garden of Eden. Although the garden entrance was locked at sundown, Tara, as one of the church's volunteer tour guides, had a key.

The first time they'd made love had been in the garden, the thick grass soft beneath them, the fragrant scent of the night jasmine, sweet olive and ginger filling their heads. The experience had been so perfect, so incredibly sweet, Mark had almost been able to forget that it had been a sin.

They weren't husband and wife. She was underage. For all intents and purposes, they were breaking into God's backyard. Sinning under his nose.

But was it a sin when they loved each other? When they had vowed to stay together forever?

Suppressing a twinge of guilt, Mark approached the garden door. The night was still; nearly 3:00 a.m., the street deserted. He saw that the latch was open. Glancing quickly over his shoulder, he sidled up to the door then ducked inside.

"Tara," he called softly, securing the door behind him. Something scurried through the underbrush. A bird roosting in one of the trees screamed protest at the noise.

Mark jumped at the sound, then moved farther into the garden. "Tara," he called again, annoyed, "I'm not in the mood to play this game tonight."

One moment became several. A sudden unease rippled over him. He opened his mouth to call out again, when she stepped out from behind one of the banyan trees at the back of the garden, a petite figure dressed in white.

Joy at seeing her warred with irritation. He felt as if she was toying with him, with his emotions. "What was that all about?" he demanded when he reached her. "For a moment I thought…something had happened to you. That you weren't here."

He saw then that she had been crying. He brought a hand to her damp cheek. "What's wrong?"

She covered her face with her hands and bent her head, her long dark hair spilling over her fingers.

"Talk to me, babe." He caught her hands and drew them away from her face. "Tell me what's wrong."

Her big, dark eyes filled with tears. "I'm pregnant!" she cried. "I went to the doctor today and he…he—"

She burst into tears. The anger and jealousy he had battled all day evaporated. He struggled to find his voice. When he did, it came out strangled. "But I thought we… Weren't we…careful?"

The force of her sobs increased. He kicked himself for his lack of tact. *Obviously, they hadn't been careful enough.*

"I'm sorry, Tara. Don't cry. I love you. It's going to be okay."

"How? What are we going to do? An abortion costs—"

"Never," he retorted fiercely. He caught her hands again, squeezing them tightly. "I love you. You love me. This is our baby, our *child*." A feeling of certainty flowed over him, easing his fear. "We'll get married. We'll be a family."

"But…how? We're… I'm afraid, Mark," she finished helplessly.

"I'll take care of you, Tara. I promise you that."

"And we'll be happy," she murmured, voice cracking. "Really happy, right?"

She sounded young and frightened. Too young to become a wife and mother.

They were both too young. They were not ready for the responsibility of raising a child. Neither emotionally nor financially.

Sudden and total panic washed over him. What was he doing? Tara had been involved in things that went against everything he believed in. What kind of pastor's wife would she make? What kind of role model for their children?

It was too late to worry about that now.

They were going to have a baby. He was going to be a father.

He needed to be strong for her, he realized. He needed to be strong for them both. Spiritually and emotionally. If he showed her the way, she would follow. Because she believed in him. She loved him.

And he loved her.

He drew her into his arms. "Babe, remember when I told you that I felt I was being called to Key West? Remember when I said I thought God had led me here, but I didn't know why? That I thought He had a special plan for me?"

"Yes," she replied weakly. "But what—"

"I think this is it, Tara. I think He led me to you. I think He meant for us to make this baby. For us to be a family."

She tipped her head back and met his eyes. "You do? Really?" The hopefulness in her voice made him ache.

"I do," he repeated, tone strong now, certain. "Let Him lead you, Tara. If you do, if we do, everything will be fine. This was meant to be. *We* were meant to be."

CHAPTER 6

Monday, November 5
8:45 a.m.

Hand to her nose, stomach rolling, Detective Carla Chapman bent over the decomposing remains of Larry Bernhardt. It appeared that the man had jumped naked from the third-floor balcony above. He had landed face-down. She would guess broken bones, internal injuries and bleeding. The fall had busted him up—but hadn't killed him. He had dragged himself a few feet before succumbing to either his injuries, pain or both.

Poor bastard. Damn uncomfortable way to go.

Carla spied an open pill bottle peeking out from under the man's left shoulder. She bent closer, examining the empty vial. Quaaludes.

Or maybe not that uncomfortable, Carla amended.

She squinted up at the still-scorching November sun. Today's forecast called for zero cloud cover and a high of ninety. The same as the last three days. Basically as unrelentingly hot as hell.

That meant Larry Bernhardt's remains had been cooking for some time, the amount to be determined by the medical examiner. Placing the time of death would be tricky, Carla acknowledged. Exposure to heat sped up the decomposition process, playing havoc with the measures they used to determine TOD: rigor mortis, lividity and body temperature.

Let the ME work the formula, she thought, glancing toward Bernhardt's housekeeper, hovering in the doorway to the house. The woman looked a hairsbreadth from falling apart, her dark eyes wide, cheeks ashen. She stared at her former boss, her mouth moving as she worked a rosary clutched in her hands.

Hail Mary full of grace, the Lord is with thee...

The prayer ran through Carla's head, a dim but still potent memory from her childhood. How long had it been since she had uttered those words? she wondered. How long since she had gone to mass? Since she had partaken in Holy Communion or confessed her sins?

Forgive me, Father, for I have sinned...

Jesus, where would she start? To be forgiven, would she have to recant all her sins or only the ones she could recall?

"I can go now, please?"

Carla blinked, refocusing on the housekeeper. She experienced a surge of pity for the woman. She had reported for work this morning only to find her boss's crushed, fly-covered body. Not the most of pleasant good mornings. To top it off, she was now out of a job.

"Go on in, but hang around a while. I expect I'll need to ask you a few questions."

Obviously relieved, the woman nodded and disappeared inside. Carla watched her go, then tipped her face to the balcony above. She found Val there, staring down at her. "You called, Lieutenant?"

"If you're finished down there, I could use a fresh pair of eyes."

"Coming up." She straightened. "By the way, got an empty bottle of 'ludes down here."

Her superior nodded. "Looks like he washed them down with Dom. Made his landing a bit softer. Leave it for the crime-scene guys. They're on their way."

Carla left Bernhardt without a backward glance. She crossed the patio, entering the house through the same door the housekeeper had used. It led to a large, beautifully outfitted garden room.

She moved her gaze over the room. White wicker furniture, French Quarter tile floors and an abundance of tropical plants. Lots of throw pillows in a fresh-looking floral print. White plantation shutters and a gently whirring ceiling fan. Very south Florida, she thought. Very Key West.

After six years on the island, Carla could recognize the style while comatose. Casual. Breezy. Easy-living, island style. It permeated everything on this floating three-by-four-mile chunk of land at the southernmost tip of the continental United States. Clothes. Food. Music. The lazy way people moved and spoke. Their laid-back attitudes and unhurried lifestyles.

She had been enamored with it at first. Key West had seemed a paradise accessible without passport. A world away from her hard-driving, industrial girlhood hometown of Pittsburg, Pennsylvania.

The garden room metamorphosed into another, more formal living space. That led to a cavernous three-story foyer. Marble floors. Chandelier. A wide, central staircase.

Carla climbed the staircase. The upstairs hallway was wide, carpeted in a pile so thick her toes would get lost in it—if she took off her shoes and socks.

She had a big picture of that. *"Oh, hey, Val. I just wanted to experience what real wealth feels like against the bottoms of my feet."*

Val appeared in a doorway at the end of the hall. "In here."

The bedroom was pure opulence. Huge four-poster bed carved out of some light, no doubt rare, wood. Satin and velvet drapes in a gold color. Tassels as big as a linebacker's fist. Mirrors, gold framed, ornate. Carla's lips lifted. Positioned, cleverly, to both the left, right and head of the bed.

Larry Bernhardt had lived like royalty. And, apparently, he enjoyed watching the fun his money could buy.

"What are you thinking?" Val asked.

Carla glanced at her boss. He stood, hands on his hips, head cocked slightly to the side as he studied her. Sometimes Valentine Lopez took her breath away—he was that handsome.

Too bad he had never given her a second glance.

"That Larry Bernhardt was self-indulgent, self-important and more than a little bit naughty."

Her boss's eyebrows shot up in question, and she smiled. "Check out the mirrors. And I'm sure with his assets, he didn't lack for company."

Her superior knew exactly what kind of assets she referred to. "Money," he murmured with a hint of bitterness, "the international language of love."

Carla nodded, agreeing with the comment and understanding the bitterness. For a woman it wasn't money, but youth. A killer body. Big breasts. The ability to suck a golf ball through a garden hose.

What about personality? Carla thought. What about brains, loyalty and a good heart? She glanced back and caught a glimpse of herself in one of the mirrors. Sun-streaked sandy hair, pert nose, wide-set hazel eyes. Too many freckles, each earned on the beach while baking.

A lump formed in her throat. She looked old, she thought with a sense of shock. Not the dewy-eyed twenty-four-year-old who had accompanied a man she barely knew for a weekend on Key West, packing little more than lip gloss and a string bikini.

Six years. It seemed impossible. She had officially become what the locals referred to as a "freshwater conch" just this past January.

The same month she had turned thirty.

She swallowed hard, remembering that twenty-four-year-old girl. She had dumped the guy and begun a passionate love affair with Key West. And like all such affairs, it had burned hotly but gone cold fast.

Not that she regretted her decision to move here. But the fact was, she was no longer twenty-four, no more a total babe in a string bikini. Now, instead of worshiping the sun, she feared it for the damage it had done to her skin. Now she recognized that the most eligible bachelors on the island were beyond her reach—they were all tourists; they didn't stay.

Carla wanted stability. A good man who loved her. Kids.

She feared she would die single and childless.

"This look like the scene of a crime to you?" Val asked.

Carla blinked and glanced at her boss, confused. "Crime? Looks like a suicide to me."

"No note."

"Leapers don't always leave a note." She moved her gaze over the bedroom. Other than the unmade bed, the room was *Home and Gardens* neat. It appeared the man had awakened, walked out onto the balcony and jumped.

She shook her head. "What makes someone like Bernhardt kill himself? Looks to me like he had just about everything a guy could want." When Val remained silent, she frowned. "You think someone helped him over that rail?"

"No, that's not what's bothering me. This place cost big money. Too much money. He was a loan officer, for Pete's sake."

"A VP. I imagine those guys make good salaries."

Val narrowed his eyes. "But Island National isn't exactly Bank One. The smaller the bank, the smaller the compensation. Come in here."

He led her to the bathroom. At first all Carla saw was the sheer size and opulence of the room. The marble garden tub, with its gold fittings, could comfortably accommodate four. A gold cherub perched on each corner of the tub; each held an urn that served as a water spout. As in the bedroom, mirrors had been strategically placed for maximum viewing pleasure. A TV had been mounted from the ceiling at one end of the tub.

"It's kind of tacky," she murmured. "Don't you think?"

"I wasn't pointing out the décor. Take a look at this." Val pressed a button hidden beneath the counter: a panel of the cabinetry below the sink popped open, revealing a chamber filled with a cache of drugs and drug paraphernalia.

Carla whistled low, under her breath. *Ecstasy. Co-*

caine. Mirrors. Razor blades. She lifted her gaze to Val's. "Drugs, sex and rock 'n' roll. So much for the image of the buttoned-down banker."

"Trust me, this guy didn't miss a trick. Check this out."

Val opened the top left vanity drawer, revealing vials of prescription drugs lined up in neat rows, like small, brown soldiers.

Carla pulled on the rubber gloves she always carried and sifted through them, reading the labels. *Zanax. Quaalude. Vicadin. Prozac.* "Seems Bernhardt had a dependency problem."

"It would seem so." Val frowned. "Notice that the same doctor's name appears on all these labels. I want you to pay him a visit. Let's make sure he had a medical reason for prescribing these drugs. Let's find out how the combination could have been affecting Bernhardt's moods."

"Got it."

"Charlie's been called?"

Charlie was a local mortician whose funeral parlor housed bodies until the medical examiner, who serviced all the keys and was located on Marathon Key, could pick them up.

She answered that he had and followed Val back out to the bedroom.

She watched as he moved his gaze assessingly over the room. Valentine Lopez was one of the smartest people she had ever known. She loved to watch him work. The truth was, he awed her.

"The pieces don't fit," he murmured, looking at her. "This is the home of a millionaire."

"He could have family money," Carla offered. "Or he could have been dealing."

"Could have," Val agreed. "When we finish up here, I want you to head over to Island National. Talk to Bernhardt's boss. Find out the man's salary, if he comes from money, if he recently came into some sort of windfall—an inheritance, big bonus, winning lottery ticket, anything like that."

Carla took out her spiral and carefully noted Val's requests, word for word. She had no illusions about being a super sleuth. She was a meat-and-potatoes kind of cop: dependable, conscientious and loyal, both to Val and the department. Those were all good qualities. Admirable. She was proud of them.

But a whiz kid she would never be. She would never be the one who broke the big case, never be the one who uncovered the missing piece of the puzzle or made the front page of the *Key West Citizen*.

Valentine Lopez was. Rick Wells was.

At the thought of Rick, her chest tightened. They had been partners and friends. Then she had made the mistake of falling in love with him. A mistake because he had been a man incapable of loving her back—first because he had been reeling over the loss of his wife, then his son.

As if loving him from afar was stupid enough, she had allowed him to use her for physical solace.

Use her? She had thrown herself at him, had all but begged him to become her lover. She had been certain he would fall in love with her. He had been in so much pain. He would be grateful. Gratitude would become need, love would follow.

She had been blinded by love. Had allowed wishful thinking to pass for logic. The moment he began emerging from his grief-induced fog, he had felt guilty. Because he didn't love her. Because he felt like a heel, an opportunist. And because only then had he realized how much she cared for him.

It had been over almost before it started.

It still hurt sometimes more than she could stand.

"Speak with the housekeeper before you leave," Val continued, cocking his head. From downstairs came the sound of the other officers arriving. "Ask about Bernhardt's mood of late, his social life, if he was dating anyone." He glanced at his watch and started for the door. "We need to contact next of kin. I heard he was divorced. Has a couple grown kids. Keep me informed."

"I will," Carla murmured, not lifting her gaze from the spiral. "You want me to take another look around here?"

"You can, but I checked it out pretty well. The evidence guys will go over the place with a fine-tooth comb."

"Gotcha." She flipped the spiral shut. "After you, Lieutenant."

They made their way down the stairs to the central foyer. There they parted company. Carla found the housekeeper in the kitchen, sitting at the table, staring blankly at the doorway. She blinked when Carla spoke.

"I'm sorry, what did you say?"

"Are you all right?"

"I don't know what to do. There's laundry. And shopping and…"

Her voice trailed off and again Carla felt pity for the woman. "I think you can go home," she murmured, tone gentle. "Before you do, I need to ask you a few questions."

The woman nodded, and Carla opened her spiral. "Your name?"

"Maria Charez."

"How long have you been in Mr. Bernhardt's employ?"

"A year last month."

"Did Mr. Bernhardt seem upset about anything?"

She shook her head.

"Was he depressed at all? Moody?"

"No, no, he seemed happy. He was good to me. Never a cross word. Generous."

"Generous? In what way?"

"When my daughter was sick, he let me stay with her. He still pay me my full wage."

"Go on."

"He always say please. And thank-you." She paused, eyes filling with tears. "He look at me when I speak. Most don't."

Carla understood. The wealthy often treated their domestics like nonentities, wanting them to be seen but not heard, to take orders but not be acknowledged.

The housekeeper looked down at her hands, then back up at Carla, expression anguished. "Why would he do this thing?"

"That's what we're trying to figure out. But I need your help." The woman nodded and Carla went on. "I understand he was divorced. When was that?"

"Last year, before Christmas." The woman's expression puckered with disapproval. "That one, she was very young. Very spoiled."

Carla cocked an eyebrow. "That one? There were other Mrs. Bernhardts?"

"Yes, a long time ago. The woman he had children with. The children, they are grown now."

Carla made a note in the spiral. "How about a girlfriend? Was he dating anyone in particular?"

She shook her head. "He had parties. He invite many girls."

Girls. A bitter taste settled on Carla's tongue. It seemed the older and richer guys got, the younger the woman they dated became. To them, thirty was over the hill. "You were here for these parties?"

"No, but I— Never mind."

Carla frowned. "What?"

The woman folded her hands in her lap; Carla saw that they trembled. "Twice I came to work, and the girls, they were still here. And once I saw...pictures."

"Pictures?" Carla repeated, straightening. "Of the girls?"

The woman shifted her gaze. "I am ashamed... I shouldn't have... Mr. Bernhardt, he would be very angry—"

"Mr. Bernhardt is dead. And anything you can tell me will help me figure out why. Where did you see these photos?"

"I can show you."

The woman led Carla back up to Bernhardt's bedroom and the highboy to the right of the bed. The evidence guys didn't even glance up. She opened the top drawer, reached inside and pushed aside the neatly arranged rows of folded handkerchiefs. "I found by accident," she explained. "I was putting away his things and...there it was."

"It" was a false-bottom drawer. And now its compartment was empty.

Carla frowned. "Did Mr. Bernhardt know you'd found this?"

"No...I was too ashamed and...what I saw—" Her face went red; she glanced at the officer kneeling beside the bed, examining it. "I prayed for him. I ask the Lord to forgive him his sins."

Carla could get little else out of her. Apparently, the girls in the photographs had been very young, naked and performing various sexual acts. The housekeeper had been unable to say if they had been underage. She had been unaware of any illegal activities occurring on the premises.

Some sins, Carla thought, glancing back at Bernhardt's home as she boarded the ferry back to the main island, even death couldn't erase.

CHAPTER 7

The Key West Police Department was located in Old Town on Angela Street. The pink, stuccoed building, the color so typical of south Florida, also housed City Hall. The unexceptional, aging two-story building, surrounded by a riot of trees, flowering shrubs and runaway weeds, hardly seemed a modern law enforcement hub.

But like everything else Liz had seen so far on this island, it possessed a casual, sometimes dilapidated, charm.

She had spent the weekend unpacking, planning and familiarizing herself with the key. She had done the latter on foot and with the motor scooter she had rented from a kiosk just up the block from her office.

It had been a difficult weekend. Everything she'd

seen had reminded her of Rachel. When her sister had first come to Key West, she had called Liz almost daily. She had described the island vividly, the people, her new church and congregation. She had described the local landscape with its wild profusion of flora in a palette of oranges, pinks and reds; its palms in so many varieties it boggled the mind—Chinese, sawtooth, coconut and windmill—and the island's architecture, with its Caribbean, Victorian and Latin influences.

Seeing the island through her own eyes had brought Rachel's conversations to life. In the moments Liz had been able to detach from her emotions, she had understood why her sister had fallen in love with this place.

Those moments had been punctuations in a narrative of pain. How could she see any beauty in the place that had taken her sister from her?

Liz turned her attention to the task before her: Lieutenant Lopez. Step number one in the plan she had put together over the weekend. She hoped to convince him to reopen his investigation into Rachel's disappearance. At the very least, she intended to put him on notice: she had loved her sister and wouldn't rest until she uncovered the truth about her whereabouts. She wanted a copy of her sister's case file and she wouldn't leave until he gave it to her.

A nervous laugh bubbled to her lips. Big bad Liz. Right. If any more butterflies landed in her stomach, she'd throw up.

Taking a deep breath, she squared her shoulders and started up the police department's front steps. She hadn't made an appointment; she had wanted the element of surprise on her side. She imagined Detective Lopez would be anything but happy to see her.

She entered the building and crossed to the receptionist's station, located to her left. The woman behind the desk greeted her with a perky smile. Liz figured her to be in her mid-fifties although she dressed more like a teenager, complete with rhinestone-studded butterfly clips in her hair.

"How can I help you, hon?" she asked.

Liz forced a confident smile. "I need to see Lieutenant Lopez. Is he in?"

"Your name?"

"Elizabeth Ames."

She drew her cotton-candy pink lips into a pucker. "Do you have an appointment?"

"No. But he'll know what this is in reference to."

"Okay, doll." She motioned the logbook on the counter. "Sign in. I'll see if he's available."

Liz did as she requested, heart beginning to race. *This was it, the moment of truth.* She scrawled her name, turned and crossed to the seating area behind her, though she didn't sit. From behind her she heard the woman asking someone named Becky if Val was available. As she listened, she stared blankly at the worn vinyl seats, struggling to get a grip on her runaway nerves. She understood cops because professionally she had crossed paths with quite a number of them over the years. That tended to happen when counseling families in crisis and delinquent teens. She had even done a stint at the St. Charles County juvenile detention center. Those six months had been a trial by fire—and had convinced her to go into private practice.

What she had learned during those months, however, had been invaluable. Including the best way to deal with police officers. They were a proud breed, independent, sometimes arrogant, often stubborn. She had to play this just right. Lieutenant Lopez could make what she had come to Key West to do easy for her…or extremely difficult.

"Lieutenant Lopez said you should come on up." Liz turned to face the receptionist. "You know where his office is?"

"No, I—"

"It's a piece of cake. Take the stairs." She pointed. "Top of the stairs, take a right. His is the one with the Dutch door. And don't worry, sugar. Unless you're one of the bad guys, Lieutenant Lopez is a real sweetheart."

Unless she was one of the bad guys. Why didn't she find that comforting?

Liz followed the woman's directions. As promised, finding Valentine Lopez's office posed no difficulty. The upper half of his door was open and she tapped on the casing. "Lieutenant Lopez?" she asked.

Valentine Lopez looked up and smiled. Liz was struck by two things: how handsome he was, and the fact that his smile didn't reach his eyes.

The man stood and motioned her in. "Ms. Ames, this is a surprise."

"I'm sure it is." She crossed to him. They shook hands, then sat. "Thank you for seeing me."

"What brings you to Key West?"

"That should be obvious." She heard the angry edge in her voice and worked to quell it. "My sister, Lieutenant."

He settled back in his chair. Its aging springs creaked with the movement. "How can I help?"

"I'd like you to reopen your investigation into her disappearance."

"I can't do that. I'm sorry. Ask me something else."

"She didn't suffer a mental breakdown and run off, Lieutenant. I'm positive she didn't."

"How do you know?"

The wording of his question caught her off guard. His slightly confrontational tone didn't. "I know my sister, Lieutenant Lopez. She's not given to emotionalism or flights of fancy. In fact, she's the most stable person I've ever known."

"That's an awfully confident claim."

"It's true."

"So, you believe her to be alive?"

"Pardon me?"

"You're referring to her in the present tense. But if she's alive and didn't run off, where is she?"

Liz felt his words like a blow to her gut. She went cold, then hot. Tears stung her eyes. "No, Lieutenant, I…I'm afraid she's…"

She cleared her throat, struggling to find her voice, to speak clearly and confidently. She had to convince him. "I'm afraid she was murdered, Lieutenant Lopez. I'm afraid she uncovered some sort of illegal activities on the island and was murdered because of it. I wish I didn't think this."

For a long moment he said nothing. When he finally spoke, his tone was patient. "If she had uncovered illegal activities on the island, why didn't she call me?"

"I don't know. Perhaps she called one of the other detectives?"

"She didn't." He softened his tone. "The most grounded of people can suffer a mental breakdown, it happens all the time. One can be precipitated by extreme stress, uncertainty, even physical conditions such as—"

"I'm a social worker," she snapped. "I'm well aware of the kind of influences that can bring about a mental breakdown."

"But you're Rachel's sister. Often it's the people closest to us we see with the least clarity."

She ignored the truth of that. "I'm her only family. More than three months have passed. If she's alive, why hasn't she contacted me?"

"I can't answer that with any certainty, Ms. Ames. Perhaps she's operating under some sort of paranoid delusions. Her behavior certainly suggested something of that sort. As did the claims she made on your answering machine. Or perhaps she's physically unable to contact you."

Liz balled her hands into fists. "Are you suggesting she's developed amnesia? That phenomenon is extremely rare, much more so than murder, I'm sorry to say."

He tossed his pen on the table, expression frustrated. "I'm suggesting nothing, Ms. Ames. I'm offering you possibilities."

"Sorry, Lieutenant, but in my opinion, they don't hold water."

"Really." He cocked an eyebrow. "How about this one? Perhaps she doesn't wish to contact you. By your own account, you two argued the last time you spoke."

Heat flew to Liz's cheeks. Guilty heat. "Yes, we argued," she retorted, tone defensive. "But not so bitterly that—"

"If she was murdered, where's the blood? The signs of a struggle? The body?" He leaned forward, gaze locked with hers. "We found nothing to indicate your sister met with a violent end. That should be a relief for you to hear, Ms. Ames. I'm a little surprised it isn't."

She ignored the comment, though it hit its mark. Why *wasn't* she eager to believe her sister alive? What was wrong with her? "I want you to reopen the case."

"I'm sorry, but there's no evidence to justify my doing so." He stood, signaling an end to their conversation.

Reluctantly, Liz followed him to his feet. "I'd like a copy of the police report."

"Sorry, can't help you." He glanced at his watch. "If there's nothing else, I have another appointment."

She had blown it, she knew. She had marched in here, all demands and accusations. Rachel had always admonished her for being a hothead. *"Liz, sweetie, try a little honey next time."*

Liz swallowed her anger and held a hand out. "Please, Lieutenant Lopez. By your own account, the investigation is closed. Perhaps I'll see something in the file you overlooked, something—"

"You won't." He met her gaze evenly. "Make no mistake, Ms. Ames, I'm extremely thorough. This is my town, my little slice of heaven on earth, and I take every infraction of the law seriously. I don't look the other way and I don't take the easy way. If I had found one *shred* of evidence indicating your sister was murdered, I would have aggressively pursued the investigation."

"And if I find evidence, Lieutenant? Will you reopen and aggressively pursue the investigation?"

"Yes, dammit. Of course I will."

"Consider yourself on notice, then. Because I intend to discover what happened to my sister. In fact, I've put my life on hold to do it. And I don't care how long it takes." She reached into her pocket and pulled out one of the business cards she'd had printed at the Speedy-print over the weekend.

He glanced at it, then back at her, one corner of his mouth lifting. "I admire your determination. I think it's misplaced, but hey, I've only been a lawman for eleven years. May I ask what your first step is going to be?"

She shot him what she hoped was a winning smile. "Your report, of course."

He stared at her a moment, then tipped back his head and laughed. "All right, you win." He held up a hand, stopping her thanks. "But you can't take it from the building or make a copy. And before you try hitting me with the Freedom of Information Act, that act applies most specifically to cases that have already been tried. Since you've just told me that I'll be reopening this case, I guess I better make certain the information isn't contaminated. Agreed?"

"Agreed."

"I'll get you set up in one of the interrogation rooms."

She smiled again, relieved. "Thanks, Lieutenant Lopez. I—"

He cut her off. "A word of warning, Ms. Ames. Key Westers are fiercely loyal to their own. Fiercely...protective. I suggest you tread carefully. Try not to step on too many toes. You won't like what happens."

CHAPTER 8

Monday, November 5
1:15 p.m.

Three hours later, Liz exited the police department, thoughts swirling with what she had read in the police report Valentine Lopez had given her. It seemed he and his detectives had, indeed, done a thorough job investigating Rachel's disappearance. They had interviewed nearly two dozen members of the congregation at Paradise Christian. All had expressed shock and dismay over their pastor's disappearance—but not surprise. Pastor Rachel had been behaving strangely, they'd said. Differently from the woman they had chosen to lead their flock. Her sermons had become bizarre, and she had been acting secretive, nervous and jumpy. One woman reported paying a call on Rachel and finding her crying. Several others had reported Rachel stopping by their home unexpectedly to ask questions about their teenage children.

The police had also spoken with her sister's housekeeper, the church groundskeeper, secretary and a handful of others Rachel had had contact with in her last days. The report mentioned a teenager in Rachel's counsel, but not the youngster's name.

The police had done a complete search of both the parsonage, church and its grounds. That search had yielded nothing out of the ordinary—and certainly not anything to indicate her sister had been a victim of violence. By that point they had begun to conclude Pastor Rachel had disappeared under her own power, but as a matter of course they had issued a statewide BOLO— police vernacular for Be On the Lookout For—then had contacted all the morgues, hospitals and medical centers in south Florida.

Their efforts had yielded nothing.

Soon after they had closed the investigation.

The scream of tires skidding to a halt startled her out of her thoughts. Liz realized with a shock that she had stepped off the sidewalk and into traffic.

"What the hell's wrong with you, lady! You got a death wish or something!"

Heart thundering, Liz scurried backward. Vivid pink petals from a low-hanging branch of the oleander tree above her fluttered to the ground. The irate driver gunned his engine and pulled past her, shooting her a disgusted look as he did.

Liz brought a hand to her chest, shaken. What was wrong with her? She could have been killed. If that driver had been distracted or traffic had been heavier...

She sucked in a shuddering breath, working for calm. Her therapist had warned her she didn't have the emotional wherewithal for this. He had warned that signs of her fragile state would manifest itself in a number of ways: emotional highs and lows, forgetfulness, feelings of being overwhelmed or confused. Inability to concentrate.

"Ms. Ames? Are you all right?"

Liz glanced over her shoulder. Lieutenant Lopez stood in the KWPD doorway, expression concerned. Obviously, he had seen her boneheaded waltz into oncoming traffic. *Dammit. The last thing she wanted him to know was just how thin an emotional thread she was hanging by.*

She forced a smile. "Fine. Thanks for asking."

"You need to be more careful. Traffic in this town can be pretty unforgiving."

She stared at him a moment, unsettled. She found something vaguely threatening in his tone, his conciliatory expression. Just as she had earlier, when he had warned her about stepping on Key Westers' toes.

Sweat beaded across her upper lip. She opened her mouth to speak, the voice that passed her lips was hardly her own, high and frightened sounding. She cringed at it, imagining his amusement. All but hearing his thoughts:

A family of fruitcakes. Her and her sister both.

Liz turned and hurried toward Duval Street, concentrating on walking with purpose and confidence, shoulders back, head held high. She felt his gaze on her and fought glancing back.

If she did, he would know. He would see.

She was losing her mind.

Liz put one foot in front of the other, again and again. Sweat pooled under her arms and rolled down her spine.

Light-headed, she focused on breathing deeply, on filling her lungs. *Oxygen in. Garbage out.*

People streamed around her. She sensed their curious glances. Her heart beat faster, out of control. She struggled to breathe, to keep moving blindly forward, to maintain.

Liz knew what was happening to her. A panic attack. Brought on by stress, by extreme anxiety. She had suffered a number of them in recent months, her first the afternoon she'd caught her husband in bed with her so-called best friend, the second a week later when one of her clients, a teenager named Shera, attempted to kill herself by taking a handful of pills.

She couldn't think about that, those things, not now. *A bench. She needed to find a place to sit.* Frantic, Liz darted her gaze from left to right, searching.

Finally, she located one. She collapsed onto it and dropped her head to her knees. She breathed deeply and slowly, as her therapist had instructed.

Oxygen in. Garbage out.

Let it go. It was going to be all right. Everything was going to be all right.

Little by little, her heart slowed, her skin cooled. The attack that had held her in its clammy grip passed. Still she sat, face cradled in her hands. Dear Lord, how could she help others, when she was falling apart herself? How could she find her sister's killer, when she couldn't even talk to one of the good guys without sliding into an abyss of anxiety?

Liz lifted her head. And realized where she was. Where her subconscious had led her.

Paradise Christian Church.

Calm poured over and through her. A sense of focus, of purpose.

Rachel.

Gooseflesh raced up Liz's arms. She whispered her sister's name, her thoughts and senses flooded with her. She felt her presence so keenly, she fully expected to see her emerge from the church. Rachel would smile, wave and cross over in that goofy loping gait of hers, the one more like a golden retriever's than a grown woman's. She would enfold Liz in her arms for a big warm hug.

And everything would be okay.

"Are you all right?"

With a start, Liz jerked her gaze from the church entrance. A woman she had never seen before stood in front of her, expression concerned.

Liz blinked. "I'm sorry, what?"

The woman held out a bottle of water. "I own the store across the street. You look like you could use this."

"Thanks. I really could." Liz managed a weak smile and took the bottle. She cracked the seal and took a long drink. She felt better immediately.

"This heat is vicious. I tell visitors to keep water with them at all times. Staying hydrated is the key."

The woman smiled again and Liz realized this was the most beautiful woman she had ever met. A natural blonde, the way some very young children are, with eyes the color of a perfect summer sky.

Liz returned her smile. "What do I owe you for the water?"

She waved aside the offer. "My treat."

"A real Good Samaritan. In this day and age no less."

"Go figure." The woman looked over her shoulder. "I better get back to the shop. Bikinis & Things." She pointed. "Stop by, I've got some real cute bathing suits."

"Thanks, I will."

A couple of teens zipped by on bicycles. One of them twisted around and waved. "Hey, Heather!"

"Hey, Melanie," she called back. "Got a new shipment of suits in."

"Awesome."

The woman turned back to Liz. "Nice meeting you. Remember, stop by."

"Wait!" Liz launched to her feet. "I didn't say thanks."

"You didn't have to." She wiggled her fingers. "Ciao."

Liz watched the other woman walk away, feeling for the first time like maybe not everyone on Key West was her adversary.

CHAPTER 9

Tuesday, November 6
Noon

Carla sat at her desk, staring at the fax she had received only moments before. It was the facsimile of an e-ticket, one-way, to the Cayman Islands. The name on the ticket: Larry Bernhardt. The travel date: November 9, 2001.

This coming Friday. A week to the day after he had leaped out his bedroom window.

She might not be an ace detective, but that didn't make sense to her.

But then, much of the information she had amassed in the past twenty-four hours hadn't. Bernhardt had been well thought of at Island National, liked and respected both by his coworkers and superiors. His boss believed he had come into a sizable inheritance this past January, though he hadn't known from where. That's when he had bought the oceanfront home.

He had been married twice; he and wife number two, the barely-out-of-her-teens Mrs. Bernhardt the housekeeper had spoken of, had divorced shortly after they'd moved into the Sunset Key home. He had two grown children, a boy and a girl, from his first marriage, both of whom he was close to. Carla had spoken with the daughter, who had been stunned. Devastated. The young woman had talked to her father the week before, she'd said; his mood had been jubilant.

His mood jubilant. Carla frowned. That had been a recurring theme. Everyone she'd talked to had described Bernhardt as happy, relaxed…on top of the world—personally and professionally. In fact, the night of his death he had been out to dinner with friends. He had talked with them about his children, his work, the future.

He hadn't mentioned a trip, however. And he certainly hadn't mentioned thoughts of taking his own life.

Carla tapped the fax, curious. The only dissenting opinion about Bernhardt's psychological state had come from his shrink. Dr. Irwin Morgenstern had stated that he'd been treating Bernhardt for severe depression and anxiety. He had prescribed a number of different medications in an attempt to stabilize him.

Considering what everyone else had said, Carla figured that was bullshit. Bernhardt had been a recreational drug user—either wittingly or unwittingly, Dr. Morgenstern had been his supplier.

A one-way ticket. She frowned. Typically, a person who bought a one-way ticket was either someone without a job or personal responsibilities or someone who was running away from something. Or somebody. A bad marriage. Financial responsibilities. The law.

So, what had Bernhardt been running away from? And why did a man with a one-way ticket to the Cayman

Islands, a beautiful home and plenty of money, on top professionally and, from what the housekeeper and other friends had said, getting laid frequently, take a swan dive out his third-floor bedroom window?

He didn't. No way.

So maybe Bernhardt had been helped out that window.

Carla shifted her attention to the evidence report. They hadn't found much. The fingerprints on the champagne bottle and pill vial were Bernhardt's. They'd collected several pubic hairs from the bed; the satin sheets had been stained with what appeared to be semen. Fresh stains, the report said. Not ones that had been laundered in.

Carla frowned, something plucking at her memory. Maybe she should head over to Bernhardt's, take another look around?

She slid her gaze to the clock mounted on the wall across from her. Just after noon. Val was at lunch. He had an appointment with the D.A. afterward. She caught her bottom lip between her teeth. Val liked to be kept abreast of his detectives' activities; she respected that, and she certainly trusted his instincts a hell of a lot more than she trusted her own.

But she didn't feel like sitting on her thumbs all afternoon waiting for him to give her the go-ahead. Screw it, she decided, pushing away from her desk and standing. Val had made it clear that Bernhardt's death was priority one, and she had nothing else to do this afternoon. She'd just go and take another look at Bernhardt's bedroom.

Within ten minutes Carla stood at the Hilton/Mallory Square boat dock, waiting for the ferry. A murder on Sunset Key presented some interesting challenges, she acknowledged. The key was accessible only by boat, a twenty-four-hour ferry that motored guests and residents to and from the mainland. With the exception of "official" battery-powered carts, no motorized vehicles were allowed on the island. And other than a sign warning Private Property, Sunset Key Residents Only, security was nonexistent. People came and went; nobody asked for proof of resort registration or residency.

Typical Key West, Carla thought. Not a care in the world.

The ferry, a handsome, thirty-two-foot powerboat, arrived. Carla waited for several passengers to disembark, then she climbed aboard. She caught the captain's curious gaze and met it. He looked away.

After waiting five minutes for more passengers to arrive, he set off. Carla faced forward, holding her hair away from her face to keep the wind from tearing at it.

"You're a cop, right?"

Carla shifted her gaze to the ferryboat captain once more. "Right. How did you—"

"I ferried you over on Monday. I heard you and your colleague talking." He looked away, then back, squinting against the brilliant sun. "Shame about Bernhardt. He seemed like a nice guy."

"You knew him?"

"Not really. I've only been on staff a month. It's just... I mean, I ferried him back and forth."

"I bet you're from Boston," she said, tilting her head, deciding he was cute. "Judging by your accent."

His lips lifted. "My family's still in shock. They just don't get why I like it here."

She slid her gaze to his left hand, found it ringless and smiled. "Mine didn't either."

"You know—" He cleared his throat. "I ferried him the night...he did it."

Carla straightened, flirtation forgotten. "That so? How'd he seem to you?"

"Same as always. Friendly. Relaxed. Nice guy," he said again, easing up on the throttle as he neared the dock.

"Anybody with him that night?" she asked as he cut the power, then maneuvered the craft against the dock.

"Not that night." He hopped up, tied off the bow, then stern. That done, he turned back to her, a frown marring his forehead. "Bernhardt seemed to have it all. So why'd he do it? I don't get that at all."

That made two of them. She stood and allowed him to help her disembark, though she was capable of managing on her own.

"I'm Detective Carla Chapman." She handed him her card. "You think of anything, give me a call."

He slid his dark gaze over her. "I'll do that...Carla."

For a split second, she thought he might suggest they get together sometime. He didn't, and she quashed her disappointment and returned her attention to Bernhardt. Since his death hadn't been officially classified yet, his home was still considered a crime scene. She ducked under the police line and entered. The interior was dim and cool. The housekeeper had drawn the drapes and closed the blinds when she left.

Carla climbed the stairs. The air conditioner kicked on. Other than the bed having been stripped by the evidence guys, she found the bedroom just as she had left it the other day. She moved her gaze slowly over the room acknowledging that she had most probably wasted her time by coming here.

Suddenly she realized what had been plucking at her

memory. The housekeeper had told her that Bernhardt had insisted on fresh bedding every day. Which meant, when he had climbed in the sack the last night of his life, the sheets had not been stained. She narrowed her eyes. Sure, the man could have jacked off one last time before taking the plunge. The hairs could be his.

But they might not be. And if they weren't, that meant Larry Bernhardt had not been alone the night of his death.

CHAPTER 10

Tuesday, November 6
3:00 p.m.

Paradise Christian Church rose up from the sidewalk, a stark, blistering white against the flat blue sky. Its bell tower and crucifix broke the sky, as if stamped from the field of blue by a baker wielding a giant cookie cutter.

Several types of palms dotted the churchyard; a royal poinciana tree with its brilliant red blossoms draped itself over the walkway.

Liz passed through the open iron gate and climbed the tile stairs to the church's front doors. They stood open, welcoming the faithful, bidding them an invitation to enter. And be saved.

She thought of Rachel and a lump formed in her throat. Liz paused to collect herself. She couldn't let emotionalism get in the way of what she had to do here.

This was her next step. The last place Rachel had been seen. The place she had loved most in the world.

If there were clues to be found, surely she would find them here.

She had made an appointment with Pastor Tim Collins, her sister's replacement. She had rehearsed what she would say to him, none of which included the whole truth. She feared that if she announced her real reason for being on Key West, he would clam up. She feared everyone would.

Liz entered the church narthex, becoming immediately aware of the stillness, the absolute quiet. She breathed deeply, registering the scent of lemon polish and candle wax.

Liz glanced around, realizing immediately why her sister had fallen in love with this church. It was old, lovely and imbued with the feeling of God's presence, one not every church possessed. Perhaps it was the stained-glass windows—of which there were an abundance—or simply the echoes of more than one hundred years of prayers.

"Are you here for the tour?" a young woman asked from the hallway to Liz's right. "You're early."

"No, not for the tour." She moved her gaze over the interior. "Though I'd love to take it." She returned her gaze to the teenager, a pretty girl of about sixteen. Liz wondered what the teenager would say if she asked her about Rachel. Would she remember her? Could she be the girl Rachel had been counseling? The one mentioned in the police report? "I have an appointment with Pastor Collins. Do you know where I could find him?"

"Pastor Tim? Sure." She smiled widely and pointed down the hallway behind her. "He's in his office. I was just talking to him."

"Thanks." Liz started past the girl, then stopped. "What time's the tour? I might try to join up after my visit with Pastor Collins."

"Three-thirty. I'll look for you."

Liz continued down the hallway, one side lined with shuttered windows that faced Duval Street, the other with what appeared to be classrooms and the nursery. She found the church office and pastor's study at the end of the hall.

The receptionist's desk was empty so Liz moved on to the study and tapped on the half-open door. "Pastor Collins? Liz Ames."

"Ms. Ames, hello." He smiled warmly, stood and waved her inside. Liz realized with some surprise that he was quite tall, over six feet, and built more like a professional football player than a preacher. "And please, call me Pastor Tim. Everybody else does."

"I will. And call me Liz." She returned his smile and crossed the room. After shaking his hand, she took the seat across from his. "Your church is lovely."

"Thank you." He swept his gaze over the study, his expression one of pure pleasure. "Paradise Christian is the oldest church on the island. It was actually St. Stephen's until 1936, when the Catholic archdiocese sold the property to build a larger facility on the other side of the island."

"It's amazing it's survived," she murmured, recalling the things Rachel had told her about the church. "Didn't I hear that it was destroyed by a hurricane and had to be rebuilt?"

"Partially rebuilt, twice actually. The first after the hurricane of 1846, then again after the one in 1935. The present building dates from 1940."

"I love old buildings. I might try to hook up with the tour later."

"If you miss today's, we offer them every day but Sunday."

"Have you been with Paradise Christian long?"

"Just a few months. My predecessor left rather suddenly and after only a short time with the congregation."

Liz's heart skipped a beat. She fought to keep her reaction from showing. "How strange. I can't imagine just up and leaving a place as beautiful as this."

"Not everyone is cut out for island life," he murmured, then changed the subject. "You said on the phone that you're a family counselor?"

"Yes." She straightened. "As I explained then, I'm a licensed clinical social worker, which is a fancy way of saying I'm a social worker who is certified for private practice. I specialize in adolescent counseling and, as you know, am new to Key West. I'm trying to get the word out that I'm here."

She dug several business cards out of her wallet and handed them to him. "I thought you might know of some within your congregation in need of counseling and that you might send them my way."

He paused as if searching for the right words. "My congregation isn't a wealthy one, Liz. Yes, there are people of great wealth on the island, but many more of moderate means. Our main industry is tourism and the majority of the island's year-round inhabitants service that industry."

He stood and crossed to his window. Sun spilled through, drenching him in golden light, making him look younger than the thirty-five she had originally guessed him to be. "As I'm sure you've already discovered, Key West is a very expensive place to live. Cost of living here exceeds that of Miami and is, in fact, one of the most expensive places to live in the continental United States."

"That surprises me."

He turned and met her eyes. "We're so isolated here. Three and a half hours from Miami, with only one road leading out. Everything has to be shipped in. Power, most food, tap water and nearly anything else you can think of. We're landlocked, so property, even rentals, go for a premium." His mouth lifted. "Not many of my flock can afford fifty to ninety dollars an hour for counseling, no matter how much they may need it."

The pastor had a rich, melodious voice and a way of looking at her when he spoke that made her think he really did care about her. That he really was a man of God.

"Which is why," she responded, "I'm willing to waive or reduce my fees for those in need. I believe that it's often the ones who need help the most who can least afford to get it."

He glanced at her business card, then back up at her, eyebrows arched. "And exactly how are *you* going to pay your rent? This address doesn't come cheap, that I know."

"As best I can," she answered evasively, then smiled. "I don't live lavishly, Pastor. As far as I'm concerned, there are things much more important than fancy cars and designer clothing."

The truth was, she had sold her parents' home to finance this endeavor. They had left it to her and Rachel when they passed away last year, and she believed her parents would have supported her decision.

He grinned. "Luckily, neither of those things fit in

here on Key West. A pair of cutoffs and a moped and you're all set."

She liked him, Liz decided. As much as she could under the circumstances. "Don't forget sunglasses and a baseball cap. Very important, I've learned that already."

"Smart lady." He glanced at his watch. "I tell you what, I'll put some feelers out. There are many confused teenagers on Key West. They run the gamut from runaways and the Rainbow Nation kids, to kids of great privilege."

He paused a moment, as if carefully considering his next words. "However, there's one girl who comes to mind immediately. Nice girl, but troubled. Her parents are frantic… She was seeing the previous pastor but refused to allow me to counsel her."

Liz caught her breath. "The previous pastor was counseling her?"

"Yes, Pastor Howard. But when she left—"

"Disappeared, wasn't it?" Liz dropped her shaking hands into her lap, praying she didn't overplay her hand. "I overheard someone talking about it. They said it was kind of a freaky thing."

"Talking about it? Really?" He frowned. "I'm surprised to hear that."

"Was it…freaky, like they said?"

He returned to his chair and sat, expression pensive. "I never met Pastor Howard, but I had to…box up her things when I took over. It was an uncomfortable task."

Liz remembered getting the boxes. Remembered looking at them and falling apart. When she had finally found the strength to go through them, she'd seen nothing to indicate her sister had been in a crisis. Or in danger.

But maybe the pastor had.

"Was there anything...in her things that suggested what happened to her?" she asked, hoping she came across as simply curious. "Anything at all?"

For a second, as the pastor stared at her, Liz was certain she had given herself away. Then he shook his head. "The police feel she suffered a mental breakdown and ran off. Everything I've heard seems to support that."

"What do you mean?" She wondered if she sounded as upset as she felt. From his expression she feared she did.

He leaned forward. "Look, I don't feel comfortable talking about this. The Ninth Commandment warns us against bearing false witness against another. In today's vernacular, that translates to not talking about others, not gossiping or spreading rumors. If I knew the facts, I would share them—"

"I understand," she said quickly. "But if there's a possibility I'm going to counsel the teenager you mentioned, or anyone else whose life was touched by Pastor Howard and her disappearance, I feel I should be informed."

"The police..." He let the thought trail off, then began again. "Pastor Howard was liked quite well by the congregation...at first. As time passed, her behavior became erratic. Or so many in the congregation told me."

He looked down at his hands, folded on the desk in front of him. Big hands, Liz noted. Callused and strong. Not the soft hands of an academician or scholar.

He returned his gaze to hers, the expression in his troubled. "She'd let her pastoral duties slip. Calls to the sick and elderly weren't made, appointments weren't kept. When I came on, I found the church office in chaos. A similar situation existed in the parsonage. So you see why I agree with the police department's belief that she suffered a mental breakdown?"

Liz struggled to keep from revealing how much his words upset her. She tried to speak but found she couldn't.

"I feel for her family," he said softly. "I can only imagine how they must be suffering."

A prickle of apprehension moved up her spine. Did he know? she wondered. Had he figured out who she really was?

And if he had, could she trust anything he had just said to her?

But how could he have figured it out?

And if he somehow had, why not confront her? He didn't seem the kind of man who would practice that kind of duplicity.

Uncertain what to do, she decided to play this out as she had begun it. She stood. "I'm sure they are." She held out her hand. "I've taken enough of your time, Pastor. Thank you for seeing me."

He followed her to her feet and took her hand. "You're welcome. I will definitely speak to the teenager's parents. I suspect you'll hear from them. They're good people, Liz. I hope you can help them."

"Me, too." She thanked him again, then walked to the door. There, she looked back at him. "How long does that tour last?"

He glanced at his watch. "You should be able to catch the tail end. They'll be in the walled garden."

He gave her directions and, sure enough, she found the group in the garden and joined them. The church, parsonage and grounds, she discovered, occupied two full blocks of valuable Key West land. The Catholic archdiocese had sold the church property after the devastating hurricane of 1935 destroyed Henry Flagler's railroad, and the city of Key West, once the wealthiest city in America, went bankrupt. No doubt they were kicking themselves now.

Liz moved her gaze over the lush garden, awed, a feeling of peace settling over her. Although the church structures had been destroyed twice, the garden had been spared. The ancient banyan trees, with their vertical roots that grew from the branches to the ground, created a kind of organic jail. Liz felt as if she had fallen through the rabbit hole and landed in a surreal fantasy land of bars, flowers and foliage.

The teenage guide discussed various pieces of statuary, one of the Blessed Virgin that dated back to the original days of the church and another of St. Francis. She pointed out the church parsonage, located at the back left of the church grounds and the small cemetery at the right. The burial ground, with its stacked tombs, Liz learned, housed the remains of a number of Key West's early, influential citizens and religious leaders.

At the conclusion of the tour, the guide showed the group out, using the entrance that faced Duval Street. As Liz exited, she spied Bikinis & Things across the street and started toward it. She had wanted to stop in and thank the woman again for coming to her aid.

Liz stepped into the shop, realizing quickly that it was one of those trendy little boutiques, the kind that carried the latest and most fashionable. She saw immediately that the store catered to young people and wealthy tourists: the bathing suits were skimpy, the prices outrageous. Other than beachwear, the shop carried the work of Key West artists and artisans, including some beautiful silver and stone jewelry.

The shop was empty save for several teenagers flipping through the Just Arrived rack and exclaiming at what they saw.

"Hi, can I help you?"

Liz turned. Her Good Samaritan stood behind her, mouth curved into a warm smile. Liz returned the smile. "Heather, right?"

"Heather Ferguson. How can I—"

"I'm the woman from the church bench. You brought me a bottle of water."

Recognition crossed her features. "Of course. How are you feeling?"

"Fine, now. Thanks."

"I'm glad to hear that." She glanced over her shoulder at the group of teenagers. "You girls need some help?" They replied that they didn't, and she turned back to Liz. "Are you looking for anything special today?"

"Actually, no. I just wanted to stop by and thank you again for coming to my aid."

"I was happy to help." She glanced at the girls again, then back at Liz. "How long are you in town for?"

"A while, actually." Her lips lifted. "I know I seem like a tourist, but I'm a new resident." She held out a hand. "I'm Elizabeth Ames. I opened a family counseling practice just down the street."

"No kidding?" Heather smiled and shook her hand. "Good to meet you."

"Go ahead and help them," Liz murmured. "I'll wait."

The other woman murmured her gratitude and scurried off to catch the girls *before* they entered the dressing room. As Liz watched, Heather carefully counted the bathing suits, then ushered them into a fitting room.

Liz understood the woman's caution. She had worked with enough teens to know that shoplifting among adolescents had reached epidemic proportions. A number of the teens she had counseled had come her way after having been caught. Only then had their parents realized their children needed help.

A moment later, Heather returned. "Thanks, you can't turn your back on these kids. You wouldn't believe the number of suits that walk out of here without being rung up."

"Actually, I would. In my practice, I've worked with quite a number of teens with sticky fingers."

"Nice way to put it." Heather laughed. "I use 'thieving yuppie larvae.'"

Liz shook her head, liking the other woman. She was not only kind, but honest and funny as well. Rachel would have liked her, Liz thought. She wondered if she and Rachel had known each other.

The bell over the shop's door tinkled as another group of young women entered. "I really have to go, Liz. But let's have lunch sometime. I'll fill you in on all the dos and don'ts of Key West."

Liz laughed. "The island's so small, surely there can't be that many."

"Are you kidding? The smaller the place, the greater the number of rules."

"Sounds intimidating."

"Not if you have an old pro like me to help you through. Give me your number and I'll give you a call."

Liz gave the woman her card and exited the shop. As she did she glanced toward Paradise Christian. And found Pastor Collins standing in the open doorway, staring her way. When she lifted her hand, he turned and disappeared into the church without returning the greeting.

CHAPTER 11

Rick strolled into police headquarters, cutting across to the receptionist. Luanne Leoni had occupied the City Hall receptionist seat since well before his time on the force. A sweet-natured grandma with the fashion sense of a teenager and a heart as big as all Key West, she remained one of his favorite people in all the world. Her tears at his son's funeral had meant more to him than she would ever know.

"Hey there, sweet thing," he murmured, leaning against the counter and ducking his head to bring it level with hers. "Miss me?"

She cocked an eyebrow. "Oh sure. My cat ran off, too. And now I don't itch no more."

"You're breaking my heart, Luanne. You really are."

"You're a very bad boy, you know that?"

"Yeah?" He flashed her a quick smile. "But I could be worse, if you'd let me. You still married to that old fart?"

"You know I am. Me and my Sonny, we're going to the grave together." She laughed. "Though I don't know who's going to kill who first."

"I'm going up to see Val." He started toward the stairs, then stopped and glanced back at her. "If you kill Sonny first let me know. I'll be waiting."

She rolled her eyes. "I'm old enough to be your grandmother, you wicked man. You'd better be gone before I get a notion to take you up on that outrageous offer."

Rick headed up. He didn't often visit Val here because it brought back painful memories. And because he invariably ran into his old partner, Carla Chapman.

When he returned to Key West from Miami, Val had partnered him with Carla. Carla had been new to the force as well, an inexperienced cop who hadn't yet honed her instincts. But she had been energetic and eager to learn. Rick, an experienced, streetwise cop with crackerjack instincts, had been emotionally dazed from his wife's death and his sudden single-parent status.

They had worked well together, playing to each other's strengths and shoring up the other's weaknesses. They had become friends.

And during the terrible time after Sam's death, she had stuck by him. She had cared for him when he had given up caring for himself; she had bullied him into eating, sleeping, sobering up.

And she had been there when he had needed physical solace, the kind of solace a man can only find in a woman's arms—and bed. They had become lovers, though the relationship had been ridiculously lopsided. He had gotten everything from it, she had gotten nothing.

Carla, he had realized too late, had fallen in love with him.

With that realization had come another—their friendship was over.

He hated having hurt her and regretted having lost their friendship. He wished to God he had never laid a hand on her.

Rick reached the second floor and braced himself for seeing her—he had to pass her office to reach Val's. If he didn't stop and she learned he had been in the building, the bad feelings between them would only intensify.

She sat at her desk. She looked up when he approached, a flicker of some strong emotion crossing her face. She looked away and he silently swore.

He wasn't about to let her get away with that. "Hello, Carla."

She lifted her face. "Hello, Rick. What's brings you down to the department?"

"Just stopped by to see Val."

"He's not in. I'll tell him you were here."

She snatched up some papers and started to stand. He stopped her. "Can't we get past this, Carla? Can't we talk about it?"

She jerked up her chin. "What's there to talk about, Rick?"

He glanced over his shoulder, then took a step into her office. "What do you think? About us, what happened."

A flush spread across her cheeks. "It's over," she said, tone brittle. "What happened between us is ancient history."

He lowered his voice, not wanting anyone to overhear them. "I'm sorry I hurt you, Carla."

"Don't flatter yourself."

"I hate that we're not... I miss your friendship. If we could start over, if we could forget the past—"

She cut him off. "You know what hurts the most? Knowing how little you thought of me. How little you respected me."

"Carla, that's not true."

"It is," she hissed. "Pretty but dim, that's what you thought of me. It's the way you treated me."

"The problem was me. It *is* me." He lowered his voice more, to a strained whisper. "I couldn't love you or anyone else, Carla. I still can't."

"Well, look who the cat dragged in." Val came up behind Rick and clapped him on the shoulder. "To what do we owe this honor?"

"It's been a couple days since I saw your ugly mug, and I figured I needed a good dose of gratitude this morning."

"Kiss mine, buddy."

"No thanks." Rick grinned. "Unlike cops, us bartenders have standards."

"Would you two mind taking your boys' club elsewhere?" Carla interrupted. "All this testosterone's making me queasy. Besides, I've got a murder to solve."

Rick cocked an eyebrow. "A murder? On Key West?"

"Carla—"

She ignored her superior's warning. "Larry Bernhardt."

Rick shifted his gaze to Val. His friend looked annoyed. "I thought Bernhardt killed himself."

"He might not have," Carla piped in before Val could respond, her tone self-important. "Trace evidence found at the scene suggests he wasn't alone the night of his death. The ME placed his TOD between 11:00 p.m. and 1:00 a.m. According to friends Bernhardt dined with that night, he parted their company in high spirits around eight. Between then and the time of his death, he managed to have sex."

"Which proves Bernhardt was a lucky guy," Rick murmured, falling into the role he had played when he and Carla were partners. "What else have you got?"

Carla made a sound of irritation. "What else do I have? What else do I need? Whoever was there that night was most probably the last person to see Larry Bernhardt alive. I want to know who she was and what time she left."

"What you should want to know," Rick corrected, "is whether the man was alive when she left."

Her cheeks flooded with color. "That's what I meant."

In police work, precision was paramount. A precisely worded question could make the difference in breaking a case and not. "Bernhardt lived on Sunset Key," he murmured. "If you haven't questioned the ferryboat captains, I suggest you do. I'd also suggest—"

"That's enough, Rick," Val muttered. "Unless, of course, you're here to rejoin the force?" He shifted his attention to Carla, his irritation with her loose talk obvious. "Have you followed up on that attempted rape from last night? I'm still waiting to see your report."

"You'll have it by lunch."

"Good." He turned to Rick and motioned toward his office. "Shall we?"

A minute later, Val shut the door behind them. "If Carla would spend a little more time on the work she's assigned and a little less time on her fantasies, she'd make my life a hell of a lot easier."

"Carla's a good cop," Rick countered, defending the woman as much from habit as from a real belief in her abilities. "She's as loyal as they come and she works her butt off for you. And you know it."

Val sighed. "True. I'm just a little frustrated with her right now." He took a seat, then indicated to Rick that he should do the same. "The last couple days she's been walking around here acting like she's Miss Supercop. She thinks she's uncovered a *murder*." Val said the last word in a melodramatic whisper.

"Obviously, you don't think she has."

"Let's put it this way, you were the talent in that partnership and I sure could use you back."

Rick ignored that. "So, what's the deal with Bernhardt?"

Val looked at him, his gaze measured. "What brought you in here today? Truth, Rick. No bullshit."

"Bernhardt's suicide."

"Just curious? Or do you have some information for me?"

"I thought it was interesting, the way Island National lost two employees in a matter of forty-eight hours. First Naomi Pearson, then Bernhardt. I wondered what the connection was."

"You're so sure there is a connection?"

"I don't like coincidences. And Pearson and Bernhardt both taking unexpected leave of Island National, so close together, is a huge coincidence."

Val leaned back in his chair, measured gaze never leaving Rick's. "I always say, you can take the cop out of the job but you can't take the job out of the cop."

Rick grinned, pleased. "So, I was right? There is a connection."

Val leaned forward; his chair screeched protest. "First, let me remind you, officially you're not a cop. And until such time as you realize what a monumental mistake you're making and decide to come back, you'll get your news the same way the rest of the civilians do—from the newspaper, radio and five o'clock news."

"And second?"

"Seeing as this particular news will be breaking tonight at five, I'll fill you in."

"I appreciate that, Val."

"I knew you would." His lips twitched. "As Island National's senior loan officer, Bernhardt wrote corporate loans in the one-hundred-thousand-plus category. It was his job to verify the applicant's financial information, then present the loan application to the bank's board. With Bernhardt's stamp of approval, the board okayed the loans."

"I'm smelling a rat here," Rick murmured, intrigued.

"A big-time rat. It seems Bernhardt began writing loans for nonexistent corporations, bilking the bank of more than a million bucks."

Rick cocked his head, fitting the pieces of the scenario together. "And since he was in charge of verifying the corporations' financial information, he simply created it, using his banking knowledge to tailor the dummy corporations' numbers."

"Correct." Val's lips lifted in a grim smile. "He was able to fool the bank so long because he had an accomplice in the bank's processing center."

"Naomi Pearson," Rick murmured. "I knew the coincidence was too much to swallow."

"Yup. She scanned in bogus payments for nonexistent corporations. For a hefty cut, no doubt."

Rick thought a moment. "Bernhardt suddenly got wealthy and the bank didn't get suspicious? From what I've heard, this guy didn't live like a pauper."

"Inheritance, or so he said. From an uncle. Nobody checked it out. Why should they? He was a well-respected bank officer." Val's lips twisted. "Apparently, he even took time off to fly to Philadelphia for the funeral."

"So, why'd he kill himself? Seems like he had a pretty sweet deal going. One he could have strung out a while."

"I can only speculate, of course. My opinion is, Naomi told him she wanted out. Without her, he's left holding a fistful of dummy loans and nowhere to go but down."

Rick frowned. "Why not just take the money and run before it all came crashing down on him?"

Val leaned toward him. "Maybe crooked old Bernhardt thought the gravy train would never end. Maybe he blew all the money on girls, that house and drugs. The guy had one hell of a lifestyle, drugs, sex and rock 'n' roll."

"And the visitor he had the night of his death?"

"If I planned to end it all, how do you think I'd want to spend my final hours?"

"Doing the horizontal mambo?"

"Without a doubt." Val looked away, then back at Rick, expression disgusted. "From what I saw, having it all wasn't enough for Bernhardt. The greedy bastard wanted to live like a king."

Much later Rick found himself thinking of what Val had said and wondering at his friend's seeming naïveté at Bernhardt's motivations. Greed destroyed lives. Desire for more drove people to unbelievable acts of selfishness and cruelty, even against those they loved. It was a sad fact of human nature Rick had seen play out in one way or another in nearly every case he had worked. It was one of the things he didn't miss about being a cop.

CHAPTER 12

Wednesday, November 7
4:00 p.m.

Within twenty-four hours of Liz's visit with Pastor Tim, the parents of the teenager he had mentioned had called for an appointment. That the pastor trusted her enough to recommend her pleased her on two levels: it moved her plan forward and led her to believe he had not seen through her ruse.

Liz greeted the couple, Inez and Dante Mancuso, at her office door. She smiled warmly, hoping to ease their obvious anxiety. "Mr. and Mrs. Mancuso, come in."

She ushered them into her office and they all sat. They looked petrified. These were people of modest means, with traditional values and limited education. He was a gardener, she a homemaker who took in ironing to help make ends meet. Nothing could be more foreign to them than the concept of psychological counseling.

The couple looked at each other, then the woman spoke. "Pastor Collins said you might be able to help us."

"I'll try, I promise you that." Liz smiled again, hurting for the two. On the phone they had told her a little about their daughter, Tara. That they were desperate was the most important thing she had learned from that conversation. That emotion had come through loud and clear then, and she could read it in their expressions and body language now. "Why don't you tell me what's going on with your daughter."

The woman wrung her hands. "We don't know what to do. Tara was such a happy child, so sweet and—" Her throat closed over the words and the man reached across and squeezed her hand.

"She's changed," he said. "It started a year ago—"

"She became sullen and disrespectful. Her grades fell. Her friends, they... They're not nice girls."

"They're fast," he added, frowning. "Insolent. Tara has become like them. She refuses to listen to us."

The woman leaned toward Liz, eyes filling with tears. "She locks herself in her room, sometimes for hours. And she has lost her faith in God. I'm so afraid... I fear for her eternal soul!"

The woman began to cry, soft tears of despair. "Nothing we've tried has helped. She was better when she was talking to Pastor Howard, but when she disappeared..."

At the mention of her sister, Liz's heart leaped to her throat. She worked to keep her focus on the teenager's needs instead of her own. "How did she respond to Pastor Howard's leaving?"

"She withdrew more," Dante said. "She was—" He stopped as if searching for a word.

His wife found it. "Frightened," she said. "Terribly frightened."

It took Liz a moment to find her voice. "Have you considered that your daughter might be using drugs?"

"Drugs?" they repeated simultaneously.

"The behaviors you describe are ones we see in kids who begin using."

The couple looked at each other, then back at her. "But where would she get them?"

They looked genuinely dumbfounded and Liz felt for them. One would think that such naïveté in this day and age would be rare, but she saw it time and again in parents. Even though drug use in teens had skyrocketed, few parents believed their children could be involved.

She softened her tone. "Anywhere, Mr. and Mrs. Mancuso. Everywhere."

Silence fell between them. Liz filled it. "Let me tell you a little bit about myself. I'm a clinical social worker. I've been in private practice for six years and specialize in family and adolescent counseling."

"Social worker?" the man repeated, looking confused. "I thought you were a psychologist."

"Actually, the two areas of study are closely related." Liz folded her hands on the desk in front of her. "Our methods differ, however. Where the psychologist focuses almost exclusively on the 'I' of a patient, the social worker aims to uncover the area of imbalance in the patient's life, be it social, professional, spiritual or familial. Once that imbalance is discovered, the social worker aims to correct it."

"Do you think you can help Tara?"

"I need to speak with her before I make a full determination of treatment, but I will tell you there are very few people who can't be helped."

A whimper escaped the woman. "But what if she's one of those? I don't think I could bear it if Tara—"

"I don't think that's going to be the case, Mrs. Mancuso," Liz inserted quickly, reassuringly. "From everything you've told me, I feel Tara can be helped. It sounds as if she had a happy, normal childhood and as if it's only recently that something has gone awry."

The woman looked at her husband, then back at Liz. "What about... Pastor Tim said you might be willing to work with us on your fees?"

"Absolutely." Liz stood. "Why don't I speak with Tara, assess how often I think I should see her and we'll go from there. Fair enough?"

They agreed it was and made an introductory appointment for their daughter for later that afternoon.

That first meeting with the teenager had gone much as Liz had expected. Tara Mancuso had barely made eye contact, let alone spoken. She'd been sullen, angry and resentful.

No surprises there: adolescents were the most difficult age group to work with, especially when they were unwilling participants in the process.

Liz had determined that she'd need to see Tara twice a week, but she knew it would be difficult to get her into the office that often. She decided to take it one session at a time, starting with this afternoon.

That had been three days ago. She hoped today's session would prove more productive.

If the girl showed up.

She did, though fifteen minutes late. Liz greeted her and ushered her into the office. "How are you today, Tara?"

The teenager looked away, lips pressed tightly together. The sun filtered through the window and fell across the girl's face, making her appear even paler than she was. In contrast, the dark circles under her eyes stood out like fresh bruises.

She could be using, Liz acknowledged. She had the look of someone strung out on drugs. Although her appearance could be a reflection of extreme emotional distress, as well.

Liz tried a different tack. "Are you eating?"

The question must have surprised the girl because she looked directly at Liz. "What?"

She repeated her question.

"Why do you care?"

"Because you look sick."

Tara hugged herself, expression transforming from defiant to miserable. Almost guilty. "I haven't been feeling well, that's all. I can't sleep and food, it makes me…"

She let the last trail off, though Liz had a good idea of what she had been about to say—that food made her ill.

"Is it something I can help with?"

A brittle-sounding laugh slipped past her lips. "I don't think so."

"Your parents are very worried about you."

Her throat worked. She glanced over her shoulder at Liz's closed door then back at her. "I know. I'm sorry about that. I'm—"

She caught her bottom lip between her teeth and lowered her gaze to her lap.

"You're what, Tara?"

The girl drew in a shuddering breath. "I…I don't want to talk about that."

"What would you like to talk about?"

"I don't want to talk to you at all."

Liz folded her hands in her lap. "We could just sit here, but it seems like a waste."

"Of my parents' money?"

"Of both our time."

"What do you care? I don't even know you."

"I heard you talked with Pastor Rachel."

Her already pale face went ashen. "I don't want to talk about her!"

"I can help you, Tara. Trust me."

"No!" The teenager leaped to her feet. "You can't help me. Nobody can!"

Liz followed her to her feet, hand out in supplication. "Let me try. You let Pastor Rachel try."

"And look what happened to her!"

Liz's heartbeat quickened. "What do you mean? What happened to her?"

"She's gone now. Gone! And I'm here. I'm—"

She brought her hands to her face. Her shoulders shook with what Liz thought were tears, but when she dropped her hands Liz saw that her eyes were dry.

She looked at Liz, expression curiously neutral. "Do you believe in God?" she asked. "Do you believe in heaven and hell? In the devil and eternal damnation?"

Startled, Liz replied that she did. "Do you, Tara?" she asked.

"Pastor Rachel did. She warned me against the devil."

For a moment, Liz couldn't find her voice. She wondered what her sister had told this impressionable and troubled young woman.

"And what did she say when she warned you, Tara?"

"That the Evil One masks himself and his army of the damned in beauty. He is seductive, his pleasures earthly and immediate. But beneath, his stench is more foul than any known to man. She warned that the price of succumbing was the eternal fires of hell."

Liz hid her dismay. Her sister couldn't have said that. The woman she had known never would have. Never.

Liz tilted her head, studying the teenager. The fanatical light in the girl's eyes troubled her. Liz suspected she had found the source of imbalance in the girl's life. She made a mental note to speak with Pastor Tim about the family's religious beliefs.

"Can I tell you a story?" the teenager asked suddenly. "It's about a miracle."

"If you'd like."

Tara inched back to her chair and sank onto it, never breaking eye contact with Liz. Liz followed suit, then waited, hands folded in her lap.

After a moment, Tara began. "In 1846, back when Paradise Christian still belonged to the Catholic church, the Blessed Virgin appeared to children playing in the churchyard. Twenty-four hours later blood ran from the hands of the statue of Christ, in the church's sanctuary."

Tara began to tremble. "Fourteen days later a hurricane hit Key West. It devastated the island and destroyed the church. A third of the island's inhabitants were killed."

Tara lowered her voice to a strained whisper. "The Catholic archdiocese decided the visions had been the work of demons and struck all accounting of them from their official records."

Liz cleared her throat. "So how did you learn the story?"

"I grew up on the island," she murmured. "Some stories can't be hushed." She fell silent a moment, expression far away. "There are those who believe the

Blessed Mother appeared to warn the faithful of the disaster to come. That like the Great Flood, the hurricane was delivered by the Lord to punish the wicked. To make them pay for their sins."

Liz swallowed hard. "Is that what you believe, Tara?"

"It doesn't matter what I believe."

"Yes, it does. It—"

"I have to go now." The girl stood so abruptly she sent her chair sailing backward. She hurried toward the door.

"Wait!" Liz jumped to her feet. "Is that what Pastor Rachel believed? Did you tell her that story? Did you—"

"Ask Father Paul, he'll tell you. He believes." Tara yanked open the door and dashed out to the waiting room.

Liz took off after her, heart racing. "Tara, please! Don't leave like this. We have to talk. We—"

She bit the last back. She was too late. Liz watched helplessly as the young woman darted across Duval Street, earning the blare of several horns as she was nearly struck by a moped.

When the teenager disappeared around the corner, Liz stepped back into her office, thoughts racing. Tara knew what had happened to Rachel; Liz was certain of it. The girl was frightened. Frightened that the same was going to happen to her.

That, Liz deduced, was why she wasn't eating or sleeping. It explained the haunted look in her eyes.

As she shut the door and turned, her gaze landed on a sheet of folded paper on the floor by her feet. She bent, picked it up and opened it. A simple message had been typed on the first line of the notebook paper:

They know. You're in danger here. Go before it's too late.

CHAPTER 13

Friday, November 9
5:25 p.m.

Mark stood behind the bar, drying glasses that came out of the washer still wet. His thoughts raced forward, to the next hours, to the promise he had made. To Tara. To their unborn child.

Dear Lord, am I doing the right thing?

"Mark?"

He glanced toward Rick, standing at the cash register, the drawer open. Mark glanced at the drawer, then back at Rick, a catch in his chest. "Problem, boss?"

"I need to make a few phone calls. You think you can hold down the fort for a few minutes?"

Mark smiled, relieved. *What? Did he think the man could read his mind?* "This crush? Are you kidding?"

The last of the afternoon boozers had trickled out

a minute ago. The evening crowd would soon begin cruising in.

Rick laughed. "Stay out of the Jack."

"No worries there, boss."

"Call me if—"

Mark shooed him toward the office. "You worry too much. Make your calls, already."

Chuckling, Rick disappeared through the doorway that led to the storage room and his office. Mark watched him go, counted to twenty once, then twice. Taking a deep breath, he inched his way to the cash register. There, he eased the drawer open.

It chimed and he froze, looking over his shoulder.

From the recesses of the bar, he heard Rick talking. *He was on the phone; he hadn't heard.*

Guilt swamped him. As did a feeling of falling, of spiraling down to the devil's dark pit.

He had to do this. For Tara. For their baby.

Tonight he and Tara were running away together. They had planned to meet in the garden of Paradise Christian at 2:00 a.m. Everything was set. About an hour before closing, Mark was going to claim illness and leave early. He would be long gone before Rick closed—and discovered what Mark had done.

Quickly, Mark scrawled an IOU to Rick, lifted the cash drawer, slid the IOU under some checks, then extracted six hundred dollars.

Hands shaking, he pocketed the money and closed the drawer. He was scared senseless. How was he going to support a wife and child? He could hardly support himself.

This decision would be easier if Tara hadn't been acting so funny. Distant and...unhappy. He had wondered if she was having second thoughts about him, about the prospect of spending her life with a humble preacher. He had wondered, God help him, if the baby wasn't his.

How could they begin their lives together with that hanging over their relationship?

Let it go, Mark. That's over. That part of her life is over.

He fisted his fingers. Tara was frightened. And not just of what their future would hold. Of her friends. They had threatened her. If she tried to leave their group, they had promised they would hurt her.

Tara feared they would kill her or the baby.

Mark didn't believe that. These were a group of spoiled rich kids, not inner-city gangbangers. They were angry and not above using intimidation to terrorize Tara.

Mark couldn't have that. He wouldn't. Lord help him, he would do whatever it took to protect his own.

He figured they'd head to Texas, back home to Humble. His parents wouldn't be happy, but they would support his decision because of the baby.

Mark sidled back down the bar and resumed his work. Rick appeared at the same moment a group of tourists entered the place, their raucous laughter the signal that Friday night had officially begun.

Rick smiled at Mark. Mark returned the smile, feeling lower than a snake's belly. He wasn't stealing, he reminded himself. He was only borrowing the money. He would pay Rick back someday, when he and Tara were settled, far away from Key West.

CHAPTER 14

Saturday, November 10
3:00 a.m.

Liz paced, her mind racing, sleep a million miles away. Thoughts of Tara and the note that had been slipped under her office door had stolen both her peace of mind and any hope of rest.

Rest? How could she rest when she was a hairs-breadth from a full-fledged panic attack?

Liz stopped pacing, closed her eyes and breathed deeply through her nose, focusing on the oxygen flowing into her, filling her lungs, then being expelled. When her heart rate slowed and the pressure in her chest lessened, she opened her eyes.

And found that she stood before her shuttered window. Light from the full moon slipped through the spaces between the slats. She unlatched the shutter and folded it open. The moonlight washed the night milky black. Below, Duval Street slept. A lone figure darted across the street.

Liz rested her forehead against the window frame. She had gone over her session with Tara a hundred times. Each time she had come to the same conclusion: the girl was frightened. Because, Liz believed, she knew what had happened to Rachel.

Liz had even wondered if perhaps her sister had been killed because of Tara. And if that was true, then by treating the teenager, she had placed herself in harm's way.

The tickle of panic returned and again Liz fought it off. She could not succumb to panic at every turn. *She would not.* She had come to Key West to discover what had happened to her sister and nothing would sway her from that mission.

Not even a threat from some creep too chicken to face her in person.

Liz had reread the note, its eleven typed words, more times than she could count.

They know. You're in danger here. Go before it's too late.

Who knew? The people who had killed her sister, obviously. And what did they know? That she was Rachel's sister and that she had come to Key West to uncover what had happened to her.

So, was the note a warning? Or a threat?

Or simply a sick joke by someone who had figured out who she was?

No, not that. She didn't think it was a coincidence that it had been left while she had been in session with Tara.

The teenager held the key, to the who and why her

sister had been killed. She had no proof to back up her conviction, she just knew it to be true.

She glanced over her shoulder. The note lay on her bedstand, beside her phone. She could take it to the police, lay it all out for them. All what? That she was counseling a troubled teen? One who seemed frightened. A teenager who, Liz believed without proof, knew what had happened to her sister?

Right. Lieutenant Lopez would laugh her out the door. He would trivialize the note and attempt to dissuade her from digging any further into Rachel's disappearance.

Liz brought her hands to her face. *Rachel...Rachel, what happened to you?*

Sudden anxiety took her breath. Her heart rate accelerated, her skin went hot, then cold with sweat. Fight or flight, she thought quickly. Not anxiety. Not a panic attack.

Do something. Now. Fast. Before it really was too late.

Liz turned and ran to the closet. She rummaged for her running shoes, grabbed them, then raced to her bureau for a pair of thick socks. She put them on, pulled her hair into a ponytail, thundered down the stairs and out into the blessedly mild night.

She started to run, sucking in one deep breath after another, realizing that she felt great. Free. Unencumbered. It was as if the debilitating anxiety had never existed. Was that all she had needed? she wondered. All this time, had she only needed to take a positive action with that moment? With her life?

Liz laughed out loud, looked to her left, then right. The street was deserted, a rare occurrence for Duval.

Apparently, even the most confirmed party animals had gone home to sleep it off.

She passed Rick's Island Hideaway, then Paradise Christian. She ran on, one block, then two.

She stopped suddenly. Heart in her throat, she turned around slowly. The street behind her was empty. She frowned and took a step backward.

It was as if her sister had called her name.

"Rachel?" she whispered.

Liz shifted her gaze to the church, ghostly white against the night sky.

Not Rachel. Her church.

Without pausing to consider how crazy that thought was, Liz started back, her feet moving slowly at first, then quickening until her breath came in ragged gasps and it felt as if her heart was going to burst through the wall of her chest.

She reached the church, shuddered to a halt and stared up at the structure, waiting. The stained-glass windows glowed subtly, as if illuminated from within. She shifted her gaze to the massive wooden doors then up to the towering spire and bell tower.

Why was she here? What had propelled her to this spot?

Maybe she really was crazy.

She heard a sound and shifted her gaze once more. To the door to the walled garden.

The sound came again. The breeze kicked up, rustling the leaves in the branches above her head. Some creature stirred, then scurried from its resting place. The clawing came again, this time accompanied by an anguished cry.

Liz ran forward, toward the garden door. It was locked at night. The tour guide had said so, to keep runaways and indigents from using the garden as a flop-house and because the garden statuary had been vandalized.

With each step closer, her heart beat faster, the urge to flee grew greater. Perspiration formed on her upper lip, she began to shake.

What was she doing? Testing herself? It was 3:00 a.m., for heaven's sake. She was a woman alone in a new town.

Elizabeth Ames, are you strong enough, bold enough, brave enough to be here? Do you, Elizabeth Ames, have the right stuff for the job?

Liz reached the heavy door, grasped the handle and twisted. The door eased open.

A large tabby cat screeched and launched itself at her.

With a cry, Liz jumped sideways, flattening herself against the door. A high laugh bubbled to her lips. The noise she'd heard had been the cat. It had gotten locked in the garden, and hungry, had begun to claw and whine at the door in an effort to escape.

And along had come big brave Liz.

Feeling more than a little foolish, she stepped into the now deathly quiet garden. A sound escaped her, one of surprise. And pleasure. The garden was beautiful in the moonlight. Exquisite. A ghostly paradise.

She moved farther into the garden, growing intoxicated on nature's perfume: night jasmine, ginger, sweet olive. She roamed her gaze over the landscape. Against the riot of flowers and foliage, the banyan roots became architectural.

Her gaze landed on something at the back of the garden, glowing unnaturally white on the carpet of green.

Frowning, she started for it. Not a blossom or toadstool, she realized.

A hand.

A scream rose in her throat. She inched closer. Trembling, she bent and brushed away the cover of foliage.

Tara stared up at her, face frozen in death.

Liz leaped backward, the scream ripping from her. That scream was followed by another and another. Turning, she ran for the garden door. Her foot landed in a hole and she pitched forward, falling on her knees. She clawed her way to her feet, whimpering, crying for help.

Tara. Dear God. They'd killed Tara.

She made it to the door and stumbled through it. Someone grabbed her, their grip crushing. She screamed again.

CHAPTER 15

Saturday, November 10
3:45 a.m.

Rick held the hysterical woman tightly against his chest. She fought him, kicking, scratching, her piercing screams ripping through the night.

She landed a blow to his shin. He swore and sprang backward, releasing her. "Dammit, lady! Shit." He rubbed his shin. "I wasn't trying to hurt you. I heard you scream and came to see what was…shit," he said again.

"I'm sorry, I—" She choked on the words. "Tara… In the… Someone—" She uttered a sound, part moan of despair, part whine of terror.

He glanced toward the garden. "Someone's in there?"

"Tara—" She brought a hand to her mouth. He saw that it shook badly. "In the garden… Tara. She's…dead."

Rick frowned, certain he had misunderstood her. "There's a girl in the garden? Dead?"

The woman nodded, her eyes filling with tears. "Murdered."

Rick glanced toward the garden once more. Key West averaged one murder—or less—a year. It hardly seemed possible that this woman had stumbled on a murder victim, in a church garden no less.

He returned his gaze to hers. "Are you certain she's dead? Did you check her pulse?"

She shook her head.

"All right, you stay put. Where is she?"

"All the way in back. Her hand. I saw…"

"I'll check it out." He started into the garden, then stopped and looked back at her. She stood, hugging herself, eyes wide and frightened. "Are you going to be all right?" She managed to nod and he made his way toward the back of the grounds.

It took a moment to locate the girl, but when he did he saw that checking her pulse would be unnecessary.

Her throat had been slit, blood loss had been extreme.

Crouching, Rick checked it anyway.

Swearing, he stood. He breathed through his nose, struggling to remain objective. Fighting against the stomach bile that rose in his throat.

Shit. Son of a bitch. Why did things like this have to happen?

He hadn't been face-to-face with murder in over four years.

It sucked just as bad now as it had then.

Turning, he headed back to the woman. She looked on the verge of falling apart.

"Is she—"

"She's dead." He unclipped his cell phone from his

belt, punched in the number for the KWPD and handed it to her. "That's the police department's number. Hit send. Tell them what's happened and where we are. Tell them Rick Wells is with you."

She did as he instructed and he returned to the garden and the dead girl.

Rick hadn't done police work in years, but some things a cop never forgot. Crime-scene procedure was one.

She had been young. And pretty. She'd had long dark hair and fine features. He narrowed his eyes. She looked vaguely familiar. He searched his memory. She was a resident, not a tourist. One of a group of teenagers he saw occasionally, partying on Duval.

He shifted his attention momentarily from the victim to her surroundings. Lots of blood. Broken foliage. Bloody footprints leading away from the body.

He inched closer and crouched beside one of the prints. He was no expert on prints, but he would bet this one belonged to an athletic shoe, maybe size nine or ten, men's.

Swallowing hard, he returned his gaze to the girl. She had been killed in a ritualistic fashion. She was naked, her body arranged in the shape of the cross, arms out, legs almost together. He noticed a tattoo, on her thigh, just below her shaved pubis. A flower, he realized. A strange flower, with curved, pointed petals.

Rick moved on. In addition to slitting her throat, the killer had split open her abdomen just above the pubis—her organs partially spilled out. He had also carved let-terlike symbols on her torso and thighs. Judging by the minimal amount of coagulated blood at the wounds, the carving had been done postmortem. Her breasts and genitals had also been mutilated, most likely after death.

He frowned. Something about the style of the murder and the victim's wounds tugged at his memory. He couldn't put his finger on just what, and once again shifted his gaze to the scene. By the amount of blood, it was obvious that she had been murdered here, not elsewhere and transported to this spot.

Rick narrowed his eyes. The condition of the brush and foliage around the corpse didn't indicate a violent struggle. Perhaps the killer had come up from behind, slit the girl's throat, killing her before she realized what was happening.

So, what had she been doing here in the middle of the night? Judging by lividity and rigor mortis, he didn't think she had been dead that long. Maybe an hour or two.

He looked at her hands. One was relaxed, one curled into a fist. From what he could see, neither exhibited defensive wounds. He bent closer. She appeared to be clutching a scrap of paper.

From behind him came voices. Val and Carla, Rick realized. He stood to greet the two officers.

"What are you doing, Rick?" Val snapped.

Rick bristled at the other man's tone. "What do you think I'm doing, Val? Examining the scene."

"That's not your job, my friend. I need you to back off. Now."

Rick stood his ground. He glanced at Carla. She met his eyes and looked quickly away. He returned his gaze to Val's. "Once a cop, always a cop. Isn't that what you always say?"

"Carla, would you escort Mr. Wells out front?"

Rick looked at Carla in silent warning—he would

not be escorted from the scene like some bimbo civilian. "What is this, Val? I was a cop for eleven years. I've handled a lot more murder investigations than you will in your entire life. It seems to me that considering my experience, you should be grateful I was first to the scene. If I were you, I'd be interested in my assessment of the situation."

Val narrowed his eyes. "Did you touch anything? Contaminate the scene in any way?"

"I checked the girl's pulse. Okay? Standard operating procedure."

"Did you touch the body in any other way?"

"Oh, sure, I French-kissed her." Rick glared at the other man. "Hell no I didn't."

Val's face flooded with color. "Dammit, Rick! You're a civilian. Not a cop. You were one of the first to the scene, that also makes you a suspect, even if only until after we question you." He scowled. "You don't belong here, and you sure as hell know it!"

"Fine! If you need to talk to me, you know where to find me."

"Bullshit, buddy. Don't leave the premises. We need a statement tonight. Got that?"

"Got it, *Lieutenant*."

CHAPTER 16

Saturday, November 10
4:28 a.m.

Thirty minutes later, Carla finished questioning Liz
Ames and Pastor Tim—who had come out to see what
the commotion was all about—and headed to where
Rick waited, pacing like a caged animal.

Carla approached him with trepidation. She had no
desire to tangle with him just now, no desire to be on
the receiving end of his fury at Val.

She understood why he was angry. A girl had been
brutally murdered. He had been second to the scene.
His every instinct told him to get involved—and his
best friend had told him in no uncertain terms that he
could not.

What Rick had said earlier had been right: he *was*
more qualified to handle this case than either she or Val.
He had more experience with murder investigations.

And he had awesome instincts. She had seen him zero in on a suspect with nothing more to go on than a gut feeling.

Truth was, even though he no longer carried a badge, Rick Wells was still more a cop than she would ever be.

Carla shuddered suddenly, chilled. Tonight, she wished she was anything but a cop. If only she hadn't seen that girl in there. If only she could go back to this morning. Or block the image from her head.

But she couldn't and she feared she would never sleep again.

Rick whirled on her. "What the hell was that all about?"

Carla glanced quickly over her shoulder. She saw that Elizabeth Ames and Pastor Tim had left the scene. She faced her old partner. "Cut him some slack, Rick. He's a little tense. This is a serious situat—"

"No shit it's serious, Carla. Tell me something I don't know."

She lowered her voice; it trembled. "This isn't Miami, Rick. We're not... Murder's not an everyday occurrence here."

His expression softened. "How're you doing?"

"Hanging in there. Barely. I puked in the bushes." She puckered up her face. "I don't even know what I'm doing here. I'm not qualified."

"Don't be so hard on yourself. That scene... Let's just say, I've seen some as bad as that but not worse."

Carla wet her lips. "A murder in this town is... It's going to shake the rafters. And the murder of one of our own, too."

"I figured. Who was she?"

"Tara Mancuso, a senior at the high school. Val knows the family. They're real conchs, just like he is."

Carla could see Rick's anger slip away. "What's he thinking?"

"As far as I know, nothing yet." She glanced over her shoulder, then back. "What're you thinking?"

He frowned. "That she knew her attacker. That she wasn't sexually assaulted." He paused. "She never knew what hit her."

"Thank God."

He leaned toward her. She caught a whiff of the spicy soap he used, and for an instant she couldn't breathe. "Carla," he murmured, "there's something about the killer's style...something that's—"

He bit the words back as Val strode over to them, his expression regretful. "Damn, man, I'm sorry. This thing...here...on my island." He looked away quickly, but Rick thought he saw tears in his friend's eyes. "I know her folks. How am I going to tell them about this?"

Rick understood how the man felt. He also knew that nothing he could say would make it better. "I'm sorry, Val."

His friend nodded, visibly pulling himself together. "Carla get your statement?"

"We were just getting to it," she said. She took a spiral notepad and pen from her front shirt pocket. "Shoot."

"There's not all that much to tell. I was closing up the Hideaway—"

"What time was that?" Val asked.

"Around three-thirty."

"That's later than usual, isn't it?"

"Yeah." He looked from Carla to Val. "It was a busy night. I was short-staffed."

"Who was out?"

"Libby, my night bartender called in sick. Again. And Mark Morgan, my boy Friday, went home sick with the flu about 2:00 a.m."

"So, you were alone at the bar from two on?"

"Two-thirty. That's when I kicked Pete out."

Pete, Carla knew, was a local old-timer and good-natured drunk. He spent his days and nights sitting on bar stools trading gossip and stories of the old days, when the navy still played a pivotal role on Key West. His favorite story was one he told about the days leading up to the resolution of the Cuban Missile Crisis.

"Then what happened?"

"I was beat, so I put the cash from the register in the safe, figuring I'd officially close out in the morning. The plan was to go home and catch some z's. I was locking up when I heard her scream."

"Her?"

"Ms. Ames. Didn't know her name then, but I do now."

"So, you don't know her at all?" Carla asked.

"Never even seen her before she landed in my arms."

Val continued. "What happened next?"

"I followed the sound of the screams here, to the garden door. As I reached it, she came flying out. She was hysterical. Once I got her calmed down, she told me about the girl—"

"What were her exact words?"

Rick frowned, trying to recall. "Something about a dead girl. In the garden. She said the girl had been murdered."

"And what did you do then?"

"I thought she was mistaken. That maybe some kid had OD'd or something. I went to see for myself. And saw right away that the woman hadn't been mistaken.

"I hightailed it back to Ms. Ames, gave her my cell phone and told her to call you guys. The rest you know. I looked over the victim, checked out the scene and got kicked out by Val. Been cooling my heels ever since."

Val nodded. "And I appreciate it, Rick. You'll be available, if we need to question you further?"

"Like I said, you know where to find me."

"That I do."

Carla watched as Rick started off, wishing she was going with him, longing for his strength and the comfort of his arms.

Tonight, for the comfort of anyone's arms.

Her head filled with the image of Tara's lifeless face, of the brutal, bloodied gash that had not only taken her life but nearly severed her head as well. She shuddered, stomach turning. She swallowed hard, fighting the queasiness.

"Learn anything interesting from Tim or Elizabeth Ames?" Val asked.

"Nothing that rang alarm bells." Carla flipped through the notebook, stopping on Pastor Tim's interview. "The pastor had gone to bed around ten. Didn't hear anything out of the ordinary. Was awakened by our cherry lights."

"He didn't hear Ms. Ames screaming?"

"I asked him that, too. He said no, he's a heavy sleeper."

Val frowned. "Rick heard her from two doors down and Tim didn't hear her from the parsonage? Interesting."

"That's what he said."

"What about Ms. Ames?"

"She couldn't sleep, went for a run. Said she heard a sound coming from the garden and went to investigate."

"Went for a run at what? At three a.m.?"

"No kidding. That one's a little off."

Val's gaze sharpened. "Go on."

"Said the church called her." He cocked an eyebrow, and Carla nodded. "Her words. Said she ran past the church, then stopped up at the corner of Fleming Street. Said it was as if someone had called her name. Said she'd felt like the church had called her."

"She actually heard a voice calling?"

"Not an actual voice. A voice in her head. A compulsion." At her boss's expression she lifted a shoulder. "I'm only telling you what she told me. Anyway, she was pretty rattled. Kept saying she could have saved the kid if she had only come sooner."

"Had she been drinking? Using?"

"She looked straight. Pupils responded to light. Her balance and speech seemed fine."

He let out a frustrated-sounding breath. "Great. Our first to the scene hears voices. The press'll love that."

"My feeling is she'll recant that bit about the church in the morning."

"Don't be too certain of that," Val muttered. "Anything else?"

"Yeah. Ms. Ames knew the victim."

"Excuse me?"

"Tara was a client of hers. Recommended by Pastor Collins. Is this one small town, or what?"

He narrowed his eyes. "Or what is right."

"I don't follow."

"Pastor Collins and Elizabeth Ames, two of the people at the scene tonight, had a relationship with the victim. Elizabeth Ames was first to the scene."

"You think it might be something?"

"Don't know. At this point, I'm not eliminating anything." Val glanced toward the garden entrance, then back at her. "Isn't that door locked at night?"

She nodded. "Ever since those kids vandalized the statuary."

"So, how did the victim…and her killer get in?"

"I didn't think to ask that question."

"Well, ask it." He glanced toward the parking lot. "The evidence guys are here. Charlie's been called?"

"I think so," she responded, rubbing her arms. "I'll double-check to be sure."

"Good. And make sure Dr. Dan up in Marathon got word. I want the autopsy results ASAP."

She nodded and glanced sideways at the evidence guys heading their way. "Anything else?"

"I want to know everything about this girl—who her friends were, who she was dating. I want you to talk to her teachers, neighbors, everybody." He shifted his attention to the other officers. "Hello, boys. Body's in the garden."

He watched them a moment, then turned back to her, expression grim. "I want to know how she spent her last twenty-four hours, who she talked with, where she went, what she ate. Everything. Got all that?"

She nodded and closed her notebook. "What about the press?"

"We'll hold them off as long as possible. I'd love to have a suspect before the story breaks. I talked to Chief Reid on my way over here, he agrees."

"What about her next of kin?"

"I'll do it." He glanced at his watch and she sensed him trying to gauge how long he could avoid making that visit. "I'm going to hang around, make sure every-thing's done to the letter. Then I'll…take care of it."

CHAPTER 17

Saturday, November 10
8:00 a.m.

Rick tapped on Val's open door. His friend glanced up. From the other man's haggard appearance, he had gotten about as much sleep as Rick had: zero.

Instead of grabbing a couple hour's shut-eye the night before, Rick had paced, unable to rest. He had recognized the killer's style. The markings on Tara's torso and limbs. The positioning of her body. But he hadn't been able to place where he recognized them from.

Not at first, anyway.

"We've got a problem," Rick said, striding into his friend's office.

Val passed a hand across his face, weary. "I'm not going to argue with you about that. I just got off back-to-back phone calls from the mayor, the head of the tourist commission and three reporters, one with the *Miami Herald*."

"Count on them continuing." Rick dropped a sheaf of computer printouts on his friend's desk. "Take a look at this."

"What is it?"

"Some stuff I got off the Internet last night." He rubbed his aching eyes, scratchy from no sleep and hours staring at his computer screen. "Remember a string of serial killings in Miami a dozen or more years back? The New Testament Murders?" Val shook his head. "How about the name Gavin Taft?"

"Refresh my memory."

"Just before I started with the Miami-Dade force, young women began turning up murdered. Their throats had been slit, their limbs and torsos carved up. The media dubbed them the New Testament Murders because of the crucifixion-style positioning of the victims and because a religious scholar claimed the 'writings' on the bodies represented Scripture passages from the New Testament.

"For years, the investigation yielded nothing. Until Taft, a twenty-four-year-old construction worker was stopped for a routine traffic violation and the officer recognized blood on Taft's arms and hands."

Val nodded. "Okay, it's all coming back now. But wasn't Taft convicted?"

"Yup. At this very moment, he's sitting on death row, awaiting an appeal."

"An appeal, of course." Val scowled. "Same as the rest of the sick bastards on death row."

"No, here's the sick part. On the Internet I discovered a Gavin Taft fan club and several chat rooms devoted to a discussion of this monster's kills." He motioned the printout. "It's all there."

While his friend skimmed the documents, Rick paced, thoughts racing. Several of the chat-room police buffs believed that Taft hadn't worked alone, that he'd had an accomplice. Still others speculated that Taft was innocent and that the real New Testament Killer roamed free.

"Dear Jesus," Val murmured, lifting his gaze to Rick's. "What do you think we've got here? A copycat?"

"Don't know, could be. The similarities between Tara's murder and Taft's killings are too great to ignore."

"If not a copycat—"

"Could be Taft had an accomplice, just like some of those folks in the chat room speculate."

Val looked skeptical. "So, what's this accomplice been doing the past four years?"

"Maybe operating in a different part of the country. Maybe serving time for unrelated crimes."

"Next you're going to suggest that Taft's not even the guy. That the wrong man was charged, tried and convicted."

"It happens."

"Not this time. They had physical evidence, Rick. DNA matches directly linking him to several of the murders."

"But not all. And no murder weapon, no trophies."

Val returned his gaze to the printouts. He thumbed through them, stopped on one and read. A moment later he looked back up. "I hear what you're saying, but no way Taft's not the guy."

Rick met his friend's gaze evenly. "Maybe an accomplice—"

Carla appeared at the door. She looked at Rick, then away. "You have a minute, Val?"

He waved her into the room. "Rick's made a rather startling find, come take a look."

She crossed to the desk, movements hesitant. Val handed her the papers. He shifted his attention back to Rick. "I appreciate you bringing me this. I'll be in touch."

Rick ignored his friend's obvious attempt to get rid of him and sat back in his chair. "What's next?"

"For you, going home and getting some sleep."

"I can live with that." Rick smiled. "What's next for you?"

"Butt out, my friend."

"The ME's report in yet?"

"Goodbye, Rick."

He narrowed his eyes. "I'm involved. I was there last night."

"You want to wear a badge, Rick? I can arrange it. Until then, however, I can't discuss an ongoing investigation with you. And you know it."

"Dammit, Val, I was there during the investigation. Just before they got him, I was assigned to the team." He lowered his voice. "Then Jill got sick and everything fell apart."

Val's expression softened. "I know, and I'm sorry. I wish I could work with you on this, Rick. You were a hell of a cop. But I can't. I need you to get uninvolved, ASAP."

"Just for once, can't you do something that isn't by the book?" Rick coaxed, sending him what he hoped was his most convincing smile. "Always following the rules, even when we were kids. Always taking the high road."

"And it cost me on more than one occasion," Val murmured. "Because I played fair, I lost Jill."

At the mention of his wife, Rick's amusement evaporated. He glanced at Carla, who had stopped reading to follow their exchange, then back to his old friend. "We both lost her, now, didn't we?"

Val paled, as if realizing just how far over the line he had crossed. "Shit, Rick, I'm sorry. I shouldn't have said that."

Rick stood. "Forget about it. We're both tired."

Val followed Rick to his feet. "I appreciate you bringing us this. But I have to ask you to stand back and let us do our jobs. Can you do that for me?"

Rick studied his friend. If Val thought he was going to sit back and wait for him and Carla to muddle their way through this, he was out of his mind. He had missed the opportunity to work on the tail end of the Taft investigation because of Jill's illness, and he wasn't going to miss it again.

Besides, he had a feeling about this case, one deep in his gut.

Rick gave Val a small salute. "Whatever you say, old friend. Whatever you say."

CHAPTER 18

Saturday, November 10
3:00 p.m.

Liz awakened with a start. She sat up in bed, disoriented. She glanced at the bedside clock and then blinked in disbelief.

Three o'clock? In the afternoon?

The events of the night before came crashing back: going for a run, finding Tara, the police questioning her, returning to her apartment and being unable to close her eyes without the horror engulfing her.

In desperation, she had taken a sleeping pill. One of the ones her therapist had prescribed back when she had been in the throes of a breakdown.

Back when? Right, she was on such an even keel now. Steady as a rock.

More like delusional. Had she really told that police

officer that the church had called her? Had she really believed it?

Did she still?

Liz moaned and dragged the comforter to her chin. She felt as if she had spent the night wrestling the devil himself. Her body ached, as if she was bruised all over. She shifted her gaze to her window, her vision blurring with tears.

Poor Tara. She had been so young. She'd had so much to look forward to—love, marriage, children. Grandchildren.

The tears welled and spilled over. Liz found herself saying a silent prayer, something she hadn't done in a long time. A prayer that Tara hadn't suffered too much. That she was safe now, in the Lord's loving and protective custody. At peace.

A lump formed in her throat. The monsters who had done this to Tara were the same ones who had made Rachel "disappear." She believed that, even without more proof than what the police would see as circumstantial. Her gut instincts told her she was right.

They weren't going to get away with it, she promised. She wasn't going to allow them to.

Liz threw back the covers and climbed out of bed, fired with steely determination. The room started to spin and she grabbed the bedpost to steady herself.

She breathed deeply through her nose, focusing on what she needed to do. She didn't have time for a nervous breakdown. She didn't have time to be weak-kneed or light-headed. She needed to pay her respects to Tara's parents today. She wanted to speak with Pastor Collins. Perhaps he could help her. She felt he knew more than he was saying—about Tara's problem and her sister's disappearance.

She released the bedpost and made her way cautiously to the closet. First, she would visit the police department. After the tragedy of the night before, Lieutenant Lopez would have to admit she was on to something. He couldn't deny the link between her sister's disappearance and Tara's murder.

Lieutenant Lopez didn't see it that way. He looked at her, expression both incredulous and annoyed. "Let me summarize," he murmured. "You believe that whoever murdered Tara also did away with your sister. You believe this to be true because…"

"Because Tara was in my sister's counsel when Rachel disappeared. Tara was somehow involved in the illegal activities my sister spoke of. They killed my sister, then when Tara began seeing me, they killed her."

The man tossed his pen on the desk. "I'm in the middle of a murder investigation, Ms. Ames. I don't have time for your imaginings."

"Imaginings!" she repeated. "A girl is dead! My sister is—"

"Missing," he supplied. "If your sister was murdered, where's the body? If she had discovered some huge, illegal operation on the island, why didn't she come to me with it? Or Detective Chapman?" he added, motioning toward the other detective, the woman who had questioned Liz the night before. He shook his head. "Or anyone else on the force, for that matter?"

Liz had to admit, their argument made sense. But she hadn't given them all of hers. She had to make them see it her way. "Tara knew who killed Rachel. She was frightened they were going to kill her, too."

Both detectives straightened. "She told you that?"

Liz hesitated. "Not just like that."

The lieutenant leaned back in his chair. He sent a glance to his detective. Liz interpreted its meaning: *nutcase.*

"Then how?" he asked. "Did the church tell you?"

"Of course not!"

His eyebrows shot up. "But didn't you tell Detective Chapman that Paradise Christian called to you last night? That the *building* urged you to come to it."

Heat flew to her cheeks. "I was overwrought. When I said the church called to me, I meant I felt a strong… pull to go there."

"That's not what you said," the woman detective murmured. "You said the building—"

"I know. I was upset. I wasn't thinking clearly."

"But you are now?"

"Yes."

Lieutenant Lopez stared directly at Liz. "Let me ask you something, Ms. Ames. Do you find it…odd that even though you've only been in town what, two weeks, you were first to the scene of the only murder this year *and* that you knew the victim?"

Liz glanced from the lieutenant to the detective, confused. "I don't follow."

"It makes you an automatic suspect. Standard operating procedure, Ms. Ames."

"That's…crazy. I was out for a run and—"

"At three in the morning," the other woman murmured. "Alone. No witnesses. With no better explanation for being there than 'the church called to you.' What do you think we should deduce from that?"

"I know it sounds crazy, but everything I told you is true. That's just the way it happened." She looked from one to the other again. "Surely you believe me?"

For a long moment, neither officer spoke. Then Lieutenant Lopez cleared his throat. "Let's get back to Tara and your claim that she feared for her life. She didn't come right out and say that, correct?"

He had wanted to shake her confidence, she realized. He had wanted her rattled, a little frightened. *Well, it wasn't going to work.*

Liz stiffened and met his gaze. "Correct," she said clearly. "I deduced it through her body language and expressions. The things she didn't say."

The lieutenant looked at his detective again. "Quick, Carla, we just learned a new interrogation technique, write down everything suspects don't say."

The woman smirked and Liz stood. "I'm a trained professional. It's my job to interpret—"

"My job," he interrupted, following her to her feet, "is to unearth the truth. Not to guess, infer or deduce. I deal in facts. Not feelings. Period."

"But—"

He cut her off. "You are overwrought, Ms. Ames. Understandably so. Go home, let us do our job."

Liz took another stab. "Take a look at this. Someone slipped it under my door while I was in my last session with Tara." She retrieved the note from her purse and held it out.

He took it from her, read it and handed it back. "So?"

"It's a threat."

"Or a joke."

"It's not a joke!" She took a deep, steadying breath. "I received this while in session with Tara. Less than twelve hours later the girl was murdered. Why don't you get it?"

The man's expression softened with compassion. "I'm really sorry, Ms. Ames. You've been through... something awful. First your sister's disappearance, now this." He glanced at the other detective. "I tell you what, I'll keep an open mind about this. I'll have Carla check out your story, see if we can discover who left you that note. Will that help?"

"Yes," she murmured, relief flowing over her. "Yes, that will help."

CHAPTER 19

Saturday, November 10
4:30 p.m.

The medical examiner for the keys was an old friend of Rick's. They had played ball together for the Key West High School Fighting Conchs. Rick had been the second-string quarterback, Daniel Carson a second-string receiver. Their sophomore year, the Conchs had won the state championship. Consequently, they had spent a lot of time on the bench together while the first string strutted their stuff. Later, when their paths had crossed professionally, they'd discovered they got along as well as men as they had as boys.

Rick knew Daniel would be much less discreet than Val. It helped that Val and Daniel had never particularly liked each other—Daniel would be inclined to share the information just for the opportunity to piss Val off.

"Daniel, Rick Wells."

"Rick." The other man laughed, his deep voice sand-papery from years of smoking. He had given up the habit the day his father died from lung cancer, but he hadn't lost the smoker's gravel. "How the hell are you?"

"Can't complain," Rick murmured. "How're Vicki and the kids?"

"Doing great. Danny's playing junior-high ball. Made first string, right off."

The pride in the other man's voice made Rick ache. Sam would have been nine this year. A fourth-grader. Playing ball. Beginning to think girls weren't the enemy.

For a split second, Rick couldn't think, let alone re-spond. In that moment he missed his child with a feroc-ity that made him want to weep.

"Shit, man. I'm sorry. I didn't think, I—"

"It's okay," Rick managed to say, finding his voice, fighting his way back from despair. "He a receiver like his old man?"

"You bet. He's got better hands, though. He's faster."

"Smarter, too, I hope," Rick teased, working to chase away the ghosts of the past.

"Without a doubt. Hold on a second." Rick heard the sound of someone in the background and Dan's reply. A moment later, he returned to Rick. "So, buddy, you call to shoot the breeze?"

"No. I need a favor."

"Thought so." Daniel's tone held no condemnation. "Does this favor have anything to do with the Mancuso murder?"

"You do an autopsy yet?"

"Finished an hour or so ago." He paused a moment. "I'd never seen anything like it before. Gang killings, suicides, overdoses. But this..." His voice thickened.

"Made me want to give this job up, open up a nice family practice. Live with a few of my illusions intact."

"It's too late for that now," Rick said grimly. "What did you find?"

"You know that's confidential information. You're not on the force anymore, Rick."

"Tell me anyway."

"Why so interested?"

"I've got a feeling about this one, Dan. Val's shut me out."

"You recognized the killing style."

"Yes."

The other man hesitated, then sighed. "You on a land line or a cell?"

"Land."

"Hold on a moment." His friend laid down the phone. Rick heard footsteps, then a door shutting. A moment later he was back. He confirmed what Rick had suspected: she had been attacked from behind, the injury to her neck had killed her, she had not been sexually assaulted and the carvings on her body had, indeed, been done postmortem.

Then he said something that took Rick by surprise.

"She was pregnant. No more than three months along."

"Oh, man."

"It gets worse, my friend. The killer cut open her womb and took the fetus."

CHAPTER 20

Saturday, November 10
5:00 p.m.

Liz climbed the steps to Paradise Christian's closed doors. She kept her gaze focused on them, afraid to look left, toward the garden. She had promised herself she wouldn't. Seeing the crime-scene tape stretched across the garden door would bring the events of the night before rushing back.

The call of that vivid slash of yellow proved too powerful, and she glanced to her left. And as she feared, the image of Tara filled her head: her face screwed into a death howl, of the blood…everywhere, of her wide, lifeless eyes. Staring up at her in accusation.

She should have been able to prevent this. Should have done something to stop it.

Liz whimpered and jerked her gaze away. She hurried up the remaining steps and crossed to the doors.

And found them locked. Confused, she tried a second door with the same results.

Of course the doors were locked. A girl had been murdered here not even twenty-four hours ago. Her killer still roamed free.

Liz searched for the bell, found it and rang. Several minutes later she saw Pastor Tim's face at the window. A moment later the door opened.

He looked as if he had aged five years since the last time she'd seen him. That she had expected—the accusation in his eyes she hadn't. She took a step back, wondering what she had done wrong. "Pastor Tim?" she murmured. "Have I caught you at a bad time?"

"Today has been difficult," he responded stiffly. "How can I help you?"

Difficult. An understatement, she was certain. "I wanted to check on Tara's parents. Have you spoken with them?"

"Of course I have. What kind of spiritual leader would I be if I hadn't?"

"I'm sorry," she murmured, taken aback, "I didn't mean to offend you. Sometimes people in pain turn away from those who can help most."

"The Mancusos are people of great faith, Ms. Ames. Their belief in their Lord and Savior will carry them through even this."

Liz recalled the fanatical light in Tara's eyes when she spoke of God, heaven and hell. "Do the Mancusos have any strange beliefs?"

"Excuse me?"

"That came out wrong," she said, cheeks burning. *I didn't mean that. It's just that Tara said some things about her Christian religion I found strange. I thought maybe she—*

"The child is dead now, Ms. Ames. Let her rest in peace."

"You don't understand."

"You might be surprised how much I do understand." He took a step back from the door. "I have to go now."

"Wait!" She shot her hand out, stopping him from closing the door, stunned by Pastor Collins's anger at her, his confrontational tone and accusatory comments. Previously, he had been warm toward her, kind and eager to help. Last night he had been conciliatory of her feelings, concerned for her safety. He had refused to leave her side until the officer that Lieutenant Lopez had assigned to walk her home had her in tow, for heaven's sake.

What had caused his attitude to change so dramatically since then?

"Please, Pastor Tim, I wanted to offer my condolences... I thought there might be something I could do for the Mancusos."

"There isn't," he said coldly. "Good day."

"It might help them to speak with me. I'm a professional counselor and—"

"They don't want to speak with you."

"How can you be so certain? They may—"

"They told me so, Ms. Ames. They asked me to keep you away from them."

She took a step backward, shocked. "They said that? I don't understand. I can't imagine why—"

"I can't help you." He sucked in a sharp breath, flushing. "A girl is dead, her parents grieving. Don't you think you've helped enough?"

On that, he shut the door in her face.

Shaken, Liz turned away from the door. And found a man standing not three feet behind her, blocking her path. His face was a nightmare: a vicious scar ran diagonally across it, from his forehead to chin. It appeared that whatever had cut him had mutilated his left eye in the process.

He stared at her with his one good eye, mouth slightly agape. She took a step toward him. "Excuse me," she said, mustering an authoritative tone.

He blinked but didn't move. Liz glanced over her shoulder at the closed church doors, then back at the man. "Excuse me," she said again. "I need to pass."

Before she realized what was happening, his hand shot out and he closed his fingers tightly around her wrist.

With a cry, she took a step backward, tugging against his grasp. He tightened his hold on her, mouth working, guttural sounds spilling from his lips.

"Take your hand off her, you monster!" Heather Ferguson strode up the path behind him. "Right now!"

The man's expression grew alarmed. He dropped Liz's wrist, whirled, then scurried off, head down.

Liz watched him go, heart pounding. He ducked through a row of flowering hedges at the end of the walkway, and disappeared.

"Are you all right?"

Liz dragged her gaze to the other woman. "I...think so." She rubbed her wrist. "He scared me, that's all."

"That character gives me the creeps. He's always lurking about. Spying."

"Who is he?"

"Stephen. I don't know his last name, if he even has one." Heather frowned. "He's the church caretaker. As far as I know he's lived at Paradise Christian all his life."

Liz swallowed hard, working to shake off the effects

of her encounter with the man. "What happened to his face?"

"I'm not from Key West, so I may be wrong, but I heard his father did that to him. Apparently, the same attack that disfigured his face damaged his brain. The church takes care of him."

Liz felt ill. That such sickness and cruelty existed in the world, that it was so often directed against children, broke her heart. "He's harmless then?"

"They say so."

Liz frowned. "You don't agree?"

"The former pastor here, Rachel Howard, caught him peeking in her windows. I told her she ought to send him packing. But she had too big a heart." Heather looked away, eyes sparkling with tears. "And now she's gone."

Liz's heart stopped, then started again, beating almost painfully against the wall of her chest. For a moment, she could hardly breathe. "You knew the previous pastor of Paradise Christian?"

"Sure, everyone around here did. I suppose you could have even called us friends."

Liz's cheeks warmed. *If Rachel and Heather had been friends, wouldn't Rachel have mentioned her sister?*

She realized the other woman was looking at her oddly and Liz forced a smile. "You suppose?"

Heather lifted a shoulder. "She was extremely busy, so was I. We were never actually able to do more than have a quick chat when we ran into each other. But I liked her. A lot."

"Have you closed up shop for the day?"

"Yes, I'm happy to say. Why, are you in sudden need of a bikini?"

"Hardly." Liz smiled again. "You've come to my rescue twice now and I'd love to express my thanks by treating you to a drink or dinner."

Heather waved the offer off. "That's absolutely not necessary."

"I'd like to anyway. If you have the time?"

Heather glanced at her watch then paused, as if considering the things she had to do and how much time it would all take. She returned her gaze to Liz's and smiled. "After the day I had, a drink would be great. I know just the place."

Five minutes later they were sitting at a small outdoor table at the Iguana Café. Liz took Heather's suggestion and ordered a rum runner, a Key West specialty made with blackberry and banana brandy, light and dark rum, cherry juice and sweet-and-sour mix. Heather ordered the same, warning Liz that the refreshing drink packed a deceptive punch.

"This place is a favorite with the locals," Heather murmured as their drinks arrived. "Great café con leche and Cuban sandwiches. The best, in my opinion."

"I'll remember that," Liz murmured. She took a sip of the frozen concoction. Tall, fruity and delicious, Liz could see why they had become a favorite with Key Westers and tourists alike.

"I heard about last night," Heather whispered, leaning toward her. "I heard you found...that girl." She shuddered. "How are you?"

Liz set her glass down hard. "Truthfully? Not so great. Shook up."

"How did you... I mean, what were you doing out so late?"

Liz told her about not being able to sleep and going for a run. "I heard a noise and went to investigate." She looked down at her drink, then back up at Heather. "I wish I hadn't."

"No kidding." Heather picked up her drink as if to take a sip, then set it back down, expression distressed. "I knew that girl."

Liz straightened. "You did?"

"Mmm, kind of. She came into the shop sometimes. Most of the local kids do." Her lips lifted. "A by-product of the kind of merchandise I sell."

"Did Tara shoplift?"

"Her name was Tara?" Liz nodded and Heather continued. "No. Not that I know of, anyway. She seemed like a nice kid."

"She was troubled," Liz murmured before she could stop herself.

"What do you mean? Was she in your care?"

Liz brought a hand to her mouth, distressed at the slip. "Please, forget I said that. I shouldn't have." She changed the topic by asking the other woman about herself.

"Me?" Heather murmured with a small shake to her head, "I'm afraid there's nothing too exciting to tell. I grew up in Miami, gave college a try but dropped out to do some modeling." She laughed, then made a face. "It wasn't for me. Or rather I wasn't for it."

"What happened?" Liz asked, honestly curious. The other woman was so beautiful, she would have thought her a natural. She told her so.

Heather laughed again. "That's a common misconception about models. Many of them aren't exceptionally pretty in real life—it's the camera that makes them so. The camera loves them. It didn't love me."

"I don't understand."

"I blame my mother," she smiled. "I inherited her

bone structure, which the camera flattens. Actually, I think she was more disappointed I didn't make it as a model than I was."

"Are you two close?"

"Not really. I rarely see her even though she lives just up the Keys in Islamorada." Heather took a long sip of her cocktail. "I drifted into retailing, then down here. I opened up my shop a few years back."

Liz wanted desperately to ask her about Rachel, but didn't know where to begin. Should she tell her who she was? That Rachel was her sister and that was why she was here on Key West? Her instincts told her Heather was an ally, but what if she was wrong? What if she told Heather the truth and alienated her?

The other woman solved the problem by bringing Rachel up herself. "I probably shouldn't have said that about that poor man, that Stephen." She sighed. "It's just that, after what Rachel said about catching him peeking in her windows…"

"I heard she disappeared. The former pastor of Paradise Christian, that is."

Heather's expression became guarded. "What about it?"

Liz fiddled with her straw, trying not to look too anxious. "It sounded a little weird to me, that's all. A pastor just up and running off like that. Is that what you believe happened to her?"

Heather sighed again. "I don't know what to believe. The Rachel I knew would never have done something like that."

"Really?" Liz leaned forward. "Why not?"

"She loved Paradise Christian. Loved Key West." Her voice thickened slightly. "She was devoted to the congregation." A frown formed between her eyebrows.

"I was on a buying trip when she disappeared. I learned what happened when I returned. I feel really bad about that. Like maybe she needed me and I wasn't here for her."

A lump formed in Liz's throat even as a surge of affection rose in her for this woman she hardly knew. Because she had known and cared for Rachel. And because she felt the same way Liz did, the same regret and guilt.

She had found a potential champion, Liz acknowledged. Someone who would back Liz up if she found any proof supporting her suspicions that Rachel had met with foul play.

"Did you talk to the police? Did you tell them the things you just told me?"

"I tried." She dropped her hands to her lap. "But the thing is, something had been bothering Rachel. She had been upset about something and acting...strangely."

"Upset about what?"

"I don't know. She wouldn't tell me."

"Was it Stephen she was frightened of?" Liz pressed.

"Frightened," Heather repeated, looking at Liz, eyebrows drawn together. "Did I say she was frightened?"

"No, I guess you...didn't. I just...I suppose I was just filling in the blanks."

Heather's frown deepened. She brought a hand to her neck, to the jeweled monogram that hung on a fine gold chain. "You know, that's a good way to describe how she acted. But of who or what, I don't know."

CHAPTER 21

Saturday, November 10
5:15 p.m.

Mark huddled in the corner of his rented room, eyes fixed on the door. His teeth chattered and he clutched a frayed blanket to his chest, unable to get warm despite the stifling heat of the room. He doubted he would ever be warm again.

Tara was dead. His unborn child, dead. Both murdered.

Mark squeezed his eyes shut, the horror of the past hours washing over him. He struggled to fit all the pieces together, to fill in some of the blanks. He had gone to meet her, as they'd planned. The garden gate had been open. He had eased through and softly called her name. She hadn't answered.

Concerned and confused, he had crept farther into the garden, careful to be quiet, not wanting to awaken

Pastor Tim or Stephen, the old caretaker. He had wondered if she had changed her mind. Or if her parents had caught her sneaking out and prevented her from meeting him.

Then things got fuzzy. He remembered seeing her lying there, covered in blood.

Mark pressed a fist to his mouth to hold back a howl of grief. From outside came the sounds of children playing in the park across the street. Although little more than a sandy patch of ground with a tired swing set and slide, the neighborhood kids didn't seem to mind.

He struggled to focus on the children, their sounds of joy. He struggled to find a calm space to speak to the Lord, to ask for guidance and strength. To turn to the one, the only one, who could help him.

That place eluded him, and instead, his head filled once again with the events of the night before. He remembered he'd called Tara's name, he'd fallen to his knees and reached for her, desperate. She had been warm. When he moved her, a gurgling sound had come from her throat, and at first he had believed her alive. Then he had seen...her throat...the extent of the blood. He had realized the sound had been the wound talking, not her.

Sobbing, he had shot to his feet. His hands, knees, arms and chest had been wet with her blood. It had been everywhere. After that, things got murky again. He had run toward the garden gate, tearing through shrubbery, blinded by tears. He had tripped and fallen, dragged himself to his feet and fallen again. His hands had been cut, his face scratched. He thought he had heard a sound, someone behind him. Breathing.

Somehow, he had made it to his car, then here. Somehow, by God's will.

Mark moaned and pressed himself closer into the corner. That had been hours ago, though he didn't know how many. Through the night and into the morning he had waited for the police to come. He and Tara had kept their relationship a secret, but any number of people could have figured them out.

Mark's teeth began to chatter again. They would think he had done it. Tara had been pregnant with his child, some would see that as a reason for him to do this. Get rid of her and the problem.

Sickness rushed up to his throat and he fought it back. Maybe the cops wouldn't discover his and Tara's relationship? And even if they had, he had been at the Hideaway until 2:00 a.m. the night before. Surely—

Dear God, the IOU. Mark searched his memory. Had he told Rick why he was borrowing the money? Had he told him about Tara? He couldn't remember. He had promised to pay him back as soon as he could. He'd told him it was an emergency.

He squeezed his eyes shut, fighting to remember exactly what he had written. He had to remember. It was important. Maybe even a matter of life and—

Rick would seek him out. Because of the money. He could be here any moment. Mark was surprised he hadn't shown up already.

He had expected to be long gone before Rick found the IOU. Mark pressed the heels of his hands to his eyes. Maybe it would be for the best. He would tell Rick everything; his friend would believe him.

Mark looked down at himself, taking in the unmistakable stains on his clothes, shoes and skin. With a growing sense of horror, he tipped his hands over. They were red from Tara's blood.

If Rick saw him this way, he would think he had done it. Everyone would.

He would go to jail.

The realization hit him with the force of a wrecking ball. With a cry, he scrambled to his feet and raced to his closet-size bathroom. The room consisted of a single sink, a slightly lopsided toilet and an old tub that had been fashioned into a shower with a barely adequate spray nozzle and plastic curtain that circled the tub. He pulled the shower curtain back and stepped into the tub to open the window behind it and let in some fresh air.

He cranked on the shower, then tore off his soiled clothes. He stepped under the stinging hot spray and started to scrub, so hard his skin burned.

He couldn't go to Rick. Rick had been a cop. The ranking detective at the Key West Police Department was his best friend. Mark had no illusions where his loyalties would lie.

He had no one else to turn to on the island. He was alone.

Fear grabbed him by the throat. For a moment, Mark couldn't breathe. He struggled to get a grip on his runaway emotions. He had to think this through. Had to stay calm, think clearly.

His survival depended on it.

He lathered his hair, thoughts racing. What were his options? Run, climb into his car and head out, ASAP. He had the six hundred bucks he had borrowed from Rick; it would take him a long way.

That felt wrong. It felt like an abandonment of Tara, of their child.

He shook his head. But they were dead. He couldn't help them anymore.

But he could. Mark cut off the water and stepped out

of the tub. Tara's friends had threatened to hurt her. She had been terrified of them.

They must have followed her to Paradise Christian's garden last night. And killed her.

Fury rose up in him, displacing the last of his fear. He dried himself, dressed and then ran to the closet. He grabbed his few possessions and threw them into his duffel bag. He needed to get the hell out. Now. Before Rick showed up at his door. Before the police did. But he wouldn't leave Key West.

Tara's friends had done this. Just as they had threatened they would. And somehow he was going to prove it.

CHAPTER 22

Rick pounded on the door to Mark's rented room. "Open up, Mark!" He waited, then pounded again. "Open up or I'll go to the cops, you thieving son of a bitch!"

He put his ear to the cardboard-thin door—no sound came from inside. He glanced down the dingy hallway, to the right, then left. His young employee lived in a building little better than a flophouse. The smell of frying bacon came from one of the units, as did the sound of a television tuned to a sports channel.

Dammit. He hadn't really thought Mark would be here, but he had hoped.

Mark Morgan was long gone, his trip financed with Rick's six hundred bucks.

He hadn't discovered the missing cash and the bogus

IOU until yesterday afternoon when he'd officially closed out Friday night's register. By then he'd known it was already too late, but he figured he couldn't not try. In truth, it wasn't the money; it was how let down he felt. He had believed in that kid. He'd trusted him.

Rick stood at the door a moment more, contemplating breaking in, then turned and walked away. What would he have to gain by doing that? Mark was gone, the money with him.

Rick shifted his thoughts from Mark to Tara's murder. The murder had been news all over the state. Not headline news, fortunately, as the more prurient aspects of the crime had been withheld from the media—the ritualistic nature of the murder, its religious overtones, the fact that Tara had been pregnant and that the killer had taken the fetus. Rick didn't have a lot of confidence that Val would be able to maintain that level of secrecy for long. One reporter smelled "cover-up" and Key West would become a media circus.

Rick didn't want that to happen. The media could big-time screw up an investigation, especially one run by rookies. Whether Val wanted to admit it or not, he needed him.

Which was the reason he had decided to pay Liz Ames a visit.

Rick swung onto his Honda Nighthawk, started the bike and headed back into Old Town, only a short drive from Mark's Packer Street address. While waiting to be questioned the night of Tara's murder, he had learned that Liz Ames lived and worked on Duval Street, in the property two down from the Hideaway. He also learned that she was new to Key West and that she was a family counselor. She had been jogging the night of the murder and, alerted by a howling cat, had stumbled upon the scene.

Something didn't add up. He had the feeling that Elizabeth Ames knew something she wasn't telling. Her story didn't ring true to him.

He found a spot in front of the Hideaway, took it, then walked up the block to Liz Ames's storefront. There, he tipped his head back and gazed up at the building's second level, then down the block, in the direction of Paradise Christian. Why would a single woman, new to a city, be out jogging in the middle of the night? She hadn't been carrying pepper spray or a cell phone, nor had she been accompanied by a dog.

It didn't add up.

Though considering how completely he had misjudged Mark, he wasn't so sure his instincts hadn't gone totally to shit. He crossed to the door that led to the second-level apartment and rang the bell. Within moments he heard the sound of someone approaching. A moment after that, the door cracked open and Liz Ames peered out at him.

He smiled. "Hi. I'm Rick Wells. I own the bar next door."

She didn't return his smile. "Yes?"

"It was me who heard you screaming the other ni—"

"I know who you are. What do you want?"

Her unfriendliness surprised him. Key Westers—even those new to the island—were typically outgoing and warm, infected with the laid-back charm of the southernmost tip of the continental United States.

He supposed he'd be suspicious, too, if he had just stumbled upon the scene of a brutal murder.

"I wanted to talk to you about the other night. About what you saw."

When she hesitated, he flashed her what he hoped was his most winning smile. "And I wanted to make sure you were okay. I know how traumatic witnessing something like that can be."

She frowned slightly. "And how do you know that?"

"Because I used to be a cop."

She paused a moment more as if carefully considering his truthfulness, then swung the door open. "Come on in."

She relocked the door after him, and started up the narrow flight of stairs. He followed her up and into her sparsely furnished living room. The furniture consisted of a comfortable-looking couch, a battered coffee table and a floor lamp. All three looked as if they could have been purchased secondhand. Nothing hung on the walls, the wooden floors were bare. A number of hardcover books lay open on the coffee table.

The room told him a lot about Elizabeth Ames, including the fact that she didn't plan to live in Key West long.

Odd, he thought. Why would a therapist open up a private practice if she didn't intend to make a long-term commitment to a location?

"Can I get you something to drink?" she asked stiffly. "Water, coffee, soft drink?"

"No, I'm good. Thanks."

"Have a seat."

He crossed to the couch, pausing to glance at the books on the table. There were several, all books on the history of Key West.

She came up beside him, bent and flipped the books closed. "I'm doing a little research."

Odd, he thought again. Elizabeth Ames was not the

typical island transplant, thrilled to be living in paradise, effusive and relaxed.

Prickly, that's what she was. And suspicious, like a
lot of folks from the mainland. No wonder she didn't
plan to stay long—she would never fit in.

He sat and smiled at her. "Looking for anything in
particular?"

She frowned at him again. "What do you mean?"

"Your research. I grew up on the island—" He spread
open his hands. "There's not much about Key West I
don't know."

She stared at him a moment, then took a seat at the
opposite end of the couch from him. "Actually, I am
looking for something in particular. Something a client
told me about."

"Shoot."

"This patient said the Blessed Virgin appeared to
children playing—"

"In what's now the walled garden of Paradise Christian," he filled in for her. "Sure, I've heard the story.
Though I don't know if it's true or not."

Her expression sharpened with interest. "I haven't
found a single record of it in any of these books."

He shrugged. "It's one of those stories everyone who
grew up here knows. In fact, I've heard several different versions of it. Why so interested?"

She looked down at her hands, clasped in her lap. He
sensed she was trying to decide whether to tell him the
truth. Whether or not she could trust him. When she
looked up he saw by her expression that she'd decided
she could. Her next words confirmed it. "Tara was a
patient of mine. She told me the story."

*Elizabeth Ames had not only stumbled upon a murder
victim, but one whom she had known.*

She suddenly didn't seem as unfriendly and suspicious as before. "I'm sorry," he murmured. "That must have been a terrible shock."

"It… Yes." Her lips trembled and she pressed them together.

"Did you tell Lieutenant Lopez about your connection to the victim?"

"Of course."

The way she said the words conveyed dislike. Not of him, of Val.

He decided to call her on it. "You don't like him much, do you?"

"I don't know him."

"He must have been interested to learn the two of you had a relationship."

"A professional relationship," she corrected. "And if you're so interested, why don't you ask him? You're friends, aren't you?"

He smiled, impressed. Seems he wasn't the only one who listened and asked questions. He decided he had nothing to lose and everything to gain by being completely honest with her. "He told me to butt out."

"Because you're not a cop anymore."

"Yes."

She smiled for the first time. The curving of her mouth altered her face, making her approachable, warm. Attractive, he realized, surprised. When she dropped her prickly, suspicious demeanor, Elizabeth Ames was actually quite attractive.

"So you decided to launch your own mini-investigation," she said.

"Basically."

"Why?"

He arched his eyebrows. "Excuse me?"

"Why launch your own investigation?"

"Because I was a cop and—"

"But you're not now. So, why do you care? Did you know Tara?"

He thought a moment before answering, searching for absolute honesty—for himself as well as her. "Because I was, in essence, first officer at the scene. Because I recognized the killer's style. Because I hate being shut out of something I know I can do better than anyone else."

"And that's it?"

"No." He silently swore, wondering how he had ended up being the one interrogated. "Because I have a feeling about this. That I need to investigate. It's stupid."

"No, it's not. I feel the same way."

They stared at each other a moment, something passing between them, something strong. Rick jerked his gaze away, uncomfortable with the connection.

"What did you mean about recognizing the killer's style?"

He returned his gaze to hers, choosing his words carefully. "A number of years ago a serial killer was operating in the Miami area. He killed young women in the same fashion Tara was killed."

Rick saw that his words shook her, but she met his gaze evenly anyway. He noticed that her eyes were a clear, light green. "How did... I saw a lot of blood, but I didn't... The paper said her throat was slit."

"Yes."

"Tell me what wasn't in the paper." When he hesitated, she leaned toward him, expression earnest. "I was there, Rick. I know there's more."

So he told her, quietly, without drama, excluding only the most gruesome details.

Liz paled. She struggled, he saw, not to cry. "And that's how...that killer in Miami—"

"Gavin Taft. Yes."

"And he was never caught?"

"He was," Rick corrected. "And convicted. At present, his address is death row at the Florida State Prison in Starke."

She frowned. "I don't understand. If these killings mirror those others and that murderer is behind bars, who..."

Her words trailed away. He picked up the thought where she had left off. "I don't understand either. Not yet anyway. Could be a copycat. Or an accomplice the police didn't know about."

Silence fell between them. She broke it first. "Have you ever heard of an old priest named Father Paul?"

Rick thought a moment, then shook his head. "I'm not Catholic."

"Tara said he knew the story about the appearance of the Blessed Virgin. I thought...if I could talk to him, maybe—"

"This might make sense?"

"Something like that." She caught her bottom lip between her teeth, expression anguished. "I can't stop thinking that I should have been able to do...something. That somehow I could have stopped this terrible thing from happening."

"She was murdered, Liz. You were her counselor, not her bodyguard."

"But she was my patient. Even though we only met twice, it was my job to help her." Liz clasped her hands together. "You said she knew her attacker. That means she put herself in the wrong place at the wrong time. It was my job to try to stop her from that kind of destructive behavior."

Rick felt for her. He understood. He thought of Sam, his senseless death. His own part in it. Yes, he understood. Only too well.

"Call the Catholic archdiocese. Or Our Lady Star of the Sea Catholic Church. I bet they'll be able to help you."

She looked away, then back. "How can I help you, Rick?"

He leaned toward her. "I wondered if there was anything you could tell me about the other night that would be helpful. Something you might not have thought was important at first. A noise? A smell? A sense of something being out of place or wrong?"

She tipped her hands up. "I told the police everything."

"Would you tell me what you told them?"

She agreed and recounted the events of early Saturday morning—she had been unable to sleep and had gone for a run. A block past Paradise Christian Church, she had felt compelled to turn toward the church. A noise had drawn her to the garden door. It had been unlocked. When she'd pushed it open, a cat had leaped out at her. She had entered the garden. And found Tara.

"And that's it? You're certain? Sometimes, in the shock of the moment, a witness can overlook something small, something that seems inconsequential. Sometimes it's that very thing that cracks a case."

Liz shook her head. "I can't—"

"Think. Carefully go over the events of that night, the sessions you had with Tara, the things she said. Your impressions."

"As I said, I only met with her twice. Her parents

were worried about her…she was obviously troubled. Frightened about somethi—"

"Frightened? Of what?"

She looked uncomfortable. "I don't know. She seemed to have a bizarre view of religion. A fanatical view of heaven, hell, the devil. That's another reason I wanted to talk to Father Paul."

He thought a moment, working to put the pieces together. "Did you know who the baby's father was?"

"Excuse me?"

"The baby's father," he repeated. "Tara knew her killer. Aspects of the crime indicate the killer was aware of her pregnancy."

The blood had drained from her face and Rick realized his mistake. She hadn't known.

He held a hand out. "I'm sorry. I thought you knew."

"A baby?" She stood. He saw that she shook. "Tara was…pregnant?"

He followed her to her feet. "I'm sorry," he said again. "I thought you—"

She started to cry, softly, the sound heartbreaking and helpless.

Rick crossed to her and took her awkwardly in his arms. She leaned into him, the tears becoming sobs that racked her thin frame.

He didn't know what to do, so he simply held her.

After a time, Liz's tears stopped and she eased away from him, obviously embarrassed. "I'm… That was so…uncalled-for." She looked at him, then away. "I just… This has been hard."

He slipped his hands into his pockets, uncertain how to respond. "Don't worry about it."

"I've made a total fool of myself."

"Not at all." He smiled. "Trust me, okay? I'm a bartender, I see lots of people making fools of themselves."

She returned his smile, hers weak. "Thanks. I wish I could have helped you more."

"If you think of anything about that night, you'll call me at the Hideaway?"

"I promise."

They crossed to the stairs that led to the first floor and started down them, stopping when they reached the front door. Liz met his eyes. "It makes sense now, how she looked. Ill, like she wasn't sleeping or eating. I thought she might be using but never that she might be pregnant."

"It could even explain why she was frightened," he murmured. "Still in high school, unmarried and pregnant. It doesn't get too much bigger than that, does it?"

CHAPTER 23

Sunday, November 11
2:00 p.m.

Liz had taken Rick Wells's suggestion and called Our Lady Star of the Sea Catholic Church. To Liz's amazement the woman who answered the phone had known not only who Father Paul was but where Liz could find him: the old priest resided at St. Catherine's, a local nursing home subsidized by the Catholic church.

The woman had assured her that Father Paul would be delighted to have a visitor, even if she wasn't a Catholic.

Liz swept her gaze over the front of the building, a one-story, flamingo-pink stuccoed structure surrounded by palm trees and palmettos. Liz guessed it had been built in the late sixties or early seventies, a period of architecture better forgotten.

She entered the residence. She had been in many such

homes over the years and although relatively small, this one wasn't much different. The air smelled faintly of antiseptic and old age. Straight ahead lay the nurses' station; to her right, a large community area, outfitted with a console television, several game tables and three sofas. The game tables were empty this afternoon, the couches full. In addition, a half-dozen residents in wheelchairs clustered around the TV, much to the irritation of a loudly complaining few whose view of the movie—Charlton Heston's *The Ten Commandments*—was obstructed.

Liz crossed to the information desk. As she did, a small dust mop of a dog darted toward her. He came to a stop at her feet, whined and assumed the "feed me" position—weight on back haunches, front paws up. Judging by his rotund appearance, he received plenty of treats. Liz squatted and scratched him behind the ears. "You're a cute little guy," she murmured. "I'm sorry, but I don't have anything to give you."

He cocked his head, as if deciding whether she was being straight with him, then dropped to all fours and waddled off. She watched him go, then stood.

The nurse smiled at her. "That's Rascal. We tell the residents not to feed him," she murmured. "But they can't help themselves. He brings them such pleasure."

"I'll bet." Liz returned her smile. "I'm looking for a resident named Father Paul Ramos. I was told he lived here."

"He does." She pointed. "He's in C wing, number fourteen. If he's lucid, he'll be delighted to have a visitor."

Liz's heart sank. "If he's lucid?"

"Father Paul's one hundred and two. Sometimes he's

with us. And sometimes he's not. So don't be alarmed if he starts talking crazy."

Liz found fourteen-C. Father Paul sat in his wheelchair, facing the window. A Bible lay open in his lap; his mouth worked as he moved the rosary beads between his fingers.

She tapped on the door. "Father Paul?"

He looked at her, squinting. "Margaret?"

"No." She stepped into the room. "My name's Elizabeth Ames. I was hoping I could ask you a few questions."

"Come in, child." He smiled and motioned her closer. "How can an old man like me help you?"

She perched on the edge of his bed and he swiveled his chair to face her. "I'm a counselor and one of my patients told me an interesting story. She said you could tell me more about it."

He laughed, the sound papery with age. "I know many interesting stories, a benefit of having lived a long time." He leaned toward her, expression almost childlike. "And I love telling them."

She laughed, too, liking this man. "This is a special story, Father. One about the Blessed Mother appearing to children in the churchyard of what is now Paradise Christian Church."

His inclined his head, expression pleased. "That is, indeed, a special story." He laid his rosary in his Bible, marking his place, then closed the book. "It is a true story, one I was told by my grandparents, children at the time.

"Key West was very different at that time. Cut off from the rest of the country by water."

He looked past her, expression faraway. "Did you know, at one time Key West was the wealthiest city in

America?" He returned his gaze to hers. "It's true. Because of the salvaging industry. Ships crashed into the reef and went down. The bells would sound and there would be a great race to see which outfit reached the sinking vessel first."

"The first to the vessel rescued the passengers and claimed the ship's bounty as their own," she murmured. "Is that right?"

"It is, indeed." His lips lifted. "There are rumors that some of Key West's more nefarious entrepreneurs actually lured the vessels to the reef."

"And you believe those rumors are true."

"One must be watchful of greed, child. There's a reason it's one of the seven deadly sins."

He sobered. "The devil is crafty, indeed. He captures us through the things that make us most human. Lust. Pride. Anger. Avarice. Envy. Sloth. Gluttony. These we must guard against, just as the Lord warned us we should."

Liz thought of Tara and shuddered. The light in Father Paul's eyes was the same she had seen in the girl's. Somehow, it seemed less disturbing in a man of Father Paul's age and religious stature.

"I've frightened you," he murmured.

She rubbed her arms. "No, of course not."

"I wish I had."

She blinked in surprise. "Excuse me?"

He looked past her once more, expression faraway. "I know, you didn't come here to be warned against the Beast. No one does anymore. It's not…fashionable."

He fell silent. His eyes closed. Liz waited, wondering if he had fallen asleep. And if he had, if she should wake him or leave.

Suddenly, he opened his eyes and looked at her,

his blue gaze as clear as a summer sky. "Back then, Paradise Christian was St. Stephen's. And there in the walled garden, among the banyan and poinciana trees, the Blessed Mother appeared as a vision to the children. She didn't speak, just hovered there, swathed in a halo as bright as the gold coins recovered from all those shipwrecked vessels. The children weren't frightened. They were awed. They understood they were in the presence of God. They fell to their knees in prayer and thanksgiving. Several ran for Father Roberto."

"Did he witness the vision?" she asked, spellbound.

The old priest shook his head. "He was too late. But he believed. After all, why would these children, good, faithful children, make such a thing up?

"For the next fourteen days," he continued, "Key West was blessed with one miracle after another. Sickness was cured. The blind could suddenly see, the crippled walk. Blood flowed from the hands of the statue of Christ."

"And then the miracles stopped," Liz whispered. "And the storm came."

"Yes. The wind first, a gentle breeze from the west. The old-timers knew. The breeze, the movement of the water. Something was wrong. Word spread. A few packed up their families and made their way toward the mainland, from key to key by boat. Others refused to leave and instead began making preparations.

"Of course, as in all things, there were disbelievers. Naysayers. There would be no storm. The Lord had always spared this beautiful place, they believed he would spare her once more."

But he didn't spare her, Liz knew. She had read about this hurricane, thought the worst Key West had suffered. The year 1846 predated hurricane naming and classification systems, so it was called only the storm of 1846.

"Back then there was no early-warning system. No hurricane center in Miami. No Weather Channel." His eyes clouded with the memory. "Only the church bells to ring. And only when it was already too late. The storm was all but upon them."

Liz shivered, imagining. She knew from her reading that in those days the only way on and off the island was by boat. Flagler's railroad didn't open until 1912; the overseas highway not until 1938.

"For forty-eight hours the storm pummeled the island. With the scream of the wind could be heard the church bells and the cries of the lost ones. Many were washed out to sea, and for weeks afterward bodies floated ashore. Entire families, lashed together." He lowered his voice. "Men, women and children. It's a miracle that anyone was spared."

"Your grandparents and their family were among the survivors."

"Yes. They were protected. The Blessed Virgin protected them."

Liz realized she was holding her breath and released it. "The church was destroyed."

"Yes," he murmured. "The church and all who had taken refuge there were washed out to sea."

"So the archdiocese decided to demonize the visions."

He shook his head, his expression unbearably sad. "The visions were a true miracle. Acts of God not demons. They were a warning to guard against the wicked, a warning of the approaching storm. The believers were saved."

He lowered his voice to a crackly whisper. Liz

leaned toward him, straining to hear. "The church lies on sacred ground. Listen well, child." He reached out and caught her hand, his skin as dry as parchment, his grip surprisingly strong. "It is a profoundly holy place and must be protected at all costs. For in the desecration of the holy, evil extends its putrid grasp."

CHAPTER 24

Monday, November 12
9:30 a.m.

Liz sat at her desk staring blankly at her far wall, Father Paul's last words still ringing in her head. She had slept with them, tossing and turning, her dreams populated with demons, and with bodies floating face-down in the water.

"For in the desecration of the holy, evil extends its putrid grasp.

For weeks afterward the bodies floated ashore. Entire families lashed together."

She had been unable to sleep for those images in her head—ones drawn by Father Paul's words—but also by Rick Wells's comments. She had been haunted by his description of Tara's death, sketchy though it had been.

He had soft-pedaled the truth for her, she knew. The newspaper had carried even fewer details. But her mind had filled in the blanks—added details including Tara's last thoughts: ones, Liz imagined, of terror, for her baby's life and her own. Liz had imagined the girl's cries for help.

Liz brought the heels of her hands to her eyes. She had totally embarrassed herself in front of Rick Wells— falling apart and clinging to him, blubbering like a baby.

All those noisy tears had made him uncomfortable. She had seen it in his eyes. She had tried to stop them, had tried to rein them in, but it had been so long since she'd had someone to hold on to, strong arms to support her. His arms, his strength, had been so comforting, such a relief. She had simply melted against him and fallen apart.

Now, he thought her an emotional wreck.

Get in line, Wells. You're not alone.

The phone rang and she jumped, startled. She grabbed it. "Liz Ames."

"Ms. Ames, it's Pastor Tim."

Something in his tone had her straightening. "Yes, Pastor?"

"The strangest thing... I found something that belongs to you."

"Something that belongs to me?" she repeated, frowning. "I wasn't aware that I'd lost anything."

"You misunderstand. I found an envelope addressed to you. In my study, under the cushion of the window seat."

Rachel. It had to be from Rachel.

"Liz?"

"Sorry, that's just so bizarre."

"Would you like to pick it up now?"

"Yes. If that's all right?"

"Fine. I'm working out of the parsonage this morning, not the church. Meet me there."

Liz agreed, and not ten minutes later she hurried up the parsonage's front walk. She found Pastor Tim waiting anxiously by the door.

"I tried to call you back," he said. "There's been an emergency... One of my flock. I have to go."

"But what—"

He thrust an oversize envelope into her hands. Her name had been printed in large, bold letters on the front. She stared at it, unsettled. The handwriting was not Rachel's. So, whose was it?

"I'm sorry, but I've got to—"

"Wait!" She caught his arm. "Where did you say you found this?"

He looked at her, gaze cool. "Under the cushion of the window seat in the parsonage study. What do you imagine it was doing there?"

She swallowed hard, feeling guilty, wondering if lying to a man of God constituted a big sin. "I wish I knew."

He glanced at his watch, then back at her, expression unreadable. "You know, I've sat in that seat more times than I can count and never noticed that envelope. I wonder why I did today?"

"I don't know," she answered. "If I had the answer to that question, I'd certainly tell you."

For a long moment, he searched her gaze. "Is there anything you'd like to tell me, Liz? Anything at all?"

Pastor Howard was my sister. I think she was murdered by the same monster who killed Tara. Can you help me?

That's what she opened her mouth to say. Instead, she murmured that there wasn't.

He looked disappointed. "I really need to go."

"Before you do, would it be possible for me to see where you found this? It might help me discover the answer to that question."

"I don't think the help you need is in my quarters," he told her, glancing at his watch once more. "I suggest you look to God, Liz. Only he can fill the empty place inside you."

With that, he shut the door in her face. Shocked, she stared at the closed door.

He knew who she really was. That was obvious. And since his attitude toward her had done a three-sixty or one-eighty after the night of Tara's murder, she suspected Lieutenant Lopez had told him.

Less obvious, however, was why she hadn't taken the opportunity to come clean. Why hadn't she told him the truth and asked for his help? He had offered it to her.

Because she didn't trust him.

A shaky laugh tripped off her lips. She didn't trust him? She was the one who had been lying. The one who had deliberately misrepresented herself.

No wonder he had slammed the door in her face. What was wrong with her?

She lowered her gaze to the envelope and the oddly printed letters across its front. She was obsessed with uncovering what had happened to her sister. And she would do anything to discover the truth.

Even lie to a man of God. Heaven help her.

Her hands began to shake. Heart in her throat, she opened the envelope. It was filled with family photographs and other mementos: a ticket stub to the Broadway musical she and Rachel had seen together; a note from their mother, Liz's graduation announcement; Rachel's baby book.

Liz shuffled through the pictures, tears choking her. Ones of her parents and grandparents, of she and Rachel as youngsters and young adults. Sisters and best friends.

It was as if Rachel had grabbed all the quickly accessible and irreplaceable pieces of her life and shoved them in an envelope for Liz.

Why? To make sure she got them? Or for another reason?

She leafed through the envelope's contents again. A sheet of unlined paper fluttered to the ground.

Liz retrieved it. The paper appeared to have been torn from a journal. Drawn on the page were several variations of the same image: an image that appeared to be a horned flower.

Liz stared at the drawing, tilting her head, then the paper. What was it? A religious symbol? A local logo of some kind?

"You're still here?"

She looked up, startled. Pastor Tim stood at his door, Bible tucked under his arm. He didn't attempt to hide his annoyance.

"Yes. I—" She held out the sheet containing the drawings of the flower. "Do you recognize this image?"

He looked at it, then away. "I have no idea what that is."

"It's not a religious symbol?" she pressed. "Or a logo from a local business?"

He didn't meet her eyes. "I said, I have no idea what it is." He snapped the door shut. "Good day."

He was lying. She didn't know why she was so certain of that, but she was. She swung around to watch him go, reviewing their brief conversation of a moment ago and the one from earlier. She recalled his expression when she showed him the drawing.

It had shifted subtly, she realized. Had it been guilt she'd seen creep across his features? Or alarm? Or some other emotion she couldn't quite put her finger on?

Liz frowned. And why, when he'd professed to be in such a big hurry, had he spent the last ten minutes in the parsonage? Could it have had anything to do with her request to take a look inside?

Her heart began to thump uncomfortably against the wall of her chest. By his own admission, he was the one who had packed her sister's things. Perhaps he had found something incriminating, something he had decided to keep to himself.

But what? And why would he? He had arrived on the island after her sister disappeared, hadn't he?

She needed to get inside the parsonage and take a look around.

Liz glanced at the door, then moved toward it. Luckily, she stood in an alcove, mostly obscured from view. She peeked over her shoulder anyway, then reached out and grasped the doorknob. Taking a deep breath, she twisted.

The door eased open. Quickly, before she could change her mind, she ducked inside, closing the door behind her.

The interior was spartan. None of her sister's homey sense of style remained. It looked like a watered-down version of a bachelor's pad: big recliner across from the TV, books stacked on the shelves and coffee table, a few framed photos. No flowers, no pretty afghan tossed across the back of the couch, no profusion of throw pillows or cutesy knickknacks.

It hurt to picture Rachel here, so Liz forced the comparisons from her mind. Fearing Pastor Tim would return before she could complete her search, she began looking for anything out of the ordinary, anything she recognized as having belonged to her sister. She made a quick but careful search of the living room, then moved on to the kitchen, then the bathroom.

Nothing jumped out at her.

From there she entered the bedroom. Again, the room was neat and spare. She glanced quickly at two framed photos on the dresser—one of Pastor Tim in full football gear, flanked by a couple of other uniformed players, the other at graduation from college, he in cap and gown, an older couple at his side, beaming.

It crossed her mind that in both photos Pastor Tim wore a costume of sorts and that every Sunday he wore another.

Would the real Pastor Tim please stand up?

She shifted her attention away from the photographs and back to her mission. She slid open the top dresser drawer. It was filled with the pastor's socks and Jockey shorts.

Liz's fingers froze. Lord help her, what was she doing? Going through someone's personal things? Violating their privacy? How would she feel if the situation was reversed?

Her own actions made her sick to her stomach. Shaking, she slid the drawer shut. She had to get a grip on herself, on her behavior. She had gone too far this time. Breaking and entering, for heaven's sake.

She grabbed the envelope from the top of the dresser, intent on getting out of the parsonage. She turned, then stopped, a scream rising to her throat.

Stephen stood at the window, staring at her with his one good eye, disfigured mouth twisted into a grotesque grimace.

The man inched closer to the window, mouth working. He lifted his hands; Liz saw that they were curved into fists. He meant to break the window, she realized. He meant her harm.

Suddenly, he pivoted away from the glass, head cocked. In the next moment he was gone.

Liz ran to the window and peered out, hoping to see which way he had disappeared. He had disappeared completely, the only evidence of his presence a broken palmetto.

She released a strangled breath, then sucked in another. Something had frightened him off. Thank God. Something—

Not something. Someone.

Pastor Tim had returned.

She heard him at the front door. Heard him insert the key into the lock. Imagined his expression as he realized it hadn't been locked. Heard the door open, then close, heard him mutter something under his breath.

Liz looked around, frantically searching for a place to hide. Her gaze landed on what she assumed was the closet. She darted toward it, yanked the door open and slipped inside.

It was, indeed, a clothes closet, and she carefully inched her way to the very back corner. The closet was deep and jammed full with clothing, sports equipment, storage boxes and even some holiday decorations. It smelled stale, faintly of sweat, aftershave and dust.

Pastor Tim entered the room. He let out a frustrated-sounding breath as he moved about. Liz's heart beat so hard and fast her chest hurt. She pressed her lips together, struggling not to make a sound, to not even breathe.

He reached the closet; she saw the shadow of his feet at the bottom of the door. She pressed herself farther into the corner. Something scurried on the wall by her ear, and a cry rose in her throat.

The doorknob turned, a sliver of light spilled into the closet. The sliver grew. Liz caught a glimpse of the man. In that glimpse he bore little resemblance to the mild-mannered pastor she had come to expect—he looked angry. And determined. A man who would level anyone who dared cross him.

Pastor Tim was not the man he professed to be.

The anxiety attack came upon her without warning. Smothering in its intensity. The weight of it upon her chest crippling. She pressed her hand over her mouth to keep from crying out and squeezed her eyes shut. In the next moment, he would find her out. How would she explain? He would almost certainly call the police. She could imagine Lieutenant Lopez's disgust. His satisfaction.

Both sisters, nutty as fruitcakes. And to think I gave her the benefit of the doubt.

Not now, Lord, she prayed. Please, not now.

The door opened a fraction wider, then snapped shut, leaving her in darkness once more. A moment later came the sound of his footsteps and the front door slamming closed.

Liz curled her arms around her middle and sank to her knees. Her pent-up breath shuddered past her lips in shallow gasps. She fought to slow her breathing, to concentrate on the steady pull and push of oxygen in and out. She willed her heart and thoughts to slow to a gallop. She had nothing to fear, she told herself. She had not been discovered.

Gradually, her breathing and heart rate returned to normal. She stood cautiously, careful to make as little noise as possible. She eased toward the door, cracked it open and peered out. As she had thought it would be, the bedroom beyond was empty.

Liz started through the door, then realized she had left the envelope behind. As she bent to retrieve it she caught the glint of metal on the floor of the closet. Curious, she bent closer. A ring, she realized. Peeking out from under a pair of work boots.

She picked it up. Her hand trembled. She recognized the ring—a circle of gold studded with rubies—it had been her mother's, one of a matched pair.

Liz shifted her gaze slightly. She wore its mate on her right ring finger.

And like Rachel, she never took it off.

CHAPTER 25

Monday, November 12
5:00 p.m.

Hours later, Liz sat alone in her office, evening shadows beginning to gather in the room's corners. After finding the ring, she had fled the parsonage. She had made it to her office, gotten the door closed and locked behind her before she'd fallen apart.

She lowered her gaze to her right hand and the twin eternity bands, nestled together on her ring finger. Her mother had given them to her and Rachel just months before she died. Liz remembered the day vividly, could recall the color of the sky, the smell of the flowers at her mother's bedside, what both she and Rachel had been wearing.

At their mother's funeral several months ago, they'd vowed never to take the rings off. A silly kind of promise, Liz supposed. A vow either one of them could have broken without the other knowing. But she hadn't. And she didn't believe her sister had either.

So how had the ring ended up at the bottom of that closet?

The answer hurt. It was further proof that her sister was dead.

Proof, unfortunately, that she couldn't take to the police.

Liz turned her gaze from the rings to her front window, to the constant stream of people passing. How could she? *You see, Lieutenant Lopez, I found it when I was sneaking out of Pastor Tim's bedroom closet.*

Right. She was already hanging on with him by a thread. One wrong move and he would have her tossed into a cell.

Or into the loony bin.

Her head hurt. She brought a hand to her temple, to the spot where the pain was most intense, and massaged it. The envelope with its mementos and cryptic drawings. The ring. The old caretaker at the window spying on her. Pastor Tim's transformation from caring clergyman to angry accuser. Her sister's disappearance. Tara's murder. How did all the pieces fit together?

The phone rang and she reached for it. "Elizabeth Ames here."

"Is this Dr. Ames, the therapist?"

Liz straightened. The voice on the other end of the line sounded deliberately muffled, and she frowned, straining to determine the caller's age and gender. "This is Elizabeth Ames, the family counselor. I'm not a doctor, however."

Total silence ensued. "Hello?" she said. "Can I help you?"

"I'm a friend of Tara Mancuso's. I need to talk to you."

For a moment, she couldn't find her tongue. It was almost as if thoughts of the girl had conjured the caller. "Did you want to make an appointment? If so—"

"I'm not calling for an appointment."

"How can I help you?"

"I have information about her death."

She caught her breath. "I'm in my office now. Do you know where it—"

"No," the caller said quickly. "Not there. I'm... I don't want us to be seen together."

A male, Liz realized.

She shifted her gaze to her front window and the gathering twilight. Something about this didn't feel right. "You say you were a friend of Tara's?"

"Yes, I..." The caller fell silent a moment. "Never mind. Calling you was a mistake—"

"Wait! Where do you want to meet? I'll be there."

For a split second, Liz feared the caller had hung up. Then he spoke, so softly Liz had to strain to hear. "Mallory Square at sunset."

"But how will I know—"

"I'll find you. And Ms. Ames? I suggest you be... really careful."

The sunset celebration in Mallory Square was a nightly Key West event, and for many it served as a kickoff for the night's revelry. Tourists and locals alike flocked to the square to watch the sun melt into the Gulf of Mexico. Placards all over town announced the exact time the fiery orb would make its descent. Today's sunset, Liz learned, was expected at 5:42.

When Liz arrived, the official celebration, which

began an hour before sunset, was already under way. The crowd was immense, a mass of half-clothed, sun-burned bodies. Street performers entertained the crowd, and every so often a roar would go up as one of the performers aced a particularly tricky move.

Liz worked her way across the square, past a fire-eater, a stand-up comedian on stilts, several jugglers and all manner of mimes. The mood was part drunken bacchanal, part Sunday-worship service. Some had come to party, some to meditate and still others to simply witness it all.

She had come for answers.

Liz stopped at the edge of a group circled around a juggler. The man tossed a half-dozen blazing hoops into the air; the group murmured their appreciation as he caught each in rapid succession.

She moved on. Minutes passed. She continued to wind her way through the crowd, studying each face, wondering which belonged to her caller. Her apprehension grew. The crowd, which she had considered a positive at first, became a negative. So many faces, she thought, a thread of panic racing through her. So many bodies. How would her caller find her?

If the call had even been legitimate. It could have been a hoax. An attempt to scare her. An attempt to get her out on the street, alone in the crowd. For in a funny way, the density of the crowd made her as vulnerable as if she were waiting in a deserted parking lot.

"And, Ms. Ames? I suggest you be...really careful."

Sweat beaded her upper lip. The crowd closed in on her. She brought a hand to her chest; her heart beat wildly under her palm.

Not now, Liz. Stay calm. Focus.

She became aware of someone behind her, standing

too close. She inched forward but found herself trapped in a sea of bodies.

"Hello, Ms. Ames."

She glanced over her shoulder.

The young man behind her wore dark sunglasses, a baseball cap and a pair of tattered cutoffs. He was shirtless. There his resemblance to the other young men on Mallory Square ended. This boy was both totally sober and as watchful as a long-tailed cat in a roomful of rocking chairs.

He caught her arm. "Come with me."

She nodded and allowed him to lead her through the throng to the bulkhead at the water's edge. The party was behind them, and it occurred to her that this boy could ever so casually push her over the side and no one would even notice.

"Sit," he murmured. "Don't look at me. Only the sunset."

She did as he requested. Several moments passed and she dared a glance at him from the corner of her eyes. He stared out at the water, expression intent.

She cleared her throat. "Why did you contact me? Why the secrecy?"

"Not yet. I need a minute."

Although difficult, she swallowed both her questions and her nerves, and focused on the constantly shifting water.

"Tara and I were in love," he began finally. "We were going to run away together."

The boyfriend, Liz realized. Tara's baby's father.

"I went to meet her. That night."

Liz looked at him, chilled. He removed his sunglasses and met her eyes. His were bloodshot.

"I found her," he said. "Like…that. I—"

Her first reaction to his declaration was pity. Her next was fear.

This young man could be Tara's killer.

And he had sought her out.

"The police are looking for me, I'm sure. Because Tara was...pregnant." His voice grew thick and he cleared it. "But they don't know who I am. We were very careful."

Liz glanced quickly to her left, then right. If she screamed, would anyone hear her? And if they did, would they react in time?

She doubted it but decided to push him anyway. "But I know who you are. I know your name. That's why you came looking for me, isn't it?"

He frowned. "What do you mean?"

"Am I a loose end?"

She saw her meaning sink in, saw disbelief and horror creep into his eyes. And realized she had nothing to fear from him.

"Tara didn't tell you about us. She was absolutely set on secrecy."

"Why so secretive?"

"Because she was afraid." He looked away, then back, features twisted with grief. "She led me to believe it was her parents she feared. They were strict, she said. They would break us up. Now I realize the truth. It was her friends' wrath she feared, not her parents'."

Liz frowned. "When you say she was afraid her friends would do her harm, what exactly are you talking about? Social alienation? Surely not bodily harm? I mean...you're not suggesting that her friends...that they—"

"Killed her," he whispered. "I think they did."

Liz shook her head, thinking of the implausibility of

it, recalling what Rick Wells had told her about the kill-ing. "Look, this isn't common knowledge, but someone close to the investigation told me that Tara's murder re-sembled the style of a serial killer who operated out of Miami a number of years ago. That killer is sitting on death row, but they believe an accomplice or copycat killed Tara."

"That's not right, I know it's not."

She leaned toward him. "How do you know?"

For a long moment, he sat silent. She sensed that he was struggling to collect himself, his thoughts. "We were going to run away together. That night. Tara was afraid. Of them. Her friends. They had threatened her."

"In what way?"

Tears flooded his eyes. He looked away. "Tara be-longed to this group. They were very possessive of one another, very jealous. Members were not allowed to as-sociate with those not a part of the Flower—"

"The Flower?" she interrupted.

"The Horned Flower. That's the name of the group."

A chill raced up her spine. *The drawings in her sis-ter's notes. Could they represent this group?*

"Tara and I had dated a few times when she told me about her friends," he continued. "'Her family,' she called them. She asked if I wanted to join."

"And you said no."

"I'm a Christian, Ms. Ames. And these kids…they were into some bad stuff. Things that I couldn't… wouldn't be a part of, even though I really liked Tara."

"What kind of bad stuff?"

"Drugs. And sex." He cleared his throat. "But it was more than that. It's what they believed. And what they didn't believe."

She waited, sensing he needed time.

"They didn't believe in God. Not in heaven or hell. Only the here and now. In earthly pleasures. They believed they owed allegiance to no one but themselves and their Horned Flower family."

Liz thought of the things Tara had said during their sessions, the comments she'd made about the devil, heaven and hell. No wonder Tara had sounded so conflicted.

"I told her I couldn't see her anymore, not if she was going to be a part of that group."

"And she chose you."

"Yes."

He sighed, shifting his gaze to the horizon and the rapidly setting sun. She, too, turned her gaze to the gulf. In the exact moment the sun sank from sight, a flash of green light appeared. A cheer rose up from the crowd.

"Dear Lord."

She looked at her young companion in question.

He met her eyes. "Did you see it? The green light?" She nodded and he continued. "It's rare. Tara used to say…" His throat seemed to close over the words and he cleared it. "She used to say if you saw the flash of green you were destined for something big."

"Did she ever see it?"

He nodded. "The last time…she saw it the day before…she found out she was pregnant."

"I'm sorry."

With the main event over, the crowd quickly dispersed. Quiet and darkness settled over them. Liz shivered.

"Tara knew who you are."

"Excuse me?"

"She knew who you really are."

Liz called his bluff. "Really? And who am I?"

"You're Pastor Rachel's sister." Liz caught her breath; he looked at her. "It's true, isn't it?"

Liz clasped her hands together. "How did she know?"

"Didn't ask."

"Did she…say anything about that? Or about my sister?"

"She liked your sister a lot. She felt bad about what happened to her."

Liz's heart beat hard against the wall of her chest. "Did she…know what happened to her?"

He shook his head and she held back a cry of disappointment, though it tasted sour against her tongue. "Why are you telling me all this?" she managed to say after a moment.

"The way I figure it, maybe your sister's disappearance and Tara's death are related."

She could have wept with relief. *This kid thought the same way she did. She wasn't crazy.*

And she wasn't alone, not anymore. "How do you figure that?" she asked.

"Tara was always so weird about your sister's disappearance," he murmured. "Besides, it just kind of makes sense to me."

"Me, too." Silence fell between them. After several moments, she met his eyes. "What do you want me to do?"

"Nothing. I called you because I wanted someone… to know everything. In case something happens to me."

"I don't understand," she said, alarmed.

"Right now I only suspect that her friends killed her. I'm going to find out for sure."

She swallowed past the lump in her throat. "How?"

"I'm going to become one of them."

"Bad idea. Very bad idea."

"It's the only way."

"Why not go to the police?"

He simply looked at her and she acknowledged the answer to her own question: as the father of Tara's baby, he would be a prime suspect. To make matters worse, by his own admission he had been there that night. And had run from the scene.

Most probably, if he went to the police, he would end up behind bars.

She let out a long breath. "You think these people are killers, for heaven's sake. If what you suspect is true, getting close to them will put you in harm's way, big-time. This is not a good idea."

"You're not going to change my mind." He glanced behind them at the nearly empty square, then stood. "I better go."

"Wait!" She followed him to his feet. "I don't even know your name."

"Mark. Mark Morgan."

"Don't go yet." She held out a hand. "Let's talk about this before you—"

He cut her off. "There's nothing to talk about. Besides, it's too late. I already contacted a couple of Tara's friends." A smile touched his mouth. "Thanks though, for...caring."

She made a sound of frustration. "But how will I know if you need help?"

"You won't hear from me," he said simply. "If that happens, go to Rick Wells. He's a friend. I trust him."

"Rick Wells?" she repeated, surprised.

"Do you know him?"

"Yes, I... We met."

He nodded and started off, then stopped and looked back at her. "Remember me in your prayers, okay? I think I'm going to need them."

CHAPTER 26

Friday, November 16
10:20 p.m.

Mark waited for Sarah, his Horned Flower connection. While he waited, he prayed. For guidance and protection. For strength.

Tonight he would be initiated into the Horned Flower. He was afraid.

Mark lifted his gaze to the sky. Dense cloud cover obliterated the full moon. This time of night Southernmost Beach—so named because it was literally the southernmost beach in the country—was deserted. From behind came the sound of traffic from Whitehead and South Streets. A Jimmy Buffet tune poured from a car's open window.

"Cheeseburger in Paradise."

Paradise. He had thought of Key West that way. Had thought her a sparkling, perfect jewel of a place.

Now he saw that her beauty masked an ugliness without compare.

Mark glanced at his watch, then toward the beach entrance. They had agreed to meet at ten-fifteen. He frowned. She was late.

Sarah, where are you?

Sarah had been the friend Tara had talked about most, the one, he knew, who had campaigned for Tara to invite him into their group. The night he met Tara for the first time, she had been with Sarah.

Mark had lied to the girl. Tara had told him about the Horned Flower and foolishly he had believed he didn't need their family. Tara had broken up with him because he wouldn't join, now she was dead.

Life seemed pointless, he'd told Sarah. He was drifting, alone without an anchor. He had always believed in God, but now he saw he had been wrong. To deny earthly pleasures for a life in heaven was wrong. Life was short. It was meant to be enjoyed.

He wanted to be a part of their family.

When Sarah resisted, he had begged her. He needed the Horned Flower. Tara had been ready to invite him into the family; she had gotten the okay. He would do anything she asked, he promised. Anything the family required of him.

In the end she had agreed to vouch for him. She had set up tonight's meeting. He was to come alone, she had instructed him. He was to wait on the bench nearest the burned-out utility light.

She had accepted him, his story, so easily.

Maybe too easily, he thought. Maybe she had no intention of meeting him here, of bringing him to the Horned Flower. Maybe she—and the others—had discovered his true purpose for contacting her.

If that was true, he was a sitting duck.

Another scenario occurred to him, one much worse. Perhaps, by convincing her to help him, he had put her in jeopardy?

An image of Sarah lying in a pool of blood, her throat slit as Tara's had been, filled his head, and his stomach rose to his throat.

He swallowed the sickness back and thought of Liz. He had called and left a message on her machine. Tonight was the night, he'd told her. He would call her tomorrow. If he didn't, she was to call Rick.

A part of him had been glad Liz hadn't been home—she would have tried to talk him out of this.

She very well might have succeeded. He could turn himself in to the police. Let them deal with this. It was their job.

It wasn't too late.

Momentarily, the clouds cleared and he saw her. She started toward him. Twin emotions of relief and fear trembled through him.

Lord, be with me now and at the hour of my death. Amen.

He didn't know why that prayer had leaped into his head but he was glad it had. No matter the outcome of the night, he knew the Lord would be with him.

Mark stood and forced a smile. "I was afraid you weren't coming."

She didn't return his smile. She held out a strip of dark fabric. "Until you're fully a part of the Flower, our total anonymity has to be maintained. Turn around, Mark."

A blindfold. He did as she requested, though his every instinct shouted he not.

She fixed the fabric across his eyes, then tied it. The

fit was snug but not uncomfortable. The dark fabric completely blinded him.

"Face me." When he did, she cupped his face in her palms. He sensed her gaze boring into his. "Remember your promise to do anything I asked?" she murmured. "Anything, without hesitation. Do you remember?"

He nodded and she stood on tiptoe. She pressed her mouth to his, and with her tongue, deposited something on his, then drew her tongue out but kept her lips pressed tightly to his.

A pill, he realized with alarm. She was drugging him! He gagged but she stood fast, her mouth against his, sealing it, forcing him to swallow.

He did and she smiled. "Good baby. Just let me make sure." She kissed him again, this time with abandon. With a passion that took him as much by surprise as her drugging him had. She moved her body against his in time to the movement of her tongue in his mouth.

With a throaty laugh she brought her right hand from his face to his shoulder, then chest, across his abdomen to his crotch. She cupped him, massaging with alternating pressure.

His body responded and guilty tears stung his eyes. How could his body betray him that way? How could he betray Tara that way?

"It will be wonderful," Sarah whispered against his ear, as if sensing his distress. "The most perfect experience ever. Just trust me."

She caught his hand again and led him slowly forward. After a few moments they stepped from sand to pavement. They took eight steps, then stopped.

A car door opened. Footsteps came around the car. Mark strained to hear, to pick up anything that would reveal the other person's identity. He couldn't even determine whether the other person was male or female.

The footsteps ceased. "He took it," Sarah said to the other's unspoken question. "I think it's starting to kick in."

She was right, Mark realized. His limbs had grown heavy, his head light. Pinpricks of colored light danced before his blindfolded eyes. He attempted to blink them away but couldn't.

The sensations were unnatural but not unpleasant. They sucked all fear and uncertainty from him.

The two helped him into a vehicle and he slumped against the seat, a smile curving his lips, his thoughts sailing—over lakes and mountains, past his life's events, people he had known and loved waving as he flew by. Buoyant as a cloud on a summer breeze, he returned their greeting, wishing he could stop and talk, frustrated that he couldn't.

Mark became aware of the vehicle moving. He fought to focus, to determine travel time and direction. His effort was wasted. Instead, his head filled with sexual images. With Sarah's mouth and touch, her voice in his ear.

"You want me, don't you?"

With a shock he realized she was beside him in the car, her mouth close to his ear, her hand in his lap. Kneading. Freeing. Stroking.

He groaned. She replaced her hand with her mouth, circling him, sucking, stroking with her tongue.

"Save it, my sweet. We're here."

The voice came as if from a great distance, echoing strangely. A man's? he wondered. Or a woman's?

The two helped him from the car. Mark didn't feel his feet touch the ground. He was levitating, he realized. Floating, like a Macy's New Year's Day balloon, being anchored by his companions' hands.

If not for them, he would float away.

He became aware of a thousand breaths being expelled, of a murmur rippling through a sea of people. They were gathered around him, he realized. Hungry.

They meant to feed on him. On his soul.

He should fight. Scream for help. Deny the unholy cravings of these walking cadavers. Instead, anticipation rippled along his nerve endings, so strong it felt as if his flesh was undulating.

Greedy hands stripped away his garments. Sarah murmured, "Drink," and brought a large vessel to his lips. He did. The liquid was warm and slightly salty.

A roar of approval rose from the gathering. Heat radiated from his lips, spreading to every nook and cranny of his being. With it came a heightened awareness, a crackling energy.

"Feed on the heat of the Flower!" someone shouted. "It opens to all possibilities. To pleasures that are its birthright."

Those assembled began to chant. "Let him see! Let him see!"

Sarah removed the blindfold. Creatures surrounded him, ones in human form. Wild animals. Exotic birds. Horrific monsters.

A scream rose in his throat. The creatures moved closer. They touched and stroked him; they whispered encouraging, loving words against his skin. Sounds of excitement slipped from their lips, of approval.

Or were those sounds slipping from his?

It was as if they were worshiping him. The physical sensations were incredible, more exciting than any sexual experience he'd ever had. Not of this world. He was infused with power. He was a god. All-knowing. All-powerful.

This was what Tara had meant, he thought. What Sarah had promised. The most perfect experience ever. If he chose the Horned Flower family, this power, this exaltation, could be his forever.

Mark felt himself levitating above the floor, floating, enraptured. He found himself upon an altar. Lips and mouths consumed him, arms enfolded, hands explored. He orgasmed, how many times he didn't know, for the spasming was all but continual.

Suddenly, light exploded in his head. Blinding. Burning like white fire. The light was followed by darkness, as black and impenetrable as hell. A darkness more frightening than anything Hollywood could fathom, more frightening than his darkest nightmare.

In it, the beast waited.

CHAPTER 27

Saturday, November 17
9:45 p.m.

Rick's Island Hideaway looked nothing as Liz had imagined. She supposed that because of the movie *Casablanca* she had expected lots of tropical plants, slowly whirling ceiling fans, women in sleek sundresses accompanied by modern-day Bogies.

Nothing could be further from reality. No plants. No sleek sundresses or Humphrey Bogart look-alikes. And instead of Sam "playing it again" at the piano, a sound system pumped out reggae music, its decibel only a notch below ear numbing.

The level needed to be heard above the raucous crowd.

She hesitated in the doorway, uncertain what to do. Obviously, her timing sucked, big-time. The crowd at the bar was six deep. Rick and another bartender, a sexy-looking twentysomething woman with a wild mane of sun-streaked hair, worked the bar—each managing to fill drink orders, run the register and socialize in what seemed to be one fluid movement.

Rick would not be happy to see her now.

Liz hung back, considering her options. According to the message Mark had left on her machine the previous evening, he expected to be initiated into the Horned Flower last night. He had been meeting his contact at ten-fifteen.

If you don't hear from me, go to Rick Wells. He'll know what to do.

She hadn't heard from him. She feared every minute could mean the difference between life and death.

If he wasn't dead already.

"Goin' in, babe?"

Liz glanced over her shoulder. She had been blocking the doorway. "Sure, sorry."

Decision made, she stepped through. A moment later, she found herself in the middle of the Saturday-night crowd, elbowing her way toward the bar. She got within shouting distance and did just that.

Rick heard his name on her first try and looked her way. A smile creased his face. "Hey, Liz Ames. What brings you in on this busy night?"

"I need to talk to you," she shouted. "It's important."

"Yeah?" He flashed her damn near the sexiest smile she had ever seen, then shifted his attention to a man sitting at the bar directly in front of him, nursing a beer. "Hey, Pete, be a gentleman. Make room for the lady."

The other man glanced over his shoulder at her. She saw immediately that he was inebriated. "You wan'to sit?"

"Thank you, but I don't mean to—"

"S'okay." He slid off the stool, landing unsteadily on his feet. "Pete g'home now."

She put a hand on his elbow to steady him. He smiled at her, then wobbled off, the crowd seeming to part for the old drunk.

Liz climbed onto the stool. "You didn't have to chase him off. I could have—"

"Don't worry about it." He cleared away Pete's glass and beer bottle, wiped the spot then replaced them with a fresh drink coaster. "Old Pete's been keeping that spot warm since just after lunch. Time to cut him off."

"Since noon?" She glanced in the direction the man had gone, amazed. "I hope he's not driving."

"Nope. Used to bicycle but landed in the ditch one too many times. Val impounded his bike."

She cocked an eyebrow at the way he said the other man's name, with real affection. "You and Lieutenant Lopez are good friends, aren't you?"

"Pretty much the best of friends. We go way back." He nodded at a couple other patrons, then returned his gaze to hers. "What can I get you?"

She really didn't want anything, but felt guilty taking up both his time and space at the bar and not ordering. "How are your frozen margaritas?"

"Killer, if I do say so myself. With salt or without?"

"With, of course."

He told her he would be right back and worked his way down the bar, taking several other orders as he did, all the while calling out humorous one-liners and greetings.

Liz dragged her gaze away, mouth going dry. She trailed her finger through a bead of moisture on the bar. Rick Wells was just one of those guys who had it all: looks, charm, personality, brains, bod. The complete, woman-eating package. No doubt he had been an athlete in high school and had had a bevy of adoring cheerleader types buzzing around him all the time.

One of those guys a smart, serious girl like her should avoid at all costs.

Her ex-husband had been one of those. But Jared had been shallow, too. A quality she hadn't noticed until too late. Liz returned her gaze to Rick and found him conversing with another patron while he shook the thick, frozen mixture into a glass.

He looked at her then, and smiled. She experienced the tickle of sexual awareness and jerked her gaze away. Don't be stupid, Liz, she told herself.

A moment later he set the drink in front of her. "One killer frozen margarita. With salt."

"Thanks," she murmured, then sipped. She had to admit, it was the best margarita she had ever tasted. She told him so.

He grinned and leaned toward her. "It's a secret recipe. My very own."

"I'm impressed."

He lifted a shoulder. "Not in the same league as curing cancer, but on a steamy Key West night, it'll do the trick."

That it would. The sweet, tangy concoction no doubt packed a deceptive wallop.

"But you didn't come here to shoot the breeze or drink margaritas, did you?"

She shook her head. "No, though I wish I had. I came because of Mark Morgan."

"Mark?" His eyebrows shot up.

"He said you were his friend. That he trusted you."

"That right? He bother to tell you he lifted six hundred bucks from my register, then left town? He trusts me, all right. To be a sap."

She shook her head, confused. "Left town? That can't be right."

"It's right, I guarantee you that. He left me a note telling me he did it."

"When did this happen?"

"The night Tara died."

The night he and Tara planned to run away together. "I've seen him since then."

His gaze sharpened. "When?"

"Last Monday."

He hesitated, as if deciding if the direction of this conversation was worth any more of his attention. He took a step away from her, signaling that he had decided it was not. "I don't really have time for this right now. The drink's on me, Liz."

"Wait!" She leaned toward him, lowering her voice. "He contacted me about Tara's murder."

He straightened and turned toward his new bartender. "Margo, can you handle the bar for a few minutes?"

She nodded and Rick indicated for Liz to follow him to his office. She did, and there he shut the door behind them. They didn't sit. "What's going on?"

"Mark's in trouble, Rick. Big trouble."

"Go on."

"He was there that night, in the garden."

"Holy shit."

"He's Tara's baby's father. He's the reason she was in the garden that night. They'd arranged to meet there. They were running away together."

"Son of a bitch." Rick crossed to his desk and sank heavily onto its edge. "The IOU he left. Of course."

"IOU?"

"The six hundred bucks. He left me a note promising to pay it back. He said it was an emergency." Rick passed a hand across his forehead. "What else did he tell you?"

Liz launched into the story, finishing with Mark's account of finding Tara dead, and running.

"No joke he's got himself in trouble," Rick muttered. "Stupid kid. Did you tell him to go to the police?"

Her silence was his answer and he narrowed his eyes. "Exactly how did you say you knew Mark?"

"He contacted me last Monday. I never heard of him before that."

"Then why call you?"

"He wanted someone to know everything in case… he disappeared."

"But why you?"

She hesitated, considering her options. She could tell him the easy part of the story and probably get away with it. But at this stage of the game it seemed not only pointless but dishonest as well.

And being dishonest with Rick Wells would be a mistake.

"Because I had counseled Tara. And because I'm Pastor Rachel Howard's sister."

She saw the moment he made the connection. "From Paradise Christian. The woman who disappeared."

It wasn't a question. She answered anyway. "Yes."

He glanced at his watch. "I have to check on Margo. It might be a few minutes."

The door shut behind him and she sank onto a chair. Only then did she realize she was shaking. She clasped her hands together and moved her gaze over the office.

No photos adorned his neat desktop, no awards, diplomas or other memorabilia hung on the walls.

No, she realized. One picture. Mostly hidden behind the in-box on his desk. She stood, crossed to the desk and picked it up. It was a picture of Rick in his full-dress police uniform and a woman in a lovely spring outfit. Liz tilted her head. Rick's graduation from police academy, she decided, judging by his crisply pressed uniform.

That the woman adored him was obvious by the way she was gazing up at him. Because of the slightly fuzzy quality of the photo and the way the sunlight fell across her face, it was difficult to make out her features. She had coloring similar to Liz's own; a slight build. She was pretty.

A lump in her throat, Liz returned the framed photo to its spot on his desk. As she did, she discovered another photo tucked into the back of the frame.

It was of a little boy with curly blond hair and Rick's smile. He looked to be about three and was smiling at the camera, pure joy radiating from him.

Who was he? she wondered. Rick's son? A favorite nephew? Was the woman his wife? That would have been her first guess, but Rick didn't wear a wedding ring.

Though these days many men didn't.

She trailed her finger lightly over the boy's image. She found something sad about the way Rick had the photographs tucked almost out of sight.

She heard Rick at the office door and quickly replaced the child's photo, then set the frame back where she had found it. She turned just as Rick stepped through the door.

"Sorry," he said. "Saturday's my busiest night."

"No, I'm sorry," she said, meaning it—just not for what he thought. By peeking at those pictures she had pried into a corner of his life he obviously preferred no one see. "My timing stinks, but I didn't... I was afraid for Mark. I think he's in danger."

Rick sat and ordered her to do the same. "Now, start at the beginning. Don't leave anything out."

Liz began. She told him why she had come to Key West, that she didn't believe the police version of her sister's disappearance. She relayed the content of the message her sister had left on her answering machine. "She said she had uncovered illegal activities on the island, something that involved the young people. She feared for her own safety. I believe those involved killed her. Nobody believed me...until Mark."

Rick leaned forward, resting his elbows on his knees and linking his fingers together. "Go on."

She repeated everything Mark had told her: that the group called itself the Horned Flower, that Tara had belonged and that they had threatened her when she tried to get out. "They describe themselves as a family and are both devoted to and possessive of other members of the family, as well as suspicious of those outside. So suspicious that Tara had to keep her relationship with Mark a secret for fear of reprisal. He said the group was into drug use and indiscriminate sex. Their shared ideology was hedonistic and atheist."

"What you're describing is a cult," he murmured. "There are thousands of loosely joined and highly organized groups in the United States that meet the criteria that defines a cult, basically a group organized around a central figure and singular philosophy. Reverend Sun Myung Moon's Unification Church, Crowleyism, the

Charles Manson family all fit the criteria though each is very different from the other."

"Whatever they are, they had great power over Tara and she was terrified of them. He believes they killed her because she tried to break away from them. He believes they killed my sister as well."

Rick looked unconvinced. She pressed on. "Mark decided the best way to expose the group was to become one of them. He left me a message saying he was being initiated last night. He told me to come to you if I didn't hear from him." She held her hands out, palms up. "So, here I am."

For a long moment, Rick was silent. When he finally spoke, his tone was low, measured. "Have you asked yourself if Mark was truthful with you?"

"No. Why wouldn't he have been?"

"Maybe he had something to do with Tara's death?"

"No way." She shook her head for added emphasis. "You didn't see him when he talked about Tara, about that night. He was in love with her."

"Do you have any idea how many victims are killed by the very people who claim to love them? A lot," he finished, answering his own question. He paused as if to allow his words time to sink in. "I was a cop, Liz. I'm thinking like a cop here. Sorting through the facts, looking at this from all angles."

"And I'm not?"

"Frankly? No, you're not. You're too close. Emotionally involved. Overwrought."

Making a sound of frustration, she stood. "I'm so tired of people telling me that. I'm not overwrought. Mark feared for his safety. He contacted me so someone would know what he was doing and sound the alarm if he disappeared. He's disappeared, we have to do something!"

Rick stood. She had to tip her head back to meet his eyes. "Okay," he murmured, tone as calm and soothing as if attempting to reason with a headstrong child. "You're fine, steady as a rock. Just hear me out. In all probability, Tara was killed by the accomplice of a man who murdered young women in Miami, or someone who is copying his crimes. There's a chance your sister fell victim to the same maniac. Or that she suffered a mental breakdown and ran off, the way the police think."

She opened her mouth to deny it was true, and he held up a hand to stop her. "Your sister's been missing what? Three months?"

"Four," she corrected. "She was last seen July twelfth."

"So, where's her body, Liz? Tara's killer made no attempt to conceal his handiwork. If you hadn't found her that night, someone else would have the next morning. Taft worked in the same manner."

He had a point; she had wondered the same thing. But she knew she was right.

"Maybe he wasn't ready to reveal himself?" she offered. "Maybe he panicked? There could be a hundred explanations for why Rachel's..."

She let the words trail off; his expression softened. "The KWPD is working in conjunction with the sheriff's department and the Florida Crime Bureau in an attempt to locate the killer. Perhaps Tara was a member of a group called the Horned Flower, but I hardly think a bunch of pampered teenagers is capable of butchering one of their friends. And trust me, Tara was butchered."

"Please help me," she whispered. "I have nowhere

else to turn. No one else to turn to. Mark said you'd know what to do."

"I'm sorry. Go home, get some sleep. In the morning—"

"In the morning Mark might be dead. Are you sure you can live with that?"

CHAPTER 28

Sunday, November 18
2:45 a.m.

"I can take it from here, Margo," Rick murmured, zipping then locking the deposit bag. "Why don't you call it a night?"

"Are you sure?" She ran a damp cloth over the seat of a chair, then set it upside down on the table. "I don't mind staying."

Rick smiled at the newest member of his staff. He had been lucky to find her. Not only was she personable, reliable and attractive, she could flat-out hustle drinks. "What, no love connection tonight?"

"Nope. I've nothing better to do than sleep. How about you?"

"When you get to be my age, sleep's a good thing."

She rolled her eyes at that. "You're what? Thirty?"

"Try thirty-six, Margo."

"Only ten years older than I am. Not that much."

Only a decade, Rick thought, amused.

"I could pour myself a glass of wine and keep you company."

He would have to be deaf and blind to miss the invitation in her question. He pretended to be both. The day after Mark disappeared, she'd walked in looking for a job. Considering Libby's reliability and Mark's sudden departure, he had all but fallen to his knees in thanksgiving. The last thing he was going to do was muck that up by getting involved with her. Besides, he believed some lines shouldn't be crossed. This was one of them.

"Help yourself to the wine, but don't stay on my account." He lifted his gaze to hers and smiled, hoping to take the sting out of his next words. "I'm alone a lot, Margo. It suits me."

Disappointment crossed her features and she quickly looked away. "That's cool." She grabbed her purse from under the register and slipped the strap over her shoulder. "Considering I've got to open tomorrow, I think I'll pass on that drink."

She crossed to the door, then stopped and glanced back at him. "So, who was that chick who stopped in to see you? Your girlfriend?"

"No such luck, Margo. Just a friend of a friend."

Where had *that* come from? he wondered as his employee left. The words had sprung so easily from his tongue, as if the meaning behind them had just been sitting there waiting impatiently to be uttered. Not in this lifetime. Even though he found Liz Ames attractive, he had no plans of becoming involved with her. Or anyone else for that matter.

With a small shake of his head, he returned his attention to closing out the bar. Or rather, he thought, a small percentage of his attention—just enough not to totally screw up the mindless jobs he had performed a million times before. The rest of his attention turned to the reason for Liz's visit tonight.

He had to go to Val. Mark had been Tara's boyfriend. Tara had been pregnant with his child. He'd been in the garden that night. The first to the scene, according to Liz. He had left that scene without reporting it and was now AWOL.

That made him a suspect. A prime suspect.

Rick frowned, thinking about the money Mark had lifted from his register and the IOU he'd left in return. Maybe Mark had needed the money to pay Tara off? Or to make her and their "problem" disappear? Maybe she had refused to abort the baby and he'd killed her? Could she have been blackmailing him? Threatening to make trouble for him?

But to whom? And blackmail him for what? Mark's wages barely kept a roof over his head. It wasn't like Mark was a married man or someone who would have a lot to lose should his predicament come out.

Typically a blackmailer used the thing a person valued most against him. Rick thought for a moment, working to pinpoint what that thing was. The Mark Morgan he knew valued his Christian faith above all. So how would Tara have been using that against him?

Rick flipped off all but the security lights, set the alarm, then stepped out into the sticky night, motorcycle helmet under his arm. He glanced up at the inky, star-studded sky. Perhaps Mark and Tara had fought. Perhaps he had discovered the baby wasn't his. He could have flown into a jealous rage and killed her.

That scenario fit the killing method. Killing with a

blade was more personal than killing with a gun. The
attacker had to actually touch his victim, physically
subdue them as they fought for their life, feel their body
spasm in death, their blood stream across their hands
or splatter against their face.

Rick swung onto the bike and started it. That took
an emotional detachment few possessed. Professional
killers. Trained military. The true psychopath. Or it
took passion. Hatred. Love. Jealousy.

Rick eased away from the curb, heading south.
Problem was, neither of those scenarios explained the
Gavin Taft connection. Mark was too young to have
been Taft's accomplice. Therefore, if Mark had killed
Tara, he would have had to have studied Taft's murders
before he did the crime. Actually, it would be an inge-
nious way to throw suspicion in another direction.

But it also placed the murder squarely in the premeditated category.

The light at Truman Avenue changed to red and Rick
slowed to a stop, the powerful engine purring beneath
him. *Premeditated murder? Mark?* That would mean
Mark had planned Tara's killing beforehand. Goodbye, crime of passion. Hello, murder in the first degree.
Which, if proven, afforded the maximum sentence the
law allowed. Which, in the state of Florida, was the
death penalty. A crime as heinous as this one had death
penalty written all over it. The prosecutor would go for
it, Rick didn't have a doubt about that.

The light turned green. Rick took a left onto Truman.
Could Mark have committed this crime? And why involve Liz Ames? Why create this whole Horned Flower
scenario?

As a backup alibi.

Rick sucked in a sharp breath. The pieces clicked

into place. Liz would be a perfect choice. Mark had no doubt learned from Tara that she was Pastor Howard's sister. At the same time, he'd learned that she didn't believe the official explanation for her sister's disappearance. And that her sister had claimed to Liz that she had uncovered some sort of evil conspiracy.

Perfect, Rick thought, checking over his left shoulder, then executing an illegal U-turn, heading back in the direction he had come. Mark would have realized that if he contacted Liz with the story, she would not only buy it, but proclaim it to any who would listen.

Mark had used Liz. He had attempted to use Rick.

Mistake, Rick thought grimly. Big mistake.

He made it to Duval Street, passed Paradise Christian and the Hideaway, drawing to a stop in front of Liz Ames's storefront. He removed his helmet, dragged a hand through his damp hair then lifted his gaze to her second-story apartment.

Despite the hour, her lights were on. He had known they would be.

He swung off the bike and glanced toward her lit windows once more. And found her standing there, gazing down at him. He lifted a hand in greeting, and pointed toward her door. She indicated she understood.

A moment later, she unlocked it. She wore a pair of running shorts and an undershirt. Her feet were bare.

"I've figured it out," he said. "I know why Mark contacted you."

Wordlessly, she motioned him inside. She bolted the door behind them, then led him upstairs.

Once in the living room, he faced her. "You might want to sit down."

She did as he suggested. He laid out his theory for

her, leaving nothing out. When he finished, she simply gazed at him, expression stricken.

"I'm sorry," he murmured.

"About what?" Her voice shook slightly. "Having an opinion?"

"Shattering your hopes. I know how desperately you want to believe this conspiracy theory. Because of your sister."

She passed a hand across her eyes. "And how did Mark learn about Gavin Taft?"

"Any number of places. Most probably the Internet."

"He was in love with her, Rick. If you had only heard him that day. It broke my heart."

"Maybe the baby wasn't his?" Rick offered. "Maybe she had broken up with him, but had agreed to meet him this last time in the garden. There, he killed her."

"It's not true, Rick." She got to her feet and lifted her gaze to his. "They were running away together that night. That's why he took the money, why he—"

"If they were running away, where was her stuff?"

"What?"

"Her stuff. She would have packed some sort of bag, one that included cosmetics, changes of clothes, mementos. I didn't see anything like that at the scene, did you?"

She sank to her seat. "But, what he said...the way he sounded, I was so certain."

Rick squatted in front of her and looked her directly in the eyes. "Were you certain because of what he said, or because you wanted to be? Because of your sister?"

Her eyes flooded with tears. "I...I don't know."

He caught her hand; it was as cold as ice and he curled his fingers around it.

"He's just a kid, Rick. How could he have done... that?"

"I don't want to believe it, either. I liked Mark. I trusted him and called him friend. But I've heard too many people exclaim after the fact how they couldn't believe some killer capable of committing whatever vicious and unconscionable act they had committed."

She released a shaky breath. "What do we do now?"

"Go to the police."

"Tonight?"

"I think we should. My guess is, after meeting with you, Mark headed out of town. He's long gone by now, but the more time that passes, the farther away he gets."

She nodded and stood. "I feel like such a fool. A gullible idiot."

"You're not the first person to be taken in by a charming psychopath. Unfortunately, you won't be the last."

Liz laughed, the sound brittle. "I was going to see the police tomorrow. I was going to bring them that." She gestured toward a large manila envelope on the coffee table, her name printed across the front. "My sister left it for me. Pastor Tim found it in the parsonage. I thought it was proof that what Mark told me was true."

"What's in it?"

"Family photographs and mementos, a page from my sister's journal." She sighed. "Take a look, if you like. I'll go change."

She left the room. Rick picked up the envelope and drew out the contents, thumbing through, stopping on the page of sketches.

The hair on the back of his neck stood up.

Tara had had a tattoo on her inner thigh. A flower. He swallowed hard, throat tight. He struggled to remember what it had looked like, but couldn't. It had been dark, his inspection cursory. The tattoo could have been of a daisy or rose, for heaven's sake.

But it hadn't been. He knew that for sure.

And there was only one person who could confirm that for him.

"What's wrong?"

He looked up. Liz stood in the doorway. She had changed into a pair of jeans and a white T-shirt. She looked scared.

"Change of plans," he murmured. "I need to make a call."

Ten minutes later, Rick thanked his old friend and hung up the phone. The medical examiner had not been happy about Rick waking him in the middle of the night. He'd made it clear it had better not happen again.

But he had told Rick what he wanted to know.

"What did he say?" Liz asked, tone almost painfully anxious. "Did Tara have a flower tattooed on her thigh?"

"Yup. Inner left. Daniel couldn't recall exactly what it looked like."

She clasped her hands together. "That's bad, isn't it?"

"Only inconvenient."

"I don't understand."

"Inconvenient because my old buddy made a sketch of it, but the only way I'm going to get a look at it is to drive to Marathon. I'll go first thing in the morning."

"And if Tara's tattoo matches the drawing from my sister's journal, what are we going to do?"

"I don't know," he answered honestly. "I guess we'll cross that bridge when we come to it."

CHAPTER 29

Sunday, November 18
1:00 p.m.

Liz paced. The night before, she had agreed that Rick would drive to Marathon and she would stay behind, just in case Mark called. She had agreed they would wait until after he had seen the medical examiner's sketch of Tara's tattoo to decide what their next step would be. They had agreed what they both needed was some sleep.

Now Liz wondered what she had been thinking. She hated this uncertainty. She hated waiting here—with nothing to do but worry—while Rick took action. She had never been one to sit back and wait for others to solve her problems.

As for sleep, that had been a joke. After Rick left, she had crawled into bed—and proceeded to stare at the ceiling for the next three hours, mind racing. She'd agonized about Mark's whereabouts, about her sister's and Tara's fate, about the factual or real existence of the Horned Flower.

When she had exhausted topics, she had focused on Rick. What was his story? He was a smart guy, that was clear. He had a passion for police work, that, too, was clear. She wondered why he had left it. The pay? Had he been hurt in the line of duty or become disillusioned by the legal system? She wondered, too, about the photographs she had seen in his office, the one of the pretty blonde and the cute little boy.

Finally, as the sun tipped over the horizon, totally disgusted with herself, she had climbed out of bed and headed to the kitchen to brew a cup of coffee. That had been a half-dozen cups ago. Her stomach burned and her head ached. She felt each of the sleepless hours of the night before. Thirty-three was too old to pull an all-nighter, she decided.

Liz stopped pacing. Anxious, she crossed to the front windows and looked out at the clear, bright day. What was happening? she wondered. Rick had promised to call the minute he had seen the ME's sketch of Tara's tattoo. She glanced at her watch and made a sound of disgust. He might not even have arrived yet. Marathon was a good two-hour drive from Key West and she was uncertain what time he'd left.

The scream of a horn dragged her back to the moment. She looked at the street. Heather was darting across, a foil-covered plate in her hands. Liz threw up her window. "Hey, you! You have a death wish or something?"

"Hey to you, too!" She held up the plate. "I come bearing gifts. Key-lime cookies."

"Be right down."

A moment later Liz swung open the door. Heather held out the plate. "I made them myself."

"You're beautiful, successful *and* you bake?" Liz said, taking the plate. "Excuse me while I turn pea green."

"I couldn't sleep, so I hit the kitchen. Baking is one of those things I resort to when I'm upset about something."

Liz drew her eyebrows together. "What's wrong?"

"Can I come in?"

"Sure. I'll make coffee."

Liz led her friend upstairs and to the kitchen. "Have a seat," she said, motioning to the table and chairs. "This will only take a minute." She quickly measured coffee into a filter and water into the carafe, then switched on the pot. That done, she turned to her friend. "What's going on?"

"Someone's been following me."

Liz's heart stopped. "What?"

Heather clasped her hands together. "Last night and...before. It's probably nothing, but after Tara, I guess I'm just...well, I'm a little spooked."

An understatement, Liz realized. She looked terrified. Coffee forgotten, Liz took the chair across from the other woman. "Tell me exactly what happened."

She nodded. "For the last few days I had this feeling that I was being followed. You know how that is? It's like you're aware that someone is there, behind you. Or you catch a movement from the corner of your eyes but when you look there's nothing suspicious."

"Yes," Liz agreed. "I know what you mean. Do you sense it's a man or a woman?"

"Man. I've no doubt." She drew in a deep breath, then continued. "Last night...I awakened suddenly. I didn't know why, because I had been deeply asleep and dreaming.

"I was confused and sat up. My window was open. About two inches."

"It wasn't open when you went to bed."

"No."

"You're certain?"

"Absolutely. The night air can give me a sinus headache, so I've learned not to sleep with the windows open."

"Did you call the police?"

She shook her head. "I was afraid... I mean, all this could just be my imagination."

"But the window—"

"What if I was mistaken? I'd look like an idiot."

"Better an idiot than—"

Liz bit back the word but it hung in the air between them.

Dead. Better than being dead.

Heather made a sound of distress. "I'm sorry," Liz murmured quickly. "I shouldn't have said that."

"No, really, I... Did Tara ever say anything about being followed?"

"No. But I only met with her twice and she never really opened up."

Silence fell between them. Liz fidgeted, uncomfortable, uncertain what to do. Should she ask the other woman about the Horned Flower? Perhaps she had heard of the group. After all, because of Bikinis & Things, she saw a lot of teenagers. She would overhear conversations. Rumors.

And if she shared her suspicions about that, should she come clean about it all, most importantly her relationship to Rachel?

The phone rang and Liz jumped to her feet, nearly toppling her chair in the process. "Excuse me a minute, Heather. I've been waiting for a call."

She crossed to the phone and picked it up, turning her back to the other woman. "Hello."

"Liz? It's Rick." By their crackling connection it was obvious he was calling from his cell phone. "The images are the same."

"My God, Rick. That means he was telling the truth."

"Not necessarily. Everything we have right now is circumstantial. Or worse, speculative."

Liz lowered her voice. "So, what do we do next?"

"Val needs to be brought up to speed. I've got to relieve Margo at the Hideaway. I'll come by your place as soon as I can get away."

"Wait! Are you sure that's a good idea? Mark said—"

"It's Mark I'm thinking of. We need to locate him fast. To do that, we need the police department's manpower."

"All right. You know your way around this kind of situation better than I do."

"Liz? You're breaking up. Look…to yourself…after we—"

His cell phone dropped the call, and she hung up, frustrated. She was pretty sure he had been asking her not to tell anyone what was going on until they had talked to Val. Which answered her question about whether she should involve Heather.

Liz glanced at her friend. Heather stared toward the window, her lovely face puckered with worry. Liz caught her bottom lip between her teeth. She didn't know why, but she felt a strong compulsion to disregard Rick's advice and tell the other woman what was going on. She felt that by not telling her she might be exposing her to danger.

Liz shook off the sensation.

Heather turned her gaze to Liz. "Everything okay?"

"Fine." She forced a smile.

The other woman's eyebrows shot up. "You seem kind of jumpy."

Liz laughed. The sound rang false even to her own ears. "Too much caffeine, that's all."

Heather saw through her lie and looked hurt. She stood. "I'd better go."

"Wait—" Liz held out a hand. "A friend's gotten himself in some trouble. I'm trying to help, that's all."

She hesitated a moment, then nodded. "Okay. If you need to talk, you know where I am."

"Thanks. I really appreciate it."

Liz accompanied her friend downstairs to the front door. There, she met the woman's gaze once more. "What about you? What are you going to do? I'm worried. I think you should go to the police."

"Forget what I said about being followed. I'm probably overreacting. I mean, why would anyone be following me?"

"Heather, don't take any chances. Please. I don't want anything to happen to you."

"I'm pretty tough." The woman grinned. "Anybody tries to mess with me, they'll regret it."

Liz watched her go, appreciating her pluck but unable to suppress a feeling of dread. No matter how tough she thought she was, Heather Ferguson would be no match for the monster who had murdered Tara.

CHAPTER 30

Sunday, November 18
3:20 p.m.

Val was waiting for Rick when he arrived back at the Hideaway. He looked pissed. "We need to talk."

"Well, hello to you, too," Rick muttered. Instead of his bike, he'd taken his battered but reliable old Jeep to Marathon. Usually reliable, he amended. The air-conditioning had gone out just outside Big Pine Key. He was hot, tired and thirsty. The last thing he wanted to do at this moment was tangle with his old friend.

"Cut the shit, Rick. I know where you were today. And I consider it a personal betrayal of our friendship."

The cat was out of the bag now. Dammit. Rick laid his cell phone and keys on the bar. "Mind if I get a cold drink first?"

"Hell yes, I mind. But you always do whatever you want anyway. Don't you, Rick?"

Margo looked from one to the other of them and ducked her head, pretending to take inventory of the drink well.

The two men exchanged a long glance. Rick swore. "Margo, we'll be in my office."

A moment later Rick closed the door behind them. They faced each other. "You crossed the line, my friend. You crossed it big-time."

"How did you find out?"

"Daniel called. He's had second thoughts about sharing that sketch with you."

Covering his ass. Smart man. Rick lifted his shoulders. "What's the big deal? No harm done."

"Bullshit. I want that sketch."

Rick stalled. "It's only a copy."

Val held a hand out. It shook slightly with the force of his rage. "The copy, please. Now."

Rick dug it out of his pocket and handed it over. Val shoved it into his pocket. No doubt he had another copy in a file at the KWPD. "Jesus, man, that's evidence you're screwing with. My investigation you're screwing with. I'd ask what the hell you were thinking, but you know what? I don't care. It's over. Do you read me? You're out of this."

He strode to the door, yanked it open and started through.

"Ever hear of a group called the Horned Flower?" Rick asked.

Val stopped but didn't turn around.

"It's a group of teenagers on Key West. They're a close-knit group, they call themselves a family. They're involved in drugs and sex for sure. And maybe murder."

Val turned. "Is this a joke?"

"Do I look like I'm joking?"

Val studied him a moment, then shook his head. "A group of teenagers here on Key West, involved in murder? Tara's murder?"

"Yes."

Val shook his head. "I don't have time for this... nonsense."

"I think you're going to want to hear what I have to say." Rick motioned to a chair. "Sit. Hear me out. If you think it's a crock of shit after you do, you won't hear from me again. Agreed?"

The other man stared at him for a long moment, then sat. "Make it fast."

"The night Tara was murdered, remember I told you one of my employees had gone home early, claiming stomach flu?"

Val nodded. "That kid who works for you—Mark."

"Mark Morgan. Worked for me. Past tense."

Val's gaze sharpened slightly. "Go on."

"I didn't close out my register until later the next day. Found an IOU for six hundred bucks."

"The kid took the money."

"Yup. It was an emergency, he said. He had to leave Key West. He promised to pay it back."

"Yeah right, in your dreams."

"I went to his place, looking for him. Car was gone, his rented room dark and silent as a tomb." Rick frowned, wondering what he would have found if he had decided to go in. "I figured the money was history and chalked it up to bad judgment on my part."

Val leaned forward slightly. "And the rest of the story?"

"A little less than a week ago Mark called Liz Ames. He arranged for them to meet that afternoon at Mallory

Square. They'd never met before but she agreed because he said he had information about Tara's death."

Val straightened. Rick could tell by his old friend's expression that he had a mouthful of questions, but to his credit he held them.

"They met. Turns out, Mark was Tara's boyfriend. They had planned to run away together the night she was killed. That's what he needed the money for."

"So he says. He knew she was pregnant?"

"Yes. But it gets worse. He was there that night, in the garden."

Val launched to his feet. "Son of a bitch! We've been chasing our tails all over this island trying to find a suspect, and you—" He bit his words back and dragged a hand through his hair. "When did you learn all this?"

"Just last night."

Angry color stained his cheeks. "You should have called me then and there. Shit, man! In an investigation like this every minute counts. You know that."

"Believe me, Val, that was what I intended to do. After I closed I went to Liz's place to collect her. I planned to insist she come with me and relay exactly what transpired between her and Mark."

"But instead you used an old friend to help you illegally obtain evidence and in the process interfere with a murder investigation. Smart, Rick. Really smart."

Rick sent his friend a level stare. "You want to hear the whole story? Or not?"

Val scowled. "What I want is to get out there and catch this killer."

"Then I guess, like it or not, you need to hear it, don't you?" The other man grunted a response and Rick continued. "Tara was a part of that group I asked you about, the Horned Flower. Mark said they had threatened Tara. If she tried to exit their 'family' they would hurt her. That's why they were running away. He went to the garden to meet her and found her there, dead. Mark told Liz that he believed they, members of the Horned Flower, had killed Tara. He also believed the Horned Flower was responsible for Rachel Howard's disappearance."

"No wonder the woman bought this whole load of shit."

"That's what I thought, too. Until I saw the drawings." Rick paused, then went on. "Liz had a journal page of her sister's. There were drawings of a strange flower, a horned flower. I remembered that Tara had a tattoo on her thigh, a tattoo of a flower. I figured if the drawings matched, it would change everything."

For a long moment, Val was silent. "And did they match?" he asked finally, softly.

"Yes, they did."

His friend digested that, then murmured, "You should have brought your suspicions to me."

"I should have." Rick shifted his gaze. "No excuses, Val. Truth is, I wanted the answer and I knew I could get it."

"And when exactly were you going to bring me on board? For the arrest?"

"Today."

"Where is he, Rick? I want Mark Morgan now."

"I don't know."

"Bullshit. Where is he?"

"Missing. Which is why Liz Ames came to me for help. Mark intended to find Tara's killer. To do that, he planned to infiltrate the Horned Flower. That was two days ago. She hasn't heard from him since."

Val laughed, the sound far from amused. "Is everybody on this island running their own private investigation?"

He began to pace. After a moment he stopped and looked at Rick. "What you're saying is, there's a secret cult operating on Key West, an island of three-by-four miles? An island where everybody knows everybody? A cult that murders its members for no obvious reason? Do they have a secret handshake? Or do they take a blood oath? Do you realize how silly this all sounds, Rick?"

"I thought the same thing, until I saw the drawings. I think there might be a connection here."

"Question, Rick. Did it ever occur to you that the reason the two images matched is because Pastor Howard had seen Tara's tattoo? Perhaps Tara even got the tattoo during the time she was being counseled by Pastor Howard. Perhaps she discussed it with the pastor. Perhaps this Horned Flower group was a figment of the girl's imagination, one she carried to obsessive lengths."

Rick thought he had considered every scenario, but he had to admit he had overlooked that one.

"Look at the facts," Val continued. "Mark had a personal relationship with the victim. He had reason to want her dead. He was at the scene. Those are the facts."

"Sometimes what looks like the truth is a lie. You know that."

"Sometimes, but it's damn rare. The guy who looks guilty is usually the one who did it. The big surprise twist at the end is Hollywood, not real life."

When Rick opened his mouth to speak, Val held up a hand stopping him. "Here are some facts you should also know. I did a little digging on your friend Liz Ames. You need to be careful who you align yourself with."

"Don't be coy, Val. Just spit it out."

"Last year was a big year for our Ms. Ames. Early in the year her mother died, a handful of months later her father. Her sister accepted this call and moved about the same time Liz walked in on her husband screwing a good friend of hers. Turns out the friend wasn't his first cheat. Her marriage fell apart. A teenager in her care attempted—and nearly succeeded—in committing suicide. Then her sister disappeared.

"Liz made her decision to come here, fresh on the heels of a total emotional and mental breakdown. A breakdown that required her to be hospitalized. Her therapist begged her not to come here, he feared she would relapse."

"A little digging?" Rick asked, voice tight. "You called the St. Louis P.D. and had them check her out. On what grounds?"

"She was first to the scene. She knew the victim. What would you have done, Rick?"

The same thing, he acknowledged. Like it or not, Val had been doing his job.

"She has issues, my friend. Serious emotional issues. I thought you'd want to know."

Rick struggled to digest what Val had told him, to place and make sense of it. Val's words explained Liz's tears, the desperation he had heard in her voice time and again. Her aura of vulnerability.

His first reaction was a sense of betrayal, of having been lied to. She hadn't been honest with him.

"What you're saying is she's a nutcase and I shouldn't believe a thing she says. Is that it?"

"Hardly. I'm checking out her claims. But I wanted to warn you. Be careful, Rick. She has an agenda, one based on emotions not logic. Desperate people do desperate things. They lie. They manufacture evidence.

Use whatever means necessary to achieve their goals. And they can be pretty goddamned convincing. That she's not playing with a full deck right now makes her a little scary."

Rick had to agree. He felt as if his old friend had delivered a swift punch to his solar plexus, momentarily knocking the wind out of him. He wanted to champion her. He wanted to deny that what Val was telling him was true.

Despite his earlier intentions, he had lost all objectivity when it came to Liz Ames and this investigation.

Val's cell phone sounded. "Lopez here."

He listened a moment, expression tightening. "Say that again, Carla." He waited. "I'll be right there."

He holstered his phone and stood. "What is it?" Rick asked. "What's happened?"

"Seems Naomi Pearson didn't run off," he replied grimly. "She turned up on Dog Beach."

"Dead, I'm guessing?"

Val hesitated, then nodded. "About as dead as you can get. Throat slit, torso carved up." He met Rick's gaze. "Looks like we've got a serial on our hands."

CHAPTER 31

Sunday, November 18
6:10 p.m.

A favorite with locals because of its "pets allowed" policy, Dog Beach was a sandy stretch between Waddell Avenue and the Atlantic Ocean, tucked up next to Louie's Backyard restaurant. Naomi Pearson had been discovered by a golden retriever chasing a Frisbee. The dog's owner had used his cell phone to call the police— after upchucking in a toy pail left behind by some kid.

Carla stood several feet from the deceased, a handkerchief doused in cologne pressed to her nose. The stench was, quite simply, unbearable.

Carla had known it would be and had come prepared. She'd been part of the team that had investigated a drowning last year. She'd gained firsthand experience that bodies decayed differently when submerged, reacting with the water to create a waxy, yellowish and rancid-smelling substance called adipocere. Over time, adipocere replaced the muscles, viscera and fatty tissues of the body, giving the corpse a bloated, nightmare appearance. The warmer the water, the faster the decomposition.

As corpses went, Naomi Pearson's was pretty damn grotesque. Bloated beyond recognition, head half-severed, gaping wounds on her torso, the corpse looked at once human and creature brought up from the bowels of hell.

Carla glanced to the right, toward Louie's dining veranda. No way Naomi had been here long. Even a light breeze in that direction would have shut the place down. So, where had she been all this time? Dragged back and forth by the currents? Hung up on something under the water?

From behind her came the sound of a car door slamming. She looked over her shoulder and saw that Val had arrived, thank God. Being alone with this vic was making her itch. She felt as though she should be doing something, but she didn't know what. She was out of her depth here. Way out of her depth.

Carla signaled to Val, then waited as he crossed to where she stood. As he neared her, he brought a handkerchief to his nose. He, too, had come prepared.

"Who found her?" he asked when he came within earshot.

"Somebody's golden retriever. Owner's pretty shook up. Questioned him, then sent him on his way. Got his name and address, of course."

"Scene's secure?"

"As well as a place like this can be. Got it cordoned off. I put Reese on the north side and McKinney on the east." She noticed a group forming on Louie's dining veranda. "Wind must have shifted."

Val glanced toward the restaurant, then turned his attention fully to the victim. For long moments Val simply studied her, then he moved closer, circling slowly, expression intent.

Finally, he lifted his gaze to her. Carla saw that his eyes were watering. "You know for sure this is Naomi Pearson?"

She nodded. "Her handbag washed up with her."

"Touch anything else?"

"Are you kidding? No way."

"She disappeared how long ago?"

"Last seen Thursday, November 1st. Seventeen days ago."

Val frowned. "It doesn't look like her killer tried to weight her with anything to keep her submerged. My guess is he tossed her and her belongings into the ocean. She must have gotten caught on something that kept her under. Her handbag, too. Tides changed, dislodged her and up she popped."

"You think the same guy who killed Tara killed her?"

"Seems obvious to me. Doesn't it to you?"

Carla always concurred with Val. Without Rick as her partner, she thought of Val as both her superior officer and her mentor. She opened her mouth to agree, but said instead, "Tara was left where she was killed, Naomi was moved. Why'd he change his ritual?"

Val looked at her, obviously surprised. "Ritual, Chapman? Have you been doing a little reading at night?"

Her cheeks heated. She had been. She didn't know why, but she had suddenly felt as though it was important for her to take a proactive approach to her career.

Maybe she was tired of feeling like the KWPD bimbo. "Yeah, a little."

"Good job." He turned his gaze back to the victim. "As for your question, I don't know the answer. Responding to his environment. Circumstances. But what I do know is, two killings on this island is two too many."

From behind them came the sound of others arriving: the evidence-collection team, a couple of guys from the sheriff's department and a medical technician.

Val met her eyes. "I need you to do something for me. Check out a kid named Mark Morgan. Run a priors on him. He rents a room over on Packer. Apparently he's disappeared, but you can talk to his landlord. If you can get a legal look around, do it."

She glanced at the approaching officers, then back at him. "What's this about?"

"If we're lucky, a murder suspect." He looked at the remains of Naomi Pearson. "We sure as hell need one."

Carla did as Val requested. Mark Morgan had no priors. No known aliases. He was twenty years old and grew up in Texas. His landlady, a Key Wester who claimed to have met Ernest Hemingway on one of his visits to Sloppy Joe's bar during the forties, had nothing but good things to say about the young man.

"Sweet as pie, that one," the woman said, leading Carla down the hall to Mark Morgan's room. She stopped in front of a door and looked at Carla, squinting against the curl of smoke rising from the cigarette dangling from her bright coral lips. "Anytime I needed something, he was happy to help. Always 'yes ma'am' and 'no ma'am' from him. I was sorry to lose him."

"He moved out for good?"

"Don't know for sure. He didn't pay his rent this

week, and I haven't seen him." Her hands, knotted with arthritis, shook as she found her master key. "That's the way it is with these kids. They rent by the week then move on. He was here longer than most."

Carla didn't hide her disappointment. "The room's been cleaned then?"

"Not yet. My girl who cleans for me, she's been under the weather." She smiled; the cigarette wobbled, its inch-long ash dropped to the floor. "Besides, I kinda hoped he'd come back."

"You ever see him with other kids? A girlfriend?"

"A girl sometimes. Dark hair. Pretty."

Tara had dark hair. "You think you could identify her from a picture?"

"Maybe." She drew her eyebrows together as if a thought was suddenly occurring to her. "Is Mark in some sort of trouble?"

"Not necessarily, ma'am. Just following up on a couple leads."

The landlady unlocked the door. Carla stepped inside. The unit consisted of a bedroom and kitchenette and smelled slightly stale, as if it had been closed up a while. She scanned the interior. The bed was neatly made. A Bible lay on the nightstand. She crossed to it and picked it up. The leather was soft and worn from use, the pages well thumbed. It was bookmarked in the Book of Revelation.

She returned it to the nightstand then crossed to the three-drawer chest. She opened the top drawer, found it empty, and opened the next two. They, too, were empty. She found the tiny closet the same way.

She turned to the landlady, hovering in the doorway, watching her. "What's through there?" She pointed at the partially closed door across from the kitchenette. "Bathroom?"

"Uh-huh."

Carla crossed to it and pushed the door open. Several pieces of dirty clothes littered the floor. It looked as if the kid had stripped, stepped into the shower and left the garments where they lay. A towel had been used and thrown over the shower ring.

Carla pushed aside the curtain and peeked at the tub. The faucet dripped. A half-empty bottle of shampoo sat on the window ledge behind the shower. A scrap of soap sat in the dish. A whisper of warm, humid air slipped through the cracked window casing.

She replaced the curtain, frowning. *Mark Morgan had left without even taking the time to pack all his things.*

She shifted her gaze to the clothes on the floor. They were heavily soiled, she saw. Bending, she carefully plucked a T-shirt from the pile. The light-blue fabric was marked with big, dark stains.

Blood, she realized, dropping the garment and straightening. Excitement bubbled up inside her. This nice "yes, ma'am, no, ma'am" kid had bloodstains all over his clothes.

"You find something?" the landlady asked from the doorway behind her.

Carla swung to face her, blocking the pile of clothing. "Would you excuse me a moment? I need to make a call."

The woman backed away to allow Carla room to pass. She closed the bathroom door behind her and dialed Val's cell. "Make one wish," she murmured when the man answered. "And I bet I can make it come true."

"Mark Morgan?"

"Bingo, boss. I think we've got our prime suspect."

CHAPTER 32

Sunday, November 18
6:45 p.m.

Liz took one look at Rick and knew that something was wrong. "What's happened."

"Can I come in?" he asked.

She swung the door wider. He stepped through, turned and faced her. "There's another victim. A woman named Naomi Pearson."

"Naomi Pears—" Then she remembered. The woman from the bank, the one linked to the man who had killed himself. The one who had been involved with fraud. She had read about it in the *Key West Citizen*. Liz brought a hand to her mouth. "How—"

"I don't know any details except that it appeared she was killed in the same fashion as Tara."

Liz felt ill. Wordlessly, she turned and crossed to the stairs. She sat heavily.

After a moment, she lifted her gaze to his. "Where did they find her?"

He paused. "A beach."

"That means the killer dumped her body into the ocean." Liz balled her hands into fists, fighting the helplessness threatening to swamp her. "I thought this guy didn't conceal his handiwork?"

Her crossed to her. "This doesn't prove Rachel's dead. It doesn't prove she fell victim to this madma—"

"Don't patronize me, Rick. Until now, the police believed Naomi Pearson had run off. Just the way they believed my sister had run off."

"Not quite. They had a good reason to believe she'd split."

"And in their estimation, they have a good reason to believe Rachel did the same."

"I don't know what to say."

"Don't say…anything. I—" She doubled over, her hands to her face. She had known all along that her sister was dead. But to have died like…that…it was too horrible.

"Have you heard from Mark?"

She shook her head but didn't look at him.

"Val was waiting for me at the Hideaway. I told him everything."

Still, she didn't speak. She couldn't find her voice. She couldn't bear to look at him. If she did, she would burst into tears.

"Liz, I have to ask you something."

His tone brought her gaze to his. Her vision swam. "What?"

"Val told me… He told me you'd recently suffered a nervous breakdown. Is that true?"

It took a moment for his question, why he had asked

it, to register. When it did, a cry slipped past her lips. She had known this would get out. That it would color everyone's opinion of her.

She wished she could have kept it from Rick. She hated the way he was looking at her, with suspicion and disappointment.

She tipped her chin up. "Yes, it's true."

"Why didn't you tell me?"

"Why should I have? We don't even know each other."

"That's bullshit and you know it."

"Do I?" She balled her hands into fists. "What would you have had me tell you? That I was hanging on by an emotional thread? That I took one too many blows this year and completely lost it? That you shouldn't have a thing to do with me because I'm a brick short of an emotional load? Is that what I should have told you?"

"It would have been honest."

She laughed, the sound brittle to her own ears. "If I had, you would have thought I *was* a brick short of a load. I can just imagine. Hi," she mocked, "I'm Liz Ames, I had a nervous breakdown this year. Want to hear about it?"

He didn't reply and she stood, facing him dead on. "What are you trying to say, Rick Wells? That nothing I have said or will say is credible? Is that it?"

He didn't answer. His silence hurt.

She tipped her chin up a fraction more. "If you want to walk out that door now, go on. No harm done."

"No. It's just that— Damn." He looked at the ceiling. "I wanted to believe you. I want to believe *in* you."

"You still can."

He returned his gaze to hers, expression naked with pain. A lump formed in her throat and she struggled to breathe past it. "Why, Rick? Why did you want to believe in me?"

He didn't answer and she waited, chest tight. Aching for him.

He turned away and crossed to the door. He rested his hand on the wooden frame. "I know what it's like to lose...everything," he said finally, not looking at her. "I know what that feels like. I know what it can do to you."

His voice thickened. "Three years ago I had everything," he murmured. "A wife and son, both of whom I adored. A career I loved."

The woman and boy from the photographs, Liz realized.

"I lost her first," he continued. "Ovarian cancer. Then Sam...he—"

Rick choked on the words. Liz remained silent, giving him time to collect himself, his thoughts. He needed her to listen.

"After Jill died, we moved back here. Val gave me a job on his team at the KWPD. It was hard but we—" Rick looked over his shoulder at her. She saw that his eyes were red. "We had to go on, right? Me and Sam. We were going to be okay. We had each other."

Liz hugged herself, knowing what was coming next. Not the details, of course, but the essence. She wished with all her heart that she could change his next words, though such wishes were futile.

"We hadn't been here that long. One night two coked-up thugs broke in. They had guns... I slept with my service weapon under my pillow. Shots broke out.

"Sam was five. He woke up. He was frightened. I heard him call out for...her. Even though she had been gone a while, when he was really scared, he cried out for her. Sometimes at night…I still wake up and hear him. He—"

His voice broke. Liz went to him. She took him in her arms and held him. He bent his head to hers. He trembled.

Seconds ticked past. His trembling ceased. He met her gaze.

"I shot him, Liz. My bullet. Ballistics proved it was my bullet that killed him."

Liz squeezed her eyes shut, aching for him. How did one rebound from that? How did one pick up the pieces and move on?

"It should have been me. I wish it had been."

She brought a hand to his mouth. "Don't say that."

"But it's true." His eyes filled with tears. "I loved him so much."

Liz cupped his face in her palms and brought his mouth to hers. She kissed him softly at first, offering the only real comfort she could. "I'm sorry," she whispered against his mouth. "So very sorry."

She moved her mouth to his cheeks, his eyelids, his chin and neck. With a soft moan, he slipped his arms around her, drawing her closer, fitting himself to her.

Their mouths met again, this time deeply. His tongue found hers. She felt his growing response to her touch. A thread of fear wound its way through her. She hadn't intended for this to happen. It wasn't smart. Or cautious. She didn't know if she was ready.

She hadn't been with anyone since Jared.

And he had betrayed her.

Liz shut her mind to the fear. Smart or not, she wanted to be with this man.

Liz broke the kiss and met his eyes. "Come with me."

She caught his right hand and led him upstairs to her

bedroom. There, wordlessly, they undressed one another and sank to the bed. Their mouths met first and for long moments they kissed, not touching in any other way.

Soon, the pressure of their mouths alone wasn't enough and Liz became bolder. She ran her hands over his shoulders, then chest. She liked his body, the feel of it under her palms—the swell of muscles, the texture of his skin, the subtle angles.

Liz skimmed her hands over his hips and abdomen, then lower. He sucked in a swift breath as she found and held him.

She would have liked to show restraint. To have held back and let him lead. But that wasn't the way she felt. She wasn't a game player, never had been. She saw a flaw, she pointed it out. She saw inequality, she worked to fix it. She wanted something, she went after it. Those weren't ladylike qualities. They didn't make her mysterious. During their divorce, her ex-husband had thrown those up at her as a reason he had strayed.

But she couldn't change who she was.

So it was she who straddled him. She who drew him inside her. And she who increased the pace to a heated frenzy.

But it was Rick who, as their passion peaked, took charge. Rick who, with a final, deep thrust, claimed her for his.

For long moments, they lay quietly, unmoving as their hearts and breath slowed, as their flesh cooled. As the seconds ticked past, their silence became heavy, awkward.

He broke it first. "I don't know quite what to say."

She swallowed hard, understanding, feeling the same. How could she explain that he had comforted her as much as she had him? That his passion had revived her. That his sounds of pleasure had restored her confidence in her ability to please a lover. She felt alive again. Desirable. Totally female.

She'd thought Jared had killed her ability to feel those things.

Her lips curved up, feeling as if a huge weight had been lifted from her. "I'm not sorry, you know. I refuse to be."

"Did I say I was?" Chuckling, he rolled onto his side, bringing her with him. "What kind of man do you think I am? Mind-blowing sex never goes in that category. It doesn't work that way."

They fell silent again, though this time without the awkwardness of earlier. After a time, Liz met his eyes. "What did Lopez say when you told him about the Horned Flower?"

Rick didn't answer immediately, and she knew. "Your friend thinks Mark did it. Right?"

"He thinks there's more than probable cause there, yes."

"Of course, he's the same one who thought Naomi Pearson ran off," she said softly, but with an edge of bitterness.

"I owe Val my life, Liz. After Sam's death I wanted to give up. Without Val, I would have." He looked away, then back. "He's my oldest friend. And he's a good cop."

"A good cop? Really? You could have fooled me. He hasn't called one right yet." He remained silent and she pressed on. "What about the Horned Flower, Rick? What about my sister's drawing and Tara's tattoo?"

"What about them?" he retorted, voice tight. "As Val pointed out, Tara could have shown your sister the tattoo and then your sister sketched it in her notes. Tara could have gotten the tattoo during the time she was in your sister's care and—"

"But none of that explains what the symbol represents... I think it represents this group Mark told us about. I think my sister was scared of them. I think the Horned Flower is the group she mentioned in her phone message."

"That's all well and good, Liz. But what proof do you have?" He didn't give her a chance to reply. "It may represent some underground group here on the island. But there's a second victim now, Liz. And I have a hard time believing this group of teenagers is responsible for killing not only Tara, but Naomi Pearson, too."

Eyes burning, she rolled onto her back and stared at the ceiling. She didn't know what or who to believe. Rick made a lot of sense. She had worked out the scenario of why the Horned Flower had killed Tara, but why Naomi Pearson? It *didn't* make sense.

But she believed in Mark. She believed in her sister. Rachel had uncovered a conspiracy. She had been afraid for her life.

"What if you're wrong, Liz?" Rick asked. "What if there's no Horned Flower and no conspiracy? What if Mark is guilty?"

She squeezed her eyes shut a moment, then turned her face to his. "But what if I'm not?"

CHAPTER 33

Sunday, November 18
8:00 p.m.

Rick entered the Hideaway, his thoughts filled with Liz and what had occurred between them. The sex had been incredible. They fit together in a way new lovers rarely did—there had been no awkward moments or ill-timed moves. No sense of having to try to please the other; pleasing had come naturally.

A swell of denial rose up in him. Rick swallowed hard against it. And against the guilt that followed.

Jill was dead. What had occurred between him and Liz hadn't been cheating.

Then why did it feel as if it had been?

Visual memories of Jill and Sam, their lives together, filled his head, one after another. The day Sam was born. His first birthday party. The adoring way he'd looked up at Rick when he tucked him into bed each night. Jill, the day they were married, looking like an angel in white lace; the first time they made love. Her laughing at his and Sam's nightly horseplay.

Beautiful memories. So sweet they hurt.

But not unbearably. Not anymore.

"About time, Rick," Margo called from behind the bar. "We were about to send out a search posse."

"That's right," Libby chimed in, grinning. "I just hope you were having a good time."

He supposed mind-blowing sex could be categorized as that.

Damn, he felt like a teenager caught in the act.

He reached the bar and forced what he hoped was a casual grin. "You girls were able to handle this crowd without me?" He shifted his gaze to the nearly empty barroom. "Wow, I'm impressed."

"Smart-ass." Margo emptied her tip jar, quickly counted the bills, then dumped the coins into her change purse. "And now you can handle it without me."

He touched her arm. "I appreciate you staying so long today, Margo. I owe you one."

"I like that." She tossed her long blond hair over her shoulder, smile sassy. "I'll make sure I collect when you least expect it."

"Anything I should know?" he asked as she hooked her purse strap over her shoulder.

"Val called. He asked when you were coming in. I told him I wasn't certain, but tonight for sure."

Rick frowned. "What time was that?"

"Half an hour or so ago."

"He say what he wanted?"

"Nope, but he asked me about that kid who used to work for you."

"Mark?" Libby asked from the other end of the bar

where she was chatting with a Hideaway regular. "What does he want with Mark?"

Margo shrugged her shoulders. "He wanted to know if I'd seen him. How could I? I don't even know what he looks like."

"How about you, Libby?" Val called from behind them. "You know what he looks like. Have you seen him?"

Rick turned. His friend stood a couple feet behind them, Carla at his side.

Val closed the distance between them. "So, Libby? Have you seen Mark?"

She shook her head. "Not since…since we last worked together. Why?"

Val ignored her question and Rick narrowed his eyes. *Standard interrogating procedure. The two weren't here to pay a social call.*

"And when was that?" Carla asked.

"I don't remember exactly." Libby looked at Rick, alarmed. "Do you?"

"Not offhand. I could check, if it's important."

"Maybe later." Val turned to Margo. "Before you go, take a look at this." He handed her what appeared to be a printout of Mark's driver's-license photo. "Have you seen this man?"

Margo studied the photo a moment, her expression altering subtly. She shook her head and handed it back. "Nope. That's the kid you're looking for?"

Was she lying? Rick drew his eyebrows together. *If so, why?*

"Sure is. Keep that," he murmured as she made a move to hand the printout back. "Call me if you see him."

She agreed, wished them all a good evening and

headed out. Rick watched her a moment, puzzled, then turned back to Val and Carla. He motioned to the bar stools. "Take a load off. I'll fix you both a drink."

"No thanks. We're here on official business."

"May I ask what kind?"

"We're trying to locate Mark Morgan. Is he here?"

Rick bristled. "You know he's not."

"Really? And how would I know that, Rick?"

Their gazes met and held, Val's challenging. Rick didn't back down. "He's not here."

"Have you seen him recently?"

"No."

"How about Ms. Ames? Has she seen him recently?"

"How would I know?"

"Don't play dumb," Carla jumped in, voice tight. "We know you were there tonight."

Rick froze. From the corner of his eye he saw Libby glance his way. He looked from Val to Carla then back. "Am I being tailed?"

Again Val ignored his question. He glanced down the bar toward Libby and the regular, and back at Rick. "We've issued a warrant for Mark Morgan's arrest."

Rick stared at his friend, stunned. "You must be joking. Two hours ago—"

"Two hours ago we didn't know what we do know."

"And what is that?"

"As you very well know, I can't tell you that."

They had found hard evidence, obviously. Whatever it was, it was solid enough to base an arrest warrant on.

Val motioned to a secluded table at the far corner of the bar. "You have a minute to talk?"

Rick nodded and looked at his employee, who

seemed oblivious to their conversation. "Libby," he called. "Bar's yours."

The three crossed to the table and sat down. Val began without preamble. "How do serial killers choose their victims?"

"Most often by opportunity. A coed is hitchhiking at the worst possible moment. A young gay man meets the wrong gaze across a crowded bar. A child is unattended in the wrong place at the wrong time. The very randomness of the perpetrator to victim is what makes serial murders so difficult to solve."

"But not all serial killers operate that way. Gavin Taft didn't."

Rick searched his memory. "Taft chose carefully, it was part of the thrill. He hunted for the perfect kill. He established a relationship with the victim first, even if only a superficial one."

"We found evidence at Mark's rented room that strongly links him to Tara's murder. We've also learned he had a relationship with Naomi Pearson."

"What kind of relationship?"

"They went to the same church. They were in a Bible-study group together. They were friendly."

"This is Key West. Lot's of people are."

"True, but he was friendly with two women who are now dead." Val paused, pursing his lips, as if weighing his options. "I did a little checking into Mark's past. He was known to have an explosive temper. To be extremely jealous. He put another teenager in the hospital for looking crosswise at his girlfriend."

"Mark did that?" Rick leaned back in his chair, stunned.

"He's been traveling for two years. I'm checking the places we know he's been, looking for similar crimes."

"The religious aspects of the crime fit as well," Carla offered. "I found a Bible in his room. He had a number of passages marked, real fire-and-brimstone, vengeance-is-mine Old Testament stuff. According to people who knew him, he was a major Bible-thumper."

Rick sat back in his seat. He moved his gaze between the two, smelling a rat. "Why are you telling me this? I seem to recall being told to butt out. Rather recently, as a matter of fact."

"We have reason to suspect that Liz Ames might be his next target."

"Liz? You're stretching, buddy."

"Am I?" Val leaned toward him. "Look at the way he contacted her. Out of the blue. With some crazy story about a cult and his being in danger. Did that ever ring true to you?"

Val didn't wait for an answer. "Why did Mark contact Liz? To establish a relationship with her. To engage her in the hunt."

For the space of a heartbeat, Rick couldn't breathe let alone speak. When he found his voice, he asked, "What do you want from me?"

"She'll tell you if he contacts her again. We need you to let us know when that happens."

As Val very well knew, no way would she call the KWPD. She considered them the enemy.

After their earlier conversation, and despite the great sex, he wasn't so sure she'd even call him.

"Think about it, Rick" Val murmured, pushing away from the table and standing. "Liz Ames's life could depend on it."

CHAPTER 34

Sunday, November 18
Midnight

Liz awakened suddenly. She looked around her bedroom, disoriented, heart pounding. She hadn't meant to fall asleep, in fact she still wore the shorts and T-shirt she had thrown on after Rick left. She had hoped Rick would call. Or Mark.

They had both been so strongly on her mind, she hadn't believed she would be able to sleep.

Liz shifted to get a look at her bedside clock, and the book on her lap slipped to the floor, landing with a thud. She made a move to retrieve it, then froze.

A sound came from the other room, a scuffling noise. The kind a cat or dog might make if trapped in a closet.

Problem was, she didn't own a pet.

Swallowing past the lump that formed in her throat,

Liz slipped quietly out of bed. The noise came again, this time louder.

Liz shook her head. She was imagining things, for heaven's sake. Letting her imagination run away with her. Still, she crept forward, her every sense on the alert.

She reached her bedroom doorway and peered through. She had left a single light on in the living room and another in the kitchen, the one over the sink. Both sent a soft pool of reassuring light spilling into the hallway.

Nothing looked out of order. She hesitated, listening. She heard a moped pass on the street below, caught the sound of distant laughter and a car door slam.

A relieved laugh escaped her. Of course, she had left several of her front windows open. The night had been mild, the humidity low. She had decided to circulate some fresh air. The sound that had awakened her had come from outside.

She headed in that direction to close the windows, then stopped as a distinct but muffled thump came from the kitchen, to her immediate right. She took a step into the room, flipping on the overhead as she did. Bright light illuminated every inch of the small area.

The scuffling sound came again. The cabinet beneath the sink, she realized. She crossed to it and ever so carefully eased the door open. Light flooded the small space. Beady black eyes blinked up at her from the garbage pail. Beady eyes belonging to a creature eight inches long with a hairless, pink tail.

A rat! Liz slammed the cabinet door closed and sprang backward. How had the thing gotten in? And how did she get rid of it? No way could she sleep knowing it was in there.

Rat poison, she thought. Or a trap. Surely she could

find a grocery or drugstore still open. Liz swung around and a scream flew to her throat.

Stephen stood in the kitchen doorway, staring at her, his mutilated face screwed into a frightening grimace. His mouth moved though no sound emerged.

She glanced quickly to her right, then left, assessing her options. The drawers behind her. She kept her knives in one of them. If she could get one, she might have a chance at defending herself.

"How did you get in here?" she demanded, backing up. "Get away from me."

He advanced. His mouth moved and garbled, words spilled forth. He raised his hands as if in an attempt to grab her.

"Get away from me." She took another step backward, reaching the counter. She reached behind her, eased open the drawer and fumbled for one of the knives.

Her fingers closed around a wooden handle. In a quick move, she drew out the knife, sprang away from the drawer and brandished her makeshift weapon at him. "Get away from me!" she shouted. "I'll cut you, I promise I will!"

He froze, his expression a mask of horror. She took another step toward him. "I mean it! I'll hurt you!"

With a cry, he inched backward. He reached the wall, but instead of stepping right to escape through the doorway, he sank to the floor. Bringing his arms up to shield his face, he cowered against the wall.

Liz stared at him, grip on the knife faltering. He whimpered, the defenseless sound childlike. Lump in her throat, she recalled what Heather had told her about the caretaker. That he had been the victim of severe child abuse. That the attack that had destroyed his face and taken his eye had also damaged his brain.

This man posed no danger to her.

Mortified at having frightened him, she laid the weapon on the counter. "It's all right," she said softly. "I'm not going to hurt you. See? I put the knife away."

He didn't lower his arms. She saw that he trembled. Her heart broke for him. She could hardly fathom the horrific abuse this man must have suffered.

She held her hands out, palms up. "I won't hurt you, Stephen. I was afraid. I'm sorry I frightened you."

He lowered his arms a fraction, peeking at her over the top of them.

She took a cautious step toward him. "You understand being frightened, don't you, Stephen?"

He did understand; she could tell by his expression, by the way he averted his gaze.

"Look at me, Stephen," she said softly, taking another step closer. He did, though tentatively. "It's all right. I'm not angry. And I won't hurt you. I promise."

She smiled to prove it. "Would you like a glass of milk and a cookie?"

He nodded. She held out a hand. "Come, sit down."

He took her hand and she helped him to his feet. She led him to the table and he sat, head down.

She poured the milk, went to the pantry and took out a package of Oreos—one of her personal weaknesses. She put three on a plate, then carried the snack to him.

"Here you go." She set them in front of him, and took the chair across from his.

He met her eyes, a ghost of a smile touching his mouth, before his gaze transfixed on the cookies. She watched as he devoured them, then reached for his milk, gulping it down.

"Would you like more?" she asked.

He nodded. This time she brought the entire package to the table, along with a glass of milk for herself. "This is how I do it," she said, and dunked one of the Oreos in the milk.

He watched her intently, then mimicked her. While he ate a half-dozen more of the chocolate-sandwich cookies, she studied him. Because of his misshapen features, she had thought this man to be a brute. Because of his inability to communicate, she'd thought he meant her harm.

Nothing could be further from the truth. Stephen was a gentle giant. An innocent trapped inside a monster's face and body.

He wanted something from her, she realized. That's why he had tried to grab her that day at the church. Why he had appeared at the parsonage window when she had been inside snooping. It was why he was here now.

But what?

"How did you get in here, Stephen?"

He turned and pointed toward the living room.

"The windows?" she asked. He shook his head yes. The side window, she acknowledged, thinking of the huge, old banyan tree on that side of the building, with its long, sturdy branches. It would have been relatively easy for him to climb the tree, traverse a branch and push through the window.

"Why are you here?"

He opened his mouth, then shut it, a look of frustration crossing his face. He stood and pointed toward the door.

Liz got to her feet. "I don't understand."

He started toward it, motioning for her to follow him.

She did until they reached the door that led to the downstairs foyer. There, she stopped. He wanted her to follow him outside.

Liz held back. "I can't go with you."

He pointed toward the door again. She shook her head. "I can't. Please try to understand, it wouldn't be smart of me to do that. Look—" She pointed at her bare feet. "I'm not wearing shoes. And there's this rat in my..." She let her words trail off.

As she had to him only minutes ago, he held out a hand to her. His eyes seemed to beg for her to trust him. They told her he wouldn't hurt her.

She hoped to God she wasn't wrong. Signaling that he should wait, she retrieved a pair of shoes, tied the kitchen cabinet shut with a belt to contain the rodent, then returned to Stephen. Taking a deep breath, she let him lead her out into the night.

CHAPTER 35

Monday, November 19
1:00 a.m.

Stephen led Liz to Paradise Christian. He took her the back way, avoiding Duval Street by cutting through the alley, staying mostly hidden behind overgrown shrubs and mature trees.

Liz's breath came in quick, shallow gasps. She was scared. No, she corrected silently. She had passed scared a half-dozen steps ago. Terrified would be a better description of her emotional state. What had she been thinking? Why should she trust this man? She knew nothing about him other than what Pastor Tim and Heather had told her.

Rachel had been afraid of him.

He could be a killer.

They reached the church's walled garden. He held a finger to his lips, warning her to be quiet, then eased open the heavy gate. They stepped through. Liz shuddered—the last time she stood in this spot had been the night Tara died.

She moved her gaze over the beautiful, silent garden, vividly reminded of that night. Of finding Tara. Her beautiful face drawn into a death grimace. Blood staining the ground around her. The sound of her own screams.

Stephen caught her hand and Liz jumped, startled back to the moment. She saw that he had relocked the gate. To keep others out? she wondered. Or to keep her from escaping?

He pointed to the opposite side of the garden. The shadow of the parsonage fell across the grounds. She saw that a single light burned in the dwelling and she wondered if Pastor Tim was up. She wondered if he would hear her if she screamed.

As if reading her mind, Stephen once again brought a finger to his lips. Keeping to the perimeter, they made their way around the garden and past the parsonage.

Then she saw it: a small building adjunct to the parsonage, not much bigger than an equipment shed.

Stephen's quarters, she realized, a chill washing over her. Why had he brought her here? Her mind ran rampant with possibilities—none of them reassuring.

They had to leave the shadows to enter the building. Stephen glanced furtively around, and motioned her forward.

"No," she whispered, hanging back.

He shook his head in the affirmative. When she still held back, he pulled on her arm.

Liz hesitated a moment more, then took a deep breath and followed Stephen into his quarters.

Basic would be the best way to describe the interior.

It consisted of one room and a kitchenette. The battered furniture was a mishmash of styles, and Liz suspected all had been charitable donations. No pictures hung on the walls, no knickknacks or personal treasures adorned the shelves.

An obviously well-loved teddy bear sat on the neatly made bed, his one button eye seeming to stare at her. In a sad way, the toy reminded her of Stephen—battered but sweet. Sympathy for this man-child welled inside her. She ached for the life he had, but more, for the one he lost.

He led her to the very back of the dwelling to a door to what she assumed was a closet. Not a closet, she realized as Stephen opened it. A small room, big enough for a single cot.

Mark sat huddled on it, knees drawn up to his chest. He lifted his face as the door opened. He looked as if he had aged five years since she had seen him last.

"Mark!" she cried. "Thank God!"

"Liz!" He scrambled off the cot and they hugged.

"I was so frightened," she said, alarmed at the way he trembled. "I was sure you were dead."

He shuddered, tears welling in his eyes. "I thought I was." He shifted his gaze to the other man, hovering in the doorway behind her. "Stephen found me."

"Stephen?" she repeated. She glanced over her shoulder only to find that the other man was gone.

"He's standing guard," Mark murmured. "I owe him my life."

She frowned. "Where did he find you?"

"Here. In the walled garden." He lowered his voice to a choked whisper. "On the spot...where Tara—"

He couldn't finish but he didn't need to. On the spot where Tara had been found murdered.

The hair on her arms stood up.

"I was unconscious. I don't remember anything after…"

His words trailed off. He looked ill.

"After what?" she asked. "Mark, what happened?"

He brought a shaking hand to his head. "I don't feel so good."

Liz caught his elbow and ordered him to sit. He did, heavily, and dropped his head into his hands. He breathed deeply and slowly, using his breath, she knew, to help steady himself.

She sat beside him, at the edge of the cot. She had so many questions for him, ones about Tara and Rachel, about the Horned Flower and what they had done to him, where he had been and whether he had recognized anyone. But she held back, seeing how easily he could be overwhelmed.

Seconds ticked past. They became minutes. Finally he lifted his head and looked at her. "The night I called you, I met a girl named Sarah at Southernmost Beach. She blindfolded me and gave me a drug—"

"What kind?"

He shook his head. "I don't know. It was a pill. It relaxed me to the point where I was no longer aware of what was real. Like I was in a bubble, floating. Removed from the physical world. Above it."

A depressant, probably. Maybe Xanax or Librium.

"Go on."

"I don't know where they took me. It didn't seem like I'd been in the car long, but it could have been hours." He paused as if using the time to prepare himself for what he was about to say next. He clasped his hands in his lap, gaze averted.

"I was aware of many people gathered around. They

gave me something else to drink. From a metal cup, like a communion chalice."

"What did it taste like?"

"Nothing I recognized. It was room temperature. Not unpleasant but weird."

"It wasn't alcohol?" He shook his head. "Was it drugged?"

"I don't know for sure, but I think it was because my memory is totally scrambled from that point." He balled his hands into fists. "How can I help Tara when I can't even remember what happened that night!"

Liz reached over and covered his hands, even as disappointment washed over her. She had hoped he would learn something substantive about Tara's murder and Rachel's disappearance. "I'll help you put it together, Mark. We can do this. Tell me what you do remember. Something that doesn't make sense to you may make perfect sense to me."

He swallowed audibly and began again, tentatively. "After I...drank from the chalice, they began to chant."

"What did they say?"

"I don't—" he pressed his fingertips to his temples "—something about heat and the flower and the light. Then they...took off my blindfold."

Liz straightened. "And? Did you recognize any of them?"

"Creatures," he said. "They weren't human. Birds and tigers and the walking...dead." On the last his voice grew thick, and he cleared his throat. "I had this sense they..."

She leaned toward him. "You sensed what, Mark?"

"That they meant to devour me, spirit and all."

For a moment, she couldn't breathe. She shook her head. "They were probably masked."

"Yes," he repeated hollowly. "Of course. Masked."

"So you couldn't recognize them."

"I guess not."

That he didn't sound convinced concerned her. She wondered again at the drugs he had been given. Some sort of hallucinogenic, for sure. As a mental health care professional, she was well versed in the effects and side effects of drugs of abuse. These days, sadly, she wouldn't be able to perform her job if she wasn't.

"They began to tear at me. As if feasting on my flesh. But they... It was sexual."

He lowered his voice to a thready whisper she had to strain to hear. He told her about their hands and mouths, about his being laid upon an altar and of floating above it, enraptured. He described his all-but-continual orgasm.

Ecstasy or cocaine might explain the intense sexual aspects of Mark's experience. Mescaline or peyote could account for the visual hallucinations. LSD for hallucinations paired with the impaired depth and time perception.

Liz swallowed against the dryness of her throat. Her heart had begun to beat faster.

"Then my head...exploded." He began to tremble. "It was like the most brilliant light in the universe flashed before my eyes, blindingly white. Then it went black." He looked at her; she went cold at the terror in his eyes. "That's when I saw it, Liz."

"It?"

"The Beast."

For the full count of five, Liz sat silent, motionless. She couldn't find her voice.

He dropped his face in his hands once more. "I'm so ashamed."

"You were drugged. Probably given a combination of something like ecstasy and LSD, a drug cocktail designed to elicit the responses you describe. You aren't responsible for what happened."

"They mean to kill me, Liz."

"Did they say that? Did anyone verbally threaten you?"

"They know what I was up to. Somehow they know."

"But how?" She frowned. "Mark, you've had a shock. You were given God only knows what combination of narcotics, ones that influenced your reactions the other night and how you feel mentally and physically right now. If they planned to kill you, they would have done it then."

"The Lord was there with me, Liz. He protected me. He sent Stephen into the garden for me."

Liz didn't know what to say. The truth was, her young friend was frightening her. The fanatical light in his eyes reminded her of the way Tara had looked that day in her office, when the girl had relayed the story of the Blessed Mother's appearance here at Paradise Christian.

He leaned toward her. "Do you believe, Liz?"

"I believe you wouldn't lie to me, Mark."

"Not my story, that's not what I mean. Do you *believe?*"

"Are you talking about God?" she asked. "About believing in God?"

Mark nodded, his teeth beginning to chatter. "In heaven, hell and all their power. In Satan and his army of darkness, in Jesus Christ and his eternal light and promise of forgiveness? He is the light, Liz. Without him we're doomed."

"You're upset," she murmured, reaching out to lay her hand on his forehead. "It's going to be okay. It's—"

"It's not!" he cried, pushing her hand away. "You don't get it. It's happening. The battle is being waged now."

Liz cleared her throat, frightened. "Mark, if you calm yourself, we can talk about what to do—"

He grabbed her hands, holding them so tightly she winced. "The outcome isn't a given, Liz. Too many people take for granted that good will win out. We can't do that." He released her hands. "The darkness is powerful, more powerful than we ever imagined."

He broke down then, sobbing like a baby. Liz took him in her arms and held him while he cried. She heard a sound and looked up to find Stephen in the doorway, gazing at Mark with affection and concern.

And fear. She drew her eyebrows together. Had they known each other before this? she wondered. The depth of emotion she saw in the caretaker's expression suggested they had, but she hardly thought it possible.

As if becoming aware of her scrutiny, Stephen shifted his gaze to hers. They stared at one another a moment, then he backed silently out of the doorway.

Liz returned her attention to Mark, who had gone still in her arms. "Are you all right?" she asked softly.

He nodded and drew away from her, wiping at his cheeks, obviously embarrassed at having broken down that way in front of her.

"I can't get them out of my head," he murmured, voice thick from his tears. "I can't get the Beast out."

Satan. Beelzebub. The Angel of Darkness.

Liz searched his expression, alarmed. In some people, drugs like LSD and mescaline proved the kindling for a prolonged psychotic event. Typically those people had either a biological or emotional predisposition to mental illness. For example, buried issues they had never dealt with or a family history of schizophrenia. The stress of the acid experience could psychically break them open. Some never recovered, their delusions persisting like the never-ending "bad trip."

Delusions involving Christ, the devil or other religious figures were common.

"I have to get you to the hospital, Mark. A doctor needs to look at you."

"No!" He jumped to his feet, expression panicked. "They'll know. They're everywhere. They see everything."

Rachel had said they were listening. That they were everywhere.

Liz shook her head against the thought, not knowing what to believe, what was fact and what was nightmare brought on by the drug cocktail. Frequently, schizophrenics heard voices and felt they were not only being watched but were in mortal danger as well.

She had to get him medical attention. She wasn't a medical doctor. She knew little about drug interactions or antidotes. She feared for his health. She told him so.

"They'll kill me, Liz! I know they will."

She opened her mouth to reassure him that the police would protect him, then closed it. They wouldn't protect him. According to what Rick told her, they thought Mark killed Tara. They thought the Horned Flower was a figment of her and Mark's imagination. They needed a suspect and had decided Mark was that man.

She thought of Rick. What did he believe? If she told him she was with Mark, would he turn him over to the police?

She feared he would. She couldn't allow that to happen.

The two of them were on their own.

Liz reached up and caught Mark's hand. "All right," she murmured. "No doctors and no police…for now. But no promises about tomorrow."

CHAPTER 36

Monday, November 19
2:45 a.m.

Rick sat alone in the empty bar, his cell phone on the table beside him. Libby had left several minutes ago. They had finished closing, but Rick wasn't ready to leave, not yet. He needed the quiet to think, to untangle his thoughts.

Too much had happened in the past twenty-four hours. His and Liz's lovemaking. Val and Carla's visit. The things they had told him. His visit with Daniel and the discovery that Tara's tattoo and the drawing in Pastor Rachel's notes matched.

Mark a serial killer? The good-natured, conscientious Christian boy who never even took a drink? The young man he had not only trusted and relied on but had come to respect?

The seasoned guys in his squad in Miami had seen

it all. They used to laugh that really bad shit was perpetrated by the ones you least suspected. The quiet ones. The handsome, smart or educated ones.

Not the penny-ante crimes. Not the everyday street crimes. But the really bad stuff. The serial killers. The drug lords. The high-tech, big-bucks operations.

Rick had seen their theory play out, time after time.

But Mark? Something, some instinct buried deep inside him, told him it wasn't true.

Everything else told him it was.

That Val and Carla believed Liz was a target terrified him. He shifted his gaze to the cell phone. He wanted to call Liz. To hear her voice. To reassure himself she was all right.

So why didn't he call? He'd gotten her number from information hours ago and had dialed it a dozen times. And had never pressed Send.

He brought the heels of his hands to his eyes. Why the hesitation? Why the knot in the pit of his gut? Guilt, he acknowledged. The feeling that he had betrayed Jill, their wedding vows.

Jill was dead. She had been gone for more than three years.

No, he admitted. She wasn't gone. She lived in his heart. She always would.

A knot of emotion formed in his throat even as a feeling of peace moved over him. He bent his head, vision blurring.

I love you, Jilly. I always will.

Love you, too, babe. It's okay to move on.

He didn't believe in ghosts or the spirit world; he knew she hadn't spoken to him. But he felt as if she had. He felt as if she were with him now.

Without examining that feeling further, he snatched up his phone and punched in Liz's number.

It rang a half-dozen times, then her machine picked up. He listened to her message, heart beginning to thunder.

He racked his brain for an explanation. She was sleeping and hadn't been able to get to the phone in time, he told himself.

She had a phone beside her bed. He had seen it.

"Liz, it's Rick." He heard the panic in his own voice and tried to temper it. "We need to talk. Call me right away, no matter the time."

He left her his cell-phone number, then hung up.

She was fine. Sleeping. It was the middle of the night, the time when normal people were in bed. Rick stood and clipped his phone to his belt, then began the last tasks he needed to complete before he could go home.

Those done, he flipped off all but the bar's safety lights, set the alarm and slipped out into the night. If she needed him, she knew how to reach him. He would head home and catch some much-needed shut-eye.

Rick ended up at Liz's place instead. He pulled his Nighthawk up in front of her storefront apartment. He cut off the engine and gazed up at her windows. A single light glowed from somewhere deep inside the dwelling. The front window stood open—an invitation to every passing maniac to break in.

Or a way for one particular maniac to get in.

He swore, unable to shake the feeling that something was wrong. That she was in immediate danger.

Calling himself the lunatic he would look like when he awakened her from a deep sleep, he swung off the motorcycle and strode to her door. He rang the bell, then pounded, fear becoming panic.

"Liz!" he shouted. "It's Rick."

Several seconds passed. Finally, the dead bolt slid back; the door cracked open.

Liz peeked around the door frame. Rick went weak with relief. "I was sick with worry. I called and you didn't answer."

A strange expression crossed her face. "I turned off the ringer."

Of course, it was something simple. Logical.

He was a lunatic.

"We have to talk. Can I come in?"

She didn't move. "Now's not a great time."

"It's important."

She hesitated, looking uncomfortable. "If it's about what happened earlier—"

"It's about Mark."

Wordlessly, she swung the door wider.

Rick stepped into the foyer. She shut the door behind him, but didn't lead him upstairs. She faced him, arms across her middle in an almost defensive stance.

Something had changed in the few hours since they parted. Something that had caused her to distance herself from him.

Thoughts of Val and Mark and Tara's murder fled his mind. "Have I done something wrong?" he asked.

"Not at all." She dragged a hand through her already tousled hair. "You said you had information about Mark."

He ignored her pointed attempt to shift the conversation away from their relationship. "Would you have let me in if I said it was about what happened earlier?"

"I don't expect anything from you, Rick. You don't have to—"

"Dammit, Liz, maybe *I* expect something."

She searched his gaze, expression altering subtly. "Oh. I...I don't know what to say."

He looked at the ceiling, frustrated by her response. After a moment, he met her eyes again. "Say anything, Liz. I'm dying here."

A hint of a smile pulled at the corners of her mouth. "All right. What do you expect... Do you have any idea what that might be?"

"Not yet." He closed the distance between them and cupped her face in his palms. "I like you, Liz. Being with you tonight... It wasn't... I've been with women since Jill. But never in a meaningful way. It's going to take me a little time to deal with this. Are you okay with that?"

"More than okay."

He returned her smile, bent and pressed his mouth against hers in a quick, possessive kiss. When he released her, he saw that she looked dazed.

He liked that, he decided. He liked it a lot.

"Val and Carla paid me a visit at the bar tonight."

She became instantly alert. "What did they want?"

"There's a warrant out for Mark's arrest. They think he killed Tara."

"Same old song, Rick. They're obviously desperate, trying to convince—"

"They believe he killed Naomi Pearson as well. They have evidence against him, Liz. Strong enough to issue a warrant."

"I don't believe it."

"There's more, Liz. They think you may be his next target."

For the space of a heartbeat she didn't even seem to breathe. Then she shook her head. "That's crazy."

"That's what I told them. But—"

"But what, Rick?" She hugged herself, as if in protection against his words. "Why are you selling Mark out this way?"

"Just listen, please. I don't want to believe he did it either, but I know enough about police work to understand that it takes real evidence to issue a warrant. The clock starts ticking the minute an arrest is made. The police have to be able to convince the D.A. that they'll be able to prove guilt. And that's tougher than you think."

"Then why are the newspapers filled with stories about new evidence surfacing that exonerates some poor guy serving time for a crime he didn't commit?"

"The system's not perfect, Liz. Mistakes happen. They're the exception, not the rule."

"So what is this strong evidence?"

"They wouldn't tell me."

"Great." She let out a long breath. "I'm tired. It's been a long night. I think I'd like you to leave now."

He ignored her. "Serials killers work in a couple different ways. Most begin their killing career with a person close to them, a neighbor, friend or coworker, then they move on to strangers."

"Stop trying to scare me."

"But some serials select their stranger, then forge a minimal relationship with them before killing them."

"You're leaving now."

She crossed to the door and began to open it. He stopped her. "The relationship, the trust is a stimulant for these killers. It increases their thrill in the kill. Gavin Taft operated that way. Ultimately, it was his undoing. Most probably it will be Mark's as well. If he's the one."

She didn't make a move, so he forged ahead.

"Naomi and Mark knew each other through their church. They were in Bible study. That would inspire a deep element of trust."

She looked shaken. "I don't want to hear any more. Please leave."

"Now he's forging a relationship with you. The frightened boy. The victim. You respond to that. You trust him because he needs you."

"Stop it."

He caught her arm. "But you do trust him. Isn't that right, Liz?"

"Why are you doing this!" She wrenched her arm free of his grasp. "Why are you trying to frighten me this way!"

"Because I don't want anything to happen to you, dammit!"

Her expression softened. "Nothing's going to happen to me. I know things you don't."

He caught his breath. "He's contacted you, hasn't he?"

She hesitated, but only a fraction of a second. And in that moment Rick knew. "He's wanted by the police, Liz. On a murder charge, for God's sake."

"I haven't heard from him."

"I don't believe you."

"Then that's your problem, isn't it?"

He swore and swung away from her, frustrated. She didn't get it. Her blind trust in this kid could get her dead.

She came up behind him and laid a hand on his arm. He looked at it, then at her.

"Thank you," she said.

"For what?"

"For caring what happens to me."

"Maybe I shouldn't." He stepped away from her hand. "Because with your reckless attitude, you may not be around that long."

CHAPTER 37

Monday, November 19
Noon

Carla parked her cruiser in front of Paradise Christian. Pastor Tim waited in front of the church for her, expression panicked.

She shook her head and climbed out of her car. A popular pastor disappears. A serial killer is slicing up young women. A prominent citizen bilks a million bucks from his employer then kills himself. Now a depression had formed in the western Caribbean, a depression with the potential to become a full-fledged hurricane. It seemed to her that paradise was going to hell in a handbasket.

The pastor rushed to meet her. "Thanks for coming, Detective. It's Stephen, the church caretaker... I didn't know what to do, so I called the police."

"Slow down," she murmured. "Tell me what happened."

He nodded and clasped his hands together. "I hadn't seen Stephen in a day or two, so I grew concerned. I went to his quarters to check on him. And I found—"

His voice broke. "Come, let me show you."

They hurried around the side of the church, bypassing the garden. Carla saw the parsonage, then a smaller building behind it.

"That's where Stephen lives," Pastor Tim said as if reading her mind. "Originally it was the buggy barn, then an equipment shed. It was converted to living quarters after Stephen returned from the sanatorium in Miami. He didn't do well there, and the church decided to accept responsibility for his full-time care."

They reached the dwelling's entrance. The door stood slightly ajar. "Was the door open before you went in?" she asked.

The pastor hung back slightly, expression queasy. "No. I knocked, then tried the knob. Maybe I shouldn't have gone in, but I was worried."

Carla didn't comment. She crossed to the door and tapped on it. "Police! Anybody home?" No one responded and she tried again. When she got the same response, she pushed the door the rest of the way open and stepped inside. The interior was neat, its furnishings basic.

Pastor Tim came up beside her. "There—" he pointed "—on the bed."

The twin bed was pushed up against the right wall, under a small, curtainless window. The baby-blue chenille spread looked worn. Ditto for the pastel, floral sheets. Carla crossed to the bed.

Pastel, floral sheets smeared with blood. Carla gazed

at the unmistakable puddles, spots and swirls, her vision blurring for a fraction of a second.

To hell in a handbasket, no doubt about it.

So much for paradise.

"Is that what I thought it—"

"Yes," Carla replied grimly. "Please stand back, Pastor. Did you touch anything earlier?"

"No, I—"

"Good."

"Do you think Stephen is—" The clergyman's voice shook. "I mean, that seems like an awful lot of blood. Is it an awful lot, Detective?"

It wasn't a little.

Carla thought of Tara. But she had seen more. A lot more.

"You say you haven't seen Stephen in a couple days?"

"That's right."

Carla fitted on a pair of rubber gloves. Bending, she carefully examined the bedding, pulling the top sheet away from the fitted. The blood appeared fairly fresh. She touched a large irregular-shaped spot and found it was still damp.

She shifted her gaze to the floor by the bed. A bloody trail led away from the bed and toward the back of the room and a door set into the wall. A bloody handprint stood out in bold relief on the pale yellow paint.

Carla's heart jumped to her throat. She swallowed past it. "That a closet?"

"I think so but I'm not sure."

She unclipped her cell phone, punched in the number for headquarters number and requested backup, ASAP. Possible homicide, she informed the dispatcher, then flipped the phone closed. She glanced at the pastor. "I think you'd better wait outside."

"But Stephen may need—"

A moan from the other side of the door interrupted his words. Carla sprang toward the door and yanked it open. Not a closet, she realized in the same instant she registered the condition of the room's occupant.

He was naked save for a pair of bloodied boxer shorts. His limbs, torso and hands were also stained red. A Bible was open on the cot beside him; pages that had been ripped from it littered the cot and floor. His face was tipped heavenward and Carla saw that his eyes were rolled back in his head.

"Stephen," Pastor Tim cried, alarmed. "Are you all right?"

The caretaker's head snapped down. For the space of a heartbeat he stared at them, his good eye wide, expression terrified. Then he opened his mouth and a terrible sound came out, the sound of a wild animal in pain. The sound tripped along Carla's nerve endings and sent shudders racing up her arms.

She saw the knife clutched in his hand. The kind a hunter might use, with an edge that was both serrated and smooth. Its four-inch blade was covered with blood.

Dammit. Carla went for her weapon. But not fast enough. With a bloodcurdling howl, the caretaker launched to his feet and charged her.

"Watch out, Pastor!" she called, lunging sideways in an attempt to protect them both.

She didn't completely elude the caretaker. He caught her shoulder and sent her crashing into the opposite wall. Pain shot through her side, and even as she righted herself and took off after him, she wondered if he had managed to cut her.

"Freeze!" she shouted. "Freeze or I'll shoot."

He didn't acknowledge her command with the slightest pause in his flight. Carla was vaguely aware of a group of tourists in the distance, of their frightened squeals. And of the sound of sirens. The cavalry. Thank God.

She darted toward the garden. She heard screaming. A shout for help. A child began to cry.

She burst through the gate. Stephen was running back and forth, knife clutched in his hand, sounds more animal than human spilling from his misshapen mouth.

She shouted for the civilians to get back. From the corner of her eyes she saw her backup storm the garden from the other entrance, weapons drawn. From Duval Street came the sound of more sirens.

"Freeze, Stephen!" He swung toward her, his expression desperate. Then he charged. She lifted her gun, ordered him to stop, once, then again.

He was nearly on top of her when she fired. The bullet caught him square in the chest. His body jerked slightly at the impact, though it didn't halt his forward momentum.

He slammed into her and sent her sprawling. Her life flashed before her, a series of brightly colored disappointments.

A moment after hitting the ground, the other officers were at her side. They eased the caretaker off her.

"You okay, Chapman?" Val asked.

She had to think a moment about that. She realized that other than having had the wind knocked out of her and being scared senseless, she was okay. She told Val so, then motioned to the caretaker.

"Is he—"

An officer at his side looked up at her. "He's alive."

"Get an ambulance," Val shouted. "Now!"

The next minutes were a blur. The ambulance arrived. A news crew. The evidence team, even the chief of police. The man congratulated her, then made his way to where the reporters waited eagerly for a statement.

"You did good, Carla," Val murmured. "Real good."

That wasn't the way she felt, though she didn't say so. She'd never discharged her weapon in the line of duty before, let alone shot another human being.

She glanced down at herself and choked back a sound of revulsion. She was covered with Stephen's blood. She went to wipe at it and realized she still wore the latex gloves she'd put on what seemed like hours ago now.

"What do you say we take a look around inside?"

She nodded and followed Val because she knew it was what he expected of her. She was shaken but unharmed. She had a job to do.

The evidence guys had already begun to do their thing. One of them was carefully combing the bedding for trace material, another was busy photographing the scene.

Val looked at her. "What happened?"

Carla filled Val in. "I was on my way to lunch when I received the call from dispatch. Pastor Tim had called in. There was a situation, he'd said. He feared someone had been hurt. He was pretty shaken up.

"I arrived at the church at approximately noon. Pastor Tim was waiting. As I had been warned, he was upset."

"How upset?"

She thought a moment. "Rattled. Shaky."

Val nodded and she continued. "He hadn't seen Stephen, the church caretaker, in a couple of days and was worried about him. He had gone to his quarters looking for him and found the bed bloodied. That's when he called us."

"He have a key to the place?"

"It was unlocked." Carla let out a breath. "He led me here. Upon a brief inspection of the bed, I noticed a trail of blood leading to what I assumed was a closet." She pointed. "I saw the handprint and feared we had a perp hiding in the closet. I advised the pastor to wait outside and I called for backup."

Val drew his eyebrows together. "But you didn't wait for backup to arrive."

"No." She met his eyes. "I screwed up. When I heard him moan, I reacted. I figured we had a victim in need of medical attention."

"Go on." Val crossed to the door and peered into the space.

"At first I thought I had been right. The caretaker was bloodied and appeared to be having some sort of seizure."

"A seizure?" Val murmured, frowning. "What indications—"

"His eyes were rolled back in his head." She shuddered, remembering. "When Pastor Tim cried out the man's name and asked if he was hurt, it was if they snapped back in place. Really creepy."

Her superior looked annoyed at her editorializing and she refocused on the facts. "That's when I saw the knife. I went for my weapon, but I was too late. He charged us and headed out to the garden. The rest I think you know."

Val moved into the narrow room. He squatted in front of the cot, careful not to disturb anything. "Bible pages," he murmured, indicating the papers that littered the cot and floor around it. "That's curious."

He tilted his head to read one. "This one's from the

Gospel of Peter. This one from Luke. Looks like mostly New Testament stuff."

He looked at her. "You read much Scripture, Carla?"

"I grew up Catholic." She rubbed her arms, at the chill bumps that dotted them. "Went to mass and confessed my sins regularly. Said my share of novenas, but that's about it. Why?"

"Don't know." His expression grew pensive. "Just trying to figure out what it all means."

He drew his handkerchief out of his jacket pocket. Using it to prevent possible contamination of the evidence, he carefully tipped the Bible over. The breath hissed past his lips.

"Carla, you might want to take a look at this."

Carla crossed to her superior and peered over his shoulder at the book. Imprinted in gold on the cream-colored leather cover was the name Rachel Howard.

CHAPTER 38

Monday, November 19
3:00 p.m.

Liz opened her door a crack. Valentine Lopez and Carla Chapman stood on the other side, their expressions grim. Her heart leaped to her throat. *They knew Mark was here. Rick had seen through her subterfuge; he had gone to the police.*

What did she do now?

She worked to hide her thoughts. "Yes, Officers?"

"There's been a development in your sister's case," Lieutenant Lopez said. "May we come in?"

"My sister's case?" she repeated, moving her gaze between the two detectives. "What—"

"May we?"

"Yes, of course." Liz opened the door wider and stepped aside so they could enter. Her hands shook as she shut and locked the door behind them.

"Do you have company, Ms. Ames?"

"I don't think that's any of your business." She moved her gaze between the two officers. "You said you had information concerning my sister?"

The man looked at the other detective. "Carla?"

She nodded and drew a book out of the canvas tote she carried. Even housed in a plastic bag, Liz recognized Rachel's Bible immediately.

Carla handed it to her. The plastic crackled. "Have you ever seen this before?"

Liz stared at the book, the leather cover marred by fingerprints. Bloody fingerprints. Tears choked her. "It was my sister's." She ran a finger over the letters of Rachel's name, stamped in gold at the bottom of the book's cover. "I gave this to her when she…" Liz lifted her gaze, vision blurred. "How… Where did you…find it?"

"Do you know Stephen St. John? The old caretaker of Paradise Christian?"

"Yes, but what does he—"

"We have reason to believe he may have been involved in your sister's disappearance."

A chill washed over her. "I don't understand."

"Detective Chapman answered a routine call to Paradise Christian this afternoon. The caretaker attacked her with a knife that fits the M.E.'s description of the one used to murder Tara Mancuso and Naomi Pearson. Among other things, we found your sister's Bible in his quarters."

Liz couldn't breathe. "Excuse me, I need to sit down."

She pushed past the two and sank heavily onto one of the stairs. She lowered her head to her knees and breathed slowly and deeply, in her nose and out her mouth.

More proof that her sister was dead. Another nail in her coffin.

"In any of your conversations with your sister, did she ever mention Stephen St. John to you? Either by name or title of church caretaker?"

She shook her head but didn't look up.

"Are you certain?"

"Yes." She lifted her face then. "You might talk to the owner of Bikinis & Things. She was friends with Rachel and she...she told me Rachel was frightened of him. That Rachel had caught him peeping in her windows."

The two detectives exchanged glances. "Do you know her name?" Carla asked, removing a spiral notepad from her tote.

"Heather Ferguson."

Carla jotted down the name. "In your sessions with Tara Mancuso, did she ever mention the church caretaker?"

"No, never."

"Do you have any idea how Stephen St. John could have come into possession of your sister's Bible?"

She shook her head.

"When did you first meet the church caretaker?" Val asked.

She struggled to collect her thoughts and put them into words. "On one of my visits to Paradise Christian. I'd just met with Pastor Tim and Stephen...blocked my path. He startled me by grabbing my wrist. Luckily, Heather Ferguson happened along. She scolded him and he ran off. Isn't he...harmless?"

"That's what we all thought," Carla said, closing the notebook.

Liz rubbed her arms. "Are you saying… You think Stephen murdered Tara and—"

Val cut her off. "Thank you for your time, Ms. Ames."

Carla crossed to where she sat. She held a hand out, expression apologetic. "I'm sorry, but we'll have to keep your sister's Bible for the time being. It's evidence."

She handed the book back, feeling light-headed. "Evidence?" She looked from Carla to her superior. "Then you think Rachel… That Stephen…"

Her voice trailed off. The lieutenant's expression softened. "In light of these new developments, I've decided to reopen the investigation into your sister's disappearance. Looks like you might have been right. We're fearful Pastor Howard may have met with foul play."

She uttered a sound of despair. *She didn't want to be right. She wanted her sister.*

"Ms. Ames?"

She lifted her watery gaze. "Yes?"

"As far as you know, did Mark Morgan and Stephen St. John know one another?"

"What?"

"Mark Morgan and Stephen St. John, did they know one another?"

"I don't… I'm not…" She looked helplessly at them, struggling to come to grips with all they had said, the implications of it. With her own conflicting thoughts and emotions. Who should she believe? Who could she trust?

"It seems like this isn't a good time," Val murmured. "If you think of anything that might help us, give me a call."

They let themselves out. For long moments, she stared at the closed door, then slowly stood, crossed to it and twisted the dead bolt. Exhaustion pulled at her. Her hands and limbs shook and she felt as if her nerves were frayed to the breaking point.

She wanted to climb into bed, pull the covers over her head and sleep. For as long as it would take for this nightmare to end. When she woke up, Rachel would be alive and all that would be left of this would be a vague, unpleasant memory.

Swallowing hard, she turned.

Mark stood at the top of the stairs. Their eyes met. A shiver of fear moved over her.

"There's a warrant out for Mark's arrest. They think he killed Tara. And they think you may be his next target."

"As far as you know, did Mark Morgan and Stephen St. John know one another?"

"I heard them." He fisted his fingers. "And it's not true. Stephen wouldn't hurt anyone. He's gentle. The most gentle person I've ever met."

Who should she believe? Who should she trust?

He frowned. "Why are you looking at me like that?"

"I'm not... I—" She shook her head and started up the stairs. "I'm exhausted, Mark. I can't talk about this right now."

"They knew exactly what they were doing to you!" he cried. "They were trying to break you down. Trying to make you question yourself and what you believe."

She reached the top of the stairs and looked him dead in the eyes. "Who should I believe, Mark? You? Or the police?"

"Me." His expression became pleading. "You can trust me. I wouldn't lie to you."

"Now he's forging a relationship with you. The

*frightened boy. The victim. You respond to that. You
trust him because he needs you."*

"Please, Liz," he begged. "Stephen's my friend. He
has this innocence, like a child. Look into his eyes,
you'll see it. He couldn't even conceive the actions
they're accusing him of."

"How do you know!" She jerked her arm free and
faced him, furious. Hurting. "I'm a family counselor, I
work with the walking wounded every day. The kind of
abuse Stephen suffered damages a person. Sometimes
in awful, frightening ways. Ways that sometimes make
them turn that anger and pain on others."

"Not Stephen."

Liz brought the heels of her hands to her eyes. A
headache jackknifed against her skull. "He had my sister's Bible."

"What does that prove? Maybe she gave it to him."

"You didn't see it! It was smeared with blood. It—
They said he had a knife, Mark. A knife like the one
used to kill Tara."

"What about Pastor Tim? He could have planted the
knife."

She started past him; he grabbed her arm. A shiver
raced up her spine. "Tara didn't like Pastor Tim. She
said there was something creepy about him. That she
had caught him in a lie. That he looked at her funny
sometimes. In a way that scared her."

"Let me go."

"He could have planted the knife, Liz. He could have
planted the Bible, to frame Stephen. To divert suspicion
from him. He lives there, too. He has unlimited access
to the garden, parsonage and Stephen's quarters."

"I said, let me go!" Confused, head pounding, she

broke free of his grasp. "He attacked a detective, Mark. Can you explain that away? Can you?"

His defiance seemed to evaporate, leaving him looking young and vulnerable.

She laid a hand on his shoulder. "We'll figure it all out, Mark. I promise. But first, I have to take some Advil and lie down. Please?"

He nodded but didn't meet her eyes.

She squeezed his shoulder, then headed to her bedroom, acutely aware of his presence. She entered her bedroom, closed the door behind her and started toward the bed. There, she stopped, turned and looked at the door.

After a moment's hesitation, she hurried back and locked it.

CHAPTER 39

Monday, November 19
5:00 p.m.

Carla paused outside Rick's Island Hideaway. She hoped Rick was here. She needed to talk to him. She needed him to tell her everything was going to be all right. That she had done the right thing.

She felt for all the world that she hadn't.

She glanced quickly behind her, looking, no doubt, as guilty as she felt, then stepped out of the blazing heat and into the bar's cool, dim interior. A half-dozen patrons were scattered throughout the room: lovers at a table in the corner, a couple of singles at either end of the bar, a group of tourists who were obviously feeling no pain.

Rick straightened when he saw her. *He'd already heard.* She wasn't surprised. News spread fast on this tiny island, and in his line of work Rick missed little of it.

Of course, the official news had been limited to the basics. The caretaker of Paradise Christian Church had freaked out, threatened a group of tourists with a knife and Key West officer Carla Chapman had been forced to shoot. The caretaker was in critical condition.

Val and the chief had managed to keep everything else under wraps. For now.

"Are you okay?" Rick asked as she sank onto the stool across from him.

"If you call feeling like total shit okay, then I'm it."

He set a draft in front of her. "No matter the circumstances, shooting another human being never feels right."

She smiled weakly and took a sip of the beer, though technically she was still on duty. "All afternoon people from the chief down have been patting me on the back and congratulating me. It feels like such a lie."

He arched an eyebrow, and Carla felt herself flush. She looked away. She'd been unable to get the image of Stephen's face as he lunged at her out of her head. Something about his expression nagged at her. Had his intent been murderous? Had he been attacking her? Or had his actions been those of a terrified, cornered animal attempting to flee?

"You want to talk about it?"

She should say no. She should sit, sip her beer and simply let his presence soothe her. If Val knew she was here, he would be furious.

She squeezed her eyes shut as Stephen's image filled her head once more. Murderous rage, she told herself. That's what she'd seen in his eyes. He'd come at her like a rabid dog, frothing at the mouth, eyes lit with blood fever. Not with helpless fear. Not with desperation.

She met Rick's concerned gaze. "Yeah," she murmured. "I think I would."

She spoke softly, starting with her call from Pastor Tim, finishing with the moment she pulled the trigger, eliminating any details that linked Stephen to Tara's and Naomi's murders.

"Sounds like a good shooting. Everything by the book."

"I'm not so—" She shook her head, biting back what she had been about to say, that she wasn't so sure. That she wondered if she could have wrestled him down. That she had second thoughts about whether he had meant her harm.

"You grew up here," she said. "What do you know about him?"

"Not a lot. That he was the victim of child abuse. That the church takes care of him. As kids we used to tell stories about him because he was different. Because he looked frightening."

"What kind of stories?"

"Ones about how he murdered his entire family but the police couldn't prove it cause they never found the bodies. Rumor was, one night he chopped them all up into little pieces then tossed them into the ocean. Stupid kid stuff."

"Was it just kid stuff?" She leaned forward. "As far as you know, did he ever threaten anyone?"

"As far as I know, no, he didn't. Why?"

She didn't answer right away. Revealing the details of this investigation would be cause for suspension.

The way she felt right now, that wouldn't be such a bad thing.

"He might be the one, Rick." She glanced toward the end of the bar, then lowered her voice. "He carved himself up. The way Tara and Naomi were. Weird shit, like writing on his torso and thighs."

Rick straightened. "Go on."

"We think they might be Bible passages."

The guy at the end of the bar to her right stood, called good-night to Rick and headed out.

She waited a moment, then continued. "He'd pulled all these pages out of a Bible. When we found him, he had the knife. There was blood…everywhere. And the pages were scattered all around him. Like he was in the act of cutting himself."

Rick glanced toward his customers, then back at her. "And the knife's consistent with the one used on both victims, right?"

"Right. How'd you know?"

"Because without that, you have little more than a crazy son of a bitch into self-mutilation." Rick narrowed his eyes. "What does Val think?"

"That we're on to something."

"What do you think?"

She never went against Val's opinion. Maybe that's why she was here. She had questions, ones she didn't trust herself to answer. Ones she had hoped Rick could help her make sense of.

"I don't know."

He leaned toward her. "Sure you do, Carla. What do *you* think?"

"I need your help."

"I'm not part of the investigation."

"I wish you were. There's something…" She swore and stood. "I've got to go."

Her caught her hand. "Give yourself some credit,

Carla. What do you think? Something propelled you in here tonight, something you wanted to run by me."

She lowered her gaze to his hand on hers. In that moment she wanted him to hold her, wanted it so badly she couldn't breathe. The feeling passed and she slid back onto the stool. "Okay, yeah. I think something about this doesn't fit. I always heard this Stephen had the mind of a child. Like he was brain damaged or something. What kind of kid could do what was done to Tara and Naomi?"

"But he's not a child," he said, playing the devil's advocate. "He's an adult."

"I know. But—" She rubbed her temple.

"But what?"

She swore, recalling the way he had looked at her, the expression in his eyes. "It doesn't feel right to me. I looked into his eyes and—"

Someone at the table of tourists signaled Rick. He nodded at them, then looked at Carla. "Hold that thought. I'm being paged."

Carla watched as Rick closed out the table's tab, brought the lovers another round and shooed old Pete off his bar stool and out the door.

"I'm taking you away from your customers," she murmured when he returned. "I'm sorry."

He flashed her a quick, breath-stealing smile. "What customers? Monday's the slowest night of the week. Last week's tourists have gone home, the majority of this week's haven't arrived and the partied-out locals are doing their best to get back to the grind." He smiled again. "I'm glad you came tonight, Carla."

Her heart skipped a beat. God help her, she was, too.

"I guess I just have so many questions. Like, how does a guy who never hurt anybody suddenly commit a string of grisly murders. Usually there's a history of some sort of violence. Cruelty to animals. A morbid fascination with death. Something. But everybody we talked to claimed he'd never hurt a fly."

"They might be wrong. He's a weird guy, Carla. Lives alone. Keeps to himself."

"I know." She picked up her beer, then set it back down without sipping. She lifted her gaze to his, anguished. "I hate my job today. I don't want it, you take it, Rick."

He reached across the bar and covered her hand with his. "He went at you with a knife. You defended yourself. He could have killed you, Carla."

She squeezed her eyes shut, the image of Stephen filling her head again. His anguished cry. The terror in his eyes.

She forced the image out. *He had meant her harm. She had been one hundred percent justified in shooting him.*

He was the one.

Rick released her hand.

"He had opportunity," she murmured. "That's for sure. Killers like this rarely stray far from their geographical comfort zone. Tara was found murdered at Paradise Christian, Rachel Howard was last seen at—"

"Rachel Howard? What does she have to do with this?"

"St. John had her Bible. Val's revised his opinion of her disappearance. He thinks she might have been the first victim."

CHAPTER 40

Monday, November 19
8:00 p.m.

"Rachel!"

Liz bolted upright in bed and looked around her dark room, confused. She had been dreaming of Rachel, she realized. In the dream her sister had been calling out for her. Alone and locked in a stifling hot box. Slowly dying.

Shuddering, Liz scrambled out of bed. She saw it was eight, crossed to the bedroom door, unlocked it and stepped out into the hall. Her apartment was dark. Totally soundless.

"Mark," she called softly. "I'm up."

Silence answered her. Frowning, she flipped on the hall light and began making her way toward the second bedroom. She tapped on the closed door. "Mark, are you there?"

He didn't reply. She tried the knob. The door eased open. She peeked into the dark room.

"Mark?" She reached for the light switch. Light flooded the empty room.

They'd come for him while she slept.

She shook her head. How would they have discovered his whereabouts? And how would they have gotten in without her knowing? If he wasn't here, he'd gone out. He'd probably left her a note.

She went into the room. The bed was made, the coverlet army barracks taut, the pillows perfectly plumped. Turning, she crossed to the closet, opened it and looked inside.

Empty. Just as she had expected it to be.

Liz shut the door and started out of the room. Suddenly, she stopped, her gaze going to the bed. To the place the dust ruffle met the wooden floor. The ecru-colored fabric was folded back. As if someone had lifted it.

So they could scurry beneath to hide.

For a moment, Liz couldn't breathe. Then she scolded herself to get a grip. Swallowing hard, she marched to the bed, bent and peered beneath.

Nothing. Of course. What had she thought she was going to find? The boogeyman hiding under the bed? Mark, grinning at her like an overgrown six-year-old? A dead body?

Mark had gone out. No doubt, he had left her a note, probably in the kitchen. A self-conscious laugh bubbled to her lips. She had better get that grip on herself before somebody had her locked up.

Liz turned off the light on her way out of the room. Smiling at herself, she headed to the kitchen. She flipped on the overhead light, then stopped in her tracks.

A lidded coffee can sat in the middle of her tiny, kitchen table in a puddle of dark liquid. The same liquid appeared to be smeared on the sides of the can and tabletop.

Liz stared at the can. She recognized the brand as the same one her mother used to buy. She hadn't realized they still sold coffee that way, ground in five-pound cans. She and Rachel had made banks out of them as kids. They had used them for butterfly houses and bug hotels, after cutting slits in the plastic top so their captured creatures could breathe.

Liz brought a shaking hand to her mouth and inched toward the table. She saw that the smears were red. The puddle a deep ruby. Blood, she realized.

A scuffling noise came from the can. With a sense of déjà vu, she reached for the can. She snapped off the lid and peered inside.

The creature peered up at her with its beady black eyes, teeth bared.

She jumped backward. The can slipped from her fingers and landed on its side on the table then rolled off and onto the floor. Blood splashed across the linoleum, the rat spilled out.

It lay there, chest heaving, near death.

Liz began to shake. Rat in a can. Sister in a box.

Slowly dying.

Slowly dying.

The words played in her head like a deranged nursery rhyme. She backed away. The doorbell rang. Liz swung in the direction of the front room, then started forward. Her slow pace quickened until she was running, tearing through the apartment to the stairwell, thundering down the stairs. Ripping the door open.

Rick stood on the other side.

With a cry, she fell into his arms.

His went around her. "You're trembling."

She pressed her face against his chest and held him tighter.

Mark was gone. Rachel was dead.

She was next.

"I heard," he said after a time, softly. "About Stephen. That he had your sister's Bible." He tipped her face up to his, searching her expression. "I know what that might mean, Liz. I'm sorry."

Emotion choked her. She couldn't speak and tears welled in her eyes.

"I'm so sorry." He cupped her face in his palms and brought his mouth to hers. He kissed her softly, sweetly, then rested his forehead against hers. "So sorry."

A movement from beyond her open door caught her eye. Someone passing by, glancing in.

Someone watching.

Her heart stopped. Liz caught his hand and drew him the rest of the way into the foyer. Reaching around him, she closed and locked the door.

She held a finger to her lips and led him upstairs. He made a move to turn on the light but she stopped him. "Not yet. Someone could be watching." She crossed to the front windows and closed the blinds, then to the side windows and did the same.

She switched on a lamp. A gentle glow fell across his features, softening them. Smoothing his concerned frown.

"What's going on?"

She brought a hand to her mouth. It shook. She realized how close she was to falling apart and it frightened her. She couldn't go there. Not now. Not again.

"I need to show you something."

She led him to the kitchen. She saw that the rat hadn't moved. Most probably it had died from lack of oxygen or of shock. Perhaps it had drowned in the blood it had been swimming in.

"Mother of God, Liz!" Rick crossed to the creature. He examined it without touching it. "Who did this?"

"After Lieutenant Lopez left, I was really tired... I had this headache... I lay down. When I woke up, he was...gone. I thought he might have left a note and I—" She cleared her throat. "I found the can and the... It was still alive."

"Who, Liz? Who was gone?"

She dragged her gaze from the rat to Rick. "We have to talk."

"Dammit, Liz. Who did this?"

"The Horned Flower." She crossed to the sink and retrieved a pair of rubber gloves and a bottle of anti-bacterial cleaner from beneath it. She put the gloves on, then took a roll of paper towels from the dispenser. She returned her gaze to Rick's. She saw by his expression that he thought she had lost her mind. "Mark was here, Rick. And now, they have him."

CHAPTER 41

Monday, November 19
8:20 p.m.

Liz refused to say more until they had cleaned up and disposed of the rat. Rick urged her to leave it as it was and to call the police; she flatly refused. What would she tell them? she had demanded. That she had been harboring a wanted man? That cultists had crept into her apartment and abducted him while she napped, leaving this lovely package behind?

Oh sure, she had continued, Valentine Lopez would love to hear that story. He would have her locked up before she had even finished talking. The only question remaining would be whether he locked her in a cell or the loony bin.

Rick glanced at her, huddled on one edge of the couch, knees drawn to her chest. He had to choose, he acknowledged. Who did he give allegiance to? Val and the police department? Or Liz and her crazy story?

As if reading his thoughts, she looked at him. "I need you to believe me, Rick. I need you on my side."

"Mark's wanted by the police, Liz. For murder. They believe he may mean you harm. Considering all that, what in God's name possessed you to harbor him here?"

"If I tell you everything, will you promise to keep an open mind?"

He hesitated a moment, then agreed. "But I can't promise anything else. You understand that, don't you? And you understand just how nuts this all seems to me?"

"Oh yeah, I understand. Half the time I think I've gone around the bend. Then someone leaves a bloody rat in my kitchen, and I snap right back to reality."

"So talk to me."

After taking a deep, fortifying breath, she began. She described how she had awakened to find Stephen in her apartment. He had led her to his quarters at Paradise Christian, where he had hidden Mark.

She met Rick's eyes. "He found him in the walled garden, Rick. Unconscious."

"The walled—"

"On the spot where Tara was found."

"Jesus, Liz, that doesn't look good. If the police had found him there—"

"They would have used it as further evidence against him. Which is exactly what they'd hoped would happen."

Then her story got weird. She described Mark's Horned Flower experience, how he had been blindfolded, drugged and driven to an unknown destination where many people waited. "He was given another drug, one he drank from a chalicelike cup. Only then did they remove his blindfold."

Rick leaned forward. "And? Did he recognize any of the other teenagers?"

"They were masked." She cleared her throat, then continued, relaying what Mark had shared with her, the sensation of being feasted upon, laid upon an altar and sexually devoured. Of continually orgasming.

"He was talking crazy, Rick. About good and evil. About the battle between the two. He spoke of the Beast."

"The Beast?"

"The devil," she murmured. "Mark's thoughts have been consumed with the experience. He insisted they wanted to kill him. He kept saying they were inside his head. And that he couldn't get the Beast out."

She rested her forehead on her knees a moment, then looked at him. "I was frightened for him. Whatever drugs they gave him caused some sort of psychotic episode."

"Did you get him medical treatment?"

"I suggested it but backed off when he became agitated. He said they would know, that they would find him."

"What about the—"

"Police?" She shook her head. "He was afraid of going to the police. He figured they'd arrest him. Rightly so."

Rick was silent a moment, absorbing what she had told him, weighing it in his mind. He met her eyes. "What's your interpretation of his experience?"

She shifted, tucking her legs under her, expression pensive. "I believe Mark was given a powerful, mind-altering combination of drugs. I believe they influenced his perception of the experience. There are a number of drugs or combination of drugs that could have elicited those feelings. Ecstasy and cocaine are powerful sexual stimulants. LSD causes bizarre visual hallucinations and distorted physical perceptions. After an acid trip, the user may suffer acute anxiety or depression for a varying period of time."

Rick pursed his lips. "Which could be what Mark's been continuing to experience."

"Exactly. In addition, because of its structural similarity to a chemical in the brain and its similarity to certain aspects of psychosis, LSD has been used as a research tool to study mental illness. The full spectrum of effects of peyote and mescaline have also served as a chemically induced model of mental illness."

She met his eyes. "These people are toying with powerful, dangerous drugs. Chemicals with the ability to cause a psychic break in the right individual."

They fell silent a moment. She pulled in a deep, fortifying breath. "This cult exists. They're dangerous. And I believe one—or more than one—of them is a murderer."

"A bold statement."

"Yes." She cocked up her chin. "What do you think, Rick? Something brought you to my door tonight and, call me cynical, but I don't believe it was my sister's Bible."

"Something's not right about this, Liz. About all of it. We've got two women brutally murdered in a manner nearly identical to the method used by a serial killer presently on death row. We've got another woman missing, now presumed murdered. Suspect number one is a twenty-year-old man from Texas. A young man who was in middle school during the height of Gavin Taft's rein of terror. Yes, he could have studied the man's crimes, but it seems unlikely. First off, there are details of the crimes difficult to come by, even with the Internet. The weapon, for one. The length and depth of the blows. The markings. The similarities are too damn close.

"That's the key, Liz. I keep coming back to those similarities. Put everything else aside and look at how those women were killed. The way Taft killed. There's a connection. And I don't believe Val, or anybody else working the case, is looking hard enough at it. They're so busy running around trying to find a suspect, they're ignoring the biggest real clue they have."

He stood and began to pace. "A killer driven to acts such as those committed by Taft is motivated by some internal compulsion, some mechanism inside that seeks release. That release can only be found through a specific and highly individual ritual, one acted out with each victim."

"I don't understand. What do you mean by a ritual?"

"Everything about the crime. How the victims are chosen and why. The manner in which they're killed. Where and how he disposes of the bodies. Whether or not they're sexually assaulted. In some cases, even the geographic location of the crimes becomes part of the ritual.

"In Taft's case, he established a cursory relationship with the women. For him, that was part of the thrill. He chose young, attractive women. The youngest in her late teens, the oldest her late twenties. He slit their throats, mutilated their genitalia and carved pseudo-religious symbols and verses on their torsos and thighs, postmortem. All were found naked, bodies arranged arms out, one foot on top of the other, as if they had been crucified."

"So you're saying it's not killing the women that satisfies these monsters, but how they kill them?"

He met her eyes, saw the horror in them and wished he could protect her from the truth. "Exactly. Serial killers are a different breed of criminal. They don't kill for the typical reasons, jealousy, greed, hatred or anger. And the way they kill is as individual as a fingerprint. Copycatting a killer to divert suspicion for a single crime, to get rid of a lover or business partner, for example, I could buy. But a serial adopting another psychopath's fingerprint for a series, it doesn't work that way."

"So, what do the police have on Mark? It must be something more than the fact he knew both women and was at the scene the night of Tara's murder. Don't you need more than that to arrest someone?"

"Yeah, you do. My guess is they found something damn incriminating in his room."

"The weapon?"

"No. Because now they've turned their attention to Stephen—"

"Who was in possession of a knife similar to the one used to kill Tara and Naomi Pearson," she filled in for him. "If they already had the weapon, that wouldn't be such a big deal." She let out a long breath. "Do you think it's possible Stephen's the one?"

"Could Stephen go over the bend and kill someone, sure. Anyone can snap that way." He stopped pacing and swung to face her. "Once again, I come back to the similarities to the Taft murders. Stephen's lived on Key West his entire life and reads at maybe a second-grade level. A guy like Stephen doesn't cruise the Internet.

He doesn't read the newspaper and he sure as hell didn't work with the man. Any way I look at it, he had zero opportunity to study Taft."

"Val asked me if Stephen and Mark knew each other."

"They're both suspects. He's wondering if they could have done this together. At this point he's exploring all possibilities."

"I didn't answer, but I think he knew. I had this feeling he could see right through me."

Rick thought of his friend, of the way his mind worked. "Val's smart. Real smart. And for as much as I believe he's not handling this investigation correctly, he's a good cop. Don't ever underestimate him."

"What about Pastor Tim?" she asked.

"What about him?"

"Mark told me that Tara didn't like him. That he scared her. He suggested Pastor Tim might have planted the Bible and the knife. Geographically, he had as much opportunity as Stephen to kill Tara."

"Tim?" Rick repeated, tone doubtful.

"You know him?"

"Sure. I played high-school ball with him, though he was two years older. So did Val."

She made a sound of confusion. "He's from Key West? I thought he only arrived after my sister disappeared."

"No, Tim grew up here. In fact, he was pretty much a hero around here his senior year. He took the Fighting Conchs to the state football championship."

Rick slipped his hands into his pockets. "He left to play ball for Florida State, then was drafted by the NFL. He only played a couple years, then dropped out to go to seminary. Said God called him. Could have knocked all of us over with a feather. I mean, who makes the NFL then voluntarily leaves? And to become a pastor?"

"What team?" she asked.

"Miami Dolphi…"

Rick's voice trailed off. He did the math.

Tim had been in Miami about the time Gavin Taft had been on his killing spree.

He could tell by her expression that she had done the calculations, too. "He told me he didn't know my sister. That he'd never met her."

"That could be true, though it's difficult to believe. His parents are members of the Paradise Christian congregation, or at least they used to be, and he visited quite often. However, your sister wasn't on the island that long. He may have had an interim position somewhere that I'm not aware of."

She glanced down at her hands, then back up at him. "There's something I haven't told you or anyone else."

She held up her right hand. "See these bands? They were my mother's. Eternity bands. Before she died, she gave one to me and one to Rachel. She asked that we never take them off—they would link the three of us for eternity."

He drew his eyebrows together, confused. "Then how did you get Rachel's?"

"Pastor Tim had it." She drew in a deep breath. "I found it on the floor of his bedroom closet."

"The floor of his… What were you…" His voice trailed off, realization dawning. "You broke into the parsonage?"

"Yes." She tipped up her chin, expression defiant. "The parsonage was Rachel's home, most probably the place she spent her last hours. I just had to see for myself that she—"

"Was really gone?"

She flushed. "I knew she wasn't there, but I...I had to see for myself."

Rick passed a hand over his face, recalling what Val had said about Liz. "*She has issues, my friend. Serious emotional issues. That she's not playing with a full deck right now makes her a little scary.*"

"Why didn't you just explain to Tim who you were and why you wanted to look around? That would seem the most rational approach."

"I felt like he was lying to me. That he knew more about my sister than he was saying. There was something about his demeanor...something about him that wasn't adding up. I had to do it, Rick. And just as I'd thought I would, I found something."

Rick acknowledged that he wanted to believe her. On some emotional level he did. Her answers made sense, even when they shouldn't.

"*Desperate people do desperate things. They lie. They manufacture evidence. And they can be pretty goddamned convincing.*"

"Rachel could have taken the ring off."

"She never took it off."

"You don't know that."

"But I knew Rachel."

"It could have slipped off one day while she was dressing. By the time she realized it was gone, she wouldn't have had a clue where she had lost it."

Liz met his gaze. "Or, Tim Collins is the killer and the ring's a trophy. I read that serial killers do that, take some memento of each victim. Often a piece of jewelry."

"Dammit, Liz! Slow down."

"He lived in Miami during the time Gavin Taft was

butchering those women. He's the right age, he had my sister's ring. Things he said are questionable. He's the one who called the police about Stephen."

Rick swung away from her and strode to the windows. He inched up one of the slats and peered out at the street. The typical Monday crowd made their way along Duval. Every night was party night in paradise.

He frowned. Why did she make so much sense? Everything she proposed was the stuff of blockbuster fiction, far from the open-and-shut reality of most murder investigations.

And entirely too possible.

Sometimes, fact proved more far out than fiction.

He turned to face her, resigned. "And how does the Horned Flower fit in?"

"Pastor Tim is one of them. Maybe the leader. Who better to attract young and impressionable people? Who better to woo adults in search of life's meaning? A former football star, a big, handsome charismatic man. And from a church pulpit, no less."

Motive. Means. Opportunity. Son of a bitch. "And why did they leave the rat?"

"As a warning. If I don't cease and desist, I'm going to end up like that rodent."

"A gruesome thought," he muttered.

"It doesn't make my day, I'll tell you that."

The image of Tara filled his head, with it the stats associated with her murder. Throat slit. Postmortem mutilation of genitalia, torso and thighs. Abdomen split wide open; fetus taken.

He had to tell her.

"There's something I haven't shared with you. About Tara's death." He paused. "It's really bad."

She went stone still. "What is it?"

"The killer cut open her womb. And took the baby she was carrying."

The blood drained from her face. She looked at him, expression anguished. "You don't mean...took."

"I do. The fetus...it wasn't at the scene, Liz."

She brought a hand to her mouth. He saw that it shook. "But why... I don't understand... Why would he do..."

Her words trailed off. He crossed to the couch and squatted in front of her. "Tomorrow, I take you to Miami. You catch a plane home to St. Louis. I sort this out and keep you apprised of the situation. Agreed?"

"Are you trying to be funny?"

"I'm trying to play it smart. And keep you safe."

"You're starting to believe me, aren't you?"

God help him, he was. He drew her up and into his arms. "Go back to St. Louis, Liz."

"I can't do that." She tipped her face up to his. "I won't let Rachel down again. And I won't let Tara, Mark or their unborn baby down. You'll just have to keep me safe right here on Key West."

Rick thought of Jill. Of how it had felt to bury her. He bent and pressed his mouth to Liz's. She melted against him, fingers curling into his pullover.

With a groan, he broke the kiss. "How early can you clear the sheets in the morning?"

"Pretty darn early when I'm motivated."

He bent and rested his forehead against hers. "I worked with a guy on the Miami-Dade force... He was one of the lead detectives on the Taft investigation. He lived, ate and slept that case. Was obsessed with it. I think I'll give him a call, see if I can pay him a visit, pick his brain a little."

She wound her arms around his neck. "While you're

with him I'll go to the library. Do a little research on Taft. I might find something everyone's forgotten. Or overlooked."

"Mmm." He kissed her again, deeply, acknowledging that he didn't want to stop. He did anyway, with a sound of regret. "And when we get back, I'm going to find out what Val has on Mark."

"All this romantic talk. It could sweep a girl off her feet."

He sobered. "I'm afraid for you to be alone, Liz."

"Then don't leave me."

Rick searched her expression, an ache of arousal in his gut. It was an invitation, he knew. They were already lovers, it would be easy to be together. Easy to fall into her bed and arms and to forget, even if only for a time, that a murderer walked the streets of Key West, mutilating young women and taking unborn babies. That he might have chosen Liz to be his next victim.

But to be with her in the shadow of the day's events felt wrong. As if the darkness around them might infect what was growing between them. He didn't want that to happen.

He told her so.

Her expression became impossibly soft. She stood on tiptoe, cupped his face in her hands and kissed him softly. "Thank you," she whispered. "I'll make up the couch."

CHAPTER 42

Tuesday, November 20
3:00 p.m.

Rick hadn't seen Bill Hunter—Wild Bill, they used to call him—since he quit the Miami force. The man hadn't changed much—still chain-smoked, still called waitresses "honey" and still had the most direct gaze Rick had ever encountered.

"Thanks for taking the time to see me," Rick said, speaking up to be heard above the din of the busy coffee shop.

"No problemo. How've you been?"

"Traded in my badge for a bar. Rick's Island Hide-away."

"Catchy name."

"Thanks." He smiled. "You ever come down to Key West, stop in. The drinks are on me."

"Apparently, you've forgotten how much cops can

drink." The other man's smile faded. "I heard what happened to your boy, Rick. I couldn't be more sorry."

Rick looked away, then back. "Thanks, Bill. I appreciate that."

The waitress stopped by their table and refilled their coffee. Bill watched her walk away, then turned to Rick. "You say you're looking into the Taft murders?"

"That's right."

"Seems you've got some kind of copycat operating down there."

"Maybe. Maybe not. That's what I'm trying to find out."

"Mind telling me why you're so interested? You're not a cop anymore."

Rick hesitated, uncertain how to respond. He decided on the direct approach. "I've got a feeling about this case. The local boys are missing something important and…I don't want anyone else to die."

"Still the cocky cowboy, I see."

"Yee-hah." Rick leaned forward. "You worked on the investigation. I figured if anybody could offer insight into how that son of a bitch thought, it'd be you."

The other man didn't deny it. "I put together a file for you. Some official stuff, my personal notes. A half-dozen pictures." He inched the legal-size envelope across the scarred Formica tabletop, then shook a cigarette out of his pack and lit up. "It's all public record now."

"Thanks, man." Rick opened the envelope, sifted through the contents, then looked at his friend. "You one hundred percent satisfied that Taft's the one."

"Absolutely." Bill drew in a lungful of smoke, then blew it out. "Taft was the creepiest SOB I ever had the pleasure of busting. Bar none."

"In what way?"

"He was proud of the way he had mutilated those women. *Proud,* Rick." He shook his head, expression faraway. "He liked telling us about it. Got off on it, you know? Like he was reliving it through us. Told us where all the bodies were." His mouth curled with remembered distaste. "I used to shower after being in the room with him. The evil…it was like it oozed out of him."

The man took another, final drag on the cigarette then tamped it out half-smoked. "But it wasn't just that," he said, leaning closer. "It was his eyes, man. They were dead. Flat and lifeless as a shark's."

A shark. A killing machine. A creature with an insatiable appetite.

In Taft's case, an appetite for killing.

"He scared the shit out of me." Bill paused for a moment to light another cigarette. "I never told anybody that before. But it's true."

The hair on the back of Rick's neck prickled. "What about an accomplice? Anything ever suggest he may not have worked alone?"

The detective narrowed his eyes, though whether with thought or against the smoke curling up from the tip of his Camel, Rick didn't know. "He could have had an accomplice, though nothing in the evidence supported that. Taft always maintained he had a spiritual adviser who offered divine help."

"Any connection to football or the Miami Dolphins?"

"Not that I know of. He may have been a fan."

"He go to college?"

"Did a semester at Florida State in Tallahassee. It didn't last. Flunked out."

Rick's heartbeat accelerated. "What year?"

"I'd have to check."

"I'd appreciate it." He cleared his throat. "Any markings on Taft or his victims?"

"What kind of marks?"

"Tattoos. Maybe of a strange-looking flower. Like a horned flower?"

Bill shook his head, and Rick shuffled the papers, digesting all that his friend had told him. "As far as you know, were any of Taft's victims pregnant?"

The other man's expression altered subtly. "Why do you ask?"

"One of our victims was. The bastard took the fetus."

"Shit." Bill took a long drag on his smoke. "Yeah," he said, voice thick. "Two of 'em. One six months along."

"Did he—"

"Yeah, he did. Sick prick."

Silence fell between them. Rick pulled a picture of Taft out of the file. The killer stared out at him, movie-star handsome. "I didn't remember that he was so good-looking."

The other man smiled without humor. "Evil takes many forms, my man. And if you're dealing with anyone associated with Taft, I suggest you don't forget that."

CHAPTER 43

Tuesday, November 20
3:30 p.m.

The main branch of the Miami-Dade library was housed in the Cultural Arts Center in downtown Miami. The coral-faced and stained stucco building all but screamed fun-in-the-sun, and Liz suddenly realized that St. Louis was going to seem awfully tepid after the fanciful pinks, corals and palm trees of south Florida.

The second floor housed microfilm issues of all the local newspapers, including the *Miami Herald*. Gavin Taft had been headline news starting in 1998. A look at the microfilm index revealed a wealth of articles on both Gavin Taft and the New Testament Murders.

Armed with a legal tablet, pen and plenty of money to pay for copies, Liz began with the oldest article and moved forward in time. She took a few notes, but for the most part learned nothing new. The first victim had been found in June of 1987. Between then and October of 1998, eleven other women were murdered. All had been killed the same way.

No connection between the women had been found.

A stupid mistake had led to Taft's capture. During a routine traffic stop for a burned out taillight, the officer thought he recognized the stains on Taft's hands and arms as blood. A thorough search of the vehicle had revealed more blood and a knife. Unbeknownst to the officer, he had caught Gavin Taft on his way home from his most recent slaughter—Jennifer Reed, a twenty-two year-old coed and the last New Testament Murder victim.

End of story until Tara turned up dead on Key West ten days ago.

Disappointed, Liz stared at the microfiche screen. She had hoped she would see a connection between the victims that no one else had. She had fantasized finding a mention of a tattoo, one of a strange horned flower.

As she moved to flip off the machine, an article at the bottom of the displayed page caught her eye.

Satanists Believed Responsible for Death of Livestock.

The story came from nearby Homestead. It detailed a rash of livestock killings—the animals had been found with their throats slit. Images associated with satanism had been drawn on fence posts and the sides of farm buildings. Pentagrams. Horned goats. An inverted cross.

A horned goat.

The Horned Flower.

Heart pounding, Liz altered her search from Gavin Taft to satanism.

CHAPTER 44

Tuesday, November 20
5:00 p.m.

"Hey, gorgeous."

Liz jumped and gasped, a hand going to her throat. She swung in her seat to find Rick standing behind her, expression amused.

She scowled at him. "You scared the life out of me!"

"I see that." He bent and kissed her, then pulled out a chair and sat. "Sorry."

She rubbed her arms. No wonder he'd frightened her, considering the things she had read in the past hour. She might never *not* be frightened again.

"What's so interesting?" He tipped one of the books up so he could read the title. *The Devil's Hour.* He looked at her, eyebrow cocked in question.

Rick wasn't going to take what she had to say well. Considering the brevity of their relationship, she shouldn't know him well enough to predict that, but she did. He would be resistant to anything that fell outside the typical law-and-order scenario of bad guy is busted by good guy—nice, neat and explainable.

A cult that worshiped Satan and murdered its wayward members and all others who might expose them fell way outside of that.

Liz changed the subject and forced a weak smile. "How'd it go with your friend?"

"Good. Seems Taft spent a semester at Florida State."

"That's where Pastor Tim went to school."

"Yup. Bill's checking the date for me." Rick caught her hand and laced his fingers with hers. "He told me something I'd never heard before. Said Taft always claimed to have a divine mentor. A spiritual adviser."

She frowned. "And?"

"Think about it, Liz. A spiritual adviser. Who in society is recognized as—"

"A pastor," she murmured, excited. "Of course."

"This might all be nothing but a coincidence. But if it turns out that Gavin Taft and Tim went to school together, I'll feel a lot more confident that what we found is solid enough to go to Val with."

"We have, I'm certain of it." She drew a deep breath. "They're satanists, Rick. The members of the Horned Flower are satanists."

He gazed blankly at her a moment, then laughed. "Very funny."

"I'm not joking." She tightened her fingers over his. "When I was looking for stuff on Taft, I found this article. Here." She slid the copy she had made out from under a pile of books and handed it to him.

He read the article then handed it back. "I saw stuff

like this when I worked on the Miami-Dade force. What about it?"

"The horned goat, the horned flower. See the connection?"

He shook his head. "You're making a pretty big leap there, Liz. My feeling is the Horned Flower is a sexual image, the group some sort of sex club. Think about it. The flower is a symbol for the female genitalia, the horn for a man's."

He had a point, but she knew she was right about this. She had to convince him. "Just listen to me, please. Satanists aren't as rare as you might think. They're not just the stuff of Hollywood. Research suggests there are more than a hundred thousand practicing satanists in the United States alone. And that figure doesn't include self-styled satanists who aren't part of a coven or those simply dabbling in the black arts. Research also supports that satanists' belief in the power of darkness predisposes them to acts of lawlessness and violence.

"According to my research, law enforcement has learned to repress any satanic elements of a crime because they don't play well in court or with juries. The defense calls it supernatural mumbo jumbo and the real evidence is discredited by association. So, they make their case without mention of black candles, altars, gutted animals or pentagrams. Can you tell me you didn't do the same when you were with the Miami-Dade force?"

She took his silence to mean he couldn't and continued. "Think about the rash of school shootings. The great majority of those kids had satanic paraphernalia in their possession."

"And a great number of them had Nazi symbols and objects, too. They were troubled kids looking for anything out there that was associated with the dark side of human nature."

From the corner of her eye, Liz saw a man at the next table glance at her. She moved her gaze and thought she saw the interest of several others. A chill washed over her.

They could be anywhere. Watching. Listening.

She grabbed her purse. "Let's talk outside."

Rick followed her out front. They stood in the cool shadow of the Cultural Arts Center's long colonnade, away from the curious stares of others. Liz picked up where she had left off. "These satanic groups lure troubled teens into the coven with promises of power and a sense of belonging. A family, if you will. Which is the exactly the way Mark told me Tara and her friends referred to the Horned Flower."

"That's typical of cults. From what I learned when I was still on the job, it is that very promise of acceptance and belonging that lures most cult devotees."

She ignored him and continued. "Of course, once in the cult, they are expected to do whatever is asked of them, whether they want to or not. Some who have escaped have told they were required to act as sex slaves to other coven members. Others were forced into prostitution.

"Then, when the member wants out, threats and intimidation are used to keep wayward cult members from leaving the group."

"Also standard cult practice, Liz. Absolute loyalty is demanded of sect members and is enforced by threats to body or spirit."

"We're on the same page here, Rick," she said, excited. "Satanists have been known to threaten to kill not only the cult member, but their family and other loved ones as well. If the member continues to try to separate from the coven, they increase their threats. For example, they might kill the member's pet, then present the mutilated animal as a very real warning."

Rick remained silent and she pressed on, encouraged. "That's what happened to Tara. She went to my sister, they found out about it and killed Rachel before she could go to the authorities. Then when Tara became involved with Mark, who insisted she leave the group, they threatened to harm her and her unborn child.

"Tara feared the Horned Flower, Rick. She told Mark she did. And sure enough, the night she was due to run away, they stopped her."

"Slow down, Liz." He held his hands up, palms out. "There's nothing to suggest Tara's murder was the act of satanists."

"No? What about the pseudoreligious carving on the body? The mutilated genitalia? Maybe the bodies weren't laid out to form a crucifix but an inverted cross, another satanic image." She took a deep breath. "Maybe Taft's spiritual adviser was the devil himself."

He sucked in a sharp breath. "Stop it, Liz. You're talking crazy. Talking like this will get us—"

"What? Laughed out of the Key West Police Department?"

"Yes." He made a sound of frustration. "You're right, when I was with Miami-Dade, we swept any ritualistic aspects of a crime under the rug because it would discredit us. But also because it wasn't really pertinent to the crime." She opened her mouth to argue; he held up a hand to stop her. "If a Buddhist or a Christian or an atheist commits a crime, their faith isn't thrown up to the jury as pertinent."

"But, Rick—"

"Listen to me. Tara, and probably Rachel, too, were killed by a sick human being acting alone, not as part of a group. In my opinion it was most probably someone who worked directly with Gavin Taft or was an admirer of his."

"Then how do you explain what happened to Mark?"

"The experience Mark described was wholly sexual with none of the chanting and ritual associated with a black mass."

"What about the altar. The ceremonial cup? And sex is often a major part of satanic ritual because it can be used in the most base and sinful way. Not as an act of love or as a beautiful gift from God, but as a sinful instrument of the devil. Aleister Crowley, the most famous satanist of all time, issued a creed declaring, 'Lust. Enjoy all of the things of sense.' He believed that sex had magical properties and practiced all kinds in his religion, even child molestation."

Rick looked shaken. He stepped away from her. "You're obsessed with this. You're starting to sound like your sister."

She froze. "How can you say that? You never even met her."

"Her words and actions discredited her. And if we press forward with the satanist angle, *we'll* be discredited. Everything we have to say will be discredited."

She recalled the most horrifying thing she had unearthed today. And perhaps the one that best illustrated what they were dealing with. "Did you ask your friend with the Miami-Dade force if any of Taft's victims had been pregnant?"

"Yes. Two were."

"And did Taft…take the fetuses?"

"Yes."

She whispered a prayer. For strength. For protection from an evil that would commit such a vile act against nature. "A satanic priest's most prized possession is a candle made from the fat of an unbaptized baby." Her voice shook slightly. "Maybe this isn't an accomplice of Taft's, but a fellow cult member continuing his lord's work."

Rick was silent a moment. "We have to be very careful here. Just because something's in print doesn't mean it's accurate or even true. What did these researchers base their fact on? What kind of studies? A few anecdotal or sensationalized incidents? Stories that were later recanted? The public has an insatiable appetite for the sick and bizarre—it sells newspapers. Liz."

Rick's cell phone rang. He took it from its holster but didn't answer. "What I know to be true, beyond a shadow of a doubt, is that there are cruel and sick people in the world, ones capable of horrific acts. Whether guided by the ultimate evil or simply broken beyond repair, they cannot be allowed to move freely with the rest of us."

He flipped open the phone. "Rick Wells here." Liz watched as Rick listened, his expression changing from intent to jubilant.

"Thanks, Bill," he murmured. "I'll keep in touch."

Rick closed the phone and turned to Liz. "My friend got that information we were looking for. Gavin Taft attended Florida State the spring semester of 1987. I'll need to confirm it, but that should have been the semester Tim graduated from FSU."

A tingling sensation started at her fingertips and spread outward. "It's him, isn't it? We've got him."

"There's more, Liz." Rick let out a short breath; Liz could see that he was excited. "One of Taft's victims was a Miami Dolphins' cheerleader."

CHAPTER 45

Wednesday, November 21
12:45 a.m.

The drive back to Key West from Miami seemed interminable. Rick spent much of the trip fiddling with the radio, scanning from one station to another, looking for the most recent weather updates. The depression that had developed in the western Caribbean had begun to move north through the Yucatán, intensifying to a tropical storm. Although late in the season, the conditions looked right for this storm to upgrade to hurricane force in the next couple of days.

News of the storm had helped fill the silence between him and Liz. They had decided to agree to disagree on the satanist issue, but still he felt it between them like a wall.

Her zeal had unnerved him. Her passionate insistence that she was right. Every step he took with her seemed to take him not a step forward but one sideways, farther into the realm of the unbelievable.

Satanists? Black masses and sacrificed babies?

As he'd admitted to Liz, during his time on the Miami-Dade force, he'd run into some of this crazy cult shit. Most of the guys had. Pentagrams and inverted crosses drawn on the walls and floors of abandoned buildings, burnt black candles that had obviously been used as part of some sort of dark mass or other pseudoreligious ceremony. Rarely had there been a crime associated with the sites and certainly never violent crime.

But it only took one individual to change those stats. One psychopath whose twisted mind told him that he had been put on earth to do the work of Satan.

"Here we are," he murmured, turning onto Duval Street. "Looks like the party's still in full swing."

"Do you need to go by the Hideaway?"

He heard the tremor in her voice. He drew to a stop at the traffic light and looked at her. "I'm not going to leave you alone, Liz."

She tilted up her chin in a show of false bravado. "You don't have to baby-sit me. I'll be fine."

The light changed and he eased forward, past a group of drunken young people. "I appreciate all that machismo, doll. But you're stuck with me."

She reached out and curled her hand around his. "What's next?"

"After sleep?"

She laughed. "After *lots* of sleep," she corrected. "Yes."

"First thing, I need to confirm that Tim and Taft were actually enrolled at FSU at the same time."

"How are you going to do that?"

"Call the university." He found a parking spot just down from her apartment and maneuvered his Jeep into it. "Pretend I'm an employer confirming résumé information. This kind of stuff isn't considered confidential. It shouldn't be a big deal."

"Then what?"

He cut the engine. "I'm going to talk to Carla. Try to catch her before she goes in this morning. I think I might be able to get her to spill what they have on Mark and Stephen. Once I'm fully armed, I'll go to Val."

They climbed out of the vehicle and made their way in silence to Liz's front door. Liz handed him her keys. He unlocked the door and they stepped inside.

Rick held a finger to his lips. She nodded and they stood quietly a moment, listening. "I'll go first," he murmured.

They made their way upstairs. When they reached the top, he turned to her. "Wait here. I want to make sure there are no surprises waiting for us."

He worked his way through each room, checking closets and under beds, looking for anything amiss. "No dead rats, bodies or burnt black candles," he called from her bedroom, closing her closet door.

"Very funny."

He turned and found her standing in the doorway watching him, her cheeks pale, eyes wide. He frowned. "What's wrong?"

She shook her head. "Needing a bodyguard is a whole new experience for me. One I could have lived without."

"I'm hurt." He started toward her. "Wounded, really."

He reached her. She smiled up at him. "I can tell."

"Beautiful and intuitive. I'm awed."

She brought a hand to his chest. "I can feel your heart beating."

"It's beating only for you."

She laughed lightly. "Corny, Wells."

He brought his arms around her. "Maybe I'm trying too hard?"

She stood on tiptoe and leaned against him. "Silly man, you don't have to try at all."

Her meaning clear, Rick caught his breath. He found her mouth and kissed her. She kissed him back, just as deeply. Sweeping her into her arms, he carried her to the bed.

Their passion didn't build slowly. It burst forth, full-blown, white-hot.

And in those minutes, Rick's thoughts emptied of everything but Liz. The sweet perfume of her body, the way she clung to him, the sounds she made as she orgasmed.

His release followed hers; she caught his sounds with her mouth. Held him until both their hearts had slowed, their flesh cooled.

He rolled onto his back. "Wow," he said, lacing their fingers, bringing her hand to his mouth.

Liz blushed and he laughed. "It's a little late for that, lady."

"I suppose it is."

They fell silent. Moments passed. Totally relaxed, he trailed a hand over her hip, enjoying the texture of her skin against his. "Tell me about your marriage," he murmured, realizing suddenly how little he knew about her. Realizing that he wanted to know all her secrets, not just those of her body. "I don't even know his name."

"Jared."

"I knew a Jared. He was a total weasel."

"Sounds like we're talking about the same guy."

"How long were you married?"

"Three years." She rested her forehead against his shoulder for a moment before tipping her face up to his. "Actually, I was married for three years but Jared was married for about three months. That's when he had his first affair. I didn't know, of course. The ignorant little wife. I walked in on him and one of my best friends."

"Some friend."

"Some husband." She paused, then sighed. "It was his birthday. I wanted to surprise him with all his favorites—prime rib, crème brûlé for dessert, chilled Tattinger's. I'd been planning it for weeks. I canceled my afternoon appointments to go home and prepare everything."

She pulled in a shaky breath. "The house...felt wrong, you know. Like something wasn't as it should be. I heard sounds coming from the bedroom. It was almost surreal, as if I was outside myself watching as I crossed to the bedroom door, reached for the knob and eased the door open. And there they were, on our bed. For one moment, I didn't believe what I was seeing. I thought there was some mistake...that I was in the wrong house, that I was dreaming. Then I thought I was going to die."

He hurt for her. "I'm so sorry, Liz. You didn't deserve that."

"Afterward, he threw his women up in my face. There'd been a lot of them."

Rick wondered what made a man like that. To have a smart, beautiful woman like Liz love you was a gift. One to be cherished.

"I'm sorry," he said again.

"Me, too." She met his gaze. "He always made me feel like I wasn't good enough. That I fell short in every way. I didn't realize how bad I'd gotten until after it was over."

"You don't fall short," he murmured. "Not in any way."

"Thank you." She rolled onto her side so she fully faced him. "You had a good marriage?"

"Yes." His chest tightened but he pushed past the sensation, the emotion behind it. "We were high-school sweethearts."

"What was she like?"

"She loved to laugh. She was a good person, kind. Sweet-natured." He smiled, remembering. "She wasn't much for school. Graduated by the skin of her teeth. She was happy to make a home for me and Sam."

Liz let out a long breath. "Well, I asked."

"What?"

"Sounds like you had the…perfect marriage. The perfect relationship. That's tough to compete with."

He trailed his thumb over the curve of her jaw. He liked her honesty. He liked the way she faced her feelings head-on.

And he liked that he mattered enough to her that she wanted to compete.

"You can't compete," he said softly. "But I don't want you to. You're not Jill."

Her eyes filled with tears. She moved to roll away; he stopped her. "You misunderstand. You're not Jill, but she wasn't you. Elizabeth Ames is a very special, very exciting woman. She's the woman I want to be with now."

Wordlessly, she moved into his arms. They made love again, slowly, with a kind of intensity that had been missing before. Each thrust brought them closer. In the final moments, they laced fingers and held tightly to one another.

Afterward, Rick held her. She snuggled against him and yawned. "Go to sleep," he murmured, exhaustion pulling at him. "It's really late."

"Mmm."

She had drifted off already, he realized, gazing at her face, soft and vulnerable in sleep. He breathed deeply through his nose, the urge to protect her rising up in him. To keep her safe and warm and close.

As he drifted off, he thought of Jill. He imagined her smiling.

Rick awakened to the smell of coffee. He opened his eyes to find Liz standing beside the bed, two steaming mugs in her hands. "I hope you take it black," she murmured. "There're lumps in the milk."

He sat up. "Black's good, thanks."

She handed him a mug, but kept her distance. He eyed her warily. "What's up? Did I sprout horns or is it my breath?"

Her lips lifted. "Just being careful. Are you a morning person? Or the other kind?"

"The other kind?"

"The ones who growl, grouse and generally curse the sun for having risen."

"You're safe." He made room for her beside him. "What time is it?"

"Late. After nine."

He groaned. There'd be no catching Carla before she went in to work.

"Hungry?"

"Starved. We could go out?"

"I have Frosted Flakes."

"But the milk has lumps."

"I forgot." She sipped her coffee. "How about toast?"

"Any strawberry jam?"

"Of course."

"Bring it on."

Thirty minutes later, they were dressed, fed and lingering over coffee. Rick brought up the day's schedule first. "I think I should go see Carla alone. Are you going to be okay?"

"Absolutely. I want to pay a visit on Father Paul."

He frowned. "Father Paul? That old priest you told me about?"

"Yes." Her expression dared him to challenge her decision. "I'm going to show him the sketch of the flower, see if he recognizes it."

"You're not going to let this satanist thing go, are you?"

"No." She looked down at her coffee, then back up at him. "I understand why it's so hard for you to accept."

"Liz—"

She laid a finger against his lips. "Let's just see how this plays out, okay? I promise I won't say the S word to anyone."

He hesitated, then stood. He bent and kissed her. "Be careful today. Really careful."

"You, too."

He searched her gaze. "I'm not kidding, Ms. Ames."

"Neither am I, Mr. Wells."

"I'll be at the Hideaway later. Meet me there."

This time, she kissed him. "It's a date."

CHAPTER 46

Wednesday, November 21
10:30 a.m.

Rick checked in at the Hideaway, found that Margo had left everything in good order, then made his call to Florida State University. The call took less than three minutes; he confirmed that Tim Collins had graduated the spring of 1987.

He dialed Carla's cell phone. She answered on the second ring. "Carla, it's Rick. Where are you?"

"Headquarters. Been here since six."

"What's going on?"

"Stephen's gone. He unhooked himself and walked out of the hospital."

"On his own?" Rick whistled. "Val must be pissed."

"He's way beyond pissed. Heads are rolling. I'm just thankful I wasn't anywhere near the hospital when it happened."

"No joke." Rick glanced at his watch. "Is he there?"

"No. He's with the chief. Why?"

"I need to talk with you. Can you meet me somewhere?"

"Not anytime soon. I've got orders to stay put. Hold on." She called out a coffee order to someone, then returned to their conversation. "Between Stephen disappearing and this damn tropical storm, it's a little intense around here."

"I could be there in ten minutes, would that work?"

"I suppose. Rick—"

He heard the question in her voice and cut her off. "See you soon, Carla. And thanks."

He found Carla in her office at the KWPD. She suggested they talk out on the smoking porch, a small balcony area off the south side of the second floor of the building.

Neither of them sat. Carla looked at him, gaze direct. "You're usually opening the Hideaway about now. This must be pretty important."

"It is." He looked at her just as directly. "I need to know what evidence you have on Mark Morgan."

"You know I can't tell you that."

"Cut the shit, Carla. You know how screwed up this investigation is. None of it is adding up."

"We're just missing something, that's all. Some link."

"Ever heard of a group called the Horned Flower?"

She shook her head.

"Tara was a member. We think they might have had something to do with her death."

"We?"

"Liz Ames and I."

She flinched. "I've got to get back to work."

She made a move to pass by him and he caught her arm. "This group's into some intense stuff. Heavy-duty drugs. Sex, some of it weird, ritualistic. They threatened Tara Mancuso. Warned her that they would hurt her if she attempted to leave the group."

"Surely you don't expect me to—"

"I have reason to believe Pastor Tim murdered Tara Mancuso and Naomi Pearson." He saw that he had her attention and pressed his advantage. "I share with you, you share with me. Agreed?"

"No way." She folded her arms across her chest and stared him down. "Tell me what you know, and I'll think about it."

Carla had changed, Rick acknowledged, proud of her. She was turning into the cop he had always believed she could be.

"Good enough," Rick said, then began, telling her about Liz's suspicions, their trip to Miami and what his friend told him. "Turns out Taft and Collins were both students at Florida State University the spring of 1987."

"FSU's a big school, Rick. Student population probably exceeds—"

"That's just coincidence number one. You may not know this, but Tim Collins played pro football for two years, then left to go into the seminary. He played for the Miami Dolphins."

"And?"

"And one of Taft's victims was a Dolphins' cheerleader."

Carla sat. For a long moment she said nothing, then she met Rick's gaze. "Collins was the one who called me about Stephen."

"I know."

"Stephen... Maybe the knife wasn't even his. Maybe

Collins engineered it all to look—" She bit the words back and brought a hand to her temple. "I shot him, Rick. I nearly killed a man who may only have been trying to defend himself."

Rick glanced at his watch, aware of time passing. "What do you have on Mark Morgan?"

"What I say goes no farther. Agreed?" He nodded. "Bloody clothes found in his rented room. Blood type matches Tara's. DNA's not back yet, but we expect it to confirm our suspicions."

"He never denied being at the scene," Rick said. "You stumble upon your girlfriend who's been hacked up, you tend to get a little bloody."

"But he ran, Rick. If he wasn't guilty, why didn't he call us?"

"How about he's young, scared and knew he would look guilty as hell?" She let out a sharp-sounding breath; he ignored it and went on. "Why try to link Stephen and Mark?"

"A witness thought he saw them together."

"Who, Carla?"

She looked toward the closed balcony door, then back at him. "You want to guess?"

"Pastor Tim."

"Bingo. He—"

The door burst open and Val stepped through, face white with rage. Carla turned, paling. "Val! Rick and I were just—"

"Don't make it worse, Detective Chapman. I'll speak with you about this in a moment."

"Val, I—"

"Excuse us, please." His tone made it clear that she was in big trouble and that she had better follow orders.

Rick stepped forward. "Don't take this out on her, Val. It's my fault."

"How noble." His tone dripped sarcasm. "But Carla knows what her responsibilities are, who her loyalties belong to. Or rather, she should." He turned his furious gaze on her. "Don't you, Detective?"

She nodded, expression devastated. "I'll be in my office."

"Good idea." When the door snapped shut behind her, Val swung to face Rick. "Are you out of your fucking mind? Do you respect me so little? Do you have so little concern for your former partner that you'd risk her career to further your ill-conceived agenda?"

"I don't have an agenda, Val. I'm trying to help."

"You arrogant prick. I don't need your help."

"I didn't mean that the way it sounded."

"Bullshit. You just want to prove you're a better cop than me."

Rick made a sound of shock at his friend's words, at the venom behind them. "That's not true."

"Then why are you sneaking around, trying to pry information out of a partner you gave up on years ago."

"I didn't give up on Carla. And I didn't give up on you or this department. I did what I had to, for me."

"I don't call hiding from life doing anything, Rick. You gave up and took the coward's way."

Rick saw red. He counted to ten before he spoke. "You were never married, Val. You never had a kid. Don't you dare call me a coward when you don't have a clue the kind of pain I suffered."

"I want you out of here, Rick. Don't test our friendship again."

"I'm afraid Pastor Tim's dirty, Val. I've uncovered some information—"

"This is my investigation. You're not a cop anymore. Stay the fuck away from my detectives."

Rick took a step toward him, realization dawning. "It's you, isn't it, Val?" He pointed at his friend. "You're the one. I can't believe I didn't see it before now."

Val knocked his hand away. "What the hell are you talking about? I'm the one what?"

"Who's so desperate to be right. To be the one to crack this case, find the killer and be the big hero."

"For God's sake—"

"You're so desperate to prove *you're* the better cop that you're even willing to overlook the truth."

They had played out this scenario time and again over the years. The stakes had changed but not the underlying motivation that drove them. Why, Rick wondered, hadn't he seen the competitive nature of their relationship before? They had competed over everything, even girls. *The* girl, actually. Jill.

"Tim's a friend, Rick. A local hero, for God's sake. A man of faith."

"Does that exclude him from suspicion?"

"Of course not. But at this point, the evidence doesn't support—"

"He and Taft attended Florida State together. One of Taft's victims was a Dolphins' cheerleader."

Val froze. "Where did you learn that?"

"I still have some friends in law enforcement, Val. Friends who don't see me as a threat. Or as a rival."

Val let out a sharp breath. "Shit, man, I don't see you as either. You're my friend. But I've got a job to do. I've got responsibilities that have nothing to do with our friendship."

"Answer me this, Val. How did Stephen, a man with the mind of a six-year-old, a man who's never been off this island, learn Gavin Taft's killing style? The similarities are not a coincidence, we both know it."

Val looked toward the closed door, as if making certain they were alone. He motioned to the chairs and table. "Sit down."

"You first."

Val pulled out one of the outdoor chairs and sat. Rick followed his lead, then waited.

"Children are easily influenced by those around them. They imitate what they see, especially when the behavior comes from someone they admire."

"And your point is?"

"We don't think Stephen's the killer. We think he's a witness. Maybe an accomplice. We think what Carla and Tim walked in on was Stephen imitating what he'd seen done. Probably to Tara. Maybe Rachel Howard as well. Think about it, Rick. How many kids play with matches and get burned? How many kids play with their old man's hunting rifle or pistol and end up blowing a hole in their head?"

Rick stiffened slightly. The image was too close to home. "What about Rachel Howard's Bible?"

"He could have lifted it from the scene. Or the parsonage. Or she could have lent it to him before she was killed. Or she might not be dead at all."

"Considering the climbing body count, I find that unlikely."

"But possible. She hasn't turned up yet."

"And you believe Mark Morgan's your man."

"Morgan ran from the scene of a murder. We found blood-soaked clothes in his rented room. The blood type matched Tara Mancuso's... We should have DNA analysis soon."

"Anything else?"

"Yeah, actually. She was holding a scrap of paper in her hand when she died. Want to guess what was written on that paper?" When Rick didn't reply, he went on. "The Hideaway's phone number. What do you think that might mean?"

Rick knew the conclusion Val had drawn. "I told you, Mark and Tara were running away together. Given that scenario, it makes sense that she would have his work num—"

"Do you know where Mark Morgan is?"

"No, I don't."

Val snorted with disgust. "And I suppose you haven't talked with him either."

"I haven't, not since the night Tara died."

Val narrowed his eyes. "But Liz Ames has, hasn't she?"

"Yes."

"Dammit!" Val brought his palm down hard on the table and jumped to his feet. "Aiding and abetting, Rick! Harboring a murder suspect! Jesus, what's wrong with you!"

"She didn't tell me until he'd gone. Yesterday, after your visit, he disappeared."

"After my visit? Convenient."

"She believes the Horned Flower has him."

He made a sound of disbelief. "Liz Ames isn't firing on all cylinders, Rick. She has you so tied up in knots—"

"That's bullshit, Val. This isn't about her."

"It's all about her. You're every action in the past few days has been motivated by a vulnerable woman who needs your protection."

"What's that supposed to mean?"

"You know damn well what it means. She even looks a little like Jill."

For one full minute Rick stared up at the other man, his world spinning. He couldn't catch his breath. Couldn't focus. It was true, he realized. Jill and Liz shared certain physical characteristics. Their coloring. Their high cheekbones and narrow, oval-shaped faces.

"Think about it, my friend. Think about why you were sucked so easily into her conspiracy theory? Because she needed you. Poor vulnerable Liz. You had to save her. The way you couldn't save Jill—"

"Shut up, Val." He balled his hands into fists and launched to his feet. "Shut the hell up!"

"If Rachel Howard had uncovered a cult on the island, one that was endangering the teenagers in her flock, wouldn't she have come to the police for help? Wouldn't she have done it as soon as possible? And how did Liz hear of this supposed cult? From Mark Morgan, suspected murderer. Everything she's told you is unsubstantiated, Rick. Her word and no one else's. No witnesses."

He lowered his voice. "You were a cop, Rick. A damn good one. Does any of this make any sense to you?"

Rick couldn't find his voice. Val made a sound of pity. "You haven't been right since Sam died. Get some help, buddy. Please, before you're in so deep you can't crawl out."

CHAPTER 47

Wednesday, November 21
10:30 a.m.

Liz entered St. Catherine's Nursing Home and headed straight to the information desk. She noticed few of the residents about today; the TV in the community area was off, the game tables empty. Even the rotund Rascal was nowhere to be seen.

"Good morning," she greeted the receptionist. "It's quiet around here today."

The woman returned Liz's smile, hers weary. "We're in lockdown mode because of the tropical storm. With the residents safe in their rooms, we can focus our attention on getting everyone ready to move, should the storm upgrade and an evacuation be ordered. If we wait too long, we're stuck."

Liz glanced at the community area's wall of windows. Maintenance workers were in the process of boarding them over. The whole thing felt slightly surreal. Although she knew a powerful storm threatened, the sky remained a perfect, cloudless blue. She recalled Father Paul's story about the hurricane of 1846, about the devastation it had wrought. No wonder there had been so many storm naysayers. The sky looked so pretty. The air felt so sweet.

"It must be difficult to evacuate a place like this."

"Difficult? Try a nightmare." She leaned toward Liz. "When a hurricane comes this late, it's most likely a whopper. And trust me, I have no plans on being a sitting duck here on Key West. And certainly not with a bunch of geriatrics."

"What are they saying?"

"It's moving fast, which is good news. The longer it churns through the warm waters, the stronger it becomes. The bad news is, we'll start seeing weather pretty quickly. The outer storm bands should reach us by midafternoon." She glanced at her watch, then smiled again, this time sheepishly. "I'm sorry, storms addle me. Are you here to see someone?"

"Father Paul. Is he up?"

"Up but agitated today. It may be the approaching storm. The change in the barometric pressure sometimes disturbs the elderly patients. You remember which room is his?"

Liz did, and after she signed in, Liz started down the C-wing hall. Most of the doors were open. She saw that the majority of the residents hovered nervously inside, some making themselves busy, others just staring into space. How frightening the threat of the storm must be to them, Liz thought. How vulnerable they must feel.

Liz reached the old priest's room and stopped in his doorway. Same as the last time she had visited, he sat facing the window, Bible in his lap, rosary beads in his hands. She tapped on the casing. "Father Paul?"

He turned. She saw by his expression that he didn't remember her. "It's Liz Ames, Father. I visited you once before." Still nothing. She took a step inside the door. "You told me the story of how the Blessed Virgin appeared to children in the garden of Paradise Christian Church."

A flicker of recognition moved across his features and he waved her into the room. "A storm's coming." He worked the rosary beads in his lap, his movements jerky.

"The staff seems to have everything under control," she murmured, crossing to the bed and sitting on the edge, facing him. "There's no need to be frightened."

"Indeed. It's in the Lord's hands. He provides for the faithful."

"Yes, He does." She cleared her throat. "I came here today, Father, because I need to ask you a question."

"Are you from the church?"

"No, Father. I'm just a friend." She opened her handbag and took out her sister's journal page, the one with the drawings of the horned flower. "Father, have you ever seen this image before?"

He took it from her. He stared at it, horror creeping into his eyes. The paper slipped from his fingers. "The battle for paradise has begun." He crossed himself; she saw that he trembled. "The Evil One and his warriors have come."

"What do you mean? Who's come?"

He met her eyes, his glassy and bright. "You know, child. The angel of light. Lucifer, the fallen one."

Satan. His worshipers.

She had been right.

A chill washed over her. She bent and retrieved the journal page, hands shaking. "You know these people?" she asked. "This group?"

He shook his head. "I know it as one of Satan's signs. Like the horned goat and inverted cross. A blasphemy. And where it resides, so does he."

"What do I do, Father?"

"Run, my child, you are in great danger. He is a soul collector. A defiler of angels and God's children alike."

She swallowed hard. "I can't do that, Father. They stole my sister from me and I…I have to defeat them."

He slowly shook his head, eyes growing bright with tears. She reached out and caught his hands. "Help me, Father. I don't know what to do."

His cheeks grew pink, sweat beaded his upper lip. "Lucifer was God's angel of light. He was our Lord's most perfect creation. But Lucifer came to believe he was more beautiful, more perfect than God."

The priest curled his fingers tightly around hers. "So God expelled him and all the angels he had coerced to his side from heaven. He sent them to the Valley of Gehenna, a place he created for them at the center of the earth."

The Valley of Gehenna. Hell. The fiery pit. The place she had feared so often during her childhood.

The devil had been real to her back then. A beast with red flesh, horns and a forked tail. Her fear of him had motivated her to behave, to pray, to *believe*.

When had she left that behind? When had Satan and the fires of hell become a religious myth to her? Had her faith in God disappeared at the same time? Or had one influenced the other?

She believed now. In heaven. And hell. The forces that drove them both.

"I'm frightened, Father."

"That's good," he murmured, inclining his head. "Never doubt, my child, he is the snake. Slick and charming. Beautiful. Ask the Lord to protect you from his evil tricks. His voracious appetite. Do not allow him to feed upon your soul, for each soul he devours makes him stronger."

"How do I fight them?" she begged, voice shaking. "What do I do?"

"Arm yourself with the Holy Spirit. For only a true messenger of God can fight the Dragon. Only the one who is the purest of heart, the one with absolute faith in Jesus Christ, our Lord and Savior."

CHAPTER 48

Wednesday, November 21
10:45 a.m.

After that, Father Paul slipped out of lucidity. He started to ramble—as near as she could tell, about events from his childhood. Soon, fatigued, he began to nod off.

Liz prepared to go. "It was nice talking with you today, Father Paul." She bent and squeezed his hand. "The Lord be with you."

He smiled and returned the pressure of her hand. "You, too, my child. May He bless and protect you."

A lump in her throat, she left his room and started down the hall, thoughts whirling with the things he had said, struggling to put his words into perspective.

"The battle for paradise has begun. The Evil One and his warriors have come."

She shuddered and rubbed her arms. How could one

take those words any way but at face value? He had recognized the horned flower immediately. She had been
right, it was a satanic image. It had frightened the old
priest. She had seen the fear in his eyes—and the resignation. As if he had known this was coming, as if he
had been waiting.

And as if he accepted that there was nothing he could
do to stop it.

Nothing but pray.

"Is everything all right?"

Liz looked up, startled. The receptionist was looking at her, her expression strange. "I'm sorry, did you
say something?"

"You looked upset. Is Father Paul all right?"

"Yes, fine," Liz said quickly. "He's sleeping now."

"His ramblings didn't upset you, did they?"

From the corner of her eye, Liz thought she saw one
of the male aides looking her way. She glanced over in
time to see him pivot and walk the other way.

Frowning, Liz turned back to the receptionist. "No,
he didn't upset me." She forced a casual smile. "Any
news of the storm?"

"Nothing new. Keep your fingers crossed."

Liz thanked the woman and left St. Catherine's. She
had walked to the nursing home, located on Whitehead
Street, only a handful of blocks from her office. She
took a left, heading toward Old Town.

*"Only a true messenger of God can fight the Dragon.
Only the one who is the purest of heart, the one with
absolute faith in Jesus Christ our Lord and Savior."*

She warned herself not to take his words too literally.
No doubt Father Paul had been speaking allegorically.
He was an old man. One steeped in the superstitions of
the Catholic church. Not the present-day Catholic faith,

but that of eighty years ago, one shrouded in mystery, superstition and ritual.

But he had recognized the horned-flower image as demonic. That meant she had been right. And that they were out there, who knew how many of them. A handful. Or many. Liz glanced quickly behind her, searching faces in the crowd. She would have no way of knowing who they were, but they would be watching her. Maybe following her now. Just like Rachel had said.

Liz's skin crawled at the thought; her heart began to drum. She glanced over her shoulder once more. The sidewalk behind her teemed with people. No one seemed to be paying her any undue attention.

Still, the hair on the back of her neck prickled. With a quick glance to the left, then right, she ducked across the street. Safely on the other side, she moved forward quickly, daring another quick glance over her shoulder.

Nothing. No one.

Just her imagination.

She laughed self-consciously and turned onto Duval Street. The sidewalk went from crowded to congested. She made her way through the throngs of tourists, stopping occasionally for groups emerging from stores.

A group with two strollers and a half-dozen other kids between the ages of six and fourteen, all of them whining about the heat and wanting ice cream, stepped into her path. Liz stopped and glanced to her left, into a storefront window. As she did, she met the eyes of a young man standing behind her to her right.

He smiled slightly and she caught her breath. She recognized him. From her first day on Key West. The Rainbow Nation kid who had looked at her with such malevolence.

He had been behind her two blocks ago.

At the realization she caught her breath. He made a move toward her; she darted forward, crashing through the stalled family, earning the father's shout of disapproval. She called out an apology and ran as best she could while having to dodge slow-moving shoppers.

She reached Paradise Christian Church and stopped, breathing hard. She glanced to her left. *Bikinis & Things. Heather would help her.*

Liz shot across the street. And found the shop closed, the door locked. She glanced at her watch, confused. Why was Heather's store closed now, midmorning on a weekday?

Frowning, she peered into the front window. Not even a security light burned inside. "Heather!" she called, rapping on the door. "It's Liz. Are you in there?"

"She's gone."

Liz jumped and whirled around, hand to her throat. A small man in a green apron stood slightly behind her.

"Sorry I scared you." He motioned to the shop next door. "I just sneaked out for a smoke."

She struggled to find her voice. "What do you mean she's gone?"

"Missing."

The word hit her with the force of an icy wave. "I don't understand. Heather's missing?"

"Didn't show up to open the shop two days ago. Still hasn't." He nodded at a husband and wife who stopped to peer into his shop window, then turned back to her. "I called her place, got no answer so I went by."

"And?"

"Closed up tight as a drum. Just like the shop. It's weird."

Liz brought a hand to her mouth. *Her sister. Naomi Pearson. Now Heather.*

She looked at the man. "Heather told me she thought a man had been following her."

"No kidding? Come to think about it, she was acting strange lately. Jumpy, you know?" He glanced nervously toward his shop. "I've got to go."

"Wait! Did you call the police?"

"You bet I did. I even talked to the big cheese, that Lieutenant Lopez. He did *nothing.* Said she had probably decided to take a trip." The man's voice dripped sarcasm. "And not even tell her employees or make arrangements for the shop to be open? Right."

Liz watched him walk away. The day seemed to close in on her. She couldn't find her breath; she began to shake. She didn't know what to do. Should she go to the police? To Rick?

She pivoted and came face-to-face with the man who had been following her. His bright blue eyes seemed to burn into hers. He grabbed her arm.

"Leave Key West," he murmured, voice low, threatening. "If you don't, you'll end up like your sister."

He tightened his grip. "Got that? Just like your sister."

He released her arm, turned and was swallowed by the crowd. For a moment, Liz stared after him, frozen. Then with a cry, she ran.

The Hideaway was located one block up on the other side of the street. She pushed through the crowds, darting across the street, earning the blare of several horns. She prayed Rick was there.

He was. He stood beside a table of customers who had to be tourists. They were discussing the storm and fell silent as she approached.

"Liz?" He moved his gaze over her, his concern growing. "What's wrong?"

"I have to talk to you," she managed to say. "It's urgent."

He excused himself from the group and led her to the back of the bar. "What's wrong?" he repeated.

She couldn't find her voice. She began to tremble, her teeth to chatter.

"My God, Liz." He laid his hands on her shoulders. "What's happened?"

For a long moment, she simply held him. Finally, she lifted her face to his. "I'm so frightened. They...they took Heather."

"Heather?"

"My friend. Rachel's friend...Heather Ferguson. She told me someone had been following her. She was frightened—"

A look of frustration tightened his features. "I'm alone here today, Liz." He glanced toward the bar and the customers looking their way, clearly eavesdropping. "Just spit it out, okay. As concisely and calmly as you can."

So she did. Quickly, she told him how she and Heather had met, what she had learned from the woman and about her visit three days ago. "She told me someone had been following her. She was frightened. Now she's missing. The shopkeeper next to Bikinis & Things said she hasn't opened her shop in two days."

"Maybe she went out of town?"

Liz drew in a shaky breath. "She would have made arrangements for the shop. She would have told her employees what was going on."

"But she didn't?"

"No." Her throat constricted with tears. "They warned me, Rick. Said I would end up like...like Rachel...if I didn't leave Key West right away."

"Who said that? When?"

"This young guy. On the way here…one of those Rainbow Nation kids. He grabbed my arm and told me if I didn't leave the island I would end up like Rachel."

He frowned as if confused. "You're saying this guy you'd never seen before stopped you and threatened you?"

"Yes…no, I'd seen him before. My first day on the island. He was standing outside my storefront window and he looked at me with such malevolence that I—"

"Stop it, Liz," he hissed. "This is too much. You're talking crazy."

"It sounds crazy, but it's not. Please, keep an open mind." She drew a deep breath. "I think the police might be in on it."

"What?"

"The man, the other shopkeeper, he went to Val about Heather. He did nothing, Rick. Explained Heather's disappearance away…just the way he did Rachel's and Naomi's."

Rick took a step back from her, expression closed. She grabbed his hands. "You've got to believe me."

"Valentine Lopez is my oldest friend."

"I know," she whispered, hurting for him. "I'm sorry."

"No, I'm the one who's sorry." He glanced past her, toward the bar and its patrons. When he met her eyes once more, the anger in his took her breath. "You're accusing my best friend of murder. Of conspiracy. Of satanism. What else? Stealing little old ladies' social security checks?"

"Just hear me out." She tightened her grip on his hands. "Please, Rick."

"Can't do it." He eased his hands from hers. "I let

myself be drawn into your drama. I used my friends and contacts in an unethical fashion. No more, Liz."

Realization dawned. It hit her with the force of a blow. "You talked to Val, didn't you? He poisoned your mind against me."

Rick didn't reply and tears flooded her eyes. "You have to believe me. Please, I have no one else."

He brought a hand to her cheek. "I want to," he murmured, voice thick. "Believe me, my every instinct shouts for me to hold you close and protect you from all the bad guys, real or imagined."

"They're not imagined," she whispered. "The Horned Flower exists."

He dropped his hand. "You don't have any real proof, Liz. You don't have one person to back up any of your accusations."

"The shopkeeper, he'll tell you Heather's missing—"

"Did she tell him or anyone else that she was being followed? Anyone but you, that is?"

"I don't know." With a growing sense of panic, she realized he was right. "I mean, I don't think so, but—"

"Did she go to the police?"

"I urged her to, but—"

"But she didn't? Just like your sister didn't go to the police even though teenagers in her flock were in danger from this Horned Flower group?"

It sounded implausible—crazy—even to her own ears. But it wasn't. "Look at the evidence, it's real."

"What evidence? A couple drawings that supposedly came from your sister's journal. A tattoo on Tara's thigh? The coincidence of two men from Florida attending the same state university. The word of a young man who's wanted in connection with a murder? A young man no one's seen since that murder—except you, of course."

He looked away a moment, then back at her. "You could have manufactured all of it. The envelope, the threats, even the dead rat."

"And the dead women, Rick?" she demanded, quivering with the force of her emotions. "Could I have manufactured them as well?"

"No, unfortunately." He let out a heavy-sounding breath. "I understand you're hurting. That you want to make sense of what happened to your sister, that you—"

"I'll never make sense of it," she corrected, tone bitter. "I just want to *know* what happened to her. Is that so wrong?"

"Only if you've used these murders to support that agenda."

Liz couldn't believe what she was hearing. Or how much it hurt. "Is that what you think I've done?"

He didn't reply; she took a step away, devastated. "Why can't you see? Who knows how many people are a part of this? And if the Horned Flower is operating with the full support of the police—"

"Stop it! This has gone too far! You're accusing upstanding citizens of murder and moral corruption. My oldest friend. A popular preacher. Who else? The mayor? The elementary-school principal?"

"Why not?" she retorted, a hairbreadth from falling apart. "Anyone could be involved."

He took another step back, expression closed. "You're the outsider here. You're the one who's crazy, not everybody else."

She brought a hand to her mouth. "How can you say that? After all we've shared?"

"Did we share anything, Liz?" he asked tightly.

"I'd begun to believe that maybe…that sometimes life offered up second chances. But now I wonder, was I simply a pawn in your desperate game?"

She moaned as if in pain. She had never felt more alone, more abandoned.

"It's over, Liz," he said softly. "I can't be a party to your delusions anymore."

CHAPTER 49

Wednesday, November 21
12:25 p.m.

Carla sat at her desk, struggling to keep her thoughts from showing. She glanced at her watch, noted that Val's secretary, Becky, would be leaving for lunch any moment. She would walk by Carla's door, call good-bye then stop and ask if Carla wanted her to pick her up anything. Same as she did every day.

What made today different was what Carla planned to do while the woman was gone.

Apprehension tightened her chest. She couldn't believe what she was thinking. She wanted to prove her suspicions wrong.

Val wasn't dirty. He wasn't involved with these women's deaths—or with this Horned Flower group Rick had told her about.

Carla lowered her eyes to the file lying open on the desk in front of her. Tara Mancuso's file. Below it lay Rachel Howard's. Below that Naomi Pearson's. Inconsistencies jumped out at her. Little ones she had missed before. Things like dates and times. Things that could be nothing.

Or something big.

She had eavesdropped on Val and Rick's conversation that morning. Something Val said had jumped out at her, bold as a street whore.

"If Rachel Howard had uncovered a cult on the island, one that was endangering the teenagers in her flock, wouldn't she have come to the police for help?"

Carla brought a hand to her temple, to the headache that pounded there. She was thinking Rachel Howard had called the police. Shortly before she had gone missing. Carla closed her eyes, trying to recall. She had been walking by Val's office; he had been on the phone. She had paused to speak to him and he had said the woman's name as he hung up.

"I'll look into it, Pastor Howard. Thanks for calling."

Why hadn't she recalled that snippet before? she wondered. The day after Tara's murder, Liz Ames had come to see Val. Carla had been there; Val had told Liz that he had never spoken to her sister. Why hadn't alarm bells sounded then?

In the past hours she had made a number of excuses for herself. That the memory had been so fleeting, so inconsequential. That she'd had no reason to suspect her superior of any kind of impropriety. That even now she was uncertain if the memory was accurate—or one conjured by exhaustion and frustration.

She was done making excuses. The truth was, Rick never would have forgotten such a detail, inconsistencies never would have escaped him. He would have involved himself so thoroughly in the investigation that inconsistencies, whether sloppy mistakes or deliberate falsification, never would have happened. Period.

Carla turned her attention to the files on her desk once more. Val had claimed to Rick that morning that Tara had been clasping a piece of paper in her hand, the Hideaway's number scrawled on it. It hadn't been paper at all, but a scrap of white fabric, most probably torn from Tara's attacker's shirt. Why had Val lied to Rick? About that and about Pastor Howard's call?

To influence him into discrediting Liz Ames. To convince him to back off.

Why?

Because Rick had been a damn good cop. Because he had feared Rick would figure out the truth.

Val was dirty.

Carla shook her head. She wasn't going to believe it, not without proof.

"I'm out of here, Carla," Becky called from the hallway outside her office. "You want me to pick you up anything?"

Carla looked up, praying she didn't look as guilty as she felt. "No thanks. I'll catch a bite later."

"Be sure to do it before Lieutenant Blood gets back." Becky made a face. "If you don't, you won't get lunch. He was on a tear this morning."

"Thanks for the tip." Carla forced a smile. "By the way, when is Val due back?"

"He thought his meeting with the chief would go through lunch. I figure I'll see him sometime after one."

Carla thanked her but the words stuck in her throat. The secretary looked at her strangely. "I think I'm coming down with a cold," Carla explained, clearing her throat.

"I have a bottle of echinacea in my top right desk drawer. Help yourself. It really works."

"I'll do that, thanks." Carla smiled and the other woman walked off. She lowered her gaze to her wrist, counting as the second hand of her watch ticked out one minute, then two, then three.

She stood and crossed to her office door. She stood there a full minute, listening for Becky's distinctive voice, wanting to be absolutely certain the woman had left the second floor.

Confident that she had, she made her way to Becky's office, a small cluttered area located to the right of Val's. In actuality, Becky worked for all the detectives; she answered the phone, directed calls and ran interference between the detectives and everybody—including witnesses, victims' families and the chief himself.

But Val was her boss; he had hired her, he could fire her. His work always came first.

Val required Becky to keep all the carbon copies from her old message pads for six months. Unless Pastor Howard had reached Val directly, which certainly could have happened, Becky would have taken a message. It was a fifty-fifty shot, but one worth taking.

The secretary kept them in the file cabinet in the corner. Bottom drawer. Carla crossed to the cabinet, squatted in front of it and pulled open the drawer. The empty pads were located in back, a stack of five of them. She choose the least recent one and began thumbing through it.

Nothing. She retrieved the next pad. And hit pay dirt.

A message to call Pastor Rachel Howard from Paradise Christian Church. Wednesday, July 11. Two days before she was discovered missing.

What that meant hit her with the force of a heavyweight's best punch.

"What are you doing, Carla?"

She jerked her head around. Becky stood in her office doorway, face screwed into a suspicious scowl. Carla forced a laugh. It sounded choked, even to her own ears. "After you left, I got to thinking about something—" She ripped the carbon copy from the pad, stood and carried it to the secretary. "This call from Rachel Howard, did Val get it?"

The woman's cheeks flooded with color. "Val gets all his messages."

Carla hurried to smooth her ruffled feathers. "That's what I thought, of course."

"Besides," Becky said, tapping the pad, "the original's gone. That means I put it on Val's desk."

"Did he return this call?"

The woman stiffened. "I imagine he did. Lieutenant Lopez is very thorough."

"Yes, he is." Carla thought of Rick, of how he would take what she was about to show him, and sadness crept over her. Everyone would be hurt by this thing—the department, Rick, her. "Thanks, Becky."

She started out of the office. The secretary stopped her. "Your voice, Carla. It seems suddenly better."

She looked over her shoulder at the other woman. "It is. Thanks for your concern."

CHAPTER 50

Wednesday, November 21
1:40 p.m.

Rick drew the ancient Jeep Wrangler to a stop in front of Carla's South Street cottage. She had called him on his cell phone a half hour ago. She needed to see him right away, she'd said. It was about the disappearance of Pastor Howard.

He cut the engine but didn't move to get out of the vehicle. He leaned his head against the rest and stared blankly up at the Jeep's canvas top, thinking of Liz. As he had watched her walk away, his every instinct had shouted to call her back. The feeling that he had done the wrong thing had grown in the hours that had passed, as had his worry over her safety.

He couldn't trust his instincts, not when it came to Liz. He saw that now. Until Val had pointed it out, he hadn't consciously acknowledged Jill's and Liz's physical similarities. Just as he hadn't seen what he had been doing—trying to save her, the way he had not been able to save Jill.

The truth of that left him feeling raw. And foolish.

He glanced at Carla's house and saw her at the window. He lifted a hand in greeting, pulled the keys from the ignition, climbed out of the Jeep and made his way up the walk.

He stepped onto the porch. It sagged slightly and the gray deck paint was peeling. In contrast, the hanging ferns and pots of multicolored flowers all but shouted tender-loving care.

Carla had always loved plants and for the longest time had tried to keep several in her cluttered, window-less office. It had driven Val nuts. Real cops, he had complained, didn't keep pansies and petunias on their desks.

Carla appeared at her door. "Hi." She smiled nervously and pushed the screen door open.

After he entered, she peered outside as if assessing if they were being watched, then closed and locked the door. He cocked an eyebrow. "What was that all about?"

"You'll understand in a moment. Come on, I've got something to show you."

She led him into her small kitchen. She went to her purse and retrieved a slip of pink paper from its side pocket. She held it out. "Take a look at this."

He closed the distance between them and took it from her. It was a carbon copy from a message pad, the kind found in most offices.

He read it then lifted his gaze to hers.

"Rachel Howard did call Val. She called him two days before she was reported missing."

Rick pulled out one of her kitchen chairs and sat, feeling as if the wind had been knocked out of him.

"This morning, I eavesdropped on you and Val. And I…remembered. He was in his office, on the phone, he said her name."

"Are you certain? Maybe he didn't get—"

"He did. I spoke to Becky about it."

"Shit." He shook his head, struggling to come to grips with this piece of information. The ramifications of it. "This doesn't mean anything. She could have called him about a…donation. About a church function or—"

"There's more, Rick," she said gently. "There was no scrap of paper with the Hideaway's phone number scrawled on it. Tara had fabric in her hand. Shirt fabric. White."

Rick thought back to that night, what he'd seen. It could have been fabric. It'd been dark, he had assumed it had been paper.

"Mark had on a light-blue T-shirt that night."

"How do you—"

"I saw it at his place. The blood looked purplish on the blue. I'm embarrassed to say I never thought about it until now. Even though that fabric was most probably torn from her attacker's shirt."

Rick felt ill. *Not Val. His best, his oldest friend. The person who had seen him through the darkest days of his life.* He felt as if he were being ripped apart.

And he thought of Liz, the way he had torn into her for suggesting Val might be dirty.

"Why, Carla?" He lifted his gaze to hers. "Why would he do this?"

"I don't know." She turned and crossed to the window behind the sink and stared out at her lush, overgrown backyard. She let out a long, disappointed-sounding breath. "I made so many mistakes. I always let him lead. Like a little puppy dog, whatever he asked of me, I did. Whatever he said, I believed."

She swung and faced him. "I never questioned, Rick." Her voice trembled. "A good cop questions everything."

"Don't be so hard on yourself. He was your boss, a lieutenant and highly thought of in the department. Who would have thought twice about—"

"You would have," she said simply, interrupting him. "I'm going to see this thing through, then I'm getting out, Rick. This isn't the job for me. It isn't the place."

He understood. But he didn't want her to go. "You're a good cop, Carla. You've turned into a good cop."

A small smile touched her mouth. "Thanks, but I know better." He started to protest. She cut him off. "I'm not you, Rick. Never will be. The time's come for me to stop kidding myself. This isn't my calling. I'll never be better than adequate, not here. Not in police work."

"You don't have to leave Key West. There are other opportunities here. You could—"

"Waitress? Work in a hotel or clothing boutique? I don't think so." Her expression became wistful. "I'm a steel mill-town girl, Rick. I don't belong in paradise."

"There's nothing I can say to change your mind, is there?"

She met his eyes, hers bright with longing. "There's one thing, Rick. Say that and I'll stay."

Tell her there was a chance for them. That he might love her.

"I can't tell you that, Carla. I'm sorry, I wish I could." He meant it. And he regretted having hurt her.

"You're in love with her, aren't you? With Liz Ames?"

He thought of Liz and his chest tightened. His instincts had been right. About everything but Val.

"I don't know. I was beginning to think there might be something—"

Dear God, he had sent her out there alone. Unprotected.

As if reading his thoughts, Carla touched his arm. "She'll be okay."

"If he hurts a hair on her head," he said fiercely, "I'll kill him, I swear I will."

"So what do we do now?" she asked, dragging his thoughts back to the issue at hand.

Rick pursed his lips. "We need more information. We need something substantive we can take to the chief."

"I'll get it. As a member of his team, I have access to things you don't. His files, desk, computer."

"That'll put you in harm's way. I can't allow that."

"It's not up to you though, is it?"

It wasn't, he knew. He swore. "Carla—"

"I told you, I'm seeing this through. Consider it my swan song." She smiled, the curving of her lips determined. "Someday I'll be telling my kids about the big case I helped crack."

He hesitated, then acquiesced—not because he approved of her solution but because he didn't see another. "Let's look at what we have. Two women dead, another missing. Rumors of a strange cult involved with drugs and teenage sex."

"Let's not forget one prominent banker's suicide. A banker who was up to his ass in bogus bank loans."

"As was one of the victims."

Rick met Carla's eyes. "Means and opportunity aren't

a problem. We need a motive. Why does one of Key West's most respected citizens, a man next in line for the chief of police's job, become a killer?"

"Is he a killer? Or is he just in bed with one?"

"Motive?"

She ticked them off on her fingers. "Love. Hate. Greed. The holy trinity of murder. Take your pick."

"Dammit!" Rick jumped to his feet, angry, itching for a fight. "I can't believe Val would do this! This is so fucked up."

"True, but that doesn't change the facts, now, does it?"

"Go to hell, Carla," he said, turning his fury on her. "Just go straight to hell."

She crossed to him and laid a hand gently on his arm. "I'm sorry," she murmured. "I know he's like a brother to you."

His fury evaporated, replaced by resignation—and determination. "How much we get done and how fast depends on what this storm decides to do. We need to move fast, if Becky hasn't told Val about your finding the message from Pastor Howard yet, she will soon. You need to—"

Carla's beeper sounded. She checked the display. "It's headquarters."

He nodded, understanding. She crossed to the wall phone and called in.

"Chapman here." She looked at Rick, eyes widening. "Another woman?"

"Where?"

Rick crossed to stand beside her.

"Big Pine Key," she repeated. "Do they have ID?" She nodded. "Keep me informed."

Carla hung up. "There's another victim. No ID yet, but she's a pretty blonde."

"Do you need to report in?"

She shook her head. "Sheriff's department is at the scene."

Rick shook his head, thoughts on his earlier conversation with Liz. "Do you know a woman named Heather Ferguson?"

Carla was silent for a moment, then nodded. "Gorgeous blonde, right? She's been in to see Val. Recently, as a matter of fact."

Rick curled his hands into fists. More proof. Son of a-bitch.

"She owns a shop on Duval," he said, jaw tight. "I'd met her at one of the Old Town merchants' meetings. Turns out she was a friend of Rachel Howard's. Liz went to see her earlier today and learned from the guy next door that she'd been missing a couple days. Apparently he went to Val, who did nothing."

"Same as he did when Rachel Howard and Naomi Pearson turned up missing." Carla clasped her hands together. "The body count's climbing too fast. Val, or whoever he's covering for, is out of control. It's like they're on a rampage."

The way Taft had been, Rick realized, there at the end, right before law enforcement had zeroed in on him. That was often the case with serial murderers. Their killing career began slowly, first through fantasizing about the crime, sometimes for years. Then came acting on the fantasy, the first kill. The thrill derived from it could last months or even years. Then they killed again. With each subsequent murder the thrill carried them a shorter period of time.

Rick met Carla's gaze grimly. "This killer's become

like a drug addict who needs a bigger fix, more often, until the time he's not high or getting high ceases to exist."

"So you're saying that our guy's reached the stage where he's either hunting or devouring his next victim?"

"Not a pleasant description," he muttered, flipping open his cell phone. "But accurate." Rick punched in Liz's number, anxious to warn her. He got a busy signal, swore and closed the phone. "Hurricane or not, friend or not, we've got to nail him. And we've got to do it fast."

CHAPTER 51

Wednesday, November 21
2:00 p.m.

Liz sat at her kitchen table, a cup of cold coffee in front of her. From the living room came the sound of the latest storm update. At this point it looked as if it would not reach hurricane force. However, forecasters warned the key to brace for intense wind and rain with the possibility of severe thunderstorms or tornadoes. A not uncommon occurrence with this type of storm.

The outer band of Rebekah—the storm's name—had reached Key West, bringing with it the first of the rain. As the storm continued to churn its way toward Key West, the rain would become heavier, the wind more severe.

And here she sat. Brokenhearted. Crying over a man who didn't believe in her. A man who had called her crazy.

She brought the heels of her hands to her eyes. With everything going on, she hadn't allowed herself the luxury of examining her feelings for him. He had been there when she needed someone. Big, strong and rock solid. He had provided emotional support—and physical solace.

She realized now her feelings hadn't needed examining. They had been growing all on their own, on a level deeper than the frantic moment.

How could she feel more for him than a kind of grateful attachment? They hadn't even known each other two weeks. It was nuts—as crazy as he had accused her of being.

Not crazy, she thought. She saw the kind of man he was. Ethical and loyal. He possessed a keen intelligence. He felt deeply and would fight to the death for what he believed in.

He didn't believe in her.

Period. End of story. Time to move on, Liz. Time to do something.

She jumped to her feet and crossed to the window. She stared out at the dark sky and madly swaying branches. Liz swallowed hard. She couldn't shake the feeling that all this had been predestined, as Father Paul had suggested. That somehow this storm was part of something greater than that of man against nature—the ultimate battle, that of good against evil. And as with the hurricane of 1846, the sinners would be swept out to sea, the believers saved.

Stop it, Liz! She wheeled away from the window. No wonder Rick had called her crazy. No wonder he wanted her out of his life.

But she wasn't crazy. She wasn't obsessed with the Horned Flower or with proving what happened to her sister. She was caught up in it. She had rattled some cages, and now she was in trouble.

Everything she had told Rick was true.

But truth on her side didn't change the fact that no one believed her. A hysterical-sounding laugh rose from her throat. Not true. Everyone who believed ended up dead or missing.

It seemed logical to assume that she would be next.

What should she do? How could she go up against the Horned Flower alone? She didn't even own a gun—let alone know how to fire one.

Rick's desertion had drained the fight out of her. She needed his cool head. The logical way he looked at things. His strength and the comfort she gleaned from simply knowing he stood with her.

But he didn't stand with her, she reminded herself. Not anymore. So what did she do next? She felt as if she had exhausted her options. She couldn't go to the police. She had neither friends nor allies to turn to. Mark and Heather had both disappeared, victims, she feared, of the Horned Flower. She could seek help from law enforcement agencies on the mainland, but without proof, they were more likely to take her for a psychiatric evaluation then to accompany her to Key West to bust up a group of murdering satanists whose ranks included members of the local clergy and law enforcement.

There had to be *something* she could do, she thought fiercely, stopping and dragging her hands through her hair. Something besides wait for the next body to turn up or for the killer to decide it was her turn to die.

Liz dropped her hands, made a move toward the living room, then stopped, realizing she was staring at the front page of the *Island News,* partially obscured by a copy of the Sunday edition of the *Miami Herald.*

She drew her eyebrows together. The weekly was out-of-date, an edition she had picked up her first few days on the island. She had glanced at it, then tossed it in a basket she reserved for catalogs, magazines and the like.

She tilted her head.

Heather Ferguson named—

Liz crossed to the basket and removed the *Herald*. The entire headline jumped out at her.

Heather Ferguson named Key West Businesswoman of the Year.

Liz lifted the folded paper and opened it. Heather smiled out at her from the large photo, her diamond-studded monogram necklace sparkling at her throat. The one Liz remembered noticing the afternoon she and Heather had drinks.

Liz stared at the necklace, seeing it as if for the first time.

H.F. Heather Ferguson.

H.F. Horned Flower.

Her hands began to shake. A coincidence, she told herself. The matching initials were simply one of those weird coincidences that life occasionally offered up. Any number of people on Key West could have the same.

It couldn't be Heather. Heather was her friend. She had been Rachel's friend. Someone had been follow-ing her.

Or so she had said. Liz had no proof of either of those. Just as she had no proof Heather had actually gone missing.

Perhaps she had gone into hiding, instead.

Feeling ill, Liz whirled around and crossed to the sink. She laid the weekly on the counter, turned on the cold water, bent and splashed her face. She twisted the faucet off and lifted her head, the cold water running down her neck and under the collar of her shirt.

Rick was right about her, she thought, glaring at her own reflection in the window above the sink. Who hadn't she accused of being part of this conspiracy of evil? A pastor? A ranking police detective? Now a woman who had never been anything but nice to her, one who may have become a victim.

Liz snatched a paper towel from the roll hanging beside the sink. She dried her face and tossed the towel in the trash.

Her anger faded. She hadn't imagined her sister's disappearance or the two murdered women. She hadn't conjured up Mark's experience with the Horned Flower, her sister's drawings or the rat left in her kitchen.

Heather probably wasn't the one. But at this point, she would follow any lead, even a flimsy one. Heather was beautiful and charismatic. Her shop afforded her access to a great number of teenagers. She had known at least one of the victims.

Liz began to pace once more, working to remember the things Heather had told her about herself and her past. Very little, Liz realized. She had grown up in Miami, had given college a try and dropped out in favor of a stab at modeling. That had gone nowhere and she had drifted into retailing. Three or four years back, Heather had opened her own store here on Key West.

Liz frowned. Had Heather mentioned family? Siblings? Father or mother—

Liz snapped her fingers, remembering. Her mother. It had been a passing mention. When Heather had been talking about her abortive attempt at modeling. She had inherited her mother's bone structure, she'd said.

Which the camera flattened. Liz had then asked about the woman, if she was still alive and where she lived. Heather had replied that she was indeed alive and that she lived on Islamorada.

Liz ran to the drawer where she kept the phone book, one with listings for the entire keys. She yanked it out, flipped it open to the section for Islamorada, praying the woman was listed. She found two Fergusons—a J. A. and a Martha.

Liz dialed J. A. Ferguson first. A young woman answered. She sounded harried and Liz heard an infant crying. Though certain this was not Heather's mother's number, she asked anyway. A moment later, she dialed Martha Ferguson.

"Hi, is this Mrs. Ferguson?"

"It is," the woman replied, tone reticent. "I'm not buying anything, if that's what you're—"

"I'm not. Actually, I'm looking for Heather Ferguson's mother. Would that be—"

The phone went dead. "Hello?" she said.

The woman had hung up on her!

Excited, Liz dialed the woman again—and got the same results. Which to her mind meant she had, indeed, located Heather's mother. But if that was true, why had she hung up on her?

Liz tried one last time. Although she let it ring for a full minute, the woman didn't pick up.

Frowning, Liz glanced at her watch. If her memory served, Islamorada was located just more than halfway between Key West and Key Largo, she would guess about a two-hour-and-forty-five-minute drive. Probably longer, considering the weather.

Liz ran to her bedroom, changed into a pair of comfortable white capri pants and slipped into her canvas deck shoes. She didn't know exactly what she wanted the woman to tell her about her daughter or how she would obtain the information, she just knew she had to do this.

She ripped the page from the phone book, grabbed her purse and umbrella and ran out into the storm.

CHAPTER 52

Wednesday, November 21
3:30 p.m.

"Is this Detective Carla Chapman?"

The voice was a man's, one she didn't recognize. "Yes," she answered. "How can I help you?"

"It's Jonathan Bell. The Sunset Key ferryboat captain. I ferried you across—"

"To Larry Bernhardt's place," she filled in, that afternoon seeming a lifetime ago now. "I remember."

"You told me to call if I remembered anything about that night, anything I'd forgotten to tell the police."

"Go on."

"That night, I ferried over a mother and her two daughters, real attractive, all of them. They said they were going to the restaurant…you know, Latitudes. But I remembered this morning that when they got off the boat they headed toward the other side of the island. Toward Bernhardt's place."

Carla digested that. "You think they were hookers?"

"No way. They looked real...fresh-scrubbed. The mother was real classy. Gorgeous."

Carla narrowed her eyes. Bernhardt's housekeeper had claimed he had liked young girls. She had found photographs of them performing sexual acts with him. Carla thought of the man's bedroom, of the mirrors placed strategically on all sides of the bed.

"How old do you think these girls were?"

He was silent a moment, as if thinking. "Fifteen, sixteen, seventeen at the most."

"The ferry's still crossing?"

"Yeah, it's a little rough 'cause of Rebekah, but we're still doing it."

Carla thanked him and hung up. Sounded to her like a quick trip out to Sunset Key was in order.

Larry Bernhardt's children had begun getting the house ready to sell. The furnishings they hadn't already taken could be sold with the house or would be auctioned. Or so the receptionist at Sunset Key Realty told Carla as she handed her the key to the property.

"I thought the investigation was complete," the woman murmured.

"You know police work," Carla replied with what she hoped was just the right note of professional boredom. "Some new little thing pops up and we have to investigate it."

"Bummer." The young woman peered out the window at the threatening sky. "You're not going to be long, are you? My boss gives the okay, and I'm out of here."

"A few minutes, fifteen or twenty, tops." She smiled again and held up the key. "I'll have it back on your desk in no time."

Minutes later, Carla let herself into Bernhardt's house. She headed directly up to his bedroom and flipped on the light.

The bedroom was empty.

With a sound of disappointment, she made her way into the room. The massive four-poster bed and matching dresser, highboy and nightstands were gone. Only the mirrors remained.

She wasn't certain what she had hoped to find, but this wasn't it. She brought her hands to her head. *Think, Carla. Think. There are answers here.*

We have one dead teenager. A girl supposedly a member of a weird sex club.

We have a dead banker, one with a fondness for teenage girls. A man who liked to watch, evidenced by the mirrors surrounding the bed and the photographs the housekeeper had found.

The night he supposedly killed himself, two teenage girls and a woman paid him a visit.

It hit her then. If Bernhardt liked the live action the mirrors provided, he would like videotapes even more. Sick self-gratification anytime, day or night. And considering his moral fiber, Bernhardt was one hundred percent capable of secretly videotaping the action taking place on his bed.

Secretly being the operative word here.

So where would the camera—or cameras—be?

Carla moved to the spot the bed had occupied. She stood quietly, listening, putting herself in Bernhardt's head. She moved her gaze over the room, imagining herself making love, wanting to watch. Now. And later.

One mirror to the right of the bed. One to the left. One at the head. Nothing on the wall at the foot of the bed. She lifted her gaze. No mirror above, just a crystal chandelier.

She frowned. No mirror above? It seemed to her, the ceiling would have provided Bernhardt with one of his best, consistently reliable views.

She narrowed her eyes, studying the chandelier, its crystal teardrops. They sparkled like diamonds. Not all of them, she realized. The bottom teardrop didn't refract the light the way the others did.

She stood on tiptoe. Once she knew what she was looking for, it was easy to find. There in the bottom crystal, a pinhole lens, no more than an eighth of an inch across. A wide angle, no doubt. Wired up the light fixture and through the ceiling.

Excited by the find, she turned to the mirrors. A guy with Bernhardt's addiction and funds wouldn't stop with one camera. No way. When the action was live, he had three views to enjoy; he would settle for no less from his video action.

She crossed to the mirror mounted where the head of the bed had been. She carefully examined the ornately carved, antiqued-gold frame inch by inch. She found what she was looking for imbedded in the top center of the frame, wired through the wall. An inspection of the two remaining mirrors revealed the same, those imbedded at bed height.

So where was the system? Carla wondered. She eased her gaze slowly over the room once more. Bernhardt had a mirror on every wall but one. The windowless wall directly across from the bed. On her previous visits it had sported a large abstract painting.

A false wall, she would bet her life on it.

She crossed to the wall and began a search for a spring or pressure release button. After nearly ten minutes, she admitted she wasn't going to find one.

Frustrated, she swung away. Her gaze landed on the doorway to the master bath. *The television in the master bathroom, mounted in the wall above the garden tub.* Of course.

She made her way there. Not just a television, she saw, but a VCR as well. She climbed into the tub and lay down, placing her head in the spot Bernhardt had most likely placed his. Sure enough, the television had been angled slightly for optimum viewing from the bath. Sick prick, she thought. Probably lay in the tub and jacked off while he watched himself committing carnal crimes with these…children. Fifteen? Sixteen. Jesus. It made her sick.

Carla stood, climbed on to the edge of the tub, flipped on the VCR and pressed eject. The machine proved empty. She ran her hand over the top and sides of the unit. Her fingers closed over not one remote, but two.

Her heartbeat quickened. One of the remotes possessed only a single button, much like a garage-door opener would.

Excited, she jumped down and hurried back to the bedroom. There, she faced the blank wall, pointed the remote and pressed the button. The corner of the wall popped free. She crossed to it and swung it the rest of the way open, revealing a two-foot-deep storage area.

Recorder. Amplifier. Video library. Hands shaking, Carla opened the recorder.

And found a tape. A tape most probably recorded the last night of Bernhardt's life.

She snatched it out, ran to the bathroom and inserted

the tape in the VCR. She rewound it, then hit play—and struck pay dirt. The tape was time and date stamped: Thursday, November 1, 11:18 p.m.

The small screen filled with naked bodies, the room with the sound of their sex. There were three people involved—two teenage girls and Bernhardt. Bernhardt was on his knees, skewering one of them from behind. The other girl was behind him, fondling and sucking.

So, where was the mama Jonathan Bell had told her about?

The cameras must have been on timers because every three minutes the view switched. When it did, Carla had the answer to her question. The breath hissed past her teeth. Heather Ferguson, she realized. Observing the action. Directing it. Feeding the participants a liquid, most probably laced with drugs.

The view changed again and Carla's eyes widened. Tara, she realized with a sense of shock. *The girl on her hands and knees was Tara Mancuso.*

Having seen all she could take, she shut off the player, popped out the tape and jumped down. She unclipped her phone from its holster and dialed Rick.

He picked up right away. The connection crackled. "Rick!" She raised her voice to be heard above the static. "It's Carla. I found tapes. Bernhardt was into young girls and he taped them. The night he died, Tara was with him. Another teenager, too, one I didn't recognize." She paused to gulp in air. "And so was Heather Ferguson."

Rick whistled and Carla continued. "From what I could tell, she was a kind of pimp. She wasn't involved in the action, she just observed it. She also administered some sort of drug."

"Did she know they were being taped?" he asked.

"I'm positive she didn't." Carla glanced toward the mirrors. "If she had, no way would she have allowed this tape to be—"

She bit back the word. "Hold on, I thought I heard something." She crossed to the bedroom door and stepped out into the empty hallway. Heart pounding, she went to the top of the stairs and peered down. "Hello, anyone down there?"

"Just me."

The Sunset Key Realty office girl appeared at the bottom of the stairs. She was dripping wet and looked miserable. "Are you almost done? My boss told me to retrieve the key and lock up. They're getting ready to stop ferry service because of the wind."

Realizing that she had been holding her breath, Carla let it out and smiled. "All finished. I'll be down in one minute."

When Carla was certain the woman was out of earshot, she continued her conversation with Rick. "No way Heather Ferguson would have allowed the tape to be found."

He was silent a moment; the connection crackled. "A pattern's emerging here, Carla. Everyone associated with Larry Bernhardt is turning up dead."

"So how did Pastor Howard fit into this twisted little scenario?"

"My guess? Tara told her what was going on and she was killed because of it."

A thought occurred to Carla and a chill washed over her. "We've got to locate the other girl in this video before it's too late. Where are you?"

"At the Hideaway. I'm storm-proofing the bar, just in case. When I'm done, I'm checking on Liz. I went by before, but she wasn't there. I haven't been able to reach her by phone either."

Carla heard the worry in his voice and hastened to reassure him. "Maybe she evacuated because of the storm."

"Maybe, but I just don't think so."

"I tell you what—" Carla glanced at her watch "—I'm heading back now. Finish there, collect Liz, then meet me at my place as soon as you can."

CHAPTER 53

Wednesday, November 21
5:10 p.m.

Liz reached Islamorada in just under three hours. Not bad considering both the traffic and the rain. The phone book listed Martha Ferguson's address as Citrus Drive. Having no clue where that might be, she turned into the first minimart she came upon, hoping the attendant would know.

"Sure, honey," the woman at the register said. She squinted at Liz through a haze of cigarette smoke. Her brown, leathery skin spoke of a lifetime spent in the brutal Florida sun. "Who you looking for?"

"Martha Ferguson. You know her?"

"Sure do. I know everybody on the island." She stamped out her cigarette. "You certain you want to visit her? She's a bit prickly, that one."

"Absolutely certain. I need to ask her a few questions about her daughter."

The woman's eyebrows shot up. "Must be pretty important questions to bring you out in this weather."

Liz didn't take the bait. She tossed out one of her own. "Have you met her daughter Heather?"

The woman frowned. "Didn't know Martha had a daughter. Never seen one come around. And I've seen almost everybody on this chunk of mud."

Interesting, Liz thought as she climbed into her car moments later, armed not only with directions to the trailer park where Martha Ferguson lived, but with her trailer number as well.

Less than five minutes later, Liz pulled up in front of a neat-looking double-wide. Light glowed from the home's interior, indicating Martha Ferguson was probably there. Liz shifted her gaze. From the darkened state of most of her neighbors' homes, it looked as if she was one of the few who hadn't evacuated.

Not so smart. Liz knew that a trailer wouldn't be the safest dwelling in forty-five-mile-an-hour winds. But she had also learned, her short time living in the keys, that Floridians were both a hardy and stubborn lot, not easily sent packing by the threat of a little wind and rain.

She opened her car door and stepped out, umbrella up. A gust of wind slammed into her, ripping both her umbrella and the door handle from her hands. Immediately drenched, Liz managed to get the car door shut, then sprinted through the rain to the woman's front door.

She knocked, and a moment later the door eased open and a woman peered out at her. "Yes?" she asked, openly suspicious.

"My name's Elizabeth Ames," Liz said, teeth beginning to chatter. "I'm with *The Keys* magazine. I'm doing an article on your daughter—"

"I have no daughter."

She began to close the door. Liz shot her hand out to stop her. "Wait! Aren't you Heather Ferguson's mother? She's recently been named Key West businesswoman of the yea—"

"I told you, I have no daughter!"

She slammed the door in Liz's face. Startled by the woman's violent reaction to the mention of her daughter's name, Liz stood frozen to the spot, the rain pouring down on her, plastering her clothes to her skin.

She had come all this way, she wasn't about to give up. She lifted her fist and pounded on the door. "I know she's your daughter!" she cried. "Why won't you talk to me? What are you trying to hide?"

"Go away!"

She pounded again. "Women are dying, Mrs. Ferguson. Please talk to me!"

For a moment Liz thought coming here had been a waste of her time, then the door cracked open. "What did you say?"

Liz took a deep breath, deciding on the truth. "That young women are dying. I'm trying to help."

"What does Heather have to do with that?"

"I don't know. Maybe nothing. That's why I'm here."

"Heather is dead to me," she said, voice heavy with pain. "She has been for a long time."

"Can I come in? Please, Mrs. Ferguson."

The woman hesitated a moment more, then nodded and allowed Liz in. She retrieved a bath towel and offered her a cup of hot tea.

Liz thanked her, and while she toweled off, the woman brewed the tea.

That done, they sat across from each other at the woman's small kitchen table. "I'm afraid I'm getting your seat cushions wet," Liz murmured.

"A little water's not going to hurt this place," the woman replied, not looking up from her tea. "Besides, if the forecasters' worst-case scenarios come to pass, a tornado will more than likely toss me into the Atlantic."

"You're not afraid?"

"I stayed for Andrew and for George. I'm not about to turn tail and run now."

They fell silent. Liz sipped her tea. The woman studied her.

"You're not a reporter, are you?"

"How did you—"

"No tablet or recorder. They always have one or the other. Nosey bloodsuckers."

"You must have had experiences with the press."

An expression of intense pain crossed her features and she looked away.

"When's the last time you saw your daughter?"

"Years ago. After her sister's—" She bit the words off and began again. "She wasn't always the way she is now. She was a sweet child. Prone to willfulness and pranks…but what child isn't?"

She didn't expect a response and continued. "Then… she began running with the wrong crowd. Fast girls. Boys I didn't like or trust. She began dabbling in the occult. With drugs. It seemed like overnight she became a girl I didn't recognize."

Martha Ferguson lowered her gaze to her hands, clasped tightly on the table in front of her. After several moments, she returned her gaze to Liz's. "She became a girl who frightened me."

Liz struggled to reconcile what this woman was saying with what she knew of Heather from personal experience. The two versions didn't fit. "How old was she when this happened?"

"Before her fifteenth birthday is when I began to see changes in her." She paused, the moment pregnant with pain. "At first I thought it was a…a phase. That given a bit of time and strict boundaries, she would return to her normal self…but it didn't go that way. Her behavior became more bizarre. Her moods blacker, more violent." The woman's voice cracked. "The Lord took both my children from me."

"Both your children?" Liz asked as gently as she could, heart breaking for this woman.

"Yes. My younger daughter, my darling Christina. She was…she was murdered by that madman Gavin Taft."

Dear God. The connection, she had found it.

Rick had been right about Gavin Taft being the link to the killer. Only that killer was a woman, not a man.

CHAPTER 54

Wednesday, November 21
5:40 p.m.

Carla stood at her front window, peering nervously out at the storm, waiting for Rick. The rain had hit during her ferry ride back from Sunset Key. It had begun as a drizzle; by the time she had reached the safety of her porch, it had become a downpour.

She swung away from the window and started to pace. *Where was he?* She couldn't quell her growing sense of dread. Shivering, she rubbed her arms.

The wind howled. Lightning flashed. She hugged herself. Every time she closed her eyes she saw dirty old Bernhardt grunting and sweating as he screwed the two teenagers doggy-style, moving between the two as if feasting at a smorgasbord. It made her sick. It infuriated her.

Bernhardt had been a sick bastard and she was glad

he was dead. Heather Ferguson, on the other hand, was evil. But worst by far had been Tara's tortured expression during the entire ordeal. A lost soul, Carla thought, squeezing her eyes shut against the haunting image. An innocent lamb to the slaughter.

A prayer popped into Carla's head, one repeated daily in the early years of her life but long ago relegated to the far recesses of her consciousness.

Our Father who art in heaven, hallowed be thy name—

From the back of her cottage came a scraping sound, like her rear door opening. She froze. "Rick?" she called. "Is that you?"

Silence answered her. Heart thundering, she drew her service revolver and made her way to the back of the house. Her hands shook as she crept forward, bits and pieces of the Lord's Prayer playing through her head.

—and deliver us from evil, for thine—

She nudged open her bedroom door. Empty.

—is the kingdom, the power and the—

She swung into the bathroom, gun out. Nothing.

—glory, forever and ever—

She reached the kitchen. The rear door had popped partially open. Rain had blown in, bringing leaves and flower petals, making a mess. She had forgotten to latch the door; this had happened before.

She laughed nervously as she laid her gun on the counter, then crossed to the door and pushed it shut.

She hated this job. She hated this place.

She wanted to go home.

"Hello, Carla."

She whirled, realizing her mistake. Metal glinted as it arced toward her; her life flashed before her eyes.

She threw her hands up, a scream ripping past her lips, a terrible sound drowned out by the howl of Rebekah's wind.

CHAPTER 55

Wednesday, November 21
6:00 p.m.

Rick tapped on Carla's front door. It drifted open. Frowning, he nudged the door wider and slipped inside.

"Carla," he called. "It's Rick."

She didn't reply and his senses sharpened. This felt wrong. Bad wrong. He swept his gaze over the room. Except for the trail of water that led from the doorway where he stood toward the back of the house, nothing appeared out of place. He narrowed his eyes. Someone had come in from the rain and walked dripping wet through the house, not pausing to wipe their feet or towel off.

Someone other than Carla, judging by the way the wooden floors gleamed. She obviously took excellent care of them.

He told himself to get out. He told himself to call the KWPD and wait on the front porch until they arrived.

But Val was the KWPD.

And he was also the enemy.

Dammit. He flexed his fingers. When Sam died, he had promised himself he would never fire a gun again. For the first time since that day, he wished for the muscle his Walther PPK 380 had provided. He wished he was the man he'd been then—arrogant, cocky, invincible.

Problem was, now he understood how tenuous life was. How fragile.

Rick moved his gaze around the room again, this time looking for something he could use to protect himself. His gaze landed on a large brass candlestick on the mantel. He crossed to the fireplace and lifted it, weighing it in his hand. Not as effective as the Walther, he acknowledged. But it would have to do.

He followed the trail of water, inching forward, straining to listen. From the back of the house came a sound, one he couldn't place. Like an ill-fitting door being dragged across the floor.

He wasn't alone.

Carla.

Rick forced himself to proceed slowly, to not abandon stealth. He found Carla in the kitchen. She lay on her side on the floor, wedged against the far cabinet, her arm hitched up the wainscoting. Then he saw the blood, an obscene smear across the light-colored tile. A growing pool around her torso.

"Carla!" he cried and raced to her side. Snatching a dish towel from the counter, he pressed it to the gaping wound in her chest. Then he saw the others.

There were so many of them. Her attacker had hacked at her as if in a frenzy.

She couldn't survive an attack like this. If the paramedics were here now, working to save her, she wouldn't survive.

Her eyes fluttered open. They looked dull already.

"No," he muttered fiercely. "Don't die, baby. You're not going to die, you hear me? You're not."

She held his gaze. Her lips moved, as if she was trying to speak. "What, sweetheart? Tell me."

He bent his ear close to her mouth. Her breath stirred against his cheek, though no sound emerged. He drew away. Her eyes closed, a small smile curved the edges of her lips.

Tears burned his eyes. "No! Dammit, Carla!" He shook her; her head lolled to the side. "Come back, baby. Come ba—"

"Get up, Rick."

Rick whipped his head around. Val stood in the doorway behind him, his gaze on Carla. He wore a hooded black rain slicker. Water dripped from the slicker onto the floor, pooling at his feet.

A trail of water from the door to the back of the house.

Fury choked him. Betrayal with it. "Is that all you have to say? Get up, Rick?"

He turned his expressionless eyes on Rick. "Is she dead?"

"What do you think?"

"I think that yes, she is."

Rick eased to his feet, shaking with rage. "What are you doing here, Val?"

"Carla called me," he replied woodenly. "She told me to meet her here, that it was urgent."

Liar! Dirty, fucking liar. "Did she?" Rick managed to say. "I wonder why?"

"Maybe for the same reason she asked you to meet her here."

"I didn't say that she did."

A flush spread up the other man's cheeks. Val drew his Colt Python revolver and aimed it at Rick. "I think you had better move away from the body."

Rick did, careful not to step in blood and contaminate the scene. He wondered if Val knew about the tape. And if he did know, whether he had already found it. He prayed he hadn't.

"Why don't you call this in, Val? Get a crew out ASAP." He folded his arms across his chest and met the other man's gaze. "There's nowhere I have to be."

Val stared blankly at him a moment, then slowly shook his head. "That's where you're wrong. You and I are going down to headquarters. We need to have a little chat."

"I think not. I prefer to be right here when the evidence crew arrives. Just want to make sure the evidence isn't contaminated. You know crime-scene procedure, Lieutenant. Leaving a murder scene unattended constitutes a serious breach."

"If I were you, I'd be a little less concerned with my duty and more concerned with your own ass."

"Meaning?"

Val narrowed his eyes. "This doesn't look good for you, does it, Rick? Finding you this way? With her?"

"Where's the weapon? Where's the blood?" Rick held out his hands, palms up. "My hands are red, from where I tried to stop her bleeding. But the way she was killed, it should be all over me.

"Her gun's on the counter," Rick continued. "Judging

by the trail of blood, it looks as if she dragged herself across the floor in an attempt to retrieve it. That's why her arm's hitched up like that, she tried to pull herself up, one drawer at a time." His voice cracked. "She didn't make it."

Val didn't even blink. "Your point?"

"My point, *old friend,* is that I didn't kill her. She went for her gun after her attacker left, probably before I arrived.

"Her killer could have exited this door," Rick continued, motioning the rear door, "then made his way around to the front. If wearing something like a—" he eyed the other man with feigned ingenuousness "—like a rubber rain slicker, he could step out into the rain and by the time he made it around the house, he'd be clean. The rain would have washed away the evidence of his deed. That make sense to you, Val?"

Val crossed to where Carla lay. He stepped over her, retrieved and pocketed her pistol. "Poor deluded Rick. He hasn't been the same since his kid died. Such a tragedy. It breaks my heart. It really does."

Rick struggled to keep his fury in check. He couldn't give Val anything to use against him. He tried another tack. "Remember that time we lifted your dad's pellet gun and decided every streetlight in town was big game? Remember how indignant we were when the cops showed up?" Rick shook his head. "Twelve years old and we thought we shouldn't have to answer to anybody."

"A couple of smart-asses." A smile tugged at the corners of Val's mouth. "The way we talked to that cop, today a kid like that'd make my blood boil."

"Your old man kicked your ass."

"What about yours? You couldn't ride your bike for a week."

"We were going to conquer the world, Val. When I think of the way we used to strut, it's a wonder anybody put up with us. Cocksure punks, that's what we were. And then we discovered girls."

"Yee-ha."

"What happened to us, Val? We were best friends. We would have died for each other." Rick lowered his voice to a soft plea. "When did it all change? When did we begin taking it all so seriously?"

Val's smile faded. "I'm tired, Rick. So fucking tired of it all. This game stinks."

"So let's stop playing." He looked his old friend dead in the eyes, aching for what had been—and regretting what must be. His friend was going down. And he had to be the one to do it. "Let's stop taking it all so seriously, let's be the boys we used to be. Cocksure punks out to save the world."

Val hesitated; his hand shook slightly. "You can't go back, Rick. We both know that."

"You can," Rick murmured, pressing his advantage. "I'll help you. Talk to me, Val. I'm here for you, buddy."

For a second, Rick saw the boy he had known and loved in Val's eyes. The kid who had been so eager to prove himself to the world, to be the people's champion, a hero.

In the next moment, that boy was gone. In his place was a man Rick didn't recognize. "Screw that. We're going to take a little ride."

He meant to kill him. And there was nobody to stop him.

"Don't do this, Val," Rick implored. "I don't know

what you've gotten yourself into, but I'll help you. You talk to me and I'll see to it that—"

"Cut the cop bullshit! You think I don't know the way it works? I've been a cop my whole life!" He motioned with his gun. "Now, shut the fuck up and get your hands behind your head. We're going for a little ride."

CHAPTER 56

Wednesday, November 21
6:20 p.m.

Rick made his way to Val's sedan, parked around the corner from Carla's cottage. Val followed closely, the barrel of the revolver pressed to the small of Rick's back.

Rick frantically scanned the area, looking for a witness to confirm his version of this nightmare, for details that would later help him create an accurate timetable of events—in case he managed to escape with his life. He came up with little. Except for several parked cars and a mangy-looking dog barking at them from Carla's neighbor's porch, the street was deserted.

"You going to kill me, Val?" Rick asked.

"Don't be so melodramatic." He pressed the gun more snugly against his back. "Although I suspect before this is all over you'll wish you were dead."

"Now who's being melodramatic?"

"Just honest, my friend."

Rick laughed at that. Valentine Lopez and honesty had parted company a long time ago. They reached the vehicle and stopped. "Why'd you park way over here? The way it's raining, I would have thought the open space right in front of Carla's would have been a better choice. But that's right, you didn't want anybody to know you were here."

"Shut up." Keeping the gun trained on him, Val yanked open the front passenger side door, reached inside and retrieved his cuffs. "Turn around."

Rick complied. "You really think cuffs are necessary? If I ran, who would bring you down?"

The other man snapped the cuffs on roughly, then shoved him against the car. He yanked open the rear door. "Get in."

Rick did, and moments later Val pulled away from the curb. Using the radio, he called dispatch, informed them he was bringing in murder suspect Rick Wells for questioning. He ended the call, a smile tugging at his mouth.

"Murder suspect? How do you figure?"

Val made a clucking sound with his tongue. "Patience. It will all be revealed to you soon. And after it is, I suspect you're going to wish I had killed you."

Dammit, he needed that tape. "Playing it close to the vest, Val? Afraid I'm going to punch holes in your little plot?"

Val looked over his shoulder and smiled, the curving of his lips as cold as ice. He held a finger to his lips. "Just a little farther. And if you play nice, I won't beat the shit out of you for resisting."

* * *

Rick faced Val across the interrogation-room table. The other man had refused to say another word until they reached police headquarters, though Rick had continued to try to goad him. Once at headquarters he'd spoken. In a singsong voice he had given Rick the option of coming peacefully with him or being cuffed and dragged in.

Rick cocked his head, studying the other man as he readied the video camera. He found Val's movements robotic, as if he was operating on autopilot. He had seen similar reactions in both victims and witnesses of violent crime. The psyche simply overloaded and shut down.

If he pushed hard enough, Rick believed, he could break him.

"So, what are we doing here, old buddy?" he asked.

Val finished setting up the camera and took the seat across from Rick's. "What do you think we're doing here?"

"Cop double-talk, tricky, Val."

"Do you know why you're here?"

"Because you're crazy. Because you killed Detective Carla Chapman and have formulated some scheme to pin it on me."

Val's eyebrows shot up. He glanced at the other officer in the room, a patrolman standing in the corner near the door. "This is Officer Walters, Rick. He's going to sit in."

Rick nodded in the rookie's direction. "Listen carefully, kid. Lieutenant Lopez is slippery. Don't let him suck you in."

"Why did you kill Carla Chapman?" Val demanded.

Rick relaxed against the chair back and returned his

gaze to Val's. Interrogation was a kind of verbal chess game. It relied on intelligence, strategy and balls-out moves meant to keep your opponent on the defensive. "I didn't, as you very well know."

"And how would I know that?"

"Because you killed her."

The other man didn't blink. "How well did you know Naomi Pearson?"

Rick hesitated, surprised by Val's shift in direction. He frowned. "Not well. She came into the bar a few times."

"How about Larry Bernhardt?"

"Larry Bernhardt? The banker?"

"Is it true he wrote your loan for the Hideaway?"

"Yes, but I don't—"

"And isn't it also true that you met Naomi Pearson for the first time at that point?"

"Yes. Bernhardt introduced me to her."

"And wasn't it also at that point you learned how loan verification worked."

"I don't follow."

"The screening and approval process for loans."

"I suppose. Although from what I've seen, it's not rocket science. Pretty straightforward stuff."

"You mean you learned how easy it would be to have fraudulent loans approved. With the right associates, of course."

Son of a bitch. Val wasn't trying to frame only Carla's murder on him, but to tie him to all of them.

Rick narrowed his eyes. He wasn't about to let the other man maneuver him into a corner. "No," he corrected, "that is not what I meant."

Before his former friend could fire another question at him, Rick fired one of his own. "Tell me something,

Val. How does it feel to know you're one of the bad guys?"

"I'll ask the questions, if you don't mind."

"But I do mind." He leaned forward, keeping his tone and body language conversational. "You see, I really want to know. What does it feel like to kill a fellow officer in cold blood? How did it feel to hack at her until her chest resembled Swiss che—"

"That's fucking enough!" Val shouted, jumping to his feet. He snatched up a file folder from the end of the table and slammed it down in front of Rick. "Take a look, my friend."

Rick flipped open the folder, aware of Val behind him, watching. It contained several copies of correspondence between him, Larry Bernhardt and Naomi Pearson. Rick read them, feeling himself begin to sweat. The correspondence detailed a plan between the three of them to begin defrauding Island National Bank by writing bogus loans.

He twisted his head to look at Val. The gleeful expression in his former friend's eyes infuriated him. "I've never seen these before."

"Is that your e-mail address?"

Rick glanced at it, though he knew beforehand it would be. Val had thought this through. And judging by the date on the correspondence, he had been planning it for some time. "Yes, it is."

"But you've never seen any of these e-mails before?"

"That's right."

"And I suppose you're going to stick to that story even after we get a search warrant for your computer. Pathetic, Rick."

They had gotten to his computer, Rick realized. Who'd helped him? Libby? Margo? Both of them?

The Horned Flower.

Rick's thoughts raced to put the pieces together. Suddenly Liz's theory about a conspiracy of evil, of a cult of Satan worshipers on a killing spree, didn't seem so wild.

But there had to be more to it than that. He took a stab. "So is it all about money, Val? About wanting more. Did you sell your soul to the devil for that?"

A muscle in the man's jaw spasmed. "You really are crazy. I feel sorry for you, Rick."

"You prepared to go to hell, Val?"

"As long as I can take you with me."

Fury took his breath. Val felt no remorse. None. Carla's life had meant nothing to him. She had been a loose end, Rick realized. Nothing more than an annoying detail to be taken care of.

"She was your colleague, you son of a bitch!" He fisted his fingers. "She thought the sun rose and set on your head."

"Carla made one fatal mistake, Rick. Besides falling for a heartless prick like you, that is."

"Yeah? And what would that have been? Trusting you?"

Val laughed. "Hardly." He bent close to Rick's ear. "She decided to grow a brain."

With a roar of fury, Rick threw back his chair, knocking Val off balance. Before he could right himself, Rick had slammed him up against the wall, arms at his throat.

"Back off!" Walters shouted, drawing his weapon. "Back off now!"

"Let him hang himself," Val managed to say, eyes on Rick's. "This would be assaulting an officer, my friend. Not a smart move for someone in your position."

"Bastard!" Rick hissed, knowing he was right. He

released him. "You're not going to get away with this. I'm not going to let you get away with it."

Val smiled and glanced at Walters. "Thanks for the backup. Holster your weapon."

The patrolman did as his superior ordered, then returned to his post by the door. Val smoothed a hand over his hair, then motioned to the chair. "Have a seat, Rick. We're not done here."

His cell phone rang, interrupting him. Val checked the display and flipped it open. "Lieutenant Detective Lopez here."

He listened, expression growing smug. "Stay calm and don't worry. I'm leaving now. It's going to be okay, I'll take care of everything."

He ended the call and looked at Walters. "I'm needed at Paradise Christian. There's been an accident." He started for the door. "Don't take your eyes off him, Walters. I'll be back as soon as possible."

CHAPTER 57

Wednesday, November 21
9:00 p.m.

Liz gripped the steering wheel tighter, fighting against gusts of wind to keep her car on the road. The muscles in her shoulders and neck hurt from the effort and her eyes and head ached from the strain of trying to see past the blinding sheets of rain and focus on the road ahead.

Thank God, she had almost made it. The last marker had announced Key West five miles ahead.

She had made good time from Islamorada. She'd done it by eschewing safety for speed. It had helped that she was alone on the road. No one else, it seemed, was foolhardy enough to be heading into Key West with a tropical storm churning steadily toward the island.

She had tried Rick before leaving Islamorada. There had been no answer at the Hideaway or his home; she had left a message on his cell phone. She had pulled over once and tried again. When she hadn't reached him that time, she'd dialed the KWPD and asked for either Lieutenant Lopez or Detective Chapman. She had come up empty again and left an urgent message that they call her.

Something was wrong. Liz darted a quick glance at her silent phone, then yanked her gaze back to the road as a gust of wind nearly forced her off. *Something had happened.*

A murderer was on the loose. A killer storm threatened. And she thought something had happened. She laughed, the sound high and nervous-sounding. Some premonition.

She was getting punchy, she admitted. She was running on adrenaline, caffeine and nerves.

When she reached Key West, the overseas highway became Roosevelt Boulevard, then Truman Avenue. Liz took a right from Truman onto Duval and eased slowly down the street. The usually bustling Duval was deserted, the windows of all but a few of the shops either boarded over or shuttered. Branches and other debris littered the way; an inverted umbrella flew past her windshield; the lid of a garbage can rolled down the sidewalk, then spun crazily on its edge before crashing into a telephone pole.

For weeks after, the bodies washed ashore. Entire families, lashed together.

She must have been crazy to come back here. To be on the road. If she had any good sense she would be inside, kitchen stocked with emergency provisions: things like a flashlight and batteries, drinking water, canned food.

Her heart sank when she saw the Hideaway. The windows were boarded over, no light shone from within.

Like every other responsible citizen of Key West, it looked as if Rick had closed shop and headed for home—or drier climes.

She had counted on his being here, she realized. She hadn't thought it through. Of course he wasn't here. Of course he wasn't open for business during the height of a tropical storm.

She stopped the car in front of the Hideaway anyway. Taking a deep breath, she flung the door open and darted for the bar's front entrance. The force of the wind was incredible, it tore at her and she had to fight her way to the sidewalk. There, she pounded, praying she was wrong, that Rick was here. She didn't even know where he lived, she realized. If he wasn't here, she might be unable to find him.

"Rick!" she shouted. "Rick! It's Liz, open up!" She waited, then pounded again. "Rick, please! It's Liz!"

A cry rose in her throat, and she choked it back through sheer force of will. She wasn't going to fall apart now. She had come this far. With or without Rick, she was going to get what she had learned to the police.

She fought her way back to her car and climbed in. She fitted the key in the ignition and twisted it. The engine sputtered but didn't turn over. Heart thundering, she tried again with the same results.

Near tears, she tried a third time. The engine came to life.

Liz made it one block before the engine began to cough. A moment later it died and she drifted to a stop in front of Paradise Christian.

Many had taken refuge in the church; they were swept out to sea.

With a feeling of predestination, she looked toward the church. The structure stood solidly against the storm, its white exterior almost brilliant against the backdrop of the dark, turbulent sky. Light glowed from within, beckoning. Seeming to call her name.

She resisted the call. Pastor Tim would be there. She suspected him of being a part of the Horned Flower, of being an accessory to murder.

She could make her way the half block to her home, she acknowledged. Wait out the storm, pray for the best. Keep trying to reach Rick and the authorities.

But she had been led here. The same as she had been the night of Tara's murder. She believed that.

Without giving herself time to reconsider, she threw the car door open and climbed out. A gust of wind caught her, propelling her forward. The driving rain stung her face and plastered her light clothes to her skin.

A loud crack rent the air. Sparks flew. She smelled smoke. A transformer had blown, she realized. One close by.

She stumbled up the church's front steps. The doors were unlocked. She inched one open and slipped through.

Quiet engulfed her. A feeling of serenity. The eternal candle burned in the sanctuary, bathing its surrounding area in a warm, reassuring light. "Is anyone here?" she called. "Pastor Tim?"

Silence answered. Frowning, she started down the hall toward Pastor Tim's office, inching her way in the dark. "Hello," she called again. "Anybody here?"

She reached the pastor's study. The door was partly open. She thought she heard a sound from within. A kind of snuffling sound. Soft. Sinister.

Someone hiding there in the dark. Waiting.

Fear caught her in a choke hold. She took a step back

from the door. The sound came again, this time accompanied by a moan.

Liz eased the door open. The lights flickered, then came on. A scream rose in her throat. Pastor Tim lay on his back on the floor, his shirt red with his blood.

She ran to him and knelt by his side. She saw the wound then and realized he had been shot. She brought a shaking hand to her mouth and glanced frantically around.

Her gaze landed on the phone. *Call 911, of course.* She jumped to her feet, got to the phone. And found it dead.

She had left her cell phone in the car.

Pastor Tim moaned, and Liz returned to his side. His eyelids fluttered, then lifted.

She covered his hand with hers. "I'll go for help. Just lie still, you're going to be okay."

He blinked, his gaze seeming to focus on her. His fingers moved, curling around hers. "Y...our...si—"

She quieted him. "Don't talk. Save your strength. The phone's dead, but I have a cell phone in my—"

"N...n...don...your...sis—"

She struggled to make out what he was saying. He coughed, the sound weak and wet. "Shh... Please, I have to call for help."

He tightened his fingers on hers. "Sis...ter—"

"Sister?" she repeated. "My sister?"

He squeezed her fingers. Her heart stopped. "What about Rachel? What are you trying to tell me, Pastor Tim?"

His mouth began to move. Liz bent her head closer; his breath stirred weakly against her ear.

"Your...she's...alive..."

A cry passed her lips. *Alive? Could it be true?*

She began to tremble, twin emotions of joy and disbelief rocketing through her. She fought to find her breath. "How can that... Where, Pastor? You have to help me find her."

"Po...po—" He moved their joined hands and she realized what he meant. She freed her hand from his and slipped it into his pocket. She closed her fingers over a folded paper and drew it out.

The lights flashed, then went off. A beam of light fell over them. She twisted around. Valentine Lopez stood in the doorway, his dark rain slicker dripping wet.

"Lieutenant Lopez!" she cried. "Thank God! Pastor Tim's been shot!"

He stepped into the room. "I got here as soon as I could."

"I don't understand. How did you—"

He motioned with the flashlight. "Move away from the body, please."

She stood and backed away. "You don't understand, he's alive."

The detective didn't reply. He squatted beside the pastor, checked his wound and pulse.

"He's gone," he murmured.

"That can't be! Just a moment ago—"

"With a wound like this, it only takes a moment. He lost a lot of blood."

"I don't understand." She began to tremble. "He can't be gone."

"What's that in your hand?"

Numbly, she shifted her gaze from the pastor's frozen face to the piece of paper clutched in her hand. Her sister's image flooded her head. She held it out. "He said... my sister's alive, Lieutenant. He gave me...this."

He took the paper, opened and read it, his features tightening. "It's a Key West address."

"Do you think that's where... Do you think it's true?" Her voice shook. "Could my sister really be alive?"

"Why don't we take a ride and find out?"

"Now?" She hung back, frightened by the intensity of his gaze.

"Your sister may be alive, Ms. Ames. If she is, I imagine your face would be the first she'd want to see."

"But Pastor Tim... Shouldn't we wait for an ambulance?"

"He can't be helped now. But maybe your sister can." He glanced at his watch, then back at her, expression grim. "Ms. Ames, your sister may be in danger from whoever shot Pastor Tim."

CHAPTER 58

Wednesday, November 21
9:15 p.m.

Minutes later, Liz huddled against the front passenger seat of the lieutenant's sedan. Cold air poured out of the air-conditioner vents, hitting the car's warm, damp interior and fogging the windows. She shuddered and hugged herself. "Where are we going?" she asked.

"To get your sister," the detective replied, maneuvering through the debris-littered streets.

"I meant...where on Key West are we—"

"Not far. You'll see."

Her teeth began to chatter. He didn't seem to notice, nor did he seem affected by the chill. "D...do you th... think she's at that address?"

He glanced at her, his eyes strangely blank. "I'm sure she is."

She stared at him, her breath quickening. "Are you all right, Lieutenant?"

"I bet you're grateful I showed up when I did. Too bad it wasn't soon enough to save Tim."

His voice sounded wrong, she realized. Tinny. Expressionless.

She cleared her throat. "How did you... I mean, what made you come by the church?"

"Tim called me." He flexed his fingers on the steering wheel. "That's what people do when they need help, call the police. Public servants. Can you believe that's what they call us, Liz? *Servants?*"

Uneasy, she pressed herself closer to the door. "No," she whispered. "I can't."

"Smart girl. You and your sister both." He shook his head. "You've handed me the last piece of the puzzle, Liz. I thank you for that."

"Excuse me?"

"Your sister. I wondered what had happened to her. I had my suspicions, but until tonight I didn't know for sure. One minute in my sights, the next—" he snapped his fingers "—poof, she was gone."

She stared at him in growing horror. *Dear God. She'd been right before; he was the one.*

"She called you, didn't she? About the Horned Flower?"

"People always trust the police." He smiled again. "Funny, isn't it? Even though we carry guns and have the power and knowledge to totally fuck them over, they trust us. Because we work for them. Because we're their *servants*."

He said the last in a high, singsong voice that sent a

chill over her. She rubbed her arms. "You went to kill her but she was gone."

His smile faded. "It was a night like this one, thunder and lightning, rain coming down in sheets. She didn't get far from Paradise Christian. Found her car wrapped around a tree. Problem was, she wasn't in it."

Liz pressed her lips together to keep from whimpering. She imagined her terrified sister, losing control of her car, seeing the tree rushing up to meet her.

"How did you get rid of her car?"

"I'm the police, Liz. Dealing with evidence is what I do, day in and out." He let out a tired-sounding breath. "I had to shoot him, you know. Tim. Bitch didn't think about how I was going to have to clean up after her. She never thinks about me and what I have to do."

Heather. They were in it together.

He let out a tight-sounding breath. "What a waste. He was a good guy, you know? A good ball player."

Pastor Tim hadn't been part of it. "Like my sister, he called you for help," she murmured. "Because he discovered Rachel was alive."

"Stephen told him."

Stephen? She didn't know he could speak.

As if he read her mind, he nodded. "Yeah, he can speak, if that's what you want to call the sounds he makes. Growing up, we gave him a hard time. Called him half-wit, retard and stuff. We were merciless when he tried to speak. Somewhere along the line, he just stopped talking." He glanced at her, then back at the road. "Sad, isn't it? Too bad Carla's bullet hadn't done the job. A person like him, what's the point? He'd be better off dead."

She hugged herself, feeling ill. She wanted nothing more than to fling open the door and make a run for it, but he knew where Rachel was. Somehow, she would have to find a way to overcome him and save her sister.

"What about my sister's Bible? And the knife?"

He shrugged. "As far as I can tell, he just freaked out. Tim thought he had seen Mark Morgan with Stephen, so I paid Stephen a visit. Showed him some crime-scene photos. Described in detail the monster we were looking for, what he'd done. Talked about Taft, quoted some Scripture. I tried to impress on him the importance of cooperating with the police. Actually, it worked out rather nicely for me."

He smiled. She found the way his lips stretched across his teeth obscene. "Some people just have no stomach for police work."

Liz could imagine gentle, damaged Stephen being forced to look at photos of Tara and Naomi. At what had been done to them. How that might cause him to react, to "freak out," as Val called it.

A brilliant flash of lightning tore across the night sky. It opened up then, unleashing a flood. Val flipped the wipers on high and eased off the accelerator. "Stephen saw them drag your sister out of the car."

She straightened. "Them? Who?"

"A couple of those Rainbow Nation kids. They're like roaches. No matter how you try, you can't get rid of them."

Liz thought of the young man who had warned her off the island earlier that day. "What did they want with her?"

"I don't think they wanted anything of her. But they'll do anything for money."

He fell silent. Liz gripped the sides of the bucket seat. "You and Heather are partners, aren't you?"

Her question seemed to jolt him. He looked at her and she smiled grimly. "Heather and Taft worked together. They killed her little sister."

His lips curled slightly and Liz realized that even though a monster, he drew the line at that. He shook his head, expression suddenly resigned. Sad. "You should have taken my threats seriously, Ms. Ames. You should have left Key West. I didn't want this to happen."

"You left the note," she murmured. "And the rat."

"And paid that little cockroach to scare you today." He slowed the automobile. "Here we are."

He pulled up in front of a beautiful old Caribbean-style home. Wide galleries circled the white structure. Dark-green storm shutters covered the windows, all closed tight against Mother Nature's fury. An iron fence circled the lushly landscaped lot, which appeared to be a block deep.

He opened his car door, stepped out of the vehicle and came around for her. She didn't resist and let him lead her across the sidewalk and through the iron gate. The wind caught it and slammed it shut behind them. She had to find Rachel and get her away from here.

He didn't ring the bell or knock. She stood back and watched as he tried the door, found it locked, drew out his gun and fired three shots into the frame, then kicked the door open.

The picture of barely controlled fury, he strode into

the foyer, dragging her with him. Candlelight cast the room in a flickering, golden light.

"Where are you!" he roared. "Show yourself, you whore from hell!"

He released her and Liz inched back, frightened.

"Where are you!" he shouted again and started toward the stairs. He passed a flower arrangement and ripped it from its pedestal and sent it crashing to the floor. The vase shattered and water spewed over the marble entryway, the exotic blooms with it.

Liz realized that for the moment he had forgotten about her. She turned and darted toward the back of the house, praying her sister was on the first floor, not the second. She checked each room she passed. Each was as beautifully appointed as the last, like something out of *Architectural Digest*.

But each was empty. She made it to the back of the house. She stepped out onto the back gallery. It faced an inground pool, created to resemble a natural spa complete with a rock waterfall. Beyond the pool lay a greenhouse and equipment shed.

Liz caught her breath, remembering her dream of the other night. Rachel locked in a hot box, dying.

The equipment shed. Rachel was there.

She ran toward it. The door was padlocked, the windows boarded over. Liz look wildly around. Her gaze fell on a shovel propped against a tree several feet away. She retrieved it. Lifting it high, she brought it down on the padlock and hinge, again and again. The metal hinge began to give; Liz hoisted the shovel once more and brought it crashing down. The hinge gave. She tore open the door.

For a fraction of a second, Liz was blinded by the absolute darkness of the shed's interior. She took a step inside. Hot and foul-smelling, like decay or human waste.

Lightning flashed. Liz saw her. Her sister huddled in the corner, hands and feet bound, head lolling to the side.

"Rachel!" she cried.

She rushed to her sister's side. She knelt beside her, cupping her face in her palms. Her skin was hot. Another flash of lightning illuminated the interior. A sound of horror rose in Liz's throat. Her sister's lips were blistered from the heat, her arms and neck peppered with cuts, bruises and burns. Liz inched aside her filthy, ripped shirt and found her back and torso in the same condition.

It looked as if her sister had been tortured. Beaten, burned. And starved. There was little to her but skin and bones.

Tears blinded her. Dear Jesus, who could have done this?

But she knew. In her heart she knew.

Heather.

Liz tore at the rope that bound her sister's wrists, freeing them, then her ankles. She got an arm around her. "I'm getting you out of here, Rachel."

"Think again, hero," a woman said softly from behind her.

Liz froze, recognizing Heather's voice.

As if the woman could read her mind, she laughed. "Surprise, Liz."

She looked over her shoulder at the other woman, not

hiding the depth of her hatred for her. "Not a surprise," she spat. "I talked to your mother."

"A loose end to be dealt with. Eventually."

"You helped Taft kill your own sister."

"No, he helped me kill her," she replied, expression serene. "He was my most devoted disciple."

Liz swallowed against the bile that rose in her throat. How could something so beautiful on the outside be so ugly inside? She shook her head in growing horror. "What kind of monster are you?"

"I'm *the* monster, Liz. I would have thought you'd have figured that out by now." She glanced behind her. "Ah, here comes my darling Valentine. Different than Gavin but just as devoted."

In the time since she last saw him, his mood seemed to have changed from furious to subdued. Liz wondered what had occurred between the two to cause the shift.

Again, as if she could read Liz's mind, Heather murmured, "He follows me. All that he now has, I've given him. I can just as easily take it all away. Isn't that right, my pet?"

"Fuck you, whore."

Instead of being angry, it was as if his obscenity excited her. She stood on tiptoe and kissed him, openmouthed, her tongue spearing in and out, quick and snakelike. She brought her hand to his crotch and squeezed. He responded by grabbing her hair in his fist and yanking her head violently backward.

She laughed and released him. "Let's get this thing done."

"Rick knows about you," Liz said quickly, bringing Rachel closer to her side. "After I talked to your mother,

I called him. By now he's contacted the sheriff, the State Bureau of Investigation, the FBI. You won't get away with—"

"She's lying," Val murmured. "Rick's under police guard down at the department. Held under suspicion of murder. Most recently, that of Detective Carla Chapman."

Rick? Under arrest?

Carla Chapman, dead?

"That's right," Heather said, responding to her unspoken questions. "Valentine has been amassing quite a lot of evidence against Rick Wells. Before this night is through, the man responsible for the Key West murders will be dead. Unfortunately, not before two more innocent women are slaughtered."

"How?" Liz asked, fear gripping her like an icy hand. "How are you going to do it?"

Heather ignored her and glanced at Val. "What about Collins?"

"Dead by now. No doubt bled to death."

Liz caught her breath. Pastor Tim hadn't been dead when she'd left him.

"You'll summon Wells?"

"As soon as we're ready for him."

"Are you certain he'll come?"

"Absolutely." The man smiled coldly at Liz. "We have his little girlfriend." Val drew out his gun. "Time to go, ladies."

Rachel moaned and shuddered. Liz fought her rising panic. She had to get her sister medical attention. "Where are we going?" she asked.

"Paradise Christian."

The church? But wh—

Then she knew. It made a twisted kind of sense. Paradise Christian Church stood on holy ground. The site of a true miracle. She closed her eyes, recalling Father Paul's words:

"For in the desecration of the holy, evil extends its putrid grasp."

CHAPTER 59

Mark battled his way up Duval Street. A downed tree three blocks back had forced him to abandon his car and make his way to Liz's on foot.

The rain blinded him. The wind made forward progress nearly impossible. He prayed. For the Lord's help. His guidance and strength.

His friends were in great danger. He had to warn them.

Rachel was alive.

He had left Liz's that day after Lieutenant Lopez's visit and gone to the hospital. He had seen what the police had been up to. They needed a murderer. Who better than a monster? Who better to single out as a mad killer than a modern-day Quasimodo? The public would buy it without a murmur. They would whisper, "Yes, it makes sense. Just look at him."

Stephen was a good, gentle creature. One incapable of cruelty. Mark had not been about to sit back and allow his friend to be framed.

He had posed as an orderly to get past the police guard. Pastor Tim had been there, praying over Stephen. He had been white as a sheet. The pastor had recognized Mark immediately and caught his hand. "We have to get him away from here," he had whispered. "They mean him harm."

And Mark's suspicions of the man had melted away.

The pastor had told him what he had learned in the past hours: that Rachel was alive. The night she had disappeared, Stephen had seen a woman on the church grounds—the woman from the boutique across the street. He had seen Pastor Howard crash into a tree and had seen the woman and others pull her from her car after it crashed.

He had been frightened. Pastor Rachel had warned him of the evil ones. She had warned him to stay away from them. She had given him the package for her sister, but he had forgotten how she'd said to get it to her.

From photos, Stephen had recognized Liz, but when he had approached her at the church, he had been chased away by the evil woman. So he had left the envelope for Pastor Tim to find. Stephen had figured that he would know what to do with it.

Together, Mark and the pastor had prayed. And planned. Pastor Tim had friends in Miami. One, a doctor and fellow pastor, would care for Stephen. Mark would stay with Stephen while Tim did a little snooping.

Then, when the guard had gone for coffee, they had unplugged Stephen and stolen him away.

A gust of wind knocked Mark back. He dug in and clawed his way forward.

But he hadn't stayed in Miami. When he'd seen that Stephen was safe, he had returned to Key West. He'd felt strongly that the Lord wanted him here, right this moment, in the midst of the storm. From the beginning, he'd believed the Lord had called him to Key West. He'd thought Tara had been the reason, but he had been wrong.

This was it. He was here to do battle for God. Against evil. Against those who would seduce and contaminate girls like Tara, those who would murder and expect to get away with it by framing the innocent. He didn't think of himself as heroic, just obedient. He hadn't a clue how he would help, what might be expected of him. But he wasn't afraid. It came down to a matter of what was worth living for—and what was worth dying for.

Mark reached Liz's storefront first. He peered in the darkened window—nothing looked out of order. Just to be certain, he tried the door. And found it locked.

Mark tipped his head back. The blinds on Liz's apartment windows were drawn, closed tight. He made his way to her door. He tried the knob and twisted. The door blew open, slamming against the side wall.

Trembling, he ducked inside, closing and locking the door behind him.

He called for her, once. Then again.

She didn't respond and he jogged up the stairs. Nothing appeared out of order in her living room. A quick search revealed the same in the rest of the rooms.

She wasn't here. And judging by the presence of her toothbrush and other toiletries in the bathroom, she hadn't left the island.

Please, Lord, let me not be too late.

Mark made his way back out into the storm. The rain had temporarily slowed to a drizzle. Taking advantage of that, he sprinted toward the Hideaway. Rick had boarded over the windows; both the front and service doors were locked.

Mark pounded and called for the man. After several moments had passed, growing desperate, he turned—and saw Liz's car. A white Ford Taurus with a Missouri tag. It sat slightly left of the center of Duval Street, driver-side door open. Mark's knees went weak with dread.

He closed his eyes and forced a deep breath into his lungs. When he expelled the breath, he expelled the fear with it. Darting into the street, he closed the distance to the car. The keys were in the ignition, her cell phone on the center console.

This was bad, very bad. Mark straightened and scanned the area. Boarded-up stores, all dark. A few automobiles, all empty. Paradise Christian, also dark.

He snatched up the cell phone and pressed the power button. The display came to life, the greenish glow the most welcoming he had ever known. Until it displayed the *no service* message.

With a sound of frustration, he tossed it onto the seat. The rain began again, with a vengeance. Thunder rumbled. *Lord, help me. I can't do this on my own. What now?*

And then, he had his answer. Mark turned and stared at the church's darkened facade.

This was where the Lord wanted him to be.

Grabbing both Liz's keys and car phone, he slammed the door and battled his way to the church's front doors.

He found them unlocked and slipped inside. Obviously the power had been out some time; the interior of the church was humid and warm. Other than the sound of the rain, the church was silent.

"Liz?" he called. "It's Mark. Are you here?"

He made his way to the sanctuary. The flame from the eternal candle cast a soft circle of light. He called out for Liz again, then Pastor Tim. His words echoed back at him, bouncing off the wooden pews, the crucifix of Christ. The large stained-glass window behind the altar alternately brightened and darkened with the flashes of lightning outside. He lifted his face. The choir loft was located above him to the right. And, like the rest of the church, was dark. Empty.

Liz wasn't here.

He didn't know why he was so certain of that but he was. He took a candle from the altar, lit it and continued his search, first through the rest of the sanctuary, then of the other rooms. The nursery and fellowship hall. The Sunday-school classrooms. The office.

He found all empty. He reached the pastor's study. The door was open. He stepped inside. And found Pastor Tim sprawled on the floor in front of his desk, the front of his light-colored shirt marred by an ominous, dark stain.

Mark gasped and rushed to his friend's side.

CHAPTER 60

Wednesday, November 21
10:00 p.m.

Heart in her throat, Liz pounded on the locked sacristy door. "Let us out of here!" she cried. "My sister needs help! Please, someone hear me!"

Val had locked them in the sacristy, a room located in proximity to the pulpit and used by priests to physically and spiritually prepare themselves for mass.

Liz looked over her shoulder at her sister, lying motionless on the floor. Her breath came in shallow pulls. Her alarmingly pale skin stretched tightly over her bones, giving her the appearance of something out of a house of horrors. Her lips and the inside of her mouth were covered with fever blisters. During the ride to the church, she had opened her eyes once. The color had been dull; she had looked at Liz without recognition.

Rachel was dying.

Panic rose up in her. She pounded on the door again. "Someone, please! Help us!"

Only the howling wind answered her, and Liz hurried back to Rachel's side. She would have to do what she could to help her. She searched her memory, trying to figure out how by assessing what was wrong with her.

Dehydration, most certainly. She had been locked in that stifling hot box for some time, deprived of water. Malnourished, obviously. She had fever. That meant she had an infection. Or...heatstroke. A friend from college had suffered a heatstroke running in sweats in August. When they'd found her, she'd been barely conscious. Burning up with fever. At the hospital they'd iced her down and administered fluids.

Heatstroke, she had learned, could lead to kidney failure, which led to death.

She needed to bring her temperature down and hydrate her.

Liz tore off her soaked shirt and went to Rachel's side. She knelt beside her, positioning herself by her head. Carefully, Liz twisted a small area of the fabric, wringing out several drops of water. They fell into Rachel's mouth. Her lips moved.

Encouraged, Liz repeated the process until she had wrung out the entire shirt. Then she folded the garment into a neat rectangle and laid the damp, cool cloth against her sister's fevered forehead.

It hurt to look at her. When she did, she imagined the hell Rachel had endured over the past months. Hell delivered at the hands of Heather Ferguson.

Liz squeezed her eyes shut, fighting tears. Why had she done it? How could one human being exact such cruelty on another? She shuddered with the force of holding back her tears. Of restraining her impotent fury. She lifted her face toward heaven, as if by doing so she would suddenly understand the why. As if somehow she would find a way to let go of her anger before it ate her alive.

"Don't cry."

Liz caught her breath and looked at her sister. Her eyes were open. And she was looking at Liz with that funny, perplexed expression Liz knew so well.

"Hi, sweetie." Liz caught her hands, a broken laugh passing her lips. "I've been looking for you."

Her sister's mouth curved up. "I…prayed…you'd come."

Liz's lips trembled and she pressed them together, working to steady herself. "Of course I came. I love you, sis."

"Lov'you…too."

"Save your strength," Liz said quickly, seeing her sister's fragile grip on consciousness slipping.

"No…sorry I…you into this."

"You didn't. Rachel, I… The last time we spoke I acted like such a jerk. I'm so sorry. If I could take back the things I said—"

"I should…told you what was happen…afraid. For you. I…" Her words trailed off; a shudder rippled over her wasted body.

"You're ill." Liz heard the fear in her own voice and worked to hide it. "Save your strength, please."

Her sister curled her fingers around hers, her grip as weak as a newborn's. "Don't you…understa…this body…just a shell. This world only a…moment in… eternity."

She closed her eyes and for one panicked moment Liz thought she had lost her. Then she stirred once more.

"My faith kept me…alive. She…didn't understa…the more she tried to turn me away, the closer we beca—"

Another shudder seized Rachel, and Liz held her. She moved slightly so Rachel's head rested in her lap. She trailed her fingers through her sister's hair, gently massaging her scalp, the way she used to when they were kids.

"I'm not going to let you die." This, Liz whispered fiercely, as if by wanting desperately enough she could will it. "I lost you once and I'm not going to lose you again."

Rachel's mouth moved. Liz bent closer. Her breath stirred against her cheek, but no sound emerged.

So she continued to stroke her hair and speak softly. "Remember the Christmas we spent in Vermont with Grandma and Grandpa? We'd never seen so much snow. We both stayed out so long that first day our cheeks were still pink the next morning."

Liz smiled at the memory. "Grandpa took us for a sleigh ride. I remember the jingle of the bells, the taste of Grandma's hot chocolate and the clouds of condensation that formed in the air as we laughed."

She lowered her gaze to her sister. Her eyes were closed but Liz could tell she was listening. And that her words were soothing to her. So she continued, recalling other stories they shared, other sweet remembrances.

From the sanctuary came the sound of voices. Liz bent close to Rachel's ear. "I'll be right back."

She eased Rachel's head off her lap, got to her feet and tiptoed to the door. She pressed her ear against it. Heather was speaking.

"—told me he was dead!"

"He should be. He took a bullet in the chest."

Pastor Tim? Were they talking about—

"Then where the hell is he?"

"When I left, he was sprawled across his office floor, bleeding like a stuck pig."

Pastor Tim was alive! If he had managed to escape—

"I am not happy about this."

"Do you think I am? If not for you, Collins wouldn't have been a problem. You were supposed to kill her that night." Val's voice vibrated with fury. "Instead, you send those Rainbow Kids to lure her to you. What were you thinking? We don't have enough problems without her?"

"Rachel Howard is not your concern."

"Not my… But you expect me to clean up your mess. You expect me to keep making everything all right."

"Yes," she murmured, "I do."

"Well, fuck you!" he shouted. "You take care of her. I wash my hands of this."

Silence followed. Liz pressed her ear closer to the door. When Heather spoke again, her voice was different: deeper, ugly. "Let's be clear on this, Lieutenant. You're in so far and so deep, your trail of slime leads all over this island. I can slip away. Can you say the same?"

"I could kill you now." He lowered his voice. "I should. Poor Heather Ferguson, another one of Rick Wells's victims."

She laughed. "But you won't, will you? Because you don't have what it takes to use the knife. And you know how it's going to look if the pastor and her sister aren't killed in the same fashion as the others. It'll be a big red flag for the investigators. And suddenly, your nice neat story is anything but. Maybe I'm wrong, but a pretty boy like you wouldn't do well in prison."

This time it was Val who fell silent. After a moment,

he spoke. "There are limits to what even I can do, Heather."

"I don't want to hear about your limitations. I've made you a very rich man, Valentine Lopez. I suggest you show me the proper gratitude."

"Fuck you to hell and back."

"That would be a lovely start. We can make that date after we finish this thing. Get Wells over here now."

CHAPTER 61

Wednesday, November 21
10:25 p.m.

Rick paced, struggling to fit the pieces of the puzzle together. They had four victims confirmed. Tara Mancuso. Naomi Pearson. The woman found on Big Pine Key. And now, Carla Chapman. Another woman, Rachel Howard, was missing and presumed dead.

They had one banker—dead by suicide—into bogus loans and young girls. Also in the mix was a cult called the Horned Flower, maybe or maybe not involved in satanism. Definitely into drugs and sex, probably underage prostitution.

And they had a once-honest, upstanding cop turned murderer.

Rick squeezed his eyes shut, working to divorce himself from the betrayal and anger that surged through him. He needed a cool head, his wits about him.

If he was going to escape this with his life. The way he figured it, Val wasn't going to allow him to walk away alive. He couldn't. Rick knew the truth.

Val, and whoever his accomplices were, had begun cleaning house. Tonight, they were tying up loose ends. They had to. He was their killer. They'd showed their hand and set the clock ticking. Time had run out on their scheme.

He thought of Liz and fear rose up in him like an icy wave. She was a loose end. Maybe their last one.

And she was alone out there.

"Son of a bitch!" He jerked his hands against the cuffs; the metal bit into his wrists and pain shot up his arms.

"Settle down, Wells," the rookie barked, trying to sound fierce but coming off prepubescent instead.

He ignored the kid and refocused on the facts as he knew—or suspected—them to be. Tara got herself involved with the Horned Flower. Her involvement included having sex with twisted old Bernhardt—and maybe others like him. She wanted out, so she goes to her pastor. Who goes to Val.

Goodbye, Pastor Howard.

He flexed his fingers. Dammit! What had transformed his friend into a murderer? Greed. That's what turned most cops. Val had probably been in on the bogus loan scheme. Hell, he may have masterminded it. Feed Bernhardt's sick addiction, then blackmail him with the very addiction he helped grow.

Of course. Rick stopped pacing. Bernhardt can't take the pressure anymore and takes a swan dive out his bedroom window. Which left Naomi Pearson hanging in the wind. With Bernhardt dead, Pearson had not only outlived her usefulness but had become a liability.

Island National would uncover Bernhardt's activities, trace them to her and she would sing like a canary.

Unless she was dead.

Goodbye, Naomi Pearson.

Then there was Carla. Obviously, Becky had mentioned the message-pad incident and Val had realized she'd caught on to him.

Goodbye, Carla.

To his thinking, the unknown vic found on Big Pine Key was either Heather Ferguson or the other teenager on Bernhardt's homemade porno. Next up, Liz Ames.

Val would have his clean house.

Rick swung to face Walters. "How long you been on the force, kid?"

"Three weeks."

"You don't say?" Rick eyed the boy, feeling sorry for him. "I used to be a cop."

"I'd heard that."

"Worked for six years with the Miami-Dade force. I tell you, I saw some shit that'd curl your hair."

"Like what?" the kid asked warily.

"Gang wars, murder, drugs, you name it. Lots of drug trade in Miami. Lots of money in it. Some of the cops went bad."

Walters glanced at the door, obviously interested but uneasy.

"You know how to spot a dirty cop, Walters?"

He shook his head. "They break regs. At first it's little stuff. The stuff everybody does even though they're not supposed to. Then it gets bigger. They tamper with evidence. They look the other way for profit. Pretty soon, they're in so deep there's more bad to them than good. Pretty soon, even murder's not too much to expect."

"I know what you're up to, Wells, and it's not going to work."

Rick ignored him. "In the academy, Walters, did they teach you the proper procedure for handling a murder scene?"

"Sure. First officer secures the scene, then calls for backup."

"Why?"

"To keep the scene from being contaminated or tampered with. When evidence is lost or destroyed, the chance of solving the crime becomes unlikely."

"And someone gets away with murder." Rick fixed his gaze on the kid's. "And if the victim is a fellow officer, what happens then?"

"Everybody's involved, from the chief on down. No stone unturned."

"Lieutenant Lopez left Detective Chapman lying in a pool of blood. He didn't call for backup. He left the scene unsecured. Why do you suppose that was?"

The rookie flushed. "So you say."

"He did, Walters. And his decision had nothing to do with law and order."

"Why should I believe you? Lieutenant Detective Lopez is a highly decorated officer. He answers only to the chief himself."

Val had picked Walters well. A rookie. Naive. Anxious not to rock the boat, anxious to impress his superior officer.

He tried again anyway. "Wake up, Walters! Lopez is dirty. He killed Carla Chapman. Before it's all over, he may kill you, too."

"Shut up!" the kid shouted. "Shut the hell—"

The wall phone rang. They both turned toward it. Looking shaken, the rookie picked it up. "Officer Walters." He paused, listening. "Yes, Lieutenant Lopez. He's right here, no problems." He listened again, then glanced at Rick. "Bring the suspect to you? At Paradise Christian?"

Now, why did Val want to get him away from police headquarters?

He didn't want any witnesses.

"Fuck him," Rick called. "I'm not going without a lawyer."

"Lieutenant Lopez, Wells is refusing to go. He's talking lawyering up." He paused, then nodded. "Yes, sir. I'll do that."

"Think regs, kid. What would the rule book say about this one? Releasing a murder suspect, a suspected cop killer, before he had been fully questioned? Refuse him his right to legal counsel? That sound right to you?"

The rookie frowned at him, obviously rattled. He cleared his throat. "Lieutenant Lopez," he said hesitantly, "I don't think—"

He paused and Rick knew it was to listen to a tirade from his superior officer. "Yes, sir."

Walters held the phone out. "He wants to talk to you."

Rick crossed to the room. The rookie brought the phone to his ear. "I have nothing to say to you, you backstabbing bastar—"

"Hello, Rick," his friend interrupted cheerfully. "Liz is with me. We're at Paradise Christian. I suggest you allow Walters to accompany you—"

"You son of a bitch! If you so much as touch her, I'll—"

"I've given Walters his instructions," he continued. "And unless you want to lose her the way you lost Jill, I suggest you cooperate."

"Let me speak with her, you prick," he said, all but

spitting the words at the man. "I'm not going anywhere until—"

Val laughed. "Of course you will. You'll do anything I tell you. And, Rick," he finished, "the clock's ticking."

CHAPTER 62

Wednesday, November 21
10:50 p.m.

The rookie pulled the cruiser to a stop in front of the darkened church. Through the stained-glass windows Rick could see the faintest flicker of light. Candles, he realized.

The young officer came around and opened Rick's door. "Get out, Wells."

Rick alighted the vehicle. "It's a trap, Walters. A setup. Why else have you bring me here?"

"Shut up, Wells." He nudged Rick forward. "It's been a long day."

"Just be careful, okay? Be ready. He's going to have to take you out." Rick glanced over his shoulder. The kid looked scared. Flat-out terrified.

Better scared than dead, Rick thought as they entered the church.

Val called to them from the sanctuary. "Walters, in here."

The rookie gave Rick a shove in that direction. Rick could feel the kid's nervous tension. Could sense his hand hovering near his gun.

Don't blow it, kid. One chance, that's all you'll have.

Val smiled as they approached. "Thanks for bringing him over, Walters. I owe you one."

"No problem." The rookie moved his gaze past Val, sweeping it over the altar area. "What's going on, Lieutenant?"

"This," Val said. He lifted his revolver, aimed and fired. The bullet struck the kid in the chest and a look of surprise crossed his face. He took a step backward, hand going to his chest. Blood seeped through his fingers.

"You son of a bitch!" Rick shouted, jumping forward. "Why'd you have to do—"

Val fired again. The rookie went down. "Don't be stupid, Rick," Val murmured, training the gun on him. "You know why."

Of course he did. No witnesses. No loose ends.

"You're not going to get away with this. I swear to God, if it's the last thing I do, I'm going to bring you down."

"Swearing to God?" Val sounded shocked. "In a church, no less." He made a clucking sound with his tongue. "I guess I will see you in hell."

"Where's Liz? What have you done with her?"

Val laughed. "Desperation suits you, Rick. I like it quite well."

"If you've hurt her, I swear I'll—"

"She's in one piece, for now. Behold—"

Liz stepped out from the shadows behind the pulpit.

She supported another woman, one who appeared too weak to stand.

"Liz!" He started forward.

"Hold it, loverboy."

This came from Heather, who stepped up behind Liz. She brought a gun to Liz's head.

"Not dead, I see," he said coldly.

"Observant."

"So who'd they find on Big Pine Key? The other teenager in Bernhardt's sleazy home video?"

"Poor Stephanie. And she had real talent, too. She and Tara both. Real wildcats in the sack. They were Bernhardt's favorites." She paused as if recalling fond memories, then continued. "It's Tara's fault Stephanie's dead. Tara asked her friend to plead with me to let her go. Because of the *baby.* Like I was supposed to give a damn about that. And I couldn't allow Stephanie to live with that knowledge, now, could I?"

She shifted her gaze to Val. "Get the chair." He hurried to do the woman's bidding and she returned her attention to Rick. "Carla did us a huge favor, finding those videos. I didn't have a clue what Larry was up to, though I should have suspected. Luckily, my disciple in the Sunset Key Realty office smelled a rat and followed Carla. You needn't worry about them, they've all been collected. I might even watch them once before I destroy them, for old times' sake."

Val brought a chair out of the sacristy and set it near Liz and directly under the choir loft. He crossed to Liz, wrenched the other woman from Liz's grasp and half carried, half dragged her to the chair. She folded into it like a rag doll.

"Rachel!" Liz cried, reaching for her.

Liz's sister? Stunned, Rick looked at Liz; she met his eyes, the expression in hers desperate.

"Secure Ms. Ames's wrists."

"No please or thank-you?" Rick shifted his attention to Heather. "Just because you're an amoral, psychopathic bitch doesn't mean you have the right to be rude."

"Amusing, Mr. Wells." Heather crossed to the altar. She bent and retrieved a length of rope from a large black plastic bag at her feet. She tossed it to Val.

"You make a good lapdog, Val," Rick said. "Valentine Lopez, Lieutenant Detective Lapdog. Nice. You must be very proud of the way you've bettered yourself."

"Shut the fuck up," Val snapped, yanking Liz's arms behind her back. He jerked hard on the rope; Liz cried out. "Unless you want me to cut off her circulation?"

Rick backed down. Val finished knotting the rope. "What about her ankles?"

"Let's live dangerously." Heather motioned him. "Bring her to me."

Val pushed her toward Heather. Liz screamed in terror as she stumbled forward.

Rick lunged. Val turned the six-inch barrel on Liz. "Think again, Wells."

He backed off, heart pounding. "Leave her be."

Val laughed. "You're such a Boy Scout, Rick. You always have been. It's sickening. By the rules, the good little public servant."

"Better than being *her* servant."

"You think so?" He circled Rick, the light in his eyes too bright. "You haven't a clue the riches afforded a man in my position. Heather taught me. Play to people's needs, their innate weaknesses. To their fears. And they will give you everything and anything you desire. Money. Power. Respect. They'll bow down, Rick. Anybody ever bow down to you? Here's a tip, asshole. It's damn nice." He tipped his head back and shouted at the heavens. "I'm the man! King of Key West!"

"Here's the tip, *asshole*," Rick retorted. "You're nothing. A common criminal who'll end up roommate and boyfriend to some guy named Bubba."

Val's face went white with rage. His hand began to shake. "Easy to be sanctimonious when everything's been laid at your feet. Your rich daddy and mommy… anything you ever wanted, they gave to you. You only had to point and it was yours."

Rick shook his head. "All of this, was it just about money, Val? About jealousy?"

"You shouldn't have come back, Rick. You should have stayed in Miami. Safe. Sam would have been safe."

Rick went cold. The other man continued. "But nothing would do but you had to come back to my island. Here, where everything was going so well for me."

"If you didn't want me here, why'd you offer me a job, Val? You acted so eager—"

"Because you talked to the chief! For Christ's sake, what was I supposed to say to him? A big-city hotshot like you wanting on the Key West force, the man practically wet himself at the thought.

"I knew you'd never go for my and Heather's version of law and order. You were too *moral*. Too self-righteous. And too goddamned smart. I needed to get rid of you quickly. So I arranged that break-in."

The breath left his body. Rick took a step backward. *Val arranged the break-in?* "Those two coked-up pieces of human refuse, you sent them to my home? Where my child slept?"

"But it didn't go according to plan. Always the cowboy, you decided to take them out all by yourself." Val lowered his voice. "I didn't mean for Sam to die. But it happened. So I used it to my advantage."

He faced Rick, expression triumphant. "I switched the ballistics report so you believed you had killed your own son."

A sound passed Rick's lips. Primal. A terrible howl of pain and fury.

"That's right, buddy, your bullet didn't kill him."

Rick sank to his knees, doubling over, the pain too great to bear. Val, who he had trusted completely, had betrayed him. Val, who he had thought of as a brother, was responsible for the incident that had taken Sam. He squeezed his eyes shut, his head filling with the memory of that night. Of holding his precious boy as his life ran out of him.

"You can't imagine how I enjoyed watching you suffer. The way I suffered, Rick. Watching you get everything I wanted. Including Jill. She was supposed to be mine. Mine!"

He growled the last. "This island and everything on it should belong to me. My people, my ancestors settled her. We fed and developed her. Yet people like you come down here and take it all—enjoy all her riches while we catch your fish, scrub your toilets and serve your food."

Val began to laugh, the sound high and wild. "Not anymore, my friend. Not anymore!"

Rick lifted his gaze to the crucifix mounted behind the altar, his vision blurred by tears. The sixteen-foot-tall cross was rough-hewn, as the real one must have been; the carved depiction of Christ beautifully rendered, showing his very human suffering.

Rick's vision shifted, moving past the crucified Christ to the stained-glass window behind it. Circular, at least twenty feet in diameter, it depicted the risen King, glorious and triumphant.

It wasn't over. Adrenaline surged through him. His vision cleared. He wouldn't give up and let this piece of shit win. Not ever.

He shifted his gaze to Liz. She met his eyes. She understood his intention—if necessary, he would give his life trying to save them. Trying to bring Valentine down.

Rick straightened. "I loved you, Val. You were my brother. My friend."

"Go to hell."

He was already there. With a roar, he charged Val. He caught him by surprise and sent them both sprawling. The gun flew from Val's hand. Rick used his height and weight advantage and pinned Val beneath him. He drew back and sent his handcuffed wrists crashing into Val's handsome face.

The man howled. Blood spurted from his nose. Rick rolled sideways, scrambling for the gun. He closed his fingers around the grip.

As he did he heard the unmistakable sound of a cylinder clicking into place. He looked over his shoulder. Heather had Liz from behind, gun to her temple.

"You have a choice," she murmured. "What's it going to be?"

Rick curled his fingers around the gun's grip, the feel of it nestled in his palms both familiar and foreign. He squeezed his eyes shut, thinking of Sam. And Liz. Assessing their options. He could take one of them out, maybe both of them.

But Liz would die. That was a given.

He couldn't do it.

"Noble," Heather murmured as he dropped the gun, amusement coloring her tone. "But stupid. Get to your feet, Wells. Now."

CHAPTER 63

Wednesday, November 21
11:25 p.m.

Liz watched as Rick got slowly to his feet. Val snatched up the gun and crossed to Rick. Blood streamed from his nose and mouth. He brought the gun up and pressed the barrel between Rick's eyes. He cocked it. Liz saw that he trembled with fury.

"Go ahead," Rick taunted. "Pull the trigger. I dare you."

"Don't push me, Wells. I'll do it, I swear I'll—"

"Go for it, you prick! Make my day!"

"No!" Liz cried. "Don't!"

Heather tipped her head back and laughed, the sound almost childlike in its glee. It was as if she fed on the negativity, the fear and hatred, the bloodshed.

"Admirable, Liz," she murmured. "Loyalty. Love. Commitment. I'm touched, really."

Heather turned to the two men. "Make sure that doesn't happen again, Valentine."

"Throw me some rope," the man responded tightly. "I'll make sure this prick doesn't move a muscle."

Heather did as he requested, then turned her attention back to Liz. "I wonder if your boyfriend here would do the same for you? Cry out, get down on his knees and beg for your life to be spared. I wonder if your *beloved* sister would?"

Heather looked over at Rachel, slumped in the chair. "Liz is in this situation because of you, Rachel. Because she loves you so much." She all but hissed the last and a chill raced up Liz's spine. "She's here because of your ridiculous faith in *Him*."

Liz shifted her gaze to the carved depiction of Christ. She thought of the little Rachel had managed to tell her, and the pieces began clicking into place.

"I don't think she would," Heather continued. "I think she might just let you die." Liz jerked her gaze back to the woman. "She let Tara die. And Naomi Pearson. Why not you?"

A sound slipped past her sister's lips. One of horror. Despair.

"Three little words, that's all I asked of her." Heather bent. From the black sack, she removed a pair of rubber gloves and fitted them on. "Three words," the woman continued. "Do you know what they were?"

Liz shook her head. Heather looked back at Rachel. "But Rachel does. Don't you, love. Say them with me. *I...deny...Him.*"

Her sister bowed her head, her shoulders shook with her tears. Fury took Liz's breath. She understood now. She thought of Father Paul, of the things he had said.

In the desecration of the holy, evil extends its putrid grasp.

"That's all I asked of her, all these weeks, day after day. As I brought her near death, then pulled her back, always giving her another chance. But she refused me. She insisted on holding on to her pathetic belief in her nonexistent savior."

Heather shook her head. "I see that you despise me, Liz. But it was she who turned away from the food I offered. The water. The end to pain. Because of Him." She pointed again to the crucified Christ, her features twisted with hate. "He is the source of her agony, not I!"

The evil that emanated from the woman made Liz's skin crawl. "You won't get away with this," she spat, struggling against the ropes that held her wrists. "Gavin Taft didn't get away with it. You'll fry just like he's going to."

"But we will," she said softly, cutting her off. She bent and retrieved a black-velvet package from the sack. Reverently, she peeled the velvet back, revealing a knife. She held it up. The blade glittered in the candlelight and Liz went weak with fear.

"Unfortunately, Val doesn't arrive soon enough to save you and your sister from the knife. But even though you and your sister die, even though Wells wrests away Val's gun and Walters is killed, in the end Rick Wells is stopped. Thanks be to *God*."

Liz shuddered at the sarcastic emphasis she put on the Lord's name. Heather Ferguson, she realized, was not just an evil being—she worshiped evil. She delighted in it.

"You see, the lieutenant's been amassing quite a collection of evidence against poor troubled Mr. Wells.

Evidence of his involvement with Larry Bernhardt and Naomi Pearson, physical evidence linking him to Tara and Carla's murders. Enough evidence that with the lieutenant's explanation of events, the case will be closed. Nice and tidy, all bodies accounted for."

"What about Mark?" Liz asked, working to conceal the hopefulness in her tone. Since the woman hadn't mentioned his name, she prayed that he had somehow escaped her grasp.

The woman's mouth tightened and she shot a provoked look at her accomplice. "He won't prove to be much trouble. He's running scared. After all, he and Wells were in cahoots. We have physical evidence to back that assumption up."

"But he knows about you and the Horned Flower. Don't you think he—"

"I think," she interrupted, "that you should shut up."

Liz ignored her. "So, you're just going to continue merrily on your way, nobody the wiser?"

"Give me some credit, I'm not stupid. I'm already missing. Presumed dead by the authorities. Just ask the fussy little man who owns the shop next to mine. It will be assumed that I'm another of Wells's victims."

She planned to move on, Liz realized, sickened. Planned to start all over somewhere else. Liz turned to Valentine Lopez. "And you? You have a fabulous future all mapped out as well?"

He smiled. "I'm so traumatized from having to kill my best friend, I leave police work and Key West behind forever."

Tears of frustration stung her eyes. How could they fight these monsters? They had nothing to fight them with, not even fear of being caught.

"Tell me," Heather murmured, "did you have any

idea your sister was so stubborn? That she would rather die than denounce Him?"

"Yes," Liz replied, lifting her chin, proud of her sister and her unshakable faith.

"However, the question of the hour is, will the good pastor rather see *you* die than to deny Him?"

"Why do you care?" Liz retorted, forcing bravado. "Her faith has nothing to do with you."

Heather laughed, the sound deep, grotesque. "That's where you're wrong, my dear. It has everything to do with me."

From the corner of her eye, Liz saw Rick struggling against his ropes. Beyond him she saw the body of the slain officer. She shifted her gaze to the officer's holster and gun.

Rick followed the direction of her gaze, then met hers again. He nodded, the movement of his head almost imperceptible.

He was going to do his best to get the gun.

"Smelling salts, Val. We can't have the good pastor passing out before the main event."

Val crossed to Rachel and waved the vial under her nose. Her head snapped up.

"Who did it?" Liz demanded in an attempt to buy time and keep Heather's and Val's attention diverted from Rick. "Which one of you sick bastards killed Tara and the others? Or was it a team effort?"

"I had the honors," Heather murmured, her face changing subtly, shifting from beautiful to horrific. "Unlike my darling Gavin, Valentine doesn't have the stomach for the knife. And it's something I enjoy."

Liz swallowed against the bile that rose in her throat. "What are you?"

Heather grinned, the curving of her mouth serpentine

in the flickering candlelight. "A defiler of paradise... The snake in the apple tree. A soul collector.

"It's so easy these days. What do you think worshiping money, power and beauty is? What is the pursuit of earthly pleasures but a turning away from God? Pride. Envy. Lust. Avarice. Sloth. Anger. Gluttony. They're a girl's best friend." She giggled suddenly, the girlish sound bizarre. "Who am I? I'm a devil for the new millennium."

"You're insane."

"Am I? Or do you just hope I am?"

A brilliant flash of lightning momentarily illuminated the church; thunder shook the building. Heather turned to Val. "It's show time."

"No!" Rick shouted, struggling to free himself.

Heather grabbed Liz from behind and dragged her back against her chest, her grip surprisingly strong. She brought the knife to her throat. "Deny Him!" she screamed. "Deny Him and I'll spare your sister's life!"

"Don't do it, Rachel!" Liz shouted. "She'll kill us anyway!"

Outside, the storm kicked into high gear. The heavens opened up; rain lashed against the building.

Liz felt Heather tense, preparing to strike. The blade burned her throat as it penetrated the skin. Liz went light-headed with terror.

"If he is truly Lord and Savior, let Him help you now!"

Rick threw himself toward the fallen officer. Val shouted a warning to Heather; he took aim at Rick. Liz screamed. A figure leaped from the choir loft.

Mark! Liz realized.

He landed on Val. They went down. The gun went off. She couldn't tell if either of the men had been hurt.

For one instant, the earth stood still, then Mother Nature unleashed her full power. Thunder shook the sanctuary. The window burst into Technicolor glory. A huge crack rent the air.

The window exploded inward as the ancient banyan tree outside it crashed through. Shards of colored glass spewed into the sanctuary.

"Cover your face!" Rick shouted.

A high scream of pain shattered the moment. Heather released Liz, and she stumbled sideways against the altar. Liz saw that a piece of glass had imbedded itself in the back of Heather's neck. The woman clawed at it, the knife slipping from her hands.

Liz dived for the knife. Heather got to it first, caught her and dragged her back. Liz fought and kicked. A second gunshot rent the air. The bullet whizzed past her head.

Mark, Liz saw. On his knees, Valentine Lopez's gun in his shaking hands. The lieutenant lay unmoving, half of his head blown away.

"Get away from her!" Mark shouted, pointing the weapon at Heather.

Heather reared up, her face contorted with hate. Blood streamed from her hand. She drew back the knife. Mark pulled the trigger. Nothing happened.

The chamber was empty.

Rick cried out her name. Liz was aware of him dragging himself toward the fallen officer. He wouldn't make it, she knew. It was over already.

Heather laughed. Thunder shook the sanctuary. A deep groan trembled across the floor, followed by a loud crack. Heather turned. The crucifix swayed slightly. Her face went white, then blank. She threw her arms up.

In the next instant, the crucifix toppled, crushing Heather beneath it.

CHAPTER 64

Liz sat beside her sister's hospital bed. Sunlight streamed through the window, creating bright patches on the white bedding. The storm had passed, leaving Key West only slightly worse for wear. Once again, paradise had been saved.

The city and her citizens had begun to clean up. Repairing the damages. Clearing away the debris. Moving on.

Liz glanced from the window to her sister. Rachel slept. She had been moved from intensive care just that morning. Liz drank in her sister's face, throat tight with tears of happiness. She'd thought she would never see her again. Never be able to hold her, laugh with her—never be able to tell her how much she loved her.

She had been given a gift so precious her heart could hardly hold the joy of it.

The color had begun to return to Rachel's cheeks. Liz, it turned out, had accurately diagnosed her sister's symptoms: heatstroke, dehydration and malnourishment. She had also suffered some secondary infection caused by untreated wounds.

The doctor had proclaimed Rachel a lucky woman. It was a miracle her kidneys hadn't shut down. That she hadn't slipped into a coma and died. Liz, he believed, had arrived in the nick of time. An hour later may have been too late.

Lucky to be alive, Liz thought. They were all lucky to be alive. Gratitude swelled in her chest. Thankfulness. She would never take life or those she loved for granted again. Would never take God's grace for granted again.

For by what else had her, Rick's and Rachel's lives been spared?

"How is she?"

Liz glanced over her shoulder. Rick stood in the open doorway. She smiled. "Good. The doctor's amazed by how she's responded."

"It's a miracle she's alive."

"I was just thinking that." She shifted her gaze to the white paper sack he carried. "Please tell me that's something to eat. Something that didn't come from the hospital cafeteria."

One corner of his mouth lifted. "Turkey sandwich from the Green Parrot. Dressed with cranberry sauce. Happy day after Thanksgiving, Liz."

He crossed to the bed, bent and kissed her. *So much to give thanks for,* she thought. *So many blessings.*

"I just left a meeting with the chief," he said, setting the bag on the bed table.

She searched his gaze. "And?"

"And…the loss of Carla and Lopez has left a huge hole in the department. He needs somebody with experience. Someone familiar with Key West and all her idiosyncrasies."

And a local hero, Liz thought. Someone who had been wronged by Valentine Lopez but didn't hold the police department liable.

Valentine Lopez's trail of slime had, indeed, led all over the island. It seemed Larry Bernhardt was not the only local businessman blackmailed into feeding Val's bank account. As he had claimed to Rick, Val had been king of his own illegal mini empire, run from his office at the KWPD.

"He offered you a job," she murmured.

Rick nodded, his expression bemused. "Yup."

"Are you going to take it?"

"I told him I'd think about it but…yeah, I might."

Rick, a cop again. Truth was, he had never stopped being one.

"What about Rick's Island Hideaway?"

He met her eyes. Something in them had her heart pounding. "I don't need a hideaway anymore, Liz."

She shifted her gaze, nervous. Hopeful. Wondering if what had occurred between them had been real or simply a side effect of the danger they had been in. She wondered if, given a chance, it would grow into something wonderful…or wither and die.

"Where's Mark?" he asked.

"Down the hall, visiting Tim."

Rick shook his head. "Another who's lucky to be alive. A bullet to his sternum, another to a rib. It's hard to believe they weren't fatal."

"Thank God."

"Yes," her sister murmured weakly. "Thank God."

They turned. Rachel had awakened and was watching them, a small, contented smile tipping the edges of her mouth.

"Hi, sweetie. Feeling okay?"

She nodded. "How long have I been asleep?"

"A while. The doctor says you're going to be fine."

"I was fine before. My Lord was with me."

Liz laced her fingers through Rachel's. "When you're strong enough, the police need to speak with you."

"Anytime," she murmured, then shifted her gaze. Her eyes widened slightly, as with surprise. "You have my ring. I couldn't find it anywhere."

Tears stung Liz's eyes. "Glad to be of help, sis." She slipped off the band and slid it onto her sister's finger.

Rachel gazed at it a moment, then turned her attention to Rick. "Hello," she said. "You must be one of my heroes."

Liz introduced them and Rick crossed to the bed. "It's good to see you looking so well, Pastor."

"Please, call me Rachel." She tightened her fingers on Liz's. "Is Stephen... Did they—"

"He's fine," Liz said quickly. "Under a doctor's care in Miami. He'll be home soon. And very happy to see you, I know."

Rachel closed her eyes, then reopened them. "He got you the envelope? With the photographs? And the drawing?"

"He did."

Rachel was quiet a moment. "I was afraid to involve Stephen that way, afraid to involve you. Afraid for my congregation. I tried to warn them through my sermons, but I only succeeded in alienating them. Then when I realized the police were involved, I didn't know where to turn."

"You did good, sis." Liz squeezed her fingers, then turned as two sheriff's officers entered the room.

"How are you feeling, Pastor Howard?" the first said, crossing to the bed. "I'm Deputy Newman, Sheriff's Department. This is Deputy Paulson. Do you feel up to answering a few questions?"

She said she was and the deputy looked at Liz and Rick. "If you don't mind, we'd like to speak with her alone."

Liz hung back. "I'd really prefer to stay."

"Go on, Liz." Rachel squeezed then released her hands. "Go on and check on your friends, I'll be fine."

Liz hesitated a moment more, and nodded. She and Rick slipped out into the hall. She glanced back as the door shut, then up at Rick.

"Did the chief say anything about the investigation?"

"They're still piecing things together, but you were right, Liz. It seems that Heather was Taft's accomplice. They believe she met him at FSU and that they became lovers. She had already dabbled in drugs and the occult, had become fascinated by the teaching of satanists Aleister Crowley and Anton LaVey. She was easily drawn into his belief in his own divine evil. They killed Heather's sister, their first victim working together as a team.

"After Taft's conviction, Heather traveled to Key West and started her cult, which they believe was a continuation of one she and Taft designed. Her first initiate was Lieutenant Lopez."

"And his allegiance afforded her not only a steady supply of the drugs she used to control her flock, but also allowed her to operate with police protection," Liz said. "Right?"

"Exactly. Like all cults, she seduced people with promises of acceptance, belonging and power. And pleasure. Sexual. Monetary. You name it. So far, they've rounded up a dozen members. They believe there might be three or four times that many."

Liz recalled how Heather had proclaimed the seven deadly sins a girl's best friend. She recalled, too, Father Paul's words. She repeated them aloud to Rick. "The devil is crafty, indeed. He captures us through the things that make us most human. Lust. Pride. Sloth. Anger. Avarice. Envy. These we must guard against, just as the Lord warned us we should."

He drew his eyebrows together in confusion and she explained about Father Paul, the things he had said. "We were there. What we witnessed was…I don't know. A part of me can't help but think…"

Again her words trailed off. She met his eyes. "What was she, Rick?"

"A psychopath. A schizophrenic with delusions of divine evil. We'll never know for sure."

Liz wanted to agree. How much more reassuring to believe Heather a terribly twisted individual than an ancient evil. Than *the* one true evil. From the things Rachel had managed to tell her, Heather really had believed herself to be the devil incarnate. She had believed herself indestructible, unbeatable. She had become obsessed with the need to break Rachel's faith, as if in doing so she would have beaten her one real adversary: Jesus Christ.

"Liz, Rick!"

They turned at the sound of Mark's voice. He was with Pastor Tim, pushing him in a wheelchair.

"How's your sister?" Mark asked as he reached them.

"She's good. Really good." Liz smiled and shifted her gaze to the pastor. "Thank you, Pastor Tim, for saving her life."

He returned her smile. "Thank you for saving mine. If not for you, Lopez would have finished the job. You scared him off."

"But I left you for dead. If you had made a sound—"

"He would have killed us both. So I played dead and prayed for God's help. He sent Mark."

She cleared her throat. "Pastor, I'm sorry for all… for my dishonesty with you. For suspecting you of such heinous crimes."

He reached up and caught her hand. "I'm sorry, too. When Lieutenant Lopez told me you were Rachel Howard's sister, I was angry. That you had lied to me. That you were continuing to lie."

"He told you?" she said, surprised. "When?"

"The morning after Tara's murder. I realize now, he wanted me to distrust you. I'm sorry. Instead of giving in to my carnal nature, I should have offered you help."

"We should go," Mark said. "It's nearly time."

"A member of my congregation is in for tests this morning," Pastor Tim explained. "I wanted to offer my support and prayers."

Liz watched them go, then turned to Rick. "I'm going to miss Mark. But he'll make a good pastor someday."

The day before, Mark had told them that he was leaving. Heading back to Texas to pursue his dream of college then the seminary.

"What are you going to do?" Rick asked softly, interrupting her thoughts.

She met his gaze. "Stay with Rachel while she heals. After that, I don't know."

He drew her into his arms. "I was hoping you might give paradise another try. We could use you here. The kids who got sucked into the Horned Flower could use you. They're going to need you."

"And what about you, Detective Wells?" she asked, searching his gaze. "Do you want me to stay?"

He was quiet a moment. She held her breath, so hopeful it hurt.

"Yes," he murmured finally, cupping her face in his hands. "You make me believe in second chances, Liz Ames. You make me glad I'm alive."

Tears of joy stung her eyes. Wordlessly, she stood on tiptoe and brought her mouth to his. For the first time, she understood the true meaning of paradise.

* * * * *

AUTHOR'S NOTE

Venturing into the unknown is one of the aspects of novel writing I find the most exciting. And the most frightening. For how does one authentically create that which they have never experienced? *Dead Run* presented me with several such challenges, ones involving both the corporeal and spiritual realm.

I surmounted these challenges only through the generous help of experts from various fields. These experts gave of their valuable time and expertise with patience and an enthusiasm I appreciated more than I can adequately express. Thank you, one and all. Any inaccuracies are mine alone. At times I bent fact to suit fiction; I hope these do not cause you consternation. To that end, I mixed historical Key West facts with fictional ones for the sake of this story. In addition, by the time this book is published, the Key West Police Department will most probably be housed in its new high-tech police complex. I will miss the charming, slightly dilapidated police headquarters depicted in *Dead Run*.

Gratitude to my experts in the corporeal realm: Lieutenant Mark Bascle, Louisiana State Police, Bureau of Investigations, Narcotics Division, for the sometimes daily answers to questions on drugs of abuse, police procedure, dynamics, protocol—the list goes on. Dr. Douglas Walker, Ph.D., for information on drugs of abuse as related to the psyche and psychosis. Chris Rush, international private investigator, Chris Rush Private Investigations, White Plains, New York, for the video surveillance expertise, technical and anecdotal.

Brian Osborne, youth director, Hosanna Lutheran Church, for bringing to life the approach of the clinical social worker. Local TV favorite Margaret Orr, WDSU TV, for her assistance with tropical storms and hurricanes.

A special thanks to Cynthia Edwards, Office of Public Information, Key West Police Department, for the tour, the explanations, the many returned phone calls. Everyone I met during my visit to the KWPD was professional, helpful and friendly—Key West–style.

And to my experts in the spiritual realm: Brian Osborne again, for spiritual insight into today's youth. Pastor Anton Kern, also of Hosanna Lutheran Church, for insights into the life and faith of a Christian pastor. The gang at CC's Coffeehouse for the thought-provoking discussions on faith, Christ and His nemesis, Satan. Particular thanks to Diane Cooper and her husband, Pastor Marvin Cooper, and to Adrienne Gilliland.

Finally, gratitude to friends and colleagues for their support and assistance: my editor Dianne Moggy and the entire MIRA crew. My assistant Kellie Crosby-Bascle. My agent, Evan Marshall. My publicist, Lori

Ames. Walton and Johnson, radio gods, whose names I jokingly promised to mention in each of my novels.

And last but never least, my husband and sons, for loving me—even when the words wouldn't come.

NEW YORK TIMES AND USA TODAY BESTSELLING AUTHOR

ERICA SPINDLER

Twenty-three years ago Anna North survived a living nightmare. A madman kidnapped her, cut off her pinkie, then vanished. Today Anna lives in New Orleans, writing thrillers under another name. She finally feels safe.

Suddenly letters start to arrive from a disturbed fan. Anna is followed, her apartment broken into. Then a close friend disappears.

Anna turns to homicide detective Quentin Malone, who's more concerned with the recent murders of two women in the French Quarter. But after a third victim is found—a redhead like Anna, her pinkie severed—Malone acknowledges that Anna is his link to the killer...and could be the next target.

BONE COLD

Available wherever books are sold.

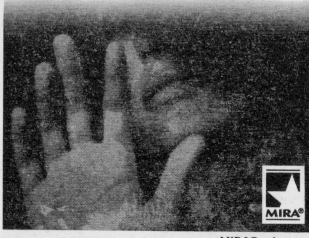

NEW YORK TIMES AND *USA TODAY* BESTSELLING AUTHOR

ERICA SPINDLER

Nearly killed as a teenager by a hit-and-run boater, Jane Killian has everything to live for—especially now, as she and her husband, Ian, are expecting their first child.

Then a woman with ties to Ian is found brutally slain and Ian is the prime suspect. Determined to prove her husband's innocence, Jane starts to have doubts. When she begins receiving anonymous messages, she's convinced they're from the boater she always believed deliberately hit her and got away with it.

Now Jane must face the tormentor who knows everything about her—including her deepest fears, which he will use mercilessly until he sees Jane dead.

SEE JANE DIE

Available now wherever books are sold.

MIRA®

www.MIRABooks.com

MES2833

REQUEST YOUR FREE BOOKS!

2 FREE NOVELS
FROM THE SUSPENSE COLLECTION
PLUS 2 FREE GIFTS!

SUS11

ERICA SPINDLER

32833	SEE JANE DIE	___ $7.99 U.S.	___ $9.99 CAN.
32832	IN SILENCE	___ $7.99 U.S.	___ $9.99 CAN.
32745	BONE COLD	___ $7.99 U.S.	___ $9.99 CAN.
32716	RED	___ $7.99 U.S.	___ $7.99 CAN.
32579	LAST KNOWN VICTIM	___ $7.99 U.S.	___ $7.99 CAN.
32445	COPYCAT	___ $7.99 U.S.	___ $9.50 CAN.
32305	KILLER TAKES ALL	___ $7.99 U.S.	___ $9.50 CAN.
31283	DEAD RUN	___ $7.99 U.S.	___ $9.99 CAN.

(limited quantities available)

TOTAL AMOUNT	$ _____
POSTAGE & HANDLING	$ _____
($1.00 for 1 book, 50¢ for each additional)	
APPLICABLE TAXES*	$ _____
TOTAL PAYABLE	$ _____

(check or money order—please do not send cash)

To order, complete this form and send it, along with a check or money order for the total above, payable to MIRA Books, to: **In the U.S.:** 3010 Walden Avenue, P.O. Box 9077, Buffalo, NY 14269-9077; **In Canada:** P.O. Box 636, Fort Erie, Ontario, L2A 5X3.

Name: _____

Address: _____ City: _____

State/Prov.: _____ Zip/Postal Code: _____

Account Number (if applicable): _____

075 CSAS

*New York residents remit applicable sales taxes.
*Canadian residents remit applicable GST and provincial taxes.

H HARLEQUIN®
™ www.Harlequin.com

MES1211BL